The Decadence of Our Souls

Claudiu Murgan

The Decadence of Our Souls was printed by CreateSpace,
An Amazon.com Company

Cover illustration by Theodore Murgan
Cover design by Costi Gurgu (Superpixel Design)
Edited by Nina Munteanu, author of "Water Is..."

First edition published in September 2017

ISBN-13: 978-1974068333
ISBN-10: 1974068331
www.claudiumurgan.com

ACKNOWLEDGEMENTS

Many thanks to my family, Gabriela, Andrew and Theodore, who stood by me while working on this novel. Especially Theodore who was my first editor and also created the cover illustration.

Thanks to my wonderful professional editor, Nina Munteanu, who brought so much value to my writing.

Thanks to all my friends who, behind the scenes, read chapter after chapter, providing invaluable feedback.

Thanks to my parents, Eugenia and Ion Murgan, for their efforts to raise me up properly. Love you both.

I also want to thank God for choosing me to deliver the message in this book to His lost Children.

Yanina,

I hope you'll enjoy it,

When a pure soul is touched by decadence...

“From the predatory jungles to the brothels of Laeta and techno-obsessed laboratories of Korobat, Claudiu Murgan’s fable about enlightenment is a compelling analysis of humanity’s search for meaning. This dichotomous tale of animal wisdom and human decadence will have you asking that meaningful question and wondering what is possible.”

—Nina Munteanu,
author of Water Is...

“The socio-economic limits that humanity has if it does not understand the difference between ‘The pleasure of living’ and ‘The joy of living in harmony with the laws of Nature’ are becoming increasingly obvious. The role of Man is more and more coherent as a thinking being, as a ‘retort’ in which the conscious reflection of Creation is synthesized, making it possible, from a certain level of spiritual development, to perceive the Creator. This true metamorphosis that mankind crosses is basically the subject of the wonderful novel, ‘The Decadence of Our Souls’. In an exciting and elegant style, Claudiu Murgan tells us the story of expanding the consciousness and awakening of the soul of the inhabitants in two very different worlds. I do not think this book is just a wonderful story but a manifesto, an invitation to a concrete involvement of many of us in the preparation for the transition to a new dimension, a Spiritual one.”

—Dr. Florin Munteanu
Center for Complexity Studies – UNESCO Center,
author of Seeds for Another World.

PROLOGUE

AT THE DAWN OF TIME, I blew life into all my creations, humans and beasts alike. You were born blind with only a burning desire to return to me, your *Creator*, to bring light to your sight for Eternity.

I specially blessed the children of the jungle and the beasts I called elephants to be bound by thought for as long as they live together and nurture each other.

I command that the time will come for the children to spread the word about me, *One Who Created All*, so all humans, through faith and cleanness of thought, come to my kingdom spiritually awake.

Kindness, warmth, intelligence and compassion I gave to the elephants, nothing less than I have given humans.

The *Trees of Life* are the womb of *My* children, and the *Book of Wisdom* is *My* written word that the children and the elephants must abide by.

I empowered the *Orange Souls* with My vibration and omnipresence to be *My* messengers on the physical plane. Listen to them and follow their guidance as you would obey *My* desire. They are sent to dispel from your minds the heavy fog of *maya's delusions.

The moment all of my children return to *Me* in the *Infinite Spirit,* I lay the rule that the elephants should roam the land on their own, and forget who they were.

* Maya – the power by which the universe becomes manifest; the illusion or appearance of the phenomenal world

CHAPTER 1

One Who Created All has released the arrows of consciousness. How many targets will the arrows reach and awaken?

From the book *We Are One* – Chapter 1

"ARE YOU AWARE OF YOUR AWARENESS?"

The voice was faint, more like the end of an echo, even though he knew that the man asking was sitting beside him. It was Bart, his master.

"Rakash, are you aware of your awareness?" the question bit him again, maybe for the hundredth time this session, but he did not move a muscle or change the rhythm of his breath, not to give away where he was mentally, or better said, where he was not.

Rakash could feel the harsh wool cover under his fingers and the growing ache of his lower back from his long meditation on the wooden bed. There were no senses anymore in the stiffened arms extended along his body. At the end of the session he had to 'come back' slowly, any abrupt moves would cause unbearable pain for the first several minutes.

The boy felt Bart moving closer to the bed, leaning on the front legs of the chair, his long black beard touching his chest. A wet cloth wiped Rakash's forehead then dropped it into a bucket filled with water behind him by a long, solid wooden table.

The water clock sounded the late afternoon. But the light in the room was dim, not only because it was facing north, but also helped by the thin crust of dirt built on the window, a mix of dust and bird droppings that couldn't be washed away by the occasional rain.

Suddenly, the room got darker, a passing cloud maybe, so Bart decided to light up a couple of half-burnt candles already stuck to the table by the melted wax. Electrical light would have interfered with the kid's meditation, as it was too bright. Bart studied the now visible orange triangle on the boy's light-brown cheeks, the stamp of his lineage and origin, proof of his yet untapped potential. A greater intensity of the orange birthmark would have indicated Bart's success in bringing to the surface century-old teachings, mental power, sensibilities and energies that no one inside the walls of this town possessed.

According to Stefano Magusti, the most prolific contemporary writer, who mentioned it several decades ago in his popular writing, *Hidden Communities of Our Time*, the brighter the orange became, the higher the mental state of a person wearing the strange signs on his cheeks. So far, Rakash couldn't recall deep memories or how to initiate the trance state that made him so valuable. There was no confirmation yet if Bart's or Magusti's guesses were right. The mark hadn't changed its intensity during the meditation sessions and the master didn't know for sure what steps to add or take out to trigger the right internal emotions preceding the *state of bliss*.

Some heard about it–the scholars, the educated, the higher ranks of the society. Few of them even claimed to have started on the path of achieving the *state of bliss*, but in fact no one was sure of the right initiation or a proven technique to follow. It was also a good icebreaker in a discussion, a clever way to meet a desirable partner, and exchange thoughts on the little literature published on the subject.

Bart knew all this. From the beginning, when he stumbled on the subject many years ago as a young scholar himself, he had decided not to change anyone's mind about what the *right way* to a meaningful living was, not until he could bring undeniable proof and become an example himself of experiencing '*the bliss*."

"Half of the hour-glass before bringing him back," the man muttered. He stood up, raised the bucket on the chair trying to avoid abrupt moves not to silence the burning candles, then left the room to prepare dinner.

The boy was not too deep into the meditation to sense when Bart left the room. It was the opportunity he was waiting for 'to come back' without being too obvious that this had been another failed session. He started by opening his eyes, then slowly moved his cold fingers and still ankles. This part was the most painful, always; somehow his legs and ankles couldn't accept this process of being immobilized for hours on end, they were kicking and screaming back to life, letting the blood flow again.

He grabbed the edge of the bed for support and pushed himself up, light-headed. He almost fell backwards and clutched the bed with both hands for a better balance.

His boots and the socks were nearby; he put them on, and then used the water from the bucket to freshen up. He arranged his entangled long hair to come straight on his shoulders. Having grown up with a shaved head; even after two years spent in Laeta, he still couldn't get used to the fluffy stuff he had to shorten from time to time, but Bart explained that it would help him integrate better with his newfound family.

Rakash still did not understand why he needed a new family when he had one already, one that provided everything for him ... the other children and the elephants. Yes, the elephants. Before being brought to this far away city, he talked to them all the time, a symphony of thoughts, knowledge, love, colours and much more that he was not taught to interpret yet. Someday he would go back so Otan, his elephant teacher, could trigger the buried meaning of his reincarnation as an *Orange Soul.*

"Hey, you are up. The food is ready," Bart, who came back to check on him, said. He smiled, showing his yellow teeth.

Rakash nodded and followed Bart into the hallway and from there to the kitchen. He found it odd to have so many enclosed spaces instead of one common open area for everyone to share. He remembered the huts and communal spaces everyone enjoyed in the village and the Library, which he'd visited only once. Maybe that's why a permanent memory of what books lined the countless shelves did not stick to him solidly.

They sat at the kitchen table facing each other ready for the dinner ritual: Rakash picking the small cut pieces of apples, pears and grapes, the pumpkin seeds, a bit of yellow, hard cheese and fish, and no more than a slice of bread with butter. Bart, gobbled the smoked meat and the red wine. Initially, the boy was encouraged to sample any meat, other than the fish, something he was familiar with, but hours later his body convulsed, sensing something that his stomach was not used to digesting. He tried again several weeks later, same symptoms, and never since.

Bart, Laeta's main scholar and his host and caretaker, just kept making notes of his behaviour and diet, avoiding pushing again for dishes that would make him sick or non-functional for more than two days. In fact this was how the scholar had set up the schedule of their sessions, every other day: enough time for Rakash to rest and potentially remember any deeper thoughts about his life in the jungle.

They ate in silence for a while, the boy nibbling at the seeds with real pleasure. Feeling the texture and the taste was part of the initial training from the moment he became aware of his surroundings in the jungle village, and of his brothers and sisters.

'*Keep it on the tongue for its texture. Each seed or leaf has its own texture and behaviour*', voices around him advised while he was still in the village. He could only remember faint voices and thoughts; faces and names of his previous family eluded him.

Bart moved his left hand through his beard removing the breadcrumbs still hanging around his mouth.

"Rakash, how is the food?" Bart asked already knowing how much the boy was enjoying the seeds and the cheese. Two years of close observations made Bart aware that the villager would not pay attention to anything else during eating, but the food. But now he wanted to ask a burning question and had to focus Rakash on what he had to say.

"Ihhmm", nodded the youngster with pleasure.

The boy sensed his master struggling to stay calm in spite of the uneasiness building inside him for reasons Rakash did not understand. He also noticed that if master spoke slowly it was because he had to share something important.

"It's been a while since the Committee left you with me to decipher the amazing treasure inside you".

The villager stopped chewing and his orange eyes fixed Bart with undivided attention.

"You might find our sessions very annoying and tiring, but believe me, they are necessary for me to understand how your community thinks, so you can become the bridge between us."

Rakash held onto the word bridge for a moment as it reminded him of the village, which was south of the bamboo crossing over the river where the elephants' herd used to go for their daily bath. Again, the sounds came alive inside him, screams of joy and water splashing, the cacophony of birds gathering on the shores, and the wooden hammers announcing that the meal was ready.

"I have to show them some results; otherwise they might take you away and ..." The man stopped talking, fidgeting with the empty mug. In reality he did not know what the Committee might do with Rakash if, in the end, he wouldn't be able to provide any indication that indeed the boy had the powers everyone expected of him. They would think they picked the wrong villager, a *Commoner*.

"We have to prove to them that you have this power within you," Bart continued in an almost desperate tone.

"Why do you keep saying that I have power? What is a *power*?" questioned the boy, putting another piece of fruit in his mouth.

"Power is not a physical thing you can touch," replied Bart, calmer this time. "You have it in here or in here," and touched his chest and his head. "This is a special kind ... to be able to feel with your heart and your mind and influence the people around you, spread love to those who lack it, change desperate thoughts into beacons of hope. You looked around town and saw that not everyone is happy; there are sad faces, some quite desperate. And even those who smile and laugh and seem to have a good time only think they are happy. It's the unfortunate life choices they made for themselves. We want to help them as well."

With his elbows pushed to the middle of the table, Bart stared into Rakash's orange eyes.

"I think ... in fact I am convinced that that sign on your cheeks makes you very special ... I feel that with my heart, with my gut. My instinct tells me that very soon you will remember more about your village and the teachings. We have to keep going through the meditation practice. Any detail I can add to my report before going in front of the Committee is important. They expect results; no more excuses. The meeting is in four days ... too soon."

Gently, Bart massaged his right leg's calf, which was shorter from birth, where most of the pain was, then poured himself more wine. Once, out of curiosity, Rakash asked to taste the liquid, but he spat it out right away.

"Play now?" Rakash was done eating and ready to do something more fun than lying dead on a hard bed.

Bart was about to reply when the door to the kitchen opened and slowly, Nayan's angular head revealed itself, keeping its body hidden on the other side. A sinister experiment of his psychotic parents when he was only two years old had turned Nayan into a human oddity. They tied his head to a triangular frame that forced the bones of his growing skull to follow that shape. A macabre experiment that landed them in jail and the boy into an orphanage.

"Here we go," said the scholar, pointing to Nayan, his young apprentice. "Here is your play mate, more suitable than me."

The boys were getting along just fine, the age difference of ten years didn't matter.

"Are you already done with the session? I hope I didn't disturb you," said the newcomer concerned.

"No worries, in fact we are even done eating and the lad here wants to play."

"I'll bring the supplies inside then I'll take him by the river to watch the birds and the other kids bathing."

"Wonderful, please don't stay too late, it's getting dark in three hours," Bart advised.

"Understood, just a bit of a walk so he shakes his legs, then we are right back," replied Nayan excited that he had another opportunity to spend time alone with Rakash.

"Did you find everything on the list?" Bart asked, thinking of the writing supplies.

"Absolutely, including the paper and ink. A package was outside by the door, I think the mailman was in a rush and didn't knock. I'll drop it in the library."

"Thank you, I'll check it as soon as you guys leave. It's the books I've been waiting for."

Rakash followed his older friend, helping with bringing all the bags in, anxious to head to the river.

He entered the kitchen and put the bread and other pastries on the middle shelf, the vegetables, fruits, all the meats and the fish to the cold room several steps down, the flour and rice on the bottom shelf.

After they were done, Bart walked them to the entrance and kept the main door ajar. He watched the boys depart and enjoyed the happiness displayed by both his protégés. Nayan was very tall for a 16 year old, slim, well-built body, with just a puff of blond hair on top of his odd-shaped head. Rakash still had a long way to fully develop and grow.

Bart hoped Nayan might be more successful in extracting any valuable knowledge from the kid. Nayan's approach was totally opposite from his own rigid method of dealing with people.

Before closing the door, he realized that he could hear the music from one of the nearby districts. The parties had already started. Laeta, the city he lived in, was ready for another day of wild entertainment.

* * *

"WE'LL TAKE THE SHORTCUT," Nayan said.

They crossed the street and squeezed into an alley between two half-timbered, three-story houses, so narrow that only kids could fit through. The alley was at a slight angle and more like a channel for the water to find its way to the main filtration station and from there, cleaned, to the fields for irrigation. There was a time when these channels were so filthy from all of the leftovers thrown down that the streets became unusable, forcing everyone to stay inside for almost a week, enough for the Committee and the sanitation department to clean it up and put in place new rules. Korobat, the city that provided all their clean technologies, had to step in and help pick up the additional garbage as the local recycling plant couldn't keep up burning it. The contamination affected even the main source of water, so it had to be taken twice through the purification process before being consumed.

The boys crossed three other main streets using similar narrow alleys, reaching an open field that was abutted the river and had a pine tree forest to its right. Behind the trees, wind turbines were moving their blades lazily in the dying wind of late afternoon. Most of the city's barren land, outside the existing boundaries, was used for generating the energy the town's nightlife relied heavily on. The other shore was crowded with three or four story buildings hosting private lounges, tattoo parlors, hotels and restaurants that, at night, all turned into decadent places of heavy drug usage, sex and drinking, all in excess. Laeta, the Entertainment City, was living up to its reputation of a place where any fantasy could be satisfied.

Since its partnership with Korobat City, Laeta had come a long way toward improving the lives of its citizens by using electricity and technology. The squalid town, whose streets at dark were dangerous to walk, became clean and safer, attracting more and more visitors each year.

"Let's run," Rakash yelled.

They broke their run meters away from the river's man-made sandy shores.

Rakash stepped on the sand and took a deep breath of the hot air. He gazed at what the locals called 'the river', which were in fact a dug channel, three km long, twenty meters wide and no more than five feet at its deepest point. It cut the town in half and borrowed water from the real river, wide and furious that ran parallel with the city, to the west of it. He liked to endlessly watch the sheer power of the tumultuous water mercilessly cutting its way through the land, admiring its determination, and comparing it with the determination and enduring existential approach of his lost community from the jungle.

The artificial beach they had just arrived at was meant to complement the pleasures found in the Entertainment District, that was just on the other side of the canal.

Only recently, after he turned six years old, was he told about the leadership structure of the city and the rules that the citizens had to obey. It was the Committee who put a lot of effort in designing the shores: easy accesses, imported sand, smooth slabs of stones for the bottom and even miniature waterfalls.

The other two bridges at the beginning and end of the channel had their own attraction, but this one by the beach was the most popular for the only reason that one could lean on the rail and watch for endless hours the hypnotic movement of bodies, in and out of the water. Very rarely, the boy would go to the bridge downstream, at the end of the channel that would offer a view of the two-story, brick-covered filtration system building, taking in the water and returning it back to the town for consumption.

The beach was less populated than usual, more adults and teenagers than parents with kids. The sun was setting, but it was still hot and humid, a perfect time for enjoying the water.

Nayan removed his sandals and blue shirt and dropped himself on the ground. Rakash followed suit. He loved to push his toes in hot sand, which to him represented a living being, evolving, transforming, adapting to the environment; billions of particles coming together as one entity, talking or just whispering in his ear a story that he couldn't yet translate. Cycles ago in the jungle, the connection with his other family – the children, the elephants and the animals – was getting stronger. Here in Laeta, he only occasionally would go outside to feel the sand, the birds and the trees. He was spending too much time inside pretending to meditate.

"How was today's session? Anything new?" Nayan asked him.

"No difference from two days ago. Don't know if I have that thing Bart is looking for: power." Rakash filled his hands with sand and started to rub it on his legs. Rough, but invigorating. The river in the jungle was lined with mud and stones. It would be nice to bring some sand when he went back. His friends would love it.

"Don't worry, it will come to you," assured Nayan, keeping an eye on the group to their right. Two couples in their thirties' laying on their towels. The women were topless, wearing just skimpy underwear. This area was still considered public, so going completely naked was prohibited.

'*They are most likely tourists getting warmed up for tonight's parties*,' thought Nayan.

Several bottles littered the sand around them. The volume of their conversation grew louder as the men were trying to wrestle the women to the ground in a contest of force and agility. But they were too drunk to coordinate themselves, only generating a good laugh for everyone else watching.

"What do you think is missing to get where master wants you to be?"

"I don't know. Maybe I've never been to that place before, so I can't recognize it." Rakash found a shell and started to scoop out sand for a miniature hole. "Back in the jungle I used to spend a lot of time with my teacher, Otan."

"We've talked about this before; there was a connection between you and the elephant. Did you always need him to turn on that deep feeling you get about your surroundings?"

"I think so. Once I spoke with a couple of older kids that were more advanced in their studies. They were able to enter a state of internal peace at any time. But they needed their teacher to open for them the door to the next level of deeper introspection. They would mentally spend time in that space inside them until they were ready to move forward," Rakash offered the few memories he had about his previous life in the village.

The topless women jumped in the water and splashed each other, while making obscene gestures towards the men, too stoned and tired to join them. The water only came to their waists; everyone could enjoy the upper part of their bodies. Both women were tall. One was white haired; the other was red-haired and muscular. An elephant head in vivid yellow and green, with piercing eyes, was tattooed on the back of the women with white hair.

"Wow," exclaimed Rakash when he saw it. "What is that?" he turned to Nayan, begging for an explanation.

"That's a tattoo, similar to your orange triangle, with the exception that she was not born with it. Someone inked it on her back. Very painful and unhealthy if you ask me," concluded the teenager trying to divert the boy's attention back to their discussion about what it means to be an *Orange Soul.* This is what master thought Rakash was based on the orange birthmark on his cheeks, an *Orange Soul.*

But the woman saw Rakash's reaction and started calling him to join them in the water. Nayan was already trying to avoid any interaction with the outsiders, let alone involve the boy with any of them.

A group of five teenagers on the other shore, already wearing their bathing suits, felt encouraged by the women's calling to Rakash and jumped at the opportunity. They thought the women would be an easy target, now that the men were dozing off on the sand, so they got in the water and closed in.

Both women heard the splashing behind them and turned. Only now could Nayan and Rakash see the back of the second woman wearing the head of a tiger, strong orange and black colours. The tiger had one point of attraction, his eyes, which were as penetrating as the elephant's on the other woman's back.

The teenagers were several feet away, not hiding their intention of touching the women, playing with them for a bit right there in the water. Nayan saw in their churlish faces that in seclusion they would even have dared to go further with or without the consent of the women.

The chased suddenly turned their backs to the chasers, but not to run. They just stood their ground for no more than ten seconds while the teenagers stopped, paralyzed, looking straight at the women's backs. It gave the women enough time to get out, put on T-shirts and wake up their partners. As the teenagers remained frozen, the visitors gathered their bags hastily, crossed the bridge and disappeared through the buildings edging the shore, toward the entertainment district.

Nayan had never seen anything like it before. Was it really the elephant and the tiger that hypnotized a group of unruly teenagers? Everyone else on both shores had watched, initially enjoying the sight of the wonderful bodies, but now looked with awe, not trying to intervene in any way. In the water, the teenagers came back to life and somehow they were not sure why they were being stared at.

Nayan waited no longer. "Let's go," he said.

"I want to see the birds," Rakash complained, not comprehending what had just happened and why his friend was in such a rush to leave.

"Next time, Rakash. Please! I just remembered that Bart asked me to copy some transcripts for next week's meeting with the Committee. And it's a lot of documents."

He didn't like lying to the young boy, but any other excuse wouldn't hold water against his sharp mind. Nayan had just witnessed two amazing events in a matter of minutes: hypnotic ink and strangers trying to make contact with a kid they had never met before. And while he was not that much puzzled about the former, the latter was the thing that worried him the most. His master always told him to stay alert and today it really paid off. They hurried back the same way, arriving home safely.

* * *

NAYAN FOUND BART IN THE library browsing the new books, additions to the one already full shelf of books on the customs and lifestyle of the jungle villagers and their partners, the elephants. His master wished to read everything that was ever published on this subject and compare it with his own experience gathered over the last two years spent with Rakash. Determining what was fiction and what was truth about this secretive community hidden in the jungle would help present his case to the Committee. The latest acquisitions ordered by the scholar from a local bookstore had leather covers and looked very old.

"Hey, Nayan, have a seat," invited the scholar. "Let me show you something interesting ... oh, where is Rakash?"

"I sent him upstairs to get ready for sleep. I also have something amazing to share with you."

Nayan didn't take the black-leathered armchair indicated by Bart, but kneeled down in front of the coffee table on which one of the books was opened.

"Look at these images," pointed the master to several coloured drawings. Two of them were images of *mutsavi* trees of different colors, blue and purple. The other images showed some roots in a desolate land, a gathering of massive stones in the jungle, and a waterfall.

"What are these?" inquired Nayan.

"Presumably, places where the villagers are being born or born from."

"You mean born from a tree or a waterfall?"

"Unbelievable, isn't it?' replied Bart. "I have no idea yet if it's true, but this is the first time I've found this information. It says that it originated from Stefano Magusti and somehow, didn't make it into any of the books about villagers. There is no indication of how Magusti came across it, and looking at the date, it was published after his passing."

Nayan loved to hear his master talk about the books as it got him excited, and made him forget for a while about the pain in his leg and the disappointment that no approach had yet shook Rakash's memory about how a regular person could achieve the *state of bliss*. The Committee was counting on turning it into a source of revenue.

"If you want I can write to the publisher, if he is still in business, and see if he has any notes left or even some unpublished material," offered Nayan.

"Good idea. Just don't show too much excitement. Say that you would like to know if they published anything else on the same subject. Rakash is our only source who can validate the information from all the books we read so far. Unfortunately, he hasn't been of much help."

"What else have you found?" Nayan took the seat across from his master.

"This book is a real gem," began Bart.

Nayan put his palms together, eyes big, upper body leaning forward, ready to absorb the newly found knowledge.

"It talks about the significance of the villagers' birthmarks and their connection with the elephants. It seems that Magusti held back some critical information."

"So this could be the proof for the Committee. They would definitely believe a record printed before I was born," said Nayan convinced that Bart had just found the missing evidence to convince the governing body of Laeta, that Rakash was indeed an *Orange Soul* that soon would lead them to what triggers an elevated state of happiness.

"I appreciate your enthusiasm, but it doesn't work like that," Bart said. "The Committee would acknowledge the resemblance between what this book says and what Rakash looks like, even behaviorally we can match them a little, but nothing more. We need to activate in the boy the state that is used to communicate with his teacher, the elephant. That will be a milestone we can celebrate. I suggest we show Rakash these images. One of these places might relate to him."

Bart closed the book and let himself be embraced by the armchair. He picked up his mug of tea, which was already cold, and looked straight through the window at the reddish sky sitting on top of his neighbor's roof.

Another long day with not much achieved. The research on Rakash was sketchy and there were only four more days before the monthly meeting to present his findings in front of the six members of the Committee. He kept sipping the tea until the dark completely engulfed the roof. Next to him Nayan was fidgeting, ready to share certain news, but Bart wanted to be by himself for a while.

"Why don't you get something to eat, then tell me today's story," suggested the scholar.

Nayan nodded and went to the kitchen.

Left alone and still holding the empty mug close to his lips, Bart studied his walls of books and maps. His keen interest in learning new things since he was nine years old could have been entirely traced by how the books were placed on the shelves, a timeline of who he was. Three quarters of his life put on display; successes and failures, but overall enough accomplishments to be proud of.

Having a real family had eluded him. The constant responsibilities of providing for a household were an unnecessary burden considering the effort and concentration he had to allocate to his work. His physical appearance didn't help in finding a wife. His nose was almost unnoticeable from profile, pushed inside his skull by an invisible force that worked on his body before being born. Small ears, a big head, and eczema on the left side of his head that didn't allow for hair to grow with the same vigor and density as the rest of his skull, forcing him to either get a haircut every other week or wear a hood.

His wobbling walk completed the list of 'qualities' that prevented him from being desired by any woman wishing to conceive children and proudly declare that she was the town's Assigned Scholar's wife. Bart squeezed his lips, producing a low toned whistle, thinking that *One Who Created All,* a higher being that no one in the city believed in, didn't want to leave him completely helpless in this world. *He* had given him a sharp mind, thick skin to withstand any vitriolic language and enough patience to sell by the bucket. He didn't have siblings as none of them passed the age of five for whatever reason, never explained to him by his parents. Bart survived against all odds, carrying his deformities devoid of shame. Too old and tired to keep trying to have more kids, his parents gave him their undivided attention.

School was fun and when the time came, his father, the owner of a medium size construction company, didn't hesitate to pay the pricey enrolment fee at the most prestigious Scholars Academy in Korobat City, as no one in Laeta had ever been to school beyond Korobat's limits. It was more than enough to get the Committee interested in him. In fact, there was only a handful of scholars in town at any given time as most of those who graduated the Scholars Academy in Korobat remained there, engaged in developing new technologies.

Nayan returned holding a large plate full of vegetables, rice and smoked fish. He was trying to stay away from red meat, to clean his body as much as possible to be ready when the breakthrough with Rakash happened. The teenager had no ego when it came to following the habits of his younger friend. Nayan knew that he could learn from him.

Nayan sat on the armchair, and mouth full, started explaining the events that happened by the river.

Bart stopped him right away.

"Finish your food first, don't swallow big gulps, just enjoy it a bit, we have time."

Five minutes later he was done. He started again, detailing everything he observed.

CHAPTER 2

Whoever understands the sound vibrations of his physical shell, has opened his internal eye.

From the book *We Are One* – Chapter 2

THE PACHYDERM WAS SITTING DOWN, leaning against the palm's thick trunk in an opening at the edge of the jungle. His voluminous belly covered in a thick crust of cracked mud rested on the crushed yellowish grass of the clearing. The front legs that bent forward were the support for his trunk, entangling his ankles like an odd colorless snake. The deep filigree of his skin was a perfect cover for his closed eyes. His tusks had several dents and scratches; the left one was shorter and with a rounded tip from much more use. Kids yelled and called meters away, but Bagham did not seem to acknowledge them, his ears showing no sign of capturing the sound. The rarefied, light-colored hair on his head moved back and forth in a gentle breeze, encouraged by the narrow opening above him, in the canopy of palm and acacia trees.

The visible side of his body had multiple marks on display in the form of circles, small hands and wavy lines. Blue and purple. Covering him unevenly, they clustered mainly on the upper side of his hind legs, towards his round back. Strange patches of joy on the otherwise dull, wrinkled skin. The shapes looked very much like an integral part of his body, not painted, but there, as unusual birthmarks. Their surface was as rumpled as the surrounding area. Other red and blackened scars dotted his ears and legs, the usual marks of a fight for an elephant of his size and age.

He felt exhausted after a night spent in the cold air of the deserted land bordering the jungle. The wet dirt chilled his hooves and sent shivers up his legs. He was not sure why his instinct brought him again to this particular spot outside the safety of the bush. Everything here was dead, no grass or animals, only the dead tree whose dried skeleton was still standing at the mercy of the heat of the day or the cold of the night. Bagham wanted to stay with the herd, but the vibrational *call* of the unborn child who would be his pupil to teach and share the knowledge left to them by their ancestors, was too strong to avoid. One had to follow and wait for events to unfold the way they were written many thousands of years ago, without anyone's consent. He was just not equipped to count how many times he had felt the *call* lately; but every other moonrise–this is what the children called the glowing circle visible at night up in the sky–he was out again, at the same desolate location, contemplating the twisted wood coming out of the bare ground like arched bony fingers, splintered in several places, all converging in a central point from where branches were shooting straight up three times his height. It was the only structure present in the desolate land outside the jungle, nevertheless lifeless and somehow out of place. It looked too fragile to brush against to stop an itch bothering him behind his left ear. He was afraid that by touching it, he would break it with a thunderous noise that, in the stillness of night, might bring unwanted attention to his whereabouts.

He expected the *call* to reinstate him as a teacher again as soon as he heard that the *Trees of Life* were in bloom. His last pupil, Maresh, transitioned nimbly to *One Who Created All* only a cycle ago, making Bagham proud of this achievement, and, at the same time, available to coach a newborn. The elephant had several other brothers and sisters going through the same torment of waiting for the *call*, but none of them went outside the jungle. The forceful vibration emitted by the *Trees* gathered the selected few elephants at various times of the day to slowly accustom them with the pain that would increase its intensity along with the intensity of the *call*. Bagham's *call* was different this time. He wanted to be there, at the *Trees*, where he had waited many times before for the arrival of his next companion. What caste will he teach this time?

Altan, the lead bull, hinted that the dead tree, was one of four locations outside the village, portals through which *Orange Souls* are born. Could he be so lucky to teach such an accomplished soul? He hoped that miraculously, the lifeless, thick branches breaking out of the parched land would come back to life, spawning seeds strong enough to carry a healthy newborn.

Footsteps rustled through the grass approaching him. Bagham slowly moved his ears to recognize whose pattern it was. Only Danish would look for him and remember to bring him water.

"Hey, Bagham," the boy greeted him with a low voice, not sure if the elephant was deep in his sleep or just resting. Danish put down the wooden bowl filled with water as the weight had started to weaken his arms. It spilled a little on the way to the clearing, but there was still enough left to keep his friend's body cool before taking him to the river for a proper wash. Danish pulled his grayish pants up, crossed his legs and dropped himself on the ground, waiting for a sign of movement, an affirmation that he could talk again.

Bagham liked Danish. He was not his companion, just a temporary helper. He reminded him of Danisha, his first assignment, many, many cycles ago. She was tall, slim, had a purple wavy mark on her cheeks, a shaved head, was gentle and above all, a good student. Of course, Danish was a *Commoner* not a *Writer*, he lacked the marks on his face; instead his hands were blue, the indication of his caste, but otherwise there was a close facial resemblance.

When Bagham came of age to receive the *call*, he was anxious and worried at the same time. The elders taught him enough to have his expectations settled. When Danisha *called* while in her peapod, his overwhelming surprise was followed by such an intense pain that his front left knee bent, almost bringing him down. The other elephants around him rapidly pushed their heads forward, providing the missing balance. He also received a faint thought-intention from his soon to be *She-Writer* companion.

Bagham moved his edge-shredded ears again and opened a lazy eye to focus on Danish.

"Here you are," his thought-intention reaching the boy.

Danish was sitting with his back straight, his blue hands on his lap with palms facing up, the position impressed upon all the kids from the moment they were able to walk.

"You did not ask me to come with you last night. I got worried when you did not return with the herd for the morning meal". Danish was not upset, he was just making a statement. By not being his companion, the boy wasn't supposed to show any sign of affection or annoyance through the tone of his voice nor through his body language, which was a sign of attachment.

"The *call* came to me very suddenly and I just felt like leaving without waking anyone. The gatekeepers let me out silently." Bagham straightened his front legs, ready to rise and follow the boy back to the village. The breeze picked up, letting the sun pierce through the canopy onto the elephant's skin. He liked the warmth of it and stopped right there, halfway up. It hit the painful spot close to his back right leg, where he was expecting the new birthmark to show up. He couldn't tell yet what it was going to be: a *Writer*, a *Builder,* an *Artist*, a *Commoner*, a she or a he. This time the pain was more confusing, deeper, not following the traditional pattern that he expected. "I forgot to take back the water pot. I dropped it somewhere in the dark close to the roots," Bagham sent a thought towards Danish.

"No worries, we can get all of them later today after the bath. So do you still feel the urge to splash water around the petrified tree?" Danish was already standing. He grabbed the pot with the intention to throw its contents onto Bagham's back.

"Don't do it, just leave it alone. I'll drink it, I'm really thirsty." Fully standing, he used his trunk to slurp water and empty it into his mouth. "I wouldn't call them petrified, I still sense a little pulse in there somewhere; nevertheless, it seems pointless to try to revive something so close to death."

Along with the *call* to come to this unusual location, the elephant had the burning desire to bring water on the trip to the edge of the jungle where the leftover of the tree jutted from the ground like a bizarre sculpture. Each time he spilled it carefully on the ground as near as possible to the base of the roots, hoping to see an immediate change only to be disappointed as the cracked ground sucked it up insatiably. It's been a while now, a fraction of a cycle, Danish clarified for him, since he kept dropping water with no visible results.

"You'll get an answer soon," said the boy confidently. "The time has come for you to get your companion. I can't think of any other reason why you were summoned outside the jungle."

He picked up the bowl, ready to go back.

"Nikor told us this morning that he *felt* his pupil too. It's a girl. He was so excited. His last two companions were boys. Not that he wasn't fond of them, but he remembers Herera, his first assignment, who was warm and gave him an amazing experience as a teacher. The buds have light colors and are of fair size now, hanging heavy on the branches. If you spend enough time under the *Trees* you will notice the kicks too." Danish updated the elephant.

Bagham moved alongside Danish; he had stopped listening to the chatter of his thoughts. Nikor was a younger elephant, only one purple and two blue hands marking his hide to display how many children he had taught so far and what caste they belong to. In his case, they were all *Commoners.* The experience the children and the elephants had was equally important as the teachings came from *One Who Created All.* It was the deep bond between humans and beasts that kept the community and the traditions perpetuating from millennia ago. Over the years, Bagham had exchanged thoughts with many in the herd about this ancient bond established with the children. The truth is that no one ever forgot their first companion and in time would only remember major natural events tied to a specific relationship or to specific items related to their caste such as a beautifully written book, a gracious mix of colours applied on bamboo paper turned into a piece of artwork, or a stronger than normal thought-to-thought tie. And his mind was etching in the common knowledge of the community his own life record of the last ten pupils using similar milestones.

One Who Created All had blessed him with good children who learnt the teachings, practiced them and achieved their caste goals while experiencing the *state of bliss.* All but two transitioned gracefully to the *Supreme Being* before turning into elders, a sign that any achievement in this existence will elude them. Those two had suffered grief from such disappointment, and Bagham hoped that they would come back in a new reincarnation for another attempt to live a meaningful life spent in awe for *One Who Created All.*

The elephant's strength of body and clarity of thought were needed to continue even further in propagating these traditions and the teachings accumulated by the herd before him. He was still young, and had a long time to wait before making the short list to become the lead bull. Bagham prayed daily to the *One Who Created All* for strength to teach as many children as possible before his physical demise.

"How many peapods are carrying lives this time?" Bagham asked.

"Last time I checked, ten," Danish answered. "Fenuku is already examining the records for the proper names. Only half of the elephants waiting for the *call* have really sensed the newborns. That's because some peapods are barely developed and incapable of sending any signal yet. Your case is different. The roots you are drawn to show no sign of life. Very strange," continued Danish.

Fenuku was the only *Builder* boy in the Council and was in charge of recording the births, deaths, and names, and who was next in line to fill any available position in the Council of five. It was the most prestigious spot in the Council. Bagham considered that perhaps he should ask Fenuku about the list of names that were about to be assigned as soon as he knew what type of companion he was expecting. "But how can I be next and even feel the *call*? The skeletal roots carry no buds."

Danish sensed the thought, powered by the annoyance and worry built inside his friend. "That, I can't explain, but I trust your instincts. They've never failed."

They continued on the mud path towards the village, passing several groups of children and elephants that were teaching in the open, in the middle of the *Supreme Being's* creation, which the community was part of. Bagham could sense Saphron, the only elephant born with small holes in her right ear, with her four *Commoners*, two boys and two girls, reading from the *We Are One* book, a daily mandatory reading for everyone until they reached eighteen cycles. Sitting on thick roots bursting from the ground, each kid was holding his own copy, trying to memorize the chapters indicated by their teacher. An exercise to test their patience and dedication, but at the same time, expand the native curiosity that they were born with.

Steps away, Manash was testing his *Writer* partner's skills on how to make bamboo paper. They were only at the first step, identifying the right type of bamboo. All the *Writers* had to go through the manufacturing process, gathering appreciation for the medium they would use to fulfill their destiny.

Other groups were hidden by the lush vegetation, and gave themselves away only when the elephants snorted or purred, showing their satisfaction with the level of knowledge their pupils displayed.

The canopy above them crawled with birds and monkeys swinging from branch to branch, used to the presence below. Scents of ripening avocado, papaya and bananas filled the air, instilling in Bagham a much needed optimism.

Otherwise, the jungle had its own sounds and breathing, its own energy vibration, a healthy organism in which each cell supported the next. There was no competition, just an awareness of everyone's place and role as written in the *Book*.

"How are your studies advancing since you have no permanent teacher?" Bagham asked. He was hungry and the slow walk allowed him to grab several branches full of leaves.

"I am halfway through the *Book*," Danish replied. "It got slower since Otan disappeared. All four of us spend no more than two hours daily amongst ourselves discussing the *Book* and every other sunrise we study with one of the available teachers, the ones who got the *call* and still have time before their pupil is born. And, if we are lucky, some mornings a Council member teaches us." He put the empty bowl on his head, bottom up, so he could eat a banana picked off the ground.

"It's a painful process, I really understand that. A calf should be born soon. Brinka is heavy with a calf and almost at the end of gestation period. She hasn't gone out during the last three sunrises," Bagham explained.

"How long before the newborn will become our teacher?" the boy inquired, throwing away the banana peel.

"At least five cycles. Like you, he will need guidance and love. There is so much knowledge we have to transfer to him and it has to be done the right way," Bagham explained.

He was aware of the children's confusion. Very few humans have ever experienced the loss of their teacher. Usually it was the elephants mourning the passing of their pupils turned into adults in the eventuality that enlightenment had not occurred. With Otan's disappearance almost three cycles ago, the amazing connection was unexpectantly broken, and four orphans left to the community.

Bagham felt the urge to urinate and stopped, letting Danish move forward, avoiding the spoil.

They walked in silence as they approached the village. The high walls were made of three layers of bamboo, enough to stop any outside physical force, and giving the villagers enough time to prepare their defense. The boys on duty pulled the thick ropes connected to the gates, letting Danish and Bagham in. This led to a forked road, which curved around the compound and united again on the other side.

To Danish's left, were the huts the kids lived in, fifteen in total, housing groups of four to six. Out of those fifteen, two were designated for the newborns and the villagers that would take care of them until the age of three. To the right, were the elephants' accommodations, an area wide enough to shelter, if necessary, the entire female population at night, as most of the bulls were out foraging in the jungle and returned in the morning. Large wooden dug outs filled with water and piles of fresh leaves lined against the interior of the bamboo wall were the only necessities the elephants needed for the short period of time they were inside. In the middle of the compound, stretching for the length of the entire village, lay the common halls, the library, meditation rooms and the workshops where the *Builders* and *Artists* tinkered with their creations. At the back, gardens provided most of their food, and beyond that, guarded by the highest portion of the fence was the most important possession they had, the *Trees of Life.* Thickened by hundreds of years of existence and covered in blue and purple bark, the *Trees* represented the portals used by *One Who Created*

All to birth *His* sons and daughters.

Danish nodded to Bagham, telling him that later on he would pick him up to go to the river, and took the left path. He passed some of his friends who were cleaning the huts and others doing kitchen chores. He would start doing his in a minute, but he wanted a bit of time by himself to process what the elephant had said about how long before he would have a new, steady teacher.

He entered the hut that he was sharing with five other boys, and dropped himself on the bed – a wood frame on top of which several layers of bamboo leaves were weaved tightly together. For a moment, he stared at the nicely arranged books on shelves that hung on the walls and at the pendants and artwork displayed above each bed, the only decoration allowed by the *Book*. He felt as empty of life as the room he was in. Then he took a deep breath and focused on the top of his head, envisioning a protective translucent energy sphere around it. Now it was safe to be alone with his thoughts.

"Five years seems like an eternity," he said to himself. "Otan, I really miss you, my friend. I hope you decide to come back to us before I transition this life. And if I recognize you, I promise I'll make you remember the experiences we had together, the same way you did with me. Yes, I was born a *Commoner* this time, but I know I've been an *Artist* in at least two previous lives." He vocalized the words for the last statement, barely spoken, but carrying enough emotion to make him cry. Danish dried the tears with his sleeve. "*We Are One*, yes, I understand that. It's the mantra we all love and make part of our daily, mundane life, at least my life. Otan, I am tired of pretending; please give me a sign. I need your help. There is no one I can confide in. My other brothers and sisters are all obedient and don't remember as much as I do."

He looked around the room for a visible sign. No sudden breeze, no movement, no energy form, no sign that his former teacher and friend was listening, and even if he was listening, not willing to intervene in any way.

"I am aware that I don't love *One Who Created All* fully. Something inside me blocks the doors of my heart from letting out waves of emotions and feeling for *Him*. This blockage also keeps away *His* love for me. Otan, tell me how I can smooth my communion with *One Who Created All.* I don't want to return to another arduous existence."

Discouraged, the boy did not expect an answer.

"*One Who Created All*, forgive me for what I'm going to do, I need to finish my training and fulfill my destiny, I can't live a *Commoner*'s life," Danish thought before dissolving the energy shield.

He gently touched the small pouch hanging around his neck in which he kept hair from Otan's tail.

"I love you my friend, wherever you are."

* * *

DANISH CLEANED HIS FACE WITH the water from the bucket sitting by the door and went straight to the gardens where he expected to find Otan's other pupils. Asman, Akello and Putri were tending the vegetables that had fallen behind in blooming. Sitting down back to back in the lotus position on the path between the rows of tomatoes, cabbage and peppers, the kids were chanting. Silently, Danish took his place close to Akello, the younger of the two girls. An instant later he visualized the mind image created by his friends. Healthy, fully ripe plants, ready to be eaten. The object of their focus was surrounded by an orange aura, a field of energy with increased effect by the vibrations of the chanting. Sometimes the elephant dung used for fertilization was not enough to keep the gardens productive. Like any other living organism of the habitat, the plants needed love and attention: the universe's energy channeled through humans. This was one of the most important lessons taught in the *We Are One* book.

Danish knew that they had all reached this level from the time spent with Otan. They were able to master helping small plants, vegetables and fruit trees, but nothing bigger than that and certainly not animals. That required a more complex energy channeling for which Otan was supposed to prepare them ... and now he was not around anymore. As the boy had just learnt, it would be five years before they could resume their training. He tried hard to stay focused on the chanting and not disturb the others.

They kept at it for a while until they all agreed that enough energy had been transferred.

"How is Bagham?" Putri asked while cleaning her purple hands on her worn, outsized shirt. Her wide, rich lips were the main attraction on her stern face. Imagining her with long hair could have improved his perception, but none of them wore hair since it added unnecessary effort to their daily activities.

"He's annoyed by the situation he's in, going to the edge of the jungle for apparently no reason. He thinks that it's *the call*, but why there?" Danish answered, getting ready for the next session by moving to the next row of plants.

"Isn't that dangerous ... to go there by himself in the middle of the night?" Akello never talked much; she used thoughts this time as well.

"Could be, but he uses his energy field to sense any enemy ahead of time and the *dapanees* never come that close to the village," Danish addressed all their worries.

The dapanees were their fiercest adversary in the jungle. They were the only creatures that the mental power of the elephants couldn't subjugate.

The lessons the children learnt through Otan's disappearance made them more cautious; their pain was still molting deep inside and they weren't sure if it would ever be put out. Being tied to one teacher was the ultimate connection and, for *Commoners*, the bond was even stronger.

"Has anyone searched the library for any record regarding this odd location?" Asman asked.

There were several extensive chapters in the *Book* that explained the main purpose of the *Trees of Life* – acting as a portal for all four castes of *Artists, Builders, Writers* and *Commoners*. It was intriguing for the children that Bagham was the only one called to a different place. But they were the pupils of Otan who, before them, taught an *Orange Soul*, Rakash, whose birth also didn't happen in the village through the *Trees*, and who also went missing ten cycles ago.

"There might be another way," Danish replied. "Altan is the oldest in the herd. I can ask him if he remembers if anything similar has happened before."

"Good idea," Akello said through her thoughts. "If he says no, then we will know how far back we have to start looking at the records."

"I'll ask Bagham if he already talked to Altan about it," Danish concluded and focused again on the papaya and avocado trees.

Danish was the oldest in their group and next in line to fill an available position with any of the elephants teaching *Commoners*. It was his only chance to continue his training that was interrupted so suddenly. He realized that he had to create such an opportunity himself, otherwise he would have to wait five cycles for Brinka's calf to become his teacher.

* * *

IT WAS EARLY IN THE MORNING, right before sunrise, when the village heard the alarm. The plank hit by wooden hammers was screaming fear, a continuous knock, so rarely used, and so different than the usual three strokes that signalled the daily meals. Nagoti was missing and a search all over the compound came up empty handed. Taber, along with her remaining pupils, Janka, Makori and Indah, frantically sent thought after thought hoping to sense any faint sign of her student. Most of the cows' herd gathered together in a small circle, heads in, combining their power to reach further and further, looking for the enemy lurking in the jungle.

All the kids assembled in the main hall and the remaining female elephants took positions by the three entrances. Torches were lit and held up on the walls.

"Quiet everyone," said Altan, the herd's lead bull, sending a mental vibratory signal to the whole community. He was the only mature bull allowed inside the village during the night to watch over Brinka, his mate. He stood in a threatening position, ears held out, head up and legs firmly planted on the ground, ready to face an invisible menace.

The alarm stopped, the kids' fearful chatter vanished. A long silence followed, in and outside the village. Altan lifted his right hooves and gently touched the ground, sending a wave of warning to the bull herd rummaging through the jungle.

"Stay calm. We can't sense anyone who doesn't belong, so we'll wait before going out to look for the child, Nagoti. The elephants that have already received *the call* of their newborn, stay behind. It might not be safe for you," the elephant continued while organizing everyone. "Taber and I will lead the search."

Bowls of seeds and fruits were passed from hand to hand as regular breakfast was already disturbed by the events.

"Taber, do you remember anything else about Nagoti's latest location?" Altan asked again after ensuring that the camp was under control and everyone was accounted for.

"The children were together right before going to sleep, but it was her turn for a quick watch on the walls. It would have been her second time training at night. She never got there," replied the She-elephant.

As part of the training, the humans had to learn how to connect and understand the nightly souls and entities that were part of the living organism surrounding them. Taber's pupils were all six years old, which was rare, since it was usually a mixture of ages among *Commoners*.

Altan did not have his own memory of losing a pupil, it was one from the common memory of the herd. He was not yet in charge when such an incident happened ten cycles ago when Rakash, one of Otan's pupils and an *Orange Soul*–so rare in the community–simply vanished. But the circumstances were different than what happened to Nagoti the other night. The search for Rakash lasted two sunrises and when they stopped at the edge of the jungle, they found faded human footprints of various sizes, some small enough to be his, but they couldn't be sure as it was quite unexpected for such a young child to reach the harsh land, stretching to the horizon. No animal had touched him either, as they couldn't locate any blood or body parts left behind by a predator.

Losing Rakash made Otan go berserk and it took him three cycles before agreeing to teach again. But only *Commoners*, because the pain he went through made his mind believe that caring for four kids would alleviate his agony.

Rakash was an *Orange Soul* with no caste limitations, a boundless potential to be discovered. The only such soul born in more than forty cycles, sent back either with a purpose by *One Who Created All* or by his own will to serve the community. It was a privilege for Otan to be his teacher.

Everything seemed to be back to normal until two and a half cycles ago. While teaching his kids at their favourite spot close to the edge of the jungle, Otan stopped in the middle of the debate about their real goal in life, raised his head towards the north and, without addressing the children a thought of warning, turned around and disappeared through the thick vegetation. This was all Altan was able to extract from Danish, the only one not completely paralyzed by the odd situation, as rarely were the kids left unattended by their teachers. Left by themselves, the *Commoners* did not follow him, but they hurled desperate thoughts of help to the closest elephant who in turn pushed them further to Brinka, the matriarch. It took a while for a searching party to come together, as everyone was spread out, and follow the tracks to the edge of the jungle, in the direction that Otan had headed.

None of the elephants could sense their missing brother. There were human footprints and elephant hooves that were probably Otan's, and several long parallel tracks dissolving into the distance. Nothing else. Their friend was gone. The herd couldn't break away and chase the tracks anywhere since each member had his or her own responsibilities within the community. They just assumed Otan was dead as the surrounding area lacked any of his patterned vibrations. Caught by the daily chores of teaching the children, the herd realized how close intruders had come to their remote location without being noticed. Nothing like this should happen again.

Altan was afraid that this same outcome would unfold for Nagoti. Their community of souls was shrinking not because they were reaching the *state of bliss*, but because of disappearances. He hoped that wherever the souls of Rakash, Otan and Nagoti were, they would come back one more time through the *Trees of Life* to elevate themselves.

It was the middle of the day when the search party left the compound looking for any trace of Nagoti. Every single path around the village was used daily, so making out the girl's footprints was impossible. In the end they had returned empty handed; sad, disappointed, and furious that another cell of an intricate organism was lost.

* * *

THAT NIGHT THE ENTIRE VILLAGE, except the guards, gathered around the *Trees* at the back of the compound. The bulls' herd was also let in for the commemoration. One by one, the child-elephant pairs walked in a slow procession carrying the grief of their recent loss, and circled the most precious treasure left to them over the centuries by *One Who Created All*: the *Trees of Life*.

Four times Altan's height, with vigorous roots going deep in the ground, the *Trees* were the transition gate for human souls coming back for a new experience. The upward-arched branches were evenly thick no matter the placement, either at the bottom or the top, to sustain the weight of peapods close to maturity. Lately, no more than six to seven buds would bloom every year on each tree, a scarce number compared to the one Altan had witnessed when he was a calf. Many souls reached their potential either as an *Artist* or *Builder* or *Writer*, and rarely came back as *Orange Souls* to help their brothers and sisters reach theirs. It was mainly *One Who Created All's* decision to send them back as they were supposed to remember previous experiences.

A few torches were scattered around the village, so in the surrounding dim light, the blue and purple peapods had a glowing aura, a pulsing energy sent like coded messages to those members of the herd that would become their teachers. The bond had been initiated at the first *call*, only to become stronger the more time the chosen elephants would spend by the *Trees*. All five purple shells of different sizes were hanging on no more than three branches, within the reach of an adult male elephant's elongated trunk. They were still not fully developed, but soon, very soon, when the energy signal became too strong and painful, a gentle touch at the base of the stem would detach the peapod from the Mother who gave birth to it.

The other *Tree* had an even number of healthy looking shells, six. There were three other hanging, quite small and whose wrinkled surfaces were not beaming with life. They represented troubled souls, unsure about having another human incarnation, stopped half way through their return journey by their own indecision and fear that maybe not even this time they would be able to reach the *state of bliss* as written in the *Book*. Those would be left hanging until all the newborns had arrived safely.

The dead peapods along with the empty ones who carried the new arrivals would be buried on the sacred land between the *Trees*.

"Sit everyone." Fenuku addressed the village.

The Council stood with Fenuku, all wearing white ceremonial robes, painted around the neck opening with their own birthmark symbol. For Fenuku and Valdina, a fifteen-cycle-old girl with dark skin and round green eyes, it was a blue and purple circle representing the *Builder* caste, and for Nukua, Akila and Fenila, a blue and purple wavy line representing the *Writer* caste. There were no *Artists* on the Council yet, since not many had come back the last two times the *Trees* had bloomed.

Everyone had learnt about the necessary balance in life, in nature and even in the number of members of their community. Each caste had its own purpose in sustaining the others and maintaining the balance those generations before them had put in place. No one was more important than another and that was why Nagoti's disappearance was a challenge that they had to face.

"It is another sad moment for our community. No matter how well we prepare for such events, the emptiness and the desolation each soul leaves behind is unbearable not only for the teacher, but for us as a whole. We all suffer knowing that Nagoti hasn't finished her journey and that her potential hasn't had the chance to be tapped. We can only hope that this broken passage through life won't deter the soul we knew as Nagoti to visit us again and enchant us with amazing additions to our common knowledge."

Fenuku paused for a second to touch Altan's rumpled skin, looking to borrow some strength, ready to continue with a steady voice.

Unexpectedly, Taber raised her trunk and screamed her agony aloud, a last attempt to reach her lost pupil by sound. The combined herd of fifty elephants joined her sorrow and, for a long moment, it seemed as if the jungle had to prepare for a stampede. But they all calmed down since the ceremony had barely started and decisions had yet to be made.

"As painful and disturbing as it is, we have to stay this course as the *Trees* are bearing fruits for us and this is a great joy. We are blessed to receive new souls to care for and guide in this life. We all know the cycle we are a part of, a cycle that we can't allow to be broken. These new brothers and sisters can prove to be amazing souls that will enrich the community beyond imagination, that can even help us reach the *state of bliss* sooner."

Fenuku spoke with passion, acting as a leader, trying to offer support and confidence.

"This *call* is even more special this time because it falls on the cycle when the *Trees* give us their seed. Every one hundred cycles they present us with this huge honour. They put their own existence in our hands, so if they were to die, we should be able to plant and grow new *Trees*."

"How do we protect the seeds?" Makora, a *Builder* girl, asked impatiently. She was third in line for a Council position.

This time the answer came from someone of her own caste, Valdina.

"Only one member of the Council knows where the seeds are kept. Our teachers are the real protectors and they select the location. From this Council only Fenuku will know." Her skin was white, showing no sign of tanning from the daily exposure to sun, so the round purple signs were quite visible on her cheeks even in the waning light of dusk.

"How many seeds are there so far?" Makora inquired. "I haven't read about it in any book yet."

It was Altan's turn to answer as the keeper of the most knowledge in the herd.

"It was decided by our ancestors that the information about the seeds was never to be written on paper. It is to be kept in our collective memory. In the past, the *Trees* offered us seeds six times, not always at equal intervals. We never had to use them since these two *Trees* we are looking at right now are still full of life and don't show any sign of fatigue."

Altan moved his ears trying to scare the hoard of insects buzzing around his head and cool himself down at the same time. "We thought we could protect ourselves, but what happened to Nagoti, Otan and Rakash, taught us that we have weaknesses. If one of you can disappear, then a book can too. We can't imagine what anyone outside this community could do with such seeds and how that could affect us. The *Book* says that any contact with humans from afar can spoil our purpose, taint our minds or change our beliefs. Who will teach the new souls if we, the elephants, are not here? What world is that without such a bond?"

Silence blanketed the gathering. Everyone's face glowed with purple and blue.

"If these *Trees* die, how long before the seeds can turn into portals?" Kakiru, a *Builder* boy quizzed his thoughts out loud.

"One hundred cycles," replied Altan, feeling the vibration of their concern. "It is a long time," he continued. "The community would shrink and we would have to apply all our knowledge and experience to survive until more souls are born."

Kakiru didn't want to let it go. "But if the seeds are too old to grow into a *Tree*, none of us will be able to come back, and with no other way to do it ... we would be gone."

Altan did not reply right away as he wanted to choose thoughts that would not create more panic, but he tried to be honest at the same time. "If the first pair of seeds is lifeless, we'll try another pair. We'll try until the *Trees* are back again. We, elephants, might also be gone by then. It is written in the *Book* that once we break our bond with humans for too long, we lose our internal direction. We will forget who we are and we will wander the jungle and even search further abroad, looking for something we lost, but we won't remember what."

"What does the *Book* say about our souls' readiness to return when the *Trees* have grown into functional portals?" asked Makora.

"We can only hope that those who still want to achieve the *state of bliss* would have the patience to wait for the gate to open, no matter how long it will take," answered Brinka, the matriarch, and the only elephant resting on the ground due to her heavy belly. "Without you, our energy powers will diminish and physical force would be the only tool to protect ourselves against any enemy. Without your love, our existence would fade away and our memories would become dormant. After a while, we might not even remember you as our dearest friends."

Silence of words and thoughts again, only the frictions of the gentle evening wind against the leaves from the garden could be heard. The gale pushed the reach of smells from the gardens against the strong odors exuded by the elephants, making the air more breathable. It was hard for anyone to imagine an existence in which the elephants would be anything other than their teachers and spiritual guides.

Fenuku tried to get everyone to focus on the subjects not yet discussed.

"I've checked the records for confirmation on who will replace Nagoti as Taber's new student. It is Danish, the oldest of Otan's *Commoners*. Danish!" he called.

The boy stepped forward. He put his bluish palms together in front of his chest and bowed towards Fenuku first, then towards Taber who, in turn, touched her chest with her trunk in acknowledgement.

"You will join their group tomorrow morning. There are a lot of *Book* teachings to catch up on. I'm sorry that you had to get a new teacher this way."

It was getting late and due to the tension that the day had started with, the energy was vanishing slowly from their human bodies. Altan sent short thought-commands to the herd members that were soon to become teachers, asking them to stay in the village for the night. They had to be protected from any harm so their still frail connection with the pods could get stronger. During Brinka's gestation, Altan stepped in to share her responsibilities in leading the cows.

"We expect Brinka to give birth at the same time the peapods will be ready to be taken down. She will be assigned a *Builder* or an *Artist* this time, while taking care of the newborn. Also Asman, Akello and Putri will help her since the calf is meant to become their teacher, growing together will only strengthen their bond." The dark was denser now and even Altan felt tired. A last thought. "Let's sleep. Stay in pairs and keep connecting with your teacher as much as possible while doing your chores."

He then helped Brinka stand and he led the pack to the other side of the village. The gates were secured behind the bulls herd heading for the waterhole for a last drink for the night. They would still look for Nagoti in a desperate attempt to find her.

CHAPTER 3

Honour your teacher, follow his advice, as he is the guide on the path to enlightenment.

From the book *We Are One* – Chapter 3

THE VIEW FROM THE TENTH FLOOR of the municipality building of Korobat City was just unbelievable–especially at sunset. The glass that covered several similar structures reflected the mélange of blue and orange piercing through the thick layer of clouds. What Hando Martinez liked the most was the colour that coated the entire city at this time of day from the reflection.

He was proud of his achievements as leader. Most of the promises he made during the elections and re-elections as mayor, when everything started ten years ago, had been implemented successfully and he could see their results by just walking through the streets.

Working on urban planning was the most challenging of all, as the locals had an inexplicable attachment to the squalid, ready to fall apart three story buildings they called homes. Martinez couldn't remember how many gatherings his team had organized to educate everyone that their ownership rights would still be protected even if the homes themselves would be leveled. He understood their fear better than any of the previous leaders as he had grown up in one of these neighborhoods in which the work was hard but honest.

The roof above their heads was necessary proof that they belonged there; it rooted them, giving them hope that the future he talked about was within reach.

Demolish every structure one square mile at a time, clean it up and rebuild. Show the citizens how promises can become reality, gain their trust and replicate the process over and over again, until the end result is a modern, well-functioning city. This was the formula he applied to all his initiatives.

He dreamt of large cobblestone streets, clean and lined with trees, houses with stone facades and rooftop terraces where people could enjoy the summer months. And slowly, using everyone's cooperation, the dilapidated houses were replaced by five to six story buildings with commercial spaces at the street level while the owners could live above and even rent the available rooms. Bakeries, coffee shops, boutique restaurants and countless small businesses enchanted his eyes every time he took a stroll to take the pulse of the city. It was a human mosaic Hando always wanted to see weaved in the fabric of the newly built urban topography. It also required a change in mentality, a sense of collaboration and sharing, which was still a work in progress.

Twenty years ago, when he was still young, the air was thick with smoke from the tanneries and metal shops spread all over town. The water, even after treatment, had a heavy taste of chemicals, which seeped into the ground and infected the main water supply.

His own family had suffered from the mounting pollution problem. First his mother passed–her weak lungs couldn't sustain the intake of heavy metals. Then, four months later, his father followed when he slipped in a cove of acidic dye. His co-workers moved quickly, but half of his body was a mushy amalgam of flesh and bones.

His own bad luck had happened during the last year of university when envy of his intellectual acumen and the contempt he held his classmates in, pushed one of his colleagues to play a spiteful joke on him: his beer was tainted with contaminated water. His vocal cords were damaged irremediably and since then he had to rely on the technological know-how that allowed him to express himself vocally only through the voice synthesizer embedded in his eyeglasses. It was his only tool of communicating with his peers.

That was the moment when Hando decided to clean his city, no matter how long it would take.

He grasped that staying healthy was a real challenge; he saw the number of young people slowly diminishing. They escaped mainly to Laeta

City, a hundred miles south of Korobat, using their bodies to pleasure others; a compromise they were willing to make as the extra money was always sent back home to help with the mounting medical bills.

As a leader he had no way to stop the migration other than showing real changes to improve their lives. And he needed to do this soon, before the city was left only with the old, the sick and some orphan kids.

Martinez knew that Laeta, the Entertainment City, welcomed this fresh blood; their slogan being ‘pleasure for everyone’. He had to work hard, to at least stop the flux, if not reverse it. People who lived hundreds of miles away were discovering this once small town where all pleasure-related activities were permitted, no boundaries, no inhibitions. There were rules in place, but to protect the guest from harm, not to stop them from having a good time.

A knock on the door brought his thoughts back to daily matters. It was Soheila, his assistant, letting him know that the council members were ready to see him.

The leader put his customized eyeglasses on, which, at the end of its right arm had a jack that fit into a socket behind his ear. He then did a sound check, “one, two, three... one, two, three”, to be sure that the voice analyzer’s volume was not too loud for the presentation he was about to do in front of his colleagues.

Hando needed to explain to his council that his new idea intended to keep their momentum going by using the brand that they’ve been building for the last ten years: *Korobat, the Technology City.* He understood early in his campaign that investing all the resources they had in every type of technology would save them.

Several years ago, Hando Martinez visited Laeta to convince its Committee to start a trading agreement beneficial for both parties. Having the Entertainment City on board would have made it easier for him to sway other cities into similar agreements. The economical invigoration of Korobat depended on his strategy, which helped him become the acting leader. He had decided to initiate such meetings only after he knew that the technology incubators, started by several established business people in a less polluted area of the city, had shown results that could be traded for goods his people needed. Buildings powered by solar and wind energy ensured year round resources; the initial entrepreneurial group was becoming larger and larger, drawing in owners of the metal shops and other similar businesses, ready for a life shift. Their creativity and desire to bring the city back to a life free of contamination was contagious. Soon after the changes took hold, a wave of enthusiasm engulfed Korobat.

The air and the drinking water became cleaner, people were less sick and much happier. Hando's intuition that Laeta would be interested in using their technologies paid off. He used them as barter for fresh fruits, vegetables and meat.

He walked out of his office and entered the room across the hall where the other decision makers of the city were waiting.

"Hello, everyone," Martinez addressed them.

They all nodded back. Elenadore Tam, the woman in charge of social services was looking much better today. Her skin lighter and the twitch of her right eye was not so obvious as the last time they met. She had also dyed her hair black, the entire look bringing her closer to her real age, fifty-five.

Elenadore had a much younger feminine colleague in the council: Mirena Vande, a thirty-four year old beauty with blonde hair, always gathered into a twisted ponytail that make her look even younger, dark blue eyes and delicate ears. Her responsibility was to implement new educational programs molded after the technologies coming out of either new or established companies headquartered in Korobat.

It was an unanimous decision to bring up a new generation of inventors and technical people this way, nurture them, challenge them intellectually as much as possible, but not to break them. Mirena was a fighter when it came to the city's kids that were now getting a proper education and a much better life. She was the fourth generation of teachers, her great-great-great grandfather being the one that put together the famed Scholars Academy. She was liked for her open attitude, low ego and the ability to deal with the male dominated business environment where emotions ran high, by not allowing herself to be pushed around.

"Before I start the presentation I want to give you a quick update,"

Martinez said, settling into his chair. "We broke ground on the north-west district, the last one that has to be rebuilt within the existing city limits. The only difference this time is the location of the business tower, on the southeast corner. The soil report came back negative to support such weight anywhere else. The low density housing and buildings can still go ahead as planned."

"How is the demand for the new tower?" Orlando Artilla asked.

A man of short height with a large, oval face, he fancied himself in expensive silk shirts of colourful nuances to bring some contrast to his pale skin. His dark brown hair was parted in the middle, exposing grayish roots. He owned the monopoly on wind turbines and solar technologies, both profitable ventures that should have allowed him to retire at any time, but the adrenaline of negotiating more deals kept him in the game.

His prosperity was also visible in the rounded shape of his body and his double chin. No one could tell if it was genetics contributing to his overweightness or the heavy eating at all the public events he loved to attend.

"It's been sitting at fifty-five percent for the last month," replied Hando. "But the selling team is working hard to attract several small businesses from cities in the far-east, less developed than ours, but with good potential. They would complement the educational initiatives and the water treatment technology."

He stood up and started pacing back and forth in front of his four colleagues, continuously playing with his ponytail of gray hair.

"And the housing is all occupied?" jumped in Huidan Banaar, the second most important businessman sitting on the council. His wealth, generated from his monopoly on the water treatment plants, made him Artilla's equal.

The two of them, Artilla and Huidan, had a mutual understanding in trying to sell each other's products by upselling the benefits of a combination of both technologies on any one renewable project. So far the agreement had worked well with no backstabbing. Somehow, they had embraced Hando's life approach of cooperation, but, most of the time, only for their own benefit.

"Korobatians are coming back as they hear good news from family left behind about the clean air, the new residential projects and the significant influx of businesses that generate more jobs. We are all well aware of how much we've improved everyone's health since the cleanup started ten years ago. They are motivated to come back to their families. Not in impressive numbers yet, but it's an encouraging trend. We also have to offer accommodations to new people settling here. As you know we have a mix of rentals and ownership; not everyone can afford to buy, especially after we raised taxes to pay for the clean-up," explained Hando.

'*As always, he had all the right answers*,' a thought flashed through Hando's mind.

Banaar was keen on verifying one more time a piece of legislation that had suffered some changes recently. "So am I still allowed to buy twenty percent of the upcoming inventory as long as I rent it to my employees at a specific rate, correct?" It was his way of diversifying his business by investing in real estate.

"Correct," confirmed Martinez. "You have to be sure that they stay employed for a minimum of five years. Look, guys, I mentioned this to you before and I'm going to repeat myself. I don't want any conflict of interest between your decisions here as citizens and the ones you make as business entities. Our initial agreement still stands."

"I still think we should revisit some of the terms. Five years is a long time and the rent control cap is killing me. I need a little bit more return on my investments," Banaar spilled out his dissatisfaction in a harsh tone and moved his body to the edge of the chair, waiting for Martinez's reaction.

Hando had no concerns with Elenadore or Mirena; he knew their actions would not contradict their contractual terms as civil servants. His worries were with the men. He wanted to keep them straight and not bring any suspicion on the Council. Things were going well and he couldn't afford a scandal that would trigger an investigation, derailing them from finishing important projects.

"We can revisit these contractual clause," said Martinez with a voice intonation suggesting that he had more to say, but, instead, he unplugged the eyeglasses' jack from his skull, took them off and started to massage the base of his nose. He was trying to buy time and think of the right approach. He needed everyone's support to pursue the initiative with Laeta.

He plugged back his eyeglasses and finished his statement. "...but only when the agreement is due. The Korobatians and the foreigners that are renting from you still need to accumulate a comfortable financial cushion before they can be charged more. Be a merciful landlord, please," Hando said jokingly to release some of the tension created by Banaar's demand.

"That might be good enough for you, but my priorities are different. I'm a pretty amenable landlord if you haven't heard already. I offer certain perks if they renew their contracts and my properties are always clean. Got only one percent complains. Don't you think that's a remarkable achievement?" Huidan shot right back at Hando, not letting the issue go.

Martinez looked around the table to get an emotional read of the other members. Attila was smiling sheepishly. He also owned real estate in the city, mainly commercial properties that had similar rent restrictions. Banaar was talking on his behalf as well, so Hando couldn't count on his full support.

The women displayed a sympathetic look, and Martinez noticed that Mirena intended to intervene several times already so Hando nodded to her.

"Huidan, you know very well that Hando can't make this decision by himself. We all need to be in agreement. This is not something we can tackle right now with so many initiatives going on. You have my support to bring your request forward and discuss it at the next official council meeting. Rent increase, as Hando said, should be treated carefully," the blonde concluded and looked straight at her council colleague, implying that she wanted him to agree with this outcome.

Martinez could see on Banaar's face the struggle of letting it go, his fingers tugging at his moustache. He was still assessing his options.

"Ok, we'll put it on the agenda for a later date," he confirmed and filled the glass in front of him with water.

The leader exhaled slowly, relieved that the issue was settled. "Thank you."

Finally, they'd come to the presentation he had prepared for more than two weeks. Involuntarily, he checked that the jack was still plugged into his skull, and then he started. "We are reaching a saturation point with Laeta and with a couple of other cities in the far east in terms of what we can offer as barter. We provided solar and wind for electricity, the water purification system, a small number of electric cars and several electronic devices. But our agreement is coming to an end soon. We have nothing else to offer for the food we get in return. The maintenance contracts are light and barely buy us anything."

Hando paced the room one more time and settled by the window, letting the warmth coming through engulf him.

"So, after some research and thinking, I realized that anything related to entertainment would interest Laeta's committee, the same way it did during my first pitch years ago. What we offered them at that time added value to their brand. Yes, it aided obscure, degrading pleasure, but in a nice lit room, candle-smoke free. Lighting the streets made the city safer and increased the number of visitors."

"What do you have in mind?" queried Mirena.

"This added value component has to be part of the new proposition. They are short on new ideas on how to increase the level of carnal and psychedelic pleasure for their existing clients and also what bait they could use to attract new ones. My contacts in Laeta kept mentioning a local scholar that has an unusual guest, a kid with an orange triangle painted on his cheeks. Not a local, he was brought from the jungles of the south. The scholar is studying this kid because he might get into a specific state of mind. It's a different kind of pleasure; a pleasure of the mind rather than of the body, that is short, but intense."

"So what exactly are we offering them?" pushed Mirena.

Martinez grinned, happy to share his marketing strategy. He pulled his long grayish ponytail over his shoulder then continued.

"This scholar, Bart Blackwood, has been working on it for a while, with no concrete results yet. It might be that he doesn't know how to handle the kid or because he doesn't have the right tools. The interesting part is that Bart did graduate from the Scholars Academy, so we have his records. Not technically inclined, but smart and stubborn. And physically grotesque. He was offered a job in Korobat right after graduation on researching future trends of technologies that could impact our lives; but he turned it down. His justification was that Laeta's river has a special attraction for him. He's a loner, with one teenager, who helps with the chores. I want to bring the village kid, Rakash, here to Korobat. We go in and offer to participate in the research with the goal of creating a device that would artificially induce this mind state. Laeta can sell the experience as a new product, like they do with sex, drugs, fake families and all the other crap."

He poured himself a glass of water while anticipating questions.

Elenadore was intrigued by the idea. "Do you really expect their Committee to agree to such an arrangement?"

"Honestly, no. A couple of characters fought me a lot last time, but even with them gone, I still anticipate a push back," replied Hando before gulping another mouth full of water.

"Then why propose it?" said Orlando.

"All I can tell you is that if my assumption is correct, their president, Kanar, will put more pressure on Bart to come up with results. In turn, this pressure would confuse Rakash so much that whatever is expected of him will not happen. This is the moment when our offer will become attractive," clarified the leader.

"If we succeed, what are we going to ask in return? Same terms as last time?" said Mirena Vande.

"No way!" Hando exploded into healthy laughter. "I want to play our cards even better this time. We'll ask for a bit less, but double the length of the contract."

"Very good," said Artilla, whose amazing negotiating skills helped him built his fortune.

A long silence followed as everyone thought of alternatives while admiring the sunset.

"Why don't we get our own villager with orange signs painted on his face, develop the technology, then charge them even more?" Banaar's greed was surfacing again.

Hando knew that he had to be prepared for any crazy ideas these two wealthy individuals spit out.

"You know I do my homework before I present any concept to you. There is not much information on this secluded community and the available published information couldn't be verified from a reliable source. If this child is as special as Laeta thinks, his absence didn't go unnoticed, so don't expect to go there and just snatch another one. From the little I read, huge beasts, called elephants, creatures of extraordinary strength and intelligence, protect this community in the jungle. I want to follow the easy path first. Why reinvent the wheel when Blackwood has already spent two years interacting with him. He is a scientist, he will help us achieve what we want; in the end it will be his reputation at stake as well. I understand that one can obtain results only after one gains the trust of the subject researched. And this is what Bart did. He gained the child's trust and treated him with dignity. It takes patience and motivation. Even if we can muster both, we lack time. We have to use his research and whatever knowledge he gathered on the boy."

"I still don't get it," stated Banaar. "What do you need our approval for?"

"For the part I've just explained. Nothing else. I want you to be aware that I'm going to reach out to Laeta on this subject. It might take two or three months before my plan unfolds, at which time we'll reconvene for updates. If everything goes well, I want your support on approving additional expenses for Blackwood's accommodations, food and a housekeeper. We want him and the kid well fed and treated as well as possible. We can even throw a small party when he arrives, maybe at one of your homes," Hando pointed to Artilla and Banaar. "In case this approach fails, we need a plan B, another product that we can present to Laeta and to our existing clients. Or we assess the option of taking our chances and organize our own trip to the south and see what we can capture. Gentlemen, please consider anything that might have potential. We need a new carrot."

"How reliable is your information?" Elenadore asked. She pushed herself back on the chair and crossed her arms over her generous breasts, waiting for an explanation that she could poke at.

"There are certain working girls that go back and forth between Korobat and Laeta," said Hando. "I've offered them the latest in hypnotic tattoo designs to bring any out of ordinary activities to my attention. Now they have better-looking bodies and more customers, making it easier to blend in. They saw the boy and tried to make direct contact."

"Wow, you really have all the answers ready," exclaimed Mirena with a large smile, then she joined Hando by the window to bask in the sun.

"Just doing my job. It kills me to know that we are not able to bring the land itself back to life yet. Yes, we cleaned it up, but it's dead land. Generations will pass before we can use it again."

Hando's words carried a lot of pain. No matter how they'd branded themselves, he knew that nature was perpetual and connecting to it was soothing. Deep inside, he was crying to see a real forest circling the city, embracing them protectively and reaching out to humans for mutual nurturing. It was another one of his dearest dreams.

The leader watched Banaar clean the perspiration off his face with a large, white handkerchief with blue dots, then pour some water in the glass in front of him. Hando knew that another question was brewing in the businessman's mind. "Martinez, we will need a bit more info on how we can translate this *mind orgasm* into a device. It has to do with brain waves and certain excitation points on the scalp, but that's just an assumption," Huidan stated.

Hando thought for a moment, left the window, and paced the room one more time.

In the end, he replied, "We can start with the same approach you used for my implant. You connected it to the cortex, excited several areas and got your feedback. Nevertheless, I'll do my best to get first hand info that you can compare to your own research. Meanwhile, Mirena, can you initiate a challenge among the final year of Technology Class from the Academy and see what they can come up with? Whoever is closer to what we want gets guaranteed employment upon graduation at one of the companies owned by our council members. Sound good?" he asked rhetorically.

Orlando and Huidan looked at each other and nodded, knowing that the selection of potential candidates for such a challenging job could only come from the Scholars Academy.

"The smarter we get them, the better," added the latter.

"We can also put together a special group joining people from both companies," suggested Artilla. His overweight body was struggling in the warm room, drops of transpiration gathering in his purple goatee.

"I like it." It was Mirena's stamp of approval. "I'll draft the content and bring it to you for review. I want to be sure I use the right words, some key words would be nice too. Give me three, four days."

"Thank you, dear," concluded Martinez ready to adjourn the meeting.

"One more thing." It was Elenadore Tam, this time not so anxious to depart. "What if we work on plan C in parallel with what we've discussed?"

Everyone turned towards her, interested in what she had to say.

"I know a handful of people who built their own small gardens with dirt brought in from the north. They did a quick contamination test, all good. Can't confirm the nutrient levels yet. The crop might be a joke or enough to feed them for a couple of months."

Martinez was aware of the small-scale agricultural initiatives. It was more of a hobby than a fulltime occupation, but he was fully supportive of it.

"Elenadore, indeed, our ultimate goal should be, to become self-sufficient. We need to start somewhere. Why don't you add it to the list of the social programs? Enroll the individuals who are ready 'to harvest their crop', if any, and let them do the presentations and even organize workshops where people can see firsthand how to do it," Hando suggested and sat again, crossing his legs under the table.

"In fact any new technology we come up with should be bartered for healthy dirt. Loads and loads of it. We'll create our own raised farms," said Huidan.

He squinted his small, green eyes as if in a gest of assessing a new business opportunity in which he could get ahead. His fat cheeks were pushed up by a large smile, his fingers continuously pulling the ends of his generous moustache.

"We'll get there, I promise you. I can't promise how soon though," the leader tried to joke. "We'll meet again next month unless something urgent requires our attention sooner."

CHAPTER 4

Knocking through meditation at the doors of One Who Created All could be a laborious task, but abundant spiritual riches await on the other side.

From the book *We Are One* – Chapter 4

NAYAN HAD LAID THE LEATHER BAG by the door; it contained all the books and documents they'd gathered for the monthly meeting with the Committee. They just wanted to buy more time, several months at least, since the scholar seemed confident that a breakthrough with Rakash was within reach.

Bart paced the hallway, fingers raking at his beard as if that would straighten out its unruly curls. His eyesight had a similar frantic movement, switching between a vague point on the horizon and the tip of his shoes. It was one of his habits to mentally peruse his prepared speech once more before delivering it to the Committee. There were a hundred places he'd rather be than in front of the six inquisitors' faces that made up the governing body of Laeta. He knew that more than half of them did not like him that much, and it was only the President's will to continue the research with Rakash that gave a little bit of rope to this endeavour. The abrasive questions that Blackwood had to endure in his previous encounters from the councilors were the statement of their disapproval that the money, time and resources allocated to studying Rakash, and, indirectly, understanding the customs of the community from the jungle, was just a waste. To them, Rakash was nothing but a savage, a kid with no useful memory or a credible personal history and no one that cared about his disappearance. But Bart knew better. Nevertheless, his influence with the President was running low and he wouldn't stick his neck out for much longer without seeing results.

"Nayan, I'll be back in a couple of hours," Bart said loudly from the hallway, not sure if he was heard since the library door where the boys were laughing copiously was barely ajar.

He liked the made-up games Nayan and Rakash were playing, enhancing their imagination, and also allowing the villager to learn new words with his friend's help. Last time Bart had the chance to passively participate, he enjoyed how, with old maps in front of them, the boys were inventing heroes and villains, crossing the line of good and evil, and fighting for honour and love. The interaction also gave Nayan the opportunity to ask Rakash about similarities between the life in his village and these invented worlds.

Bart pulled on his hood to cover the damaged side of his skull, picked up the leather bag and stepped outside to wait for the car that the Committee usually sent for him. Bart would have avoided even this favour, but recently the pain in his shorter leg increased ten-fold, forcing him to limit his walking.

Since the number of tourists had gone up several years ago, no carts and animals, the old way of Laeta's transportation, were allowed on the inside streets, only bicycles or electric cars provided by Korobat City, and most of them were used for and by visitors.

The town could afford to purchase only a limited number of such vehicles since the barter was quite taxing and went for a significant number of years. He had to admit that improvements had been made at all levels of society, including those involved with the entertainment industry, which was bringing in most of the town's revenue.

The car, a small, square-like, metal box, painted white, arrived on time. The scholar stiffly got in the back seat, muttering a curse because of how little space he had to extend his feet. The seat was hard with barely any cushion stuffed underneath: a first generation model sold to them by Korobat almost ten years ago. The driver was new so Bart didn't bother to even say "hello."

It was a short drive across the bridge to the municipality building, a two-story structure with small windows and entrances on all four sides from four different streets. The outside walls had a lighter nuance of brown, contrasting nicely with the darker colour of the mahogany-framed windows. Large, green ceramic pots housing feriga leafs and several of the heart-shaped bright red flamingo flowers were placed on the stone stairs. The scholar walked through the wooden doors into the main lobby. It was empty except for a couple of women that vanished into one of the offices in the opposite direction. He headed towards the stairs to his right, and his heavy steps snatched a loud screech from several loosened boards on the floor. He started the slow ascent to the second floor to a large wooden-paneled room used for their private meetings. There were twenty-five steps, but he counted them anyways, not thinking that, somehow, their number had mysteriously decreased, but to keep his mind busy from the intensified pain that was numbing his leg.

Even from the beginning, the Committee decided this initiative was to be kept off the books unless something tangible could be paraded to the citizens as a huge success that had used their own resources.

For a while now, the scholar had the impression that Laeta was trying to compete with Korobat, and capturing Rakash was part of that plan. Two years ago he had no idea of the Committee's intention when he explained in detail the fascinating stories about a group of humans and elephants living together in the jungle, far south of Laeta. But they asked more and more questions, so he kept talking, drunk from all the attention he was getting from a group of people often so scarce in spreading compliments. Not long after, interest on the subject vanished. A year passed before the President shared with Bart how Rakash was captured by a special unit, trained specifically in surviving harsh conditions. The men were instructed to go south, reach the jungle, and capture a villager. This was how he ended up with Rakash, studying him to reproduce an instantaneously *state of bliss.*

Everyone except the President was in the room. The councilors, seated on one side of the long wooden table, were talking amongst themselves, barely noticing Bart entering and pulling out a chair. He dropped the bag on the table with a thud. The noise got their attention for a moment. They looked at him annoyed, but did muster a nod of acknowledgement, then continued their conversations. Bart sat down and released a loud exhale, while massaging his muscles, battered from the additional effort.

Artwork that had come with Rakash hung high up on the wall opposite the door. Bart raised his head to have another look at them, and recollected one more time what the leader of the expedition shared with him two years ago about how they found Rakash: the wooden masks representing crude features of human and elephant faces, the paintings on bamboo leaves depicting elements of village's daily activities, and the colourful weavings were laying out in the sun outside of the jungle. Rakash had been sitting in the middle of these items, said the leader. The boy was touching them with care, and even talking to them. Rakash did not see the foreign men approaching; he might have been too absorbed in his mental exercise. But even when he did see them, he wasn't scared of them, the captain had told Bart. The boy accepted the liquid that he took as water. The dose of tranquilizer was strong enough to put him out for the duration of the entire trip back. Bart couldn't convince the Committee to let him keep the artwork for more than two months, since it might induce the boy's *state of bliss.* Now, as he glanced at the art pieces again, he recognized the village's topography in one painting, and the body posture of someone ready for an energy healing in another. His experience with Rakash made him identify almost immediately the meanings and symbols that previously were hidden due to lack of knowledge. The artwork had tremendous spiritual value for the villagers, contrasted by the slight value placed on them by Laeta's citizens; it was mainly an egotistic display of a conqueror.

Only one woman, Victoria Kaft, succeeded to be elected in this male dominated governing body. She proved herself effective in keeping the female population of the Entertainment District safe and healthy by pushing various regulations in this respect. No more sexual transmitted diseases, no more beatings, just the occasional bruises if the escorts happened to be at the wrong time and place when a brawl had started. One could expect that her short stature, powered by legs thick as the trunk of a ten-year-old butter tree, which spiked with pain from time to time from bad blood circulation, might have kept her still, but it was just the opposite. Her colleagues were quite pleased with the results.

The door to the left opened and the President, Kravis Kanar, strode into the room with loping steps. Kanar's inflated personality was on display, Bart noticed, especially when guests from outside the inner circle of the council were present. It was his way of showing territorial strength over those with less decisional power. The chatter stopped. He was a tall man, taller than anyone else in the room. His white hair was combed backwards, and started just above his eyebrows. Kravis had almost no visible forehead. He smiled to the room, acknowledging his colleagues with a short nod of his head, and then sat at the end of the table, two seats away from Bart.

"Hello, hello," the president addressed the scholar directly and a jovial tone. "I really hope to hear good news today as we are all anxious to see results."

He was not the chitchat type of person, Bart reflected; so getting down to business was what he liked to do. Bart did not reply right away; he kept arranging in front of him the papers and books he had pulled out from his bag. They all stared at him, expecting the same lamentations and excuses for the lack of results. The shuffling continued for several moments, reverberating on the high walls.

On his way to the meeting, Bart had made a decision that was against his moral principles: to lie to the Committee if necessary. It was outrageous hypocrisy, but any other approach would have Rakash removed from his care in a matter of hours. He knew how dangerous it was to go down this path. He might lose his status, reputation and even be forced to leave the city for good. This last option might have been radical to someone building his life in one place, and potentially unbearable–unless one could knock at a door that was opened for him after university graduation in Korobat City. For now he had to remain optimistic and be as excited about the lies he was about to tell as the truth he had revealed in the past.

Bart energetically opened one of the books in front of him to the page showing the colourful trees and other special places in the jungle.

"We came across new and reliable information about jungle locations where individuals like Rakash are being born," he said, looking straight at the president. “And I refer to the individuals with the orange triangle on their cheeks. All the other ones are coming through the trees.”

The members of the Committee smiled politely, not sure if they could laugh loudly, and indirectly waited for the President’s reaction.

Kanar did not laugh, but he wanted more details. “How did you confirm what the book says? You know that most of the time these writers can’t be trusted.”

Bart saw in their faces that they all had questions; but hierarchy was important.

“I let Rakash browse the book and because he doesn’t understand all the words, his only reactions came when he saw the pictures. His face lit up and his fingers touched each location gently, trying to get a connection that seemed so easy to initiate. Something clicked inside him as he closed his eyes and did not lay down as he does for the meditation. For a brief moment the orange triangle on his cheeks came to life and I could sense that mentally he was somewhere else. Unfortunately, I did not have the chance to expose him to these images any longer and correlate them with a duration increase of the meditations as I just received this book days ago. This validation tells me that moving forward, Rakash’s memories are slowly surfacing and more content will be validated. I’m telling you, this is encouraging.”

Kanar looked at his colleagues, nodding to them with permission to ask their questions.

Gerald Misk, a lean man in his fifties, rested his bearded chin on his palms, then with a soft voice he asked. “Have you found a way, an easy way, to trigger this *state of bliss* in our tourists? We have to be able to commercialize it.”

Misk was the one that had to keep the continuous flow of guests happy by offering new ways that they could pleasure themselves, new twists to existing products. It was not an easy job as a high percentage of tourists were returning visitors that expected to be challenged.

“That will come as soon as Rakash goes through a fully induced session. I take detailed notes on his behaviour and it is very unlikely that I would miss something so significant,” replied Bart.

"I hope you understand that time is not on your side," Misk said then pushed himself back on his chair, signaling for someone else to ask a question.

Orgil Nurkan, the next one ready to grill Bart, was the meanest of all the councilors. He was blind in his left eye from a medical problem that no doctor could identify and treat, hence the odd angle of his head when trying to look at the person he was addressing. Thin hair only shielded the sides of his round skull, the remaining area was just a shiny ball covered in sweat most of the time.

"Mr. Blackwood," he started in that official tone that characterized him. "Have you initiated yourself yet with this process that the kid is going through? If yes, have you felt anything unusual?"

Bart had not expected such a question, but he didn't flinch.

"Of course, I tried. At this point, without having much information to generalize, the experience should be personal. Mine would differ from Rakash's, and from yours. But to answer your question, I didn't feel like I was getting closer to this state."

Nurkan's tough attitude helped the city negotiate the barter deals with Korobat City years back when electricity was a novelty that changed the history of this strategically located town and its citizens.

Most of the Committee members kept their seats for multiple election cycles mainly because the contracts and transactions they signed on behalf of the city made a significant impact for everyone's betterment.

"I still think that if Rakash was the right person, you would have found a way by now to break down any internal barrier he might have," continued Nurkan, showing that he was not done yet. "What if the kid needs a drastic shake-up, maybe some pain-induced motivation." He shrugged his shoulders, almost distancing himself immediately from such a crazy statement. But the thought was out in the open, hanging for all to assess and judge its validity and practicality.

"Mr. Nurkan, we are not savages. We can't just hurt him!" exploded Bart, who was immediately on his feet and was close to smashing his chair on the ground. "When did we start torturing people? Let alone kids." Saliva spotted his beard and he started gesticulating frenetically as if that would protect Rakash from harm. The boy being taken away and put in school with other children was expected, but hurting him was unthinkable. "If the Committee is not interested in him let me know and I'll continue the research at my own expense. Rakash would become my responsibility entirely," Bart said defiantly.

The scholar's desperation was visible in his body language, leaning low over the table. Somehow, he became blinded, not fully realizing how eager these people were to provide new experiences to the Entertainment District, which was booming with tourists, and how easy it would be for them to take drastic measures to attain this goal.

"Look, Bart," president Kanar intervened, "what we want to get across to you is that our leniency has limits and this open-ended research can't keep going on forever. Orgil's statement was a bit extreme and we would like to avoid such an outcome. No matter what our final decision is, Rakash is our responsibility, not yours." He gestured towards Nurkan, knowing that he was not done with what he had to tell Bart.

"Mr. Blackwood, since I am responsible for assessing any opportunity presented to us for the benefit of the city, I have to keep an open mind. And if opportunity comes from someone or somewhere who was proved worthy in the past, I'm even more willing to listen," Nurkan explained slowly, as if talking to a retarded person.

'*Same tone of voice, same cold look, insensitive to the irresponsible declaration he had just made about Rakash,*' thought the scholar, and took his seat, suddenly concerned with more potential bad news.

"Your research isn't a secret anymore, at least not to Korobat's Council," Nurkan continued.

"What! How did they..?"

"It's not important anymore, they know, there is no point in denying it. They offered to help develop a device that could induce a *state of bliss* within minutes for anyone to try."

Bart scrutinized their faces intensely. They had no sympathy for him and no regard for the effort he had put in deciphering Rakash's enigmatic world. They were seriously considering the offer. '*Do they really think that they would be able to achieve this feat when I couldn't in two years? This is insane!*'

Kanar defended their offer. "Korobat has proved trustworthy many times in delivering on its promises. It might be a long shot, but they wouldn't have proposed to do it unless they knew they could. They are not aware of our decision yet. We still want you to succeed in delivering a gift we all want to enjoy. Two months. This is the final stretch. After that, we take over," the president ended and signaled for the others to leave.

After the door closed behind the last member of the Committee, Kravis Kanar shifted to sit beside Bart. "What we told you today seems harsh, but I want you to put yourself in our place. We have a city to run. Remember that we chose you for this job. There is no shame in admitting your own limitations. Nothing like this was ever been tried before."

The President was sweetening the sour pill, but at the same time he was being firm in not giving Bart any false hopes. This was the end, for real.

"What will happen to Rakash?" the scholar asked.

"If there are still no results after two months, we will allow Korobat to start their research under your supervision. You'll both be going there for one year."

Bart couldn't believe this turn of events.

"Am I forced to go or is it my decision?"

"We prefer that you go with Rakash, but no one will force you," replied the Committee's elder. "He is familiar with you, so your absence could put a strain on his mental health, jeopardizing the outcome. Your monthly salary will stay in place and be provided to you once you come back or at your convenience. Korobat will pay for any other expenses, including accommodation. Nevertheless, I don't want to get ahead of myself and assume a negative result. It's up to you to focus the experience you've accumulated over the last two years in such a way that no one can deny your achievements."

Blackwood slowly began to put his materials back in his bag. He finally said resentfully, "I read that some of the villagers could not attain the *state of bliss* in one lifetime. Their desire for fulfillment brings them back again and again until the great communion is achieved. The *We Are One* book is mentioned in several publications, but no copy has ever reached us. I'm telling you this, so you can understand how daunting my task is to work with a child that barely started training with his elephant teacher. I can't replace that type of tutor, a creature that embodies thousands of years of knowledge and secrets so foreign to us."

The President was speechless in hearing this information for the first time.

"This book contains spiritual wisdom passed from generation to generation, protected carefully by the herd,: Bart continued. "We have nothing similar, most of us don't even clearly understand the notion of *spirituality*. Based on all my reading, it is connected to the *state of bliss* and *He, Who Created All*, is supposedly the same person who wrote the book." Bart held the bag over his chest like a weight keeping him grounded against an invisible wind. "*He* is the *Creator* of this world and other which we don't have access to. They believe in this supreme energy *Being* and each of their daily activities only have one purpose: to please *Him*, as they are judged on their spiritual path by their actions. There are so many amazing things we can learn from them ... all we need is the desire to do it."

He raised his eyes to the beautiful artwork on the walls and continued, "Another amazing fact is that some of these kids grow into adults, but they are barely mentioned in any of the books I have. It's not a badge of honour to become old in the village, that's why the written proof is scarce."

Kravis Kanar stood up and walked to the window. Blackwood watched the old man frown at his statement, unsure if he had correctly read between the lines of what Bart had just said.

"Are you telling me that you are not bothering to try anything with Rakash during the remaining time?" the president asked.

Bart wanted to show his rage and frustration by screaming at the President and making him understand that sometimes a lifetime is just a drop of what is needed for the soul to find itself concisely, but instead he kept his voice calm. "What really makes it to this wonderful state is what the villagers call a *soul*, an entity we all have within our bodies. They know about it and they keep learning about it from the moment the connection with their elephant teacher is active. So, two years of hard work means nothing in terms of what's required to obtain any tangible results. If the books are a bit accurate, these guys are spending at least a quarter of their day meditating, talking to the *One Who Created All* and finding themselves. Do we do anything like that? We are continuously moving, laughing, fucking, drinking, drugging, and we do not take a break to calm down and think deeply."

The President turned around intrigued by Bart's language, which was usually carefully chosen.

"My reason for working with Rakash is different from yours," Bart continued. "A saleable product that can attract more visitors and double the city's revenue is what you care about. A change in mind set and behaviour is my goal. Do you find any satisfaction in running a city whose main preoccupation is to find new ways of prostituting itself?"

Bart remained calm, yet openly letting his sadness and disappointment show on his weary face. In that very moment he felt purposeless. He had accumulated so much knowledge for nothing; short-term benefits and gratification proved once more that undisputable arguments cemented old mentalities even firmer.

The scholar watched Kanar drum his fingers on the window, regretting staying behind and trying to offer him consolation. The evening's dim light was casting an orange glow on his profile, turning him into an allegoric character so commonly found on Laeta's streets on the days of the annual carnival.

"Bart, your frustration is understandable. I have moments like this when I see my life as an endless blurry line of meetings, put-out fires, deals, and parties; but I also evaluate the results of all that 'wasted time': betterment for our city and its citizens. You know that back in the day it was an almost unanimous decision that our town wouldn't change its century-old engrained mentality of facilitating and offering pleasures to others. I jumped on the bandwagon as a true believer because I couldn't envision another future for us. Trying to compete with Korobat or any other city with technology, luxury goods or any other industry, would have been suicidal. This is our niche and we have to hold onto it by any means.

Think of it like a service we are providing. We make people happy. Do we care about the colour of their skin or their political conviction?" Kanar challenged. "No. In Laeta all barriers are eliminated in the name of pleasure and happiness, being either real or false."

Bart didn't understand how the President's confession could help with the dire situation he was in. Bart snapped his bag shut and stood up, ready to leave.

But Kanar was not finished. "You are right in saying that we have no idea of the *soul* entity residing inside us. How can we be sure of that? Just by trusting some old books? You will be laughed at. People want to think that they are in control of every action and decision, good or bad, which they make. In order for their mentality to change, they will have to witness an event of great magnitude."

Kanar left the window, once again becoming the calculated leader that couldn't put feelings ahead of what was best for the city, and went to Bart's side as he made for the door.

"Nevertheless, I can bet my career on it, that even if the belief that we are possessed by *souls* entered our narrow minds, the thirst for what we provide in Laeta today wouldn't be extinguished."

He patted Bart dismissively on the shoulder, obviously already thinking of his next meeting. "Do your best with the kid, my friend. I don't want you to stay in Korobat for such a long time." Then he opened the door and pushed Bart out gently.

* * *

THE ORDERS FROM KOROBAT'S LEADER had been clear: he'd described the target and the necessary action to be taken, so both women had no reticence in going ahead with it. Their families back home had confirmed that they'd been moved into new apartments in nice areas of the city and Mariam's brother even got an entry job at the local solar plant.

The women were enjoying a drink on one of the outdoor patios of Laeta's Entertainment District, keeping an eye on a specific shop that specialized in nuts and seeds, most of them grown locally. Mariam, the one with locks of red hair coming out of her fancy hat, sat facing the store, while Tandar, the white-haired one, was checking the opposite direction, from where the target of their stake out was supposed to come. The street was narrow and busy with tourists, pressing the women to look sharply, yet remain nonchalant.

For this particular undertaking they wore T-shirts so that their large hypnotic tattoos remained hidden, exposing only inoffensively black flames coming out of a small dragon's head on their upper arms.

'*Maintain a low profile, no one must link you to Korobat,*' explained the leader before sending them off.

The women became so used to Laeta's easygoing atmosphere, that Martinez's advice seemed out of place. Here the rhythm of life was laid-back, but animated by an incessant movement of people, always under the impression that a new experience in this city would fulfill them and give their lives purpose in the long run. Being unassuming or eccentric wouldn't have made a difference in this amalgamation of normal and odd. Anyone's wildest dreams could be commercialized in the Entertainment District; so, in a way, "normality" was strange.

Laeta's success was so overwhelming that expansion past the initial city blocks became necessary, forcing the Committee to purchase more buildings and relocate its inhabitants to the fringes of the city in newly constructed apartments. Some people realized the potential for steady revenue by leasing their homes instead of selling them. The fun was there to stay for a long time, guaranteeing a stream of cash for generations to come.

Tandar kicked her friend under the table and nodded in the direction she was facing. Now it was Mariam's turn to keep her eyes peeled and confirm that the kid would use the same store for replenishing his master's cupboards.

They'd been following him for a month now, checking that the youngster didn't make unexpected changes to his weekly itinerary. This shop, Vargas' Seeds and Nuts, was their best chance to implement the plan given to them. Its owner had his own weaknesses, and so it was not hard convincing that this was just a prank being played against Nayan, nothing more. The women had all the necessary tools to accomplish this task.

Nayan did not spend more than ten minutes inside the store since Vargas knew exactly what to bag for him and had it ready for pick up. Vargas' Seeds and Nuts was the first stop on his route and the one he liked the most. Being a long-term customer allowed him to try new varieties on display and even nibble on sweets that were not on his list. He had to hurry back as his master was not well at all, and he didn't know how to help. Bart had returned from his meeting with the Committee in a dark mood, but the outcome of the discussions, for the first time, was off limits to Nayan. The effort of having Rakash remember went to another level, and the master's mood in reverse direction.

Nayan left the store preoccupied, unaware that he was being watched.

The women finished their drinks, then, unhurriedly, approached the store themselves.

Inside, Vargas was behind the counter engrossed in writing in a small notebook, while his helpers were arranging jars of dried fruits and various teas on shelves, and positioning the bags and barrels of nuts and seeds in such a way to leave a narrow path to walk through. One could have bought a handful of seeds or a bushel; any measure was welcome as long as a sale was taking place.

Mariam looked in awe at the uncountable varieties of nuts she had no idea existed. She stopped by a large bag full to the brim with overgrown macadamia nuts. Without a second thought, she placed one in her mouth, slowly biting it. She expected a spicy taste, but was disappointed.

'*Maybe it goes better with a food dish or mixed with other seeds*,' she said to herself, and moved along the narrow aisle.

She really enjoyed the novelty of the store that they had never walked into before.

"Ladies, how may I help you?" Vargas asked with a big smile.

From the moment they got the assignment, Tanar had shadowed Nayan to learn his weekly routine. Mariam offered to trail Vargas to learn his habits and something that they could use to bargain with to their advantage. After several days, it became clear how easy it would be to convince him to go along with their plan with nothing in return, except a threesome at one of his favourite hotels in the District.

Mariam took the lead.

"Just browsing for something tasty that could increase a certain potential ... if you know what I mean," she said winking at him and returning his smile.

"You came to the right place," said Vargas. "There are nuts that can help with that and there are ... spices meant to do a better job. I don't advertise too much since they are very rare and extremely expensive. They're mainly kept for my own use or for special customers."

Vargas came out from behind the counter. Short, thick legs sustaining an elongated body covered by a dress-like shirt. His hair was the main feature of his appearance, bluish, with a darker nuance in his beard. He was not only trying to hide his age, but also blend in at the parties organized for tourists.

"Spices, interesting," Mariam commented to Tanar. "We never tried it before." She moved closer to the man, touching his shoulder then asked, "What would it take for us to get some of that amazing stuff?"

Vargas had the feeling that he was onto something promising, two gorgeous escorts looking for the good stuff that could turn a regular night into one to remember years later. Their darker skin gave away that they were not locals, but they adapted well to the Entertainment District's rules, bringing as much pleasure as requested by the clients.

"Nothing more than joining me tonight at Deer's Heights. I got a room from 8 pm onwards, so plenty of time for us to have some fun."

The women exchanged a quick look. It was that easy. Much better to explain what they really wanted in a casual atmosphere.

Tanar moved closer to him. "Can we be assured that you'll bring enough spices for all of us?" she asked.

Playing with him was part of the plan, not to raise any suspicion for giving in too soon.

"Last of your worries, ladies. I treat my escorts with respect and pay well. If we get along tonight, we can become regulars."

Vargas passed his fatty hand over Mariam's firm breasts with a normal gesture, part of knowing each other's ritual. He liked them. Classy ladies, but with a rough edge at the same time. “Any more interesting tattoos under those T-shirts?” He pointed at the visible flames.

“Let’s not spoil the surprise that you are going to have tonight. You won’t be disappointed,” replied Tanar, playing with locks of her hair.

“Are we going to meet downstairs or will you give us your room number now?” Mariam asked.

The man paired the women by gently taking Mariam’s hand and bringing her beside Tanar. Quite a lovely sight. He didn’t have a favourite. He wanted them both. “Ask for Vargas room at reception. I’ll let them know that you’re coming,” he said, after which he put four macadamia nuts in a paper bag and handed it to Tanar. “For your walk back to the District. Tasty, soft and very fulfilling.”

Tandar took the bag, patted the back of his hand and left, followed by Mariam.

* * *

DEER’S HEIGHTS WAS A NICE PLACE, not located in the middle of the District, but not at its fringes either. It was a former inn, in which the owners added two more storeys to keep up with the demand for discreet meeting places. Every other building on the street was almost at the same height, but painted different colors, creating an amazingly refreshing view during the day that would brighten the mood of even the most depressed person.

Mariam and Tanar dressed for the occasion. They were determined to convince Vargas to go along with their plan, but at the same time—as the man put it during the conversation in his store—to ‘become regulars’.

Vargas had the money to pay for his eccentric taste, but he also had his circle of local friends as weird as he was. There were rumors that his real estate holdings in town were significant and the store was just a way to keep with the image his family had built over time.

The women discussed how to do their best to turn this appointment into a long-term lucrative operation, and even take the ‘regulars’ term to the next level, ‘exclusive’.

The young brunette working at the reception desk gave them the room number without a question. She seemed used to Vargas's visitors. The women had the impression that this inn was his lair, and if everything went well, this is where they would spend most of their working time.

The fourth floor only had two apartments extended down the length of the building. They overlooked the main street just above the entrance, blocked by the building across the street. The view at the back showed multiple lower roofs, and further down, the green line of the forest encircling the city.

Neither of the women had been there before so they only knew from discussions with other girls in the business that the top apartments were divided into four rooms each, so a larger group could split up and still have privacy. This setup considered the fluidity and extremes of human moods, appealing to all tastes.

Mariam knocked at the heavy-looking door on the left side of the hallway and opened it without waiting for confirmation.

He stood in the middle of the room, glass in hand, wearing a shirt similar to what he wore earlier in the store, but longer, to cover his stunted, overgrown legs. As expected, the main room was windowless, and had four doors leading to more intimate spaces. There were three large couches, several chairs lined up against the wall, and on the opposite side, a long narrow table with enough food and drinks to last a week for a party of four.

Tanar closed the door behind her and moved forward a bit, to the edge of the colourful carpet that covered the entire floor. She moved her boot over it. It was made from noise-absorbent fibers, thus nothing unwanted would slip through the walls. It gave the women a hint that Vargas might own the place. The furniture looked relatively new, but the oil paintings and rugs hanging on the walls, had some sentimental value and passed through generations.

Vargas looked at them pleased, imagining the tasks he had for them. He wanted to challenge their skills to see how far they were willing to go. The women's nipples already aroused Vargas, protruding through their semi-transparent blouses and their long legs disappearing under short, flashy dresses.

"Welcome to my humble playground. Please, help yourself," he encouraged them towards bottles of various shapes and colors. "Have you ever tried this ticklish wine from the far east? It's tasty." He waited for them to fill their glasses, then toasted. "To a lasting business relationship."

All three of them drank to that. '*The wine had an interesting taste indeed,*' Mariam thought and emptied her glass.

"No one will bother us tonight so we can stay in this room or use any of the other ones. Your choice."

"If it's only us, this will do it," Mariam moved closer to the wall to dim the light a bit. "Are you ready for your surprise?"

Vargas liked them more and more. Facing him, Mariam started to pull up her blouse, revealing her breasts and firm belly. Tanar waited for her friend to finish, then started the same moves. They let him enjoy the view for a minute.

"Put the glass down," advised Tanar smiling.

Docile, Vargas did.

Slowly they turned around exposing their vivid tattoos, the elephant and the tiger heads, as real as ever. The intense, hypnotic look of their eyes froze Vargas who remained standing. The women could see his gaze reflected in a small mirror hanging on the wall in front of them. Complete surprise, mixed with a sudden detachment from the present.

"How much longer?" Tanar asked her friend.

"Just a bit more. We really have to impress him at this phase and blow him away in the next one," replied Mariam, still checking the man in the mirror.

They had become quite skilled in using the perks offered by Hando, and together, the tattoos were an effective defense gadget.

"Enough."

They turned around and helped Vargas sit on the couch, so he wouldn't lose his balance when coming out of the trance. He slowly recovered his focus and realized that he wasn't standing anymore. He panicked for a second not sure how long he was incapacitated.

"Don't worry, dear, nothing happened to you," Mariam assured him.

"Give me a glass," demanded the man. "Am I supposed to get thirsty?"

"The reaction is different from person to person. We used it only with our special clients, and honestly, not many have deserved that label so far or had the money to pay for it," explained Tanar.

"Where did you get those tattoos? They're impressive."

Vargas's head was clear again, ever better than before arriving at the inn.

"It's not officially on the market yet. It was a gift for us. We have even more to show you," Mariam replied and gave him a pair of eyeglasses she'd taken out of her purse.

"For what we want to show you, you'll still have to look at the tattoos, but these eyeglasses will protect you from falling into a trance again."

Vargas put them on.

Tandar turned around letting the elephant head face their new patron.

"Touch the right ear," she said, waiting to sense his fingers on her skin. He did, and took them away immediately.

"Don't be shy," she joked. "Do you feel the bump?"

"Feels like a cushion underneath the skin. What's in there?"

"This is how our special customers take our type of *spices*," Mariam giggled. "Bring your nose close to the right side of the trunk and inhale."

By now he knew that there was no point in looking surprised. He put his nostrils on top of the tattooed spot Mariam indicated, and gasped a healthy intake.

A second later his nose exploded in a soft pain that split in two, moving up to his brain, and down his throat, passing his stomach, and splitting again down his legs. He felt happy, a very good happy, in a space that suddenly had vibrations he never saw before, more crisp and with a higher frequency. The elephant's trunk was moving towards him, but he was not afraid of its strength acting on him, it was just a friendly gesture of touching his colored hair and beard. The tiger was harmless too. Two wild animals suddenly tame and ready to listen to his commands. A thought raised within him, more of an experiment, to have the beasts disappear. That thought or the intention of having it, triggered an impulsive energy fluctuation that disintegrated realistic images into infinitesimal colourful pieces, instantly absorbed by the bright space surrounding him.

His view was unobstructed now. White, powerful light stretched to the horizon, revealing a long path one could follow to another dimension.

"Let's bring him back. I really want to try his stuff." Mariam said, anxious to get a taste of the spices.

She gently pushed Vargas's head towards the same spot on Tanar's back. This time to the left part of the trunk, and forced the man to inhale by covering his right nostril. He jerked backwards on the couch, eyes fixed on the ceiling. The women knew how to administer the right dosages for both phases of the experience, so he should be fully operational in a few seconds.

Vargas gasped for air several times. He was sweaty, but excited by what he remembered of his experience. And ready to ask questions.

"I've had this drug before. It's synthetic, isn't it?" the man asked.

"Yes," acknowledged Mariam. "The trick is in the tubes implanted in the trunk. The friction accelerates the particles that enter the body at double the speed than when using a short tube. And you felt the effect."

"Very ingenious," admitted Vargas, using his sleeves to clean the sweat off his face. "I haven't used synthetic in a while, so it's a bit unpredictable for me. My turn to treat you, ladies," and he extended his hands asking for help to stand up.

A box with silver incrustations sat on the table. He opened it and pulled out a small transparent bag containing a brownish powder.

"Here it is. A mix of hammer-tree bark and red moss. Made in the woods of the far East, where the secret of the right combination is being kept. All natural. Can't get healthier than this," he said visibly satisfied. "You can take it as I do, but on another day we could use the elephant's trick to see if it enhances its strength."

He poured some powder on a piece of glass and moved it aside so they could try it.

"Before we do it, could we ask you for an insignificant favour?" started Mariam.

"Anything."

"You have a client who several days ago took advantage of us and did not pay for our services."

"He might have been a big strong guy that you two couldn't handle," commented Vargas. "Not even with the tattoos."

The women looked at each other smiling.

"Actually he was more like a teenager, but we underestimated him. He vanished before we could take any action."

"And he is my client?" asked Vargas incredulously.

"Yes, he comes in weekly to pick up product you already bag for him," Tanar clarified.

"Nayan, the scholar's helper? I didn't think he was the District type of guy. What do you have in mind?"

"He is just a kid so we don't hold a grudge; nevertheless, he needs to be taught a lesson. It's more of a prank than anything else," intervened Mariam to steer the discussion in the direction they wanted.

"How can I help with this prank?" he offered.

Tanar took a small bottle out of her purse and explained.

"The next time you prepare nuts and seeds for him, sprinkle this liquid over them. You can use it all. It will give him an upset stomach for several days. Nothing radical."

"I like it. Now can we go back to where we left it off?" said Vargas anxiously.

That answer gave the women the confidence that the assignment was accomplished successfully, and nothing could stop them from solidifying the relationship with Vargas.

They took the powder in and dropped their skirts, ready to extend the man's sensorial limits.

CHAPTER 5

One Who Created All, unlock my heart and pour your love into it so, in return, I can share it with everyone around me.

From the book *We Are One* – Chapter 5

THE SCREAM WAS SOUNDLESS even if the expression on Nagoti's face showed deep puzzlement. Her hands grabbed the air, desperate for another breath as murderous fingers clutched at her throat. Danish had her locked physically and mentally, no thought would slip through his mental barrier to alert anyone.

He had chosen her as a justified sacrifice because his chances of overpowering her were higher than with any of the other children. Danish also knew that her skill level of protecting her thoughts was inferior to his, increasing his chances of cleanly eliminating her.

For the last several days after the murder, Danish had been waking up before everyone else just to be sure that none of his nightmares would be understood by mistake by any of the children he was sharing the hut with.

Nagoti was family and he had betrayed her and the entire community. A sacrilege that could be forgiven if he ever reached the *state of bliss* in this existence. And if that would happen, he would not reincarnate to help his brothers and sisters, but he would try to continue purifying his soul for its next level.

Pushing Nagoti down the latrine hole was the hardest part. He thought of so many possibilities of disposing her body, but all, in one way or another, had weaknesses that could have given the herd a chance to discover her. Leading her outside the village would have been an almost impossible task due to the protective energy layers imposed by the elephants and because he did not have enough time to gain her trust completely. The smelly pit was an undignified way to end her existence, but it was the only place where a decomposing body could go unnoticed. Nagoti's hand sticking out was an obsessive dream that he was attempting to remove through meditation and creating art pieces after his reading and chores were done.

'*Busy your mind during the day, be active, don't think about her. Forget her, push her memory down, deep, deep, where no one can find it, hide it even from yourself, so no mental protection is required,*' he kept telling himself at the beginning of each day.

At least the sacrifice was worth it, as the teachings kept getting better and better. He felt like an efficient cell of their community again. On his first day with the new group, Taber tested his knowledge of certain chapters from the *Book*, and was pleased with his comprehension of its meanings. She had him excused from the morning chores for several sunrises so he could find a quiet place in the Library to study, then in the afternoon to join the others–Janka, Makori and Indah–to discuss the significance of a specific line that they all had a hard time understanding. Due to his recent reassignment, Danish was now the oldest of the group, but by no means did his age give him any more authority over the others. A cell was a cell, with no official leader. The elephant teacher educated them all at once and guided each of them on his or her own path.

One afternoon, while coming out of the Library, Danish saw Bagham and Asman, the elephant's new temporary helper, returning to the village. Holding the *Book* under his arm, Danish ran towards them.

"Hello to both of you. How do you feel, Bagham?"

Since joining Taber's group, the boy couldn't spend as much time with Bagham, so Asman did chores for him. The elephant's rumpled skin was clean, which made the marking of his previous child partners very visible.

"I'm glad to see you." The elephant sent a happy thought. "I was looking for you to share something amazing. The dead tree has come to life. Two sunrises ago, a small orange peapod broke through one of the branches. Just like a wet spot on cracked wood. We have spread more water since, and it has grown overnight even more. Today it is almost one third of the peapod's size from the *Trees*. It's quite unbelievable."

Danish smiled, beaming with love. His friend's mood was entirely changed, pleased that it was not a false call, and indeed, the desolate emptiness was showing unexpected signs of life.

"I'm so glad, Bagham. In fact, Asman and I wanted to ask Altan if any other herd member had his pupil born at that location."

"Asman did mention to me how you all wanted to help. Thank you. I talked to Altan about it and he confirmed that there are several other locations throughout the jungle–portals for orange souls that are known only to a few."

"Why didn't he tell you as soon as he saw you going over there?" Danish asked, and opened the *Book* at the same time, looking for something.

"There were many deceitful calls in the past, this is how he justified his lack of sharing. He wanted to be sure that this time the soul decided on a new experience. Also, I'm not high enough in the hierarchy to become the herd's leader for Altan to pass that knowledge to me. What are you trying to find in there?" Bagham watched Danish, who was absorbed in flipping through the pages at the end of the *Book*.

"I'm looking for any reference to that location. Could it be written somewhere else if not in here?" replied the boy.

"It's in there, coded throughout several pages. It's not the right time for you to fully know how to decipher it. I was told that the *Orange Souls* are special and rare. Rakash was one of them. He vanished shortly after I was born. Otan, his teacher and your teacher as well, also disappeared several cycles ago. We still don't know if their disappearances are connected in any way. With faith in *One Who Created All*, this mystery will be revealed to us."

"When can we learn more about *Orange Souls*?" Asman inquired, trying to be part of the discussion. The elephant didn't want to share too many details with the children.

"If my new partner is an *Orange Soul*, it will be a great honour not only for me, but for all of us as a whole. They are souls who have reached beyond the *state of bliss*. They purified themselves and are coming back to spread new teachings. Their awareness of their surroundings happens within days after birth, but they will still need guidance in awakening all the innate knowledge they have. Their clarity of thought is marvelous. I had almost no direct contact with Rakash, so everything I'm telling you, I know from Altan."

"Does this mean that the herd will share more knowledge with us about these special souls?" Danish sat himself on the grass, the *Book* on his knees, looking up at Bagham.

"It's expected to happen that way," confirmed the elephant.

"Would this soul remember all his previous experiences in the village?" Danish had so many questions.

"I'm not sure how many he will remember. It could be all of them or only a few. He or she might identify you as a dear memory from fifty cycles ago or as one from even deeper in his timeline. My focus is on his safe arrival, then we can consider any next steps," said Bagham, circling Danish to go back on the path.

"Are you leaving already? Can I come with you when you feel it's time to detach the peapod?" asked the boy.

Without turning his head, the elephant responded, "*Orange Souls* are to be welcomed only by their partners and Council members. Sorry, Danish."

Asman followed behind Bagham, but had the time to hear Danish's reaction before running towards his hut. "These are stupid rules."

Back in his hut, Danish dropped the *Book* on his bed. A rage had risen inside him and he walked towards the gardens to calm down. His favourite spot was hidden close to the bamboo fence just before the clearing where the *Trees of Life* stood. There, the grass was left wild, as the shade from the fence would stop anything else from growing without the villagers' miraculous intervention. The bamboo sticks were refreshingly cold on his back when he leaned against them. He stopped his thoughts for a moment to generate a protective energy layer. Bagham, a knowledgeable teacher, would have brought lasting happiness and sparked a feeling of love in anyone but Danish.

"What's wrong with me? Why do I get so upset every time I meet him?"

The boy pushed his head against his palms in a failed attempt to extract beliefs that could clarify his questions. It was an unbreakable pattern no matter what approach he took: an inoffensive discussion generating disturbing ideas, tormenting him for days afterwards.

"What's wrong with me?" he asked himself again, hoping that someone else would answer.

He removed the piece of bark covering a hole in the ground that he had dug as a hiding place for his artwork. He pulled out several palm tree leaves along with other leaves that were much longer and thinner, and used for intricate weaving. His breathing calmed down so he started the last step in assembling the parts of a necklace whose beads were dried avocado seeds mixed with purple, white and black perforated stones. Hanging in the middle was a round polished piece of bark. One side was painted with markings he had found in the *Book*, celebrating the communion between elephants and humans; the other side displayed a stylized version of the *Trees of Life*. This was going to be a gift for the *Orange Soul*.

Danish was very proud of his artistic achievements even if he was the only one assessing himself; he hadn't dared to gather up his courage and present his work to anyone else. The offerings to new arrivals were part of millennium-old customs, and the members of the higher castes were expected to prepare meaningful gifts. It was not mandatory for the *Commoners*, but even a fruit or a food dish would have been appreciated.

Being a part of the *Commoner* caste, it was impossible for Danish to offer his precious necklace. What was expected of him was a food dish or just a flower, the embodiment of humbleness.

The boy raised the finished piece in the air for another look. It was beautiful. The leaf's colour on one side had yellowish nuances, making the ancient markings even more visible. He put it on the grass with exaggerated care and started to pull out more items from the hole, arranging them in front of him.

Bamboo was his favourite material. It was strong, but flexible, and docile if one knew how to handle it. Danish would expose the areas he wanted to bend with energy vibrations that would weaken the fiber without leaving cracks, making it smooth to the touch. He created bamboo frames of various sizes, pinning dead bugs, dried leaves or sacred passages found in the Library, and painted on carefully carved pieces of wood inside them. He had something to present to the Council if he ever came to the decision to publicly declare himself as an *Artist,* in spite of any consequences.

Danish had no idea what to expect of their reaction, since he had found no records of anyone else claiming that they felt they were part of a different caste than the one they were born into.

He felt completely calm now. Meditating was an efficient way to bring himself back; but working with his hands was also good. He suddenly realized that he had to stop asking Bagham questions whose answers would upset him. Focusing on the *Book* and the follow up discussions should be his main goal. Going in front of the Council with the request of being assessed and recognized as an *Artist* might be too soon after joining Taber's group. He lacked patience to achieve his goals, and the risks were high.

"I will present my request to them at the end of the dry season," Danish said aloud, rationalizing this dangerous thought. "It gives me enough time to claim that Taber's guidance opened new windows of understanding in me."

The wind ruffled the grass on the ground and prickled the boy's ears with unexpected sounds. A round shaved head appeared from behind some mango trees, then Baqar's full body. He was garbed in grayish pants and shirt, both waving on his tiny frame. Food stains that couldn't be removed by numerous washes, and mended rips in his clothing made him look shabby.

His brother's arrival made Danish panic for a moment, only to remember immediately the clandestine invitation made to Baqar, one of the older males from the *Artist* caste. Danish didn't have too many choices if he wanted to move ahead with his plan. There were only three unrealized *Artists* in the village, two males and one female. While in the prime creative phase of their life, neither of them was able to create unique artwork that could have generated the approval of the other members of the *Artists'* caste. Ten inimitable pieces of art was the threshold imposed during the immemorial time of the *Book*. It was a necessary condition to lift any mental burden, which could have pulled the soul back from its journey of reaching the *state of bliss*.

After attentive observations and sporadic interaction with all of them, he concluded that Baqar was not only the oldest of them, at thirty-five cycles, but also the most depressed. Any initiative or statement coming from him would get symbolic acknowledgement from the Council as his end was near. Baqar's time left in the village was less than a cycle. His soul's journey this time did not accomplish much, not enough to embed the ecstatic feeling of the *state of bliss* in him and secure his safe transition to the next astral level.

His dark brownish skin was wrinkled wherever visible, most notably on his head and hands, making the marks on his cheeks, a small blue palm tree leaf, barely noticeable. His body posture and slumped walk left no doubts about how defeated he felt. He slowed his pace approaching the area before the *Trees of Life*, and looked around.

Danish waived his hand at him. Another piece of his plan seemed to unfold peacefully this time. If Baqar listened to his offer, his chances of presenting himself as an *Artist* when the time was right would increase dramatically. From his view, he was offering Baqar an opportunity for redemption and, thus, a good deed that should count for his soul's evaluation when facing the *Supreme Being*.

Baqar found his way to Danish's spot and squatted with his back to the fence.

"How are you feeling?" asked Danish.

He really didn't care too much, just enough to be sure that what he had in mind would be accomplished.

"Tired. Like the previous sunrise and the sunrise before that. A blank mind is an unbelievable weight to carry around," answered Baqar.

The *Commoner* was impressed by the *Artist*'s bluntness about his situation.

"I've wasted everyone's time. My teacher couldn't help either. I know it was not his fault, but mine. Something is broken inside me. At this age no one can tell me what to do. The rules don't apply to me anymore. A fulfilling satisfaction arises inside me when helping in the kitchen or in the garden."

Baqar was resigned to his inescapable condition.

"My name will be mentioned in the records as a failure, a burden that my soul will have to carry in its next return."

"I want to help ease your pain," said Danish. "Like you, I also feel different. On the outside, I'm a *Commoner*, but on the inside, I feel like an *Artist*."

Baqar looked at him intensely, not sure if he could believe the statement. "An *Artist* soul returned as a *Commoner* who remembers?"

Danish got on his knees excitedly. The wind was still and the garden heavy with the smell of the ripe fruits and plants. "Yes, I remember. Only fragments, but I do remember. Otan, my teacher, helped me to reconnect with my soul's previous experiences."

"I pity you, the same way I pity myself."

"I don't need your pity!" exclaimed Danish, who recognized that the discussion was on the edge of escaping his control. He knew that he needed to show compassion towards the older man to persuade him to play along.

"Look, it's my burden to carry, no one else's. Just as you carry yours. My artwork is not worthy yet for what I feel I am, but it is still adequate as a gift."

"What do you want from me?" Baqar's hands had a visible tremor, so he locked them onto his knees. A body reaching thirty cycles had noticeable signs of deterioration.

"Here are my creations." Danish pointed to the items on the ground. "The *Trees* will give birth soon and a gift is expected. And maybe not just from the mature villagers ..." He left the words hanging, hoping that Baqar would make the connection with ease, but the unrealized *Artist* waited patiently. "I'm offering one of my artworks for you to take credit. I have only one condition. Your gift will go to Bagham's new pupil. An *Orange Soul*."

Baqar's eyes grew unexpectedly wider. He didn't need any more convincing. "Being in the presence of such a soul is an additional blessing to one's life," he muttered looking at the artwork.

"Everyone will be surprised, but the justification is that *One Who Created All*, in his immeasurable kindness, sent a jolt of inspiration to an otherwise deserted mind, to share the joy of such a wonderful birth," the *Commoner* explained as he'd rehearsed.

Baqar didn't seem to notice the insult. It didn't matter anyway. He felt the struggle of his soul in this tarnished body, it's sadness that it couldn't leave it's physical shell and enter an experienceless existence sooner. At least this lie would turn events in his favour, a positive entry under his name in the record, ending a dull reality.

"I'll do it," decided Baqar, "but I also have a condition."

Danish didn't expect attitude from someone who was already assessed as emotionally distraught and would accept any type of offer. He smiled sheepishly.

"You will help me create a piece of artwork of my own, which I'll hand over to the Council just before my soul transitions."

The *Commoner* nodded his head in agreement. It was a good deed that would wash away some of his sins.

* * *

THE ELDERS GATHERED IN TWO of the biggest huts of the village. All of the castes were mixed together, but separated by gender. *Commoners, Builders, Artists and Writers* mingled daily, waiting for their soul to find its way up to the astral level where, after assessing the existence it had just been released from, would decide if and when to come back.

Every several cycles, three or four unrealized children turned adults would move to this part of the village, their responsibilities reduced and the community's expectations of them diminished.

Their prime time in which creativity was supposed to be abundant had eluded them, leaving some with the desire to keep trying to fulfill their customary obligations. And if that was not possible, at least get involved in the diurnal chores.

The most rewarding of all was taking care of the newborns right after the peapods released them. The caste sign would be barely noticeable on the babies' faces and only the small coloured hands of the *Commoners* would distinguish them for a quick count.

Baqar sat at one end of a wooden table inside the hut, looking down at his toes, but his thoughts focused on his discussion with Danish. An unbelievable shiver of energy passed through his body as soon as his mind processed the fact that before the end of this existence, a piece of artwork would bear his name.

This regained strength made the last couple of sunrises pass much faster. Positive thoughts and ideas swirled in an otherwise quiet mind. He realized that this gift offering to the *Orange Soul* could be turned into another opportunity.

Baqar walked to the women's hut, looking for Alanda, the only unrealized *Artist* female. She was sitting on her bed reading a book. The man sat beside her tenderly.

"What are you reading?"

"Nukua's latest addition to the library. He is so talented. It's an allegory about what other worlds *One Who Created All* could have created. He contemplates the question: "*Are we alone*?"

"If you think it's good, I'll get a copy too. It will be refreshing for me to browse through the library as I haven't done so in a while. My thoughts are so far away," replied Baqar.

"What's bothering you?" Alanda had a high level of empathy towards everyone. She was only two cycles younger than the man, but her physical degradation was more pronounced. The skin around her eyes sagged, making them barely visible, and her cheekbones protruded pointedly.

"We are going to witness very soon the arrival of an *Orange Soul*, Bagham's new partner."

"That's wonderful!" interrupted Alanda with a spark of energy in her voice.

"Yes, indeed. Since I found out about it, an untapped vigor came over me, enlightening me with creative thoughts lost a long time ago."

"What are you trying to tell me, Baqar?" Alanda put the book on the bed and gently grabbed his hand.

"I finally created my own artwork. I can't describe the ecstatic elevation I had. The chains of creative inability unshackled, temporarily offering me this amazing break."

"*One Who Created All* is good with you, Baqar. He sees our weaknesses, listens to our prayers, and garnishes us with his blessings or difficult lessons to toughen us. He has to remind us that our internal love for ourselves and for him has to spill out and embrace everyone in the village, the jungle, the world beyond the limits we know."

Alanda's devotion couldn't be shattered. If it wasn't for the caste she was born into, her soul could have already been in the astral level, liberated and happy.

"When can I see it?"

The woman's reaction had no trace of envy. Baqar's revelation had touched her deeply, silently thanking *One Who Created All* for this miracle.

"I'll show it to you soon, but I wanted to ask if you would pair with me to care for the *Orange Soul*."

Alanda started crying. Emotions overwhelmed her, aware of the honour given to her in the last cycles of this existence.

"Unwavering faith is what our souls need for a smooth transition. Determination on the spiritual path ignites the locked energies inside us, under the protection of the *Supreme Being*." Baqar knew very well the essence of the *Book* and how to express it for Alanda to follow him unconditionally. "Neither you nor I lack faith. We both had wonderful teachers who opened our mind's eyes on the spiritual path," said Baqar, pleased with his achievement.

"In our case, *One Who Created All* left us short of creativity, but only because *He* loves us. We are chosen for another return and given the chance to share life with our brothers and sisters, thirty or fifty cycles in the future, whenever we decide to return. We will experience an *Orange Soul*'s contribution to the community in real life, and not have to learn about it from books." Excitement engulfed her. "Let's ask Bagham for permission to be his partner's caretakers." Alanda embraced her caste brother.

Baqar returned her hug. He felt content. Suddenly, the vision of his purpose in his remaining cycle was revealed to him with stunning clarity. The positive vibrations of the *Orange Soul* would partially clear his karma, allowing his soul to return shamelessly to the astral level.

CHAPTER 6

When eating, one gets full easily. When praying to One Who Created All, one never becomes full of His love.

From the book *We Are One* – Chapter 6

ON HIS WAY HOME, Bart struggled to breathe deeply. Even now, while standing in the hallway, the unbearable pain, still clutching at his chest, made his inhalations short and fast, and had him gasping for more air. He understood the reaction of his body to the subconscious painful thought that he might lose Rakash and, at the same time, an entire intangible world of energy and vibrations, of delicate connections within the boy's body and mind, that Bart tried to bring forward through meditation. A world too difficult to be understood by the people he was living amongst.

Following Rakash's example, Bart had found some calm with his own meditation, searching within, the omnipresent *soul.* He created his own affirmation, words he thought to have meaning and impact when addressing the *soul* and *One Who Created All.*

Bart was not sure if the *Supreme Being* was able to spend time on anyone else other than the community in the jungle. But the scholar tried to keep his activities in line with what would draw the attention of such an entity towards him. Unfortunately, with the new developments adding even more pressure on him, he was not consistent enough to keep morning meditation in his schedule.

He needed to re-evaluate what new approach would 'internally activate' Rakash. The scholar didn't know yet how the connection between *One Who Created All* and individual *soul* worked, in fact only his intuition let him think that there was a connection.

Nayan was waiting to release him from the burden of the heavy bag.

"How did it go?" he inquired excitedly, taking the bag from Bart. The scholar knew that the boy hoped to hear the good news of having Rakash around for many more months to come.

Bart, still short of breath, held onto the youngster's arm, avoiding a direct answer. "I'm a bit tired now, let's talk tomorrow morning. Please take care of Rakash and bring some wine to the library," he instructed and Nayan scurried off. Bart had no appetite, but a drink would help him clear his mind and decide on next steps. He dropped his coat on an armchair and sat on the couch, visually browsing the rows of books related to the villagers. "What else can I use?" he muttered, mentally indexing and discarding potential options. He decided to write it down, so his mind would register it even better. "Images, words, sounds, stories, smell ... anything else we used?"

Nayan came in carrying a small carafe of wine. He poured some in a glass for his master and headed towards the door quietly not to disturb his deliberations.

"Don't go," said Bart. "Have a look at this list and let me know if we exposed Rakash to any other stimuli. Try to add examples under each category. We have to narrow down what else can trigger his deep meditative state."

The teenager was more than eager to help his master. He picked up the piece of paper and started drawing lines in between key words. "We showed him all of the images and drawings related to his former way of life," Nayan said, taking the initiative. "There are not too many in the books we gathered so far, but important enough for him to recognize them immediately."

"What was his general reaction to these images?" asked the scholar.

"Happiness, satisfaction, joy, a good feel overall as he is still under the impression that he will go back to his village soon enough."

"Write down Happiness and Joy. Next category is Words. Which ones have we focused on?"

Nayan thought for a moment. "Strength, power, thought, vibration, energy, presence, light, elephant, brother, sister, *One Who Created All*, harmony ... many more and combinations of them."

"During each session I asked him to focus on selected words and none of them worked. No internal or external change." Bart sipped the wine and stared at Nayan intensely. "What if the trigger is based on words that generate feelings such as happiness, joy, love, loyalty, gratitude," said the scholar. "We exposed him to stories and familiar sounds, but his reaction was not profound. Not more different than yours or mine. We should try a combination of *One Who Created All* and love or any of the other words you've just written down. It has to work."

Nayan drew a big circle around the new key words, a protective layer against any malefic influence that could have changed their meaning if left bared on paper. "Should we adjust the meditation posture as well?" offered the youngster. "I told you he complained about the pain in his legs from extended stays on his back. Maybe the lotus position is what he needs, but shorter sessions."

"That's a good idea," Bart concurred. "We'll try it tomorrow."

Nayan was about to leave the room, but he turned around and asked, "Master, what happened at the Council meeting? How much longer can we keep Rakash?"

Bart finished his wine, pulled out his shoes and laid down on the couch, ready to sleep. "Don't want to talk about it tonight. Overall, it was a good chat, very informative. They liked what they heard," Bart said equivocally to divert his protégé's attention.

"So this is good news then," smiled Nayan.

"You could say so," concluded Bart closing his eyes. "Turn off the light, good night."

* * *

THE NEXT DAY, the frenetic rhythm of work started. Bart was determined not to hand over Rakash to Korobat so easily. If he had to capitulate, the scholar would definitely go with the boy; no matter what the President had said, the villager was his responsibility more than anyone else's.

Key words were written in big letters on pieces of cardboard and displayed in the meditation room in front of Rakash.

"How are you feeling?" Bart asked, getting ready to apply the changes. He was making a considerable effort to shake off from his mind the outcome of yesterday's meeting. "Nayan mentioned that you would prefer to sit in the lotus position and have shorter sessions. Let's try it."

The child was ready to start.

"I'm not going to time the sessions anymore. Meditate for as long as you are comfortable in this position. Also focus on feelings, which are represented by words such as happiness, joy, love, gratitude. Think of your elephant teacher, feel him next to you, exchanging thoughts. Remember one of your discussions that really filled you with joy," Bart explained the new format.

"Joy?" Rakash still lacked an understanding of some of the new words he had to learn.

Bart looked at Nayan for help.

Nayan happily conceded. "Rakash, you told me about taking Otan to the river for his bath and how you would move your little hand over his wrinkled skin, feeling his physical strength and the stream of warm thoughts."

"Yes, I remember that discussion."

"That feeling for us is joy or happiness and even love. Get that feeling inside of you, then think of *One Who Created All*, and of your favourite teachings from the *Book*. Focus on that as hard as possible, remove your mind from this physical plane," Nayan guided his younger friend.

Rakash nodded and repositioned himself on the hard surface of the bed.

"We'll be outside in case you need anything or have something to share," said Bart and, along with Nayan, he left the room, leaving the door ajar.

The villager closed his eyes, and started the breathing exercises his teacher had taught him. Inhale, hold, exhale, several times for the mind to quiet, heart to slow down, so the energy used at the extremities of the body would be slowly moved and focused to the most important location, the forehead. Sitting straight was so much more comfortable than laying on his back. The energy flow circulated so naturally inside him now; no blockages, no nerve pinching.

Otan smiled in front of him, balancing his trunk left and right between his tusks, stomping excitedly. Around him, the herd was similarly involved in his happiness. This was Rakash's first memory of his teacher, which he had to dig up from within, after considerable effort.

Soft warmth engulfed his body and he enjoyed it. He held Otan's image for a little longer then he morphed it into thoughts about *One Who Created All.*

The "*One Who Created All* is Love, *One Who Created All* is Energy, *One Who Created All* is Vibration, *One Who Created All* is Omnipresent," he repeated silently over and over again, getting lost in the depth of its meaning, trying to pierce through the veil of delusion that was still blocking a deeper understanding of this wisdom.

The warmth grew in intensity on his cheeks and at the base of his spine. Rakash tried to maintain focus on the mantra, somehow aware of the new sensations he was experiencing.

One Who Created All was responding to his calling by enhancing his mental image of an opened energy channel along his back. The point between his eyebrows was hurting, but nothing close to what he felt before.

He repeated the mantra with more concentration and mental force. It was just him and the *Supreme Being,* a request and an immediate answer through boosts of energy and vibrations sent to every part of his body.

Rakash was able to visualize a golden light ball forming inside the lower part of his abdomen, pulsating continuously up and down, undecided about which direction to go.

At the same moment Nayan peeked into the room to check on Rakash. He saw something that everyone was waiting for a long time: the orange triangles were alive on his cheeks, an internal throbbing light bringing them to life.

He froze for a moment, unsure if he should go get Bart or enjoy this unique view a bit longer. He removed himself from the door and rushed to get his master so he could witness the results of his hard work.

"Master, come quickly," whispered Nayan and he vanished immediately from the library.

Bart trotted as fast as his short leg allowed him and gasped at seeing the child through the sliver of space. Satisfaction, relief, and a bag of mixed feelings hit his weakened confidence. Rakash's birthmarks came to life, their orange color pulsing from internal energy. His pupil had moved closer to spiritual attainment.

Suddenly a tremor took over Rakash's hands and legs and, for a moment, he almost lost his balance. Ignoring his own rules about protecting the sensitivity of the meditation environment, Bart pushed his shoulder into the door. He burst in to grab the child from a potential fall.

The door knocked the bucket behind it, making enough noise to bring Rakash back to reality. The brutal rupture from what he was experiencing made him dizzy and he fell sideways on the bed. Bart rushed to the boy, followed by Nayan.

"Are you ok? I'm so sorry. I saw you shaking and ready to fall and I forgot that it might be a normal reaction when reaching the *state of bliss.*"

Rakash straightened his legs, but was not ready to climb down. He couldn't see the light ball anymore, but the concentrated energy still hovered in the same place, less intense. The vibrations bouncing between his cells and internal organs were slowly dissipating as well, returning his body shell to a normal state. Then he noticed the excitement on Nayan and Bart's faces and understood that what he just went through was the 'power' they were looking for.

"The changes worked," he said, smiling.

"Yes, they have," confirmed the scholar, barely believing how much time he wasted using the wrong method. "The signs on your cheeks came alive, not burning hot, but just enough to prove that an intense process was going on inside of you. From the outside you were a picture of calm. It's unbelievable what amazing developments can occur in the calmness of our mind." Bart grinned.

Rakash thought for a long moment on what the scholar just said and replied with unexpected maturity. "It is more than calmness of the mind. It's *One Who Created All* who talked to me because I called *Him*. I wanted *Him* to hear me, so I opened my heart to *Him*. I let *Him* in voluntarily, asking for nothing in return. While chanting the mantra, I remembered that selflessness is part of who we are as a community. Helping and caring for each other."

"Nayan, go get ink and paper and write everything down," instructed the happy scholar.

"Why did you mention the heart?" inquired Bart intrigued.

"In the village we communicate by thought with the elephants, but our hearts sing our blessings, compassion, and gratitude for their spiritual guidance."

Finally, Bart had tangible proof that the stories about the power of thought and the heart were true and could be considered, up to a point, a reliable source.

Rakash was feeling different, as though a blockage inside his head had completely disappeared during meditation. Knowledge he didn't know he possessed was surfacing, like a bubble of air released from the mud of a deep lake.

Nayan returned holding a notepad, ready to record every word of the incredible experience he had just witnessed.

"It's the heart that hosts the soul, the gate we work hard to open for communicating with *One Who Created All*," said Rakash. "Rational thinking has nothing to do with it. No one born outside of the village can understand such a powerful bond ingrained into us for thousands of cycles."

"Do you remember anything else?" Bart was hungry for more details.

The youngster closed his eyes, searching for particulars that his consciousness might have left out due to the sudden come back. "I remember that many previous births have preceded this one and, in one of them, I was able to reach a *state of bliss* deep enough for *One Who Created All* to offer me free passage to the next astral level. But he also asked me if I want to return to help my siblings achieve their potential," concluded Rakash, exhaling several times to energize his body.

Nayan wrote frenetically, already finishing the first page of notes. His eyes were glued to the page, focused on adding, if possible, any nuance and meaning that were revealed to his level of understanding.

"Have you unlocked any knowledge about the additional purpose of the *Orange Soul*?" asked Bart a question he had posed a long time ago and for which he couldn't find an answer in any of the books he had already studied.

The boy didn't pause to think about it, he just replied instantly. "I did not ask this question yet. I asked for love as you instructed and this is what I received. Unlimited, unconditional love."

"So *One Who Created All* is answering your questions?" intervened Nayan, still scribbling row after row of knowledge that they were hungry for.

"He answers all our prayers, questions and doubts."

Rakash was very convincing in his responses.

"Will *He* answer mine too?" Nayan almost whispered his question, in case *One Who Created All* was listening.

The villager climbed down and walked to the table, grabbing a glass of water, then addressed his friend. "I don't remember much because I never read the *Book*. It was read to me now and then. One existence is not enough to understand it, but if your communion with *One Who Created All* is strong enough and one has achieved his purpose, then reaching the *state of bliss* and transitioning to the next level can occur. The *Book* mentions the '*Lands beyond the Dead Stretch and the humans*', but I don't know of any other details. I can't answer this question on *His* behalf."

Rakash voiced his doubts: "Are we the same?" He put the empty glass back on the table, straightened his back, and answered his own question: "Physically we look the same, but we behave differently." Then suddenly, another thought struck him: "What do you believe in?"

Bart and Nayan looked at each other embarrassed. It seemed that the sudden connection with the wisdom of *One Who Created All*, released in Rakash a new understanding of his environment that also required more answers from his caretakers.

"No one in the city has a moral compass similar to the one followed by your community," Bart replied. "The Laetanians believe in a decent life, punctuated by physical accumulation as a social status, and having a good time because life is relatively short. Why bother with anything else?"

A quick introspection provided Bart with an unsettling truth: he would have followed the same path if hadn't been for the books on the villagers and his keen curiosity. There was no prayer or gathering of any kind to worship an entity like *One Who Created All.* There was no one to listen to their daily challenges and answer them with hope, decency, and care. The Laetanians, Korobatians and people in every other city and town that dotted the horizon were at the mercy of what life threw at them unexpectedly, and had to deal with it on their own.

The adrenaline of seeing Rakash igniting his inner potential wore off, and the pain bit into Bart's muscles again like a hungry creature that needed his energy to survive, forcing him to sit. A lightheaded sensation overcame him. The smell of wine touched his nostrils and he realized that it was his own breath since recently indulging on wine was his refuge from the pain and lack of results with Rakash.

"We don't have your belief compass, that's for sure," confessed the scholar. "We make plans for the future and work hard or steal or cheat to see them accomplished. If it doesn't happen, we say it was bad luck and start all over again or quit, if the will is not there."

"Otan told me that what we think, what we do, is all *His* will," said Rakash. "We act to please *One Who Created All* and in return *He* helps smooth our path to enlightenment."

'*Such a foreign concept,'* Bart thought to himself. *'Anyone looking to reach the state of bliss was driven by the desire of a new experience and not because of a belief in a higher invisible entity. It was a trend, that was all.'*

"Life's purpose for all the other castes is very clear, but not for me. I don't know what plans *One Who Created All* has marked for an *Orange Soul. He* will send me a message when I'm ready." Rakash went deeper and deeper into his newfound well of ancient wisdom. "How are you going to use this 'power'?" he asked, looking at both Nayan and Bart.

The master and the disciple had puzzled looks as they had imagined the moment when the boy would bring his priceless inner resources to the surface, but never put much consideration on what would come next.

Believing in *One Who Created All* was one aspect of what the villagers termed *faith.* Calling *Him* with an inward voice was a quality that they were not sure they possessed, and not yet sure how to activate, as it was hidden deep down inside them.

'Nevertheless, we are ready to try. But how to convince the masses to seriously consider such an approach?' Bart continued his inner evaluation.

"We need your help, Rakash," Nayan broke the long silence. "If this higher state of consciousness is achieved by everyone around us, good things will happen to them. All of these worldly desires deceive them from the reality that the teachings of your community have revealed to us. We want to give them the chance to taste the elusiveness of a new realm. These types of humans don't believe in the omnipresence of an intangible being, including us, until we met you," Nayan admitted and pushed the notepad sideways, so he could rest his elbows on the table. "More sessions are needed to establish a pattern of how to consistently induce the deep trance. Based on today's results, I'm confident that we will get the Council off our backs," he concluded, displaying a grin similar to his master's a bit earlier.

The anxiety of presenting tangible proof in such a short period of time had never left Bart's mind since the latest official meeting. He would have to invite them over for a live demonstration. But not until he was certain that Rakash could deliver consistent results every session.

"Let's rest now. We'll try again the day after tomorrow, until then you can spend as much time as you like outdoors," Bart said, knowing this would be happy news for Rakash.

* * *

RAKASH WAS INDEED HAPPY. His contentment exuded from every fiber of his being; it was a joy that stayed with him permanently. He found inner peace and the following three sessions were successful, taking him through the same succession of sensations and interaction with *One Who Created All.*

His hosts were equally pleased, as the prospect of leaving for Korobat was less and less likely to happen. The boy didn't fully understand what exactly master meant to say when he confessed to him that the Council's intention was to send all three of them away to a distant town for different types of sessions, if he couldn't reach the *state of bliss* soon. But now that pressure was lifted, Bart had explained, and they would be able to continue their work in Laeta.

Rakash was proud of himself for evolving spiritually without Otan's help. He had so many stories to share with all his brothers and sisters upon returning to the village.

He was not aware that anyone else from the community left the jungle for the '*Lands Beyond the Dead Stretch*'. He was the first. He would fill a thick book, with story after story, as part of his life's purpose.

The door of the meditation room was closed, but he could hear some noise from the kitchen, where Panette, a young girl recently hired by Bart to cook for them, was preparing lunch. He went through his usual stretching steps, slowly, having learnt to control each muscle, tensing it from low to intense strength. Using this technique at the beginning and end of his sessions helped create better blood circulation while in the lotus position, and also allowed him to meditate for longer periods.

Gentle light poured in through the windows, touching the wall opposite from where he was standing. It was warm inside. The good weather of the hot season would stick around for two to three more weeks before giving in to cold rain and strong winds.

"The rainy season is upon you, my friends," said Rakash out loud, sending a symbolic message to his siblings in the jungle, and trying to remember all the blessings associated with the divine rain sent to them by *One Who Created All.*

The downpour would allow everyone outside, except maybe the elders, to feel the splash on their hot skin; rivulets of water would find adhoc trenches between stretched muscles or entangled locks of hair. Moments later they would be ankle-deep in the mud, moving sluggishly like wild honey running down a bamboo stick. The elephants would join the madness with happy shrieks, stomping hard and covering the children with layers of fluid brownish skin, washed away almost instantly by resilient showers.

Blissful memories of his unique community.

Rakash put on his sandals, ready to share with Bart and Nayan the new perceptions he felt through his recently enhanced skills. He stopped in the hallway to watch Panette in the kitchen moving between the stove and sink, tasting from the steaming pan, nodding to herself, then continuing her cooking rituals. Her dishes were tasty; he tried them a couple of times, but he wasn't ready yet to give up his favourites: nuts, fruits and cheese.

Rakash moved to the library. Bart was not reading, just holding his regular tea mug, deep in thought.

"Where is Nayan?" asked the boy, looking around for his friend. Bart didn't move. "Hey," said Rakash louder this time.

Bart jumped out of his reverie. "He went to get some supplies. He should be back soon. How did it go?"

Recently, his beard had more speckles of gray and the eczema on his head was a darker nuance of red, as if the blood underneath the skin had become thicker.

Rakash sat on the armchair facing the scholar, legs pulled up to his chin. "I've experienced some new sensations," he said.

That was the signal for Bart to lay down his mug and grab the notebook.

"I heard sounds inside my body. The vibrations of my heart sped up, colliding with the slower ones from other organs. It generated a powerful wailing that reverberated up and down, through my bones and skin. Its intensity puzzled me, almost bringing me back. It took me a moment to adjust my consciousness to understand the message."

"Interesting," was all what Bart could say, still processing this information. "Is the message from *One Who Created All?*"

"I told you before that all the messages are from *Him*. How *He* communicates with us might be different each time. Maybe this is an indication that my body and soul purification are naturally progressing. There are symptoms that I can't explain on my own. I need Otan's guidance."

Rakash wanted to say something else, but paused, waiting for Bart to finish the sentence he was writing.

"Master!" The boy had heard Nayan use the term so many times, that he decided to use it as well. "When will I return to the village? I miss them all."

His voice was grave and sincere. The scholar did not expect the question; he had tried hard since he received the boy, to divert his mind from those he had left behind. Of course, there were still instances when only those memories would generate results in meditation, but Bart had included enough distractions in Rakash's daily activities that he hoped the fog of time would make the jungle community invisible.

"I don't know yet. We have to please the Council first, then we can make the request."

Bart wanted to see Rakash returned to his people. He ever hoped that he would be allowed to join him, even if it was only for several days, so he could see the elephants, the elders, the library, and the remote, undisturbed ancient community with his own eyes. Only after experiencing them first hand, would he be able to validate the content from all of the books he studied.

There was a bit of a racket in the hallway. Nayan had just returned, and Panette rushed to help with the heavy bags he was carrying. Giggling followed, then silence as the kitchen door shut behind them.

Bart was not sure if he had made a good decision in hiring the girl. Being only three years older than Nayan, she liked him and the interest was mutual. The scholar needed Nayan to focus on their work now more than ever.

Moments later, the apprentice entered the library carrying three bowls of walnuts and various seeds.

"Here are some snacks before dinner. Panette will be ready soon," he said, entering the library.

Bart, chewed absent-mindedly on a few of them, still thinking about Rakash's desire to go back.

"I delivered your message to the President's office, master," Nayan confirmed, enjoying the snack.

"Good. We have to be ready. Two weeks will pass fast. I can't wait to see their reaction ... hhhmmm... these seeds are quite tasty," Bart said, taking another handful.

He tried to keep his mouth full to avoid answering any more questions from Rakash.

But the villager was not satisfied with Bart's answer, so he asked again. This time Nayan was his target. "I asked master when I could return to the jungle."

Nayan was sitting across from Blackwood and glanced at him, looking for acceptance on his vague answer.

The young boy almost choked, spitting some of the seeds out. "Whatever the master told you, there is nothing I can add," he replied, coughing to clear his throat.

"I will talk to the Council when they come to visit us," Rakash continued seriously. "I want to go back and see Otan. I need his guidance now." He kept chewing on the walnuts.

"Agreed, we are all going to mention your request to the President," Bart concluded, hoping to remove any worries that might impact Rakash's concentration.

They heard Panette calling from the kitchen. The faint smell of food suggested another delicious dish, so they hurried to try it.

* * *

THE NEXT SEVERAL DAYS WERE a blur for all of them, including Panette, who could barely find a few hours for a nap, while Bart, Nayan and Rakash were doing the same from the exhaustion generated from the continued vomiting and lasting weakness in the whole body.

The first symptoms appeared on Rakash, initially mild, but slowly intensifying. Waves of fever, warmth, and cold shook his body, followed by overall feebleness, which culminated with vomiting. When nothing was left in his stomach to come out, the muscle contraction didn't recede, his whole frame convulsed like it was hung from strings and manipulated by a bad puppeteer.

He had everyone else worried since they didn't know what to do other than listen to the doctor who had no solution either. He had never seen all these symptoms present in one patient.

Nayan then fell sick, so there were two of them lying in the same room. Panette and Bart took turns emptying smelly buckets and changing the damp cloth on their burning foreheads. When Bart soon ailed with the same symptoms, Panette grew hysterical, overwhelmed and afraid that she would be next. She almost gave up on them, but changed her mind at the last minute, and brought her mother to help out.

Bart was settled in the library since no bed could fit in the other room.

The girl felt guilty, thinking that her cooking had had something to do with the sickness that was consuming the house. However, she had eaten the food too and was perfectly fine. The effort of staying awake added to her burden and the thought that she caused all of this took her normal smile away. Her hair, always combed and caught in a ponytail, was in disarray.

This was what the Council members saw when they knocked at the door on the day scheduled for validating Rakash's capabilities.

Panette froze with her mouth open, unsure of what to do.

"Where is Blackwood?" questioned Kravis Kanar, carrying himself straight and stiff like the wooden cane in his hand. "Can we come in?"

"Everyone in the house is sick, Mr. President," Panette explained. "Mr. Blackwood, too. Sick, very sick," she nodded multiple times very compellingly.

Kanar turned to his entourage, who had no initial desire to come, but their support pledged to the leader made them. They all smiled, unconvinced by the girl's performance.

"Is this another one of his tricks to buy more time?" said Victoria Kraft hastily.

"No, mam, no tricks. Not even doctor Trengle knows what the disease is," Panette defended her employer.

"Let's go inside," Orgil Nurkan said, pushing his way in past the distressed girl. The whole Council stepped in and spread out from the hallway, opening doors in search of Bart.

Kraft and Kanar pulled out handkerchiefs to cover their noses as the air inside smelled heavily of stale medicines and spoiled food.

"Girl, how can you survive in this pestilence?" Victoria Kraft asked rhetorically. "Open the windows immediately," she ordered to a still confused Panette, who rushed to do so.

The President found Bart in the library, half conscious, saliva coming down from the corner of his mouth. The affected side of his scalp was visible and looked worse than usual, covered by an unhealthy reddish coating. The bucket beside the couch was half full and stank profusely. The stench was even worse in that room from sweat and soiled clothing that Panette didn't dare remove.

Misk and Nurkan reported a similar scene from the room where the boys were resting.

"Do you think he's playing us?" Nurkan asked, not trusting anyone.

"Hard to say," Kanar replied. "He is two weeks away from the deadline, so what better time to try something so desperate. I don't know what to say, people. It could be real or induced to soften us up and delay the handover. What do you think?" he glanced among them.

Victoria joined them, just catching the President's last words. "I've asked the girl when it started–the disease I mean. It was almost two weeks ago, right after he invited us over to display the 'amazing results' he achieved. It's too obvious," Kraft finished her assessment.

"Maybe he's too proud to accept defeat and staged the sickness as an easy way out," suggested Misk.

Gerald Misk wanted the villager to go to Korobat because he was assured by Hando Martinez that his experts would add as much 'spice' as possible to the induced *state of bliss*, and that he would be one of the few selected for testing it. Kravis was not sure which version to accept as the truth but, being the leader, he had to decide quickly. "We'll stick to the latest conditions. If he can't provide firm evidence within two weeks, we will send all of them to Korobat. No more delays." Then he turned around, leaving the room and the house. The other members followed.

Kraft addressed Panette who was still bewildered by the important unannounced visit. "Tell Blackwood when he wakes up, two weeks, nothing more."

* * *

IT TOOK BART four more days to recover just enough to stand by himself with precarious balance. He took small steps through the house like a baby learning how to walk. The boys' symptoms were also fading, the pain and the feeling of the insides of their bodies being eviscerated diminishing.

Panette's mother, Anaria, still helped with some tasks that her daughter was initially entrusted with. The girl tried to gather enough courage to face Bart several times to let him know about the awkward visit that the council had made. "Master, please try this soup, you need to eat something," said Anaria, carrying the bowl and, at the same time enforcing the idea that it was her doing the cooking and not her daughter who couldn't be trusted with such a mundane task anymore.

"Thank you for all your help," the scholar addressed the older woman. His voice was weak, his vocal cords not yet strong enough to produce powerful sounds. "Panette, don't hide. Come in," he called the girl who was listening from the hallway.

She came in, looking down, with her hands behind her back, expecting a scolding for her ineptitude.

"I want to thank you, too. For taking care of the boys and me." He sipped twice from the soup, proving that he still had confidence in their cooking. "It wasn't your fault. We didn't get sick because of your dish. You eat with us and nothing happened to you," Bart explained.

"Master, maybe it had something to do with me being a woman," Panette explained, still willing to carry the blame.

"Not at all."

Bart could see the worry and distress on her face, enforcing his instincts that it was something or someone else that had made them sick. "Did you eat any of the nuts and seeds that Nayan bought?"

"No, master. They're too dry for my taste. I don't like any of them," Panette confessed as she got the courage to sit down ready to mention the other burning issue on her mind.

"Take some of those seeds, mix them with regular food, and feed it to a stray dog or cat. I bet they'll get sick as well," Bart instructed.

The girl nodded, not completely convinced that she had the heart to sicken an animal. She would find another way to prove the master's theory. "Master, there is something else I have to tell you. The Council was here. All four of them. They said that you invited them," she spoke very fast, avoiding any eye contact.

Bart knew that he was missing an important item, but couldn't remember what. His immediate thoughts were totally erased by his painful suffering and worry for his protégés. "Did they see us in this state?"

"I couldn't stop them. They busted in looking for you."

"What did they say?" asked the scholar, panic rising in his chest.

"Two weeks, nothing more. This is what the lady councilor said before she left. I hope you know what she meant." Panette had delivered the message. She was relieved and suddenly all the pressure was gone. She realized that she needed Bart's absolution of the imaginary guilt. She stood up, reinvigorated, ready to tend to the boys.

The man tried one more time to understand if there was still enough time to salvage the situation. "When did they come?"

"Four days ago."

"So much effort for nothing," Bart muttered, realizing that Rakash would not be able to recuperate in time to show the Council that he had in fact achieved the results promised.

He would have to focus on getting the boys stronger each day, to be ready for the trip to Korobat. Maybe tomorrow his strength would permit him to face the Council.

* * *

"MASTER, THIS ISN'T FAIR; we were very sick," said Nayan's when Bart broke the news that they had to pack and go to Korobat for a year or at least until their team of experts could find a way to induce the *state of bliss*, while avoiding the lengthy and intense meditation sessions. Blackwood didn't want to argue with his disciple, especially when he was right.

He met with the Council while the boys were still recovering, thinking that he could find some compromise given the circumstances and extend the deadline, but he couldn't shake their belief that it was faked. Bart had exhausted any good faith gathered with the Council over the years, and helping Korobat to achieve what he was not able to would be the only smart and advisable thing to do.

"They won't listen to me anymore," Bart tried to find another way of explaining matters, so Nayan would leave him alone. "Even if they were to see Rakash's birthmarks come alive, it would only give them the certainty that Korobat can find a way to commercialize it. This is what the Council wanted from the beginning."

Rakash was sitting on the floor in the lotus position, turning the pages of the book that contained the drawings of the *Trees of Life*. Still feeling weak, he listened to the verbal exchange between the two, tacitly acknowledging Nayan's waste of energy in his argument. *'Why doesn't he face the final decision? At least he isn't forced to come. Master got approval for him to join if he wants to. But I have no choice,'* Rakash thought, not losing sight of the *Trees*. *'I'm moving further and further away from everyone I love.'* He froze for a second, nothing too obvious for the other two to notice. *'Forgive me, One Who Created All. I'm much closer to you now, closer than ever. I have You, and I almost have everything I need spiritually. I'll let You guide me in this new world void of any beliefs and love, even real love for themselves. Can You help them, too?'*

The boy silently repeated the same question Nayan posed before they got sick. Rakash had no certainty that *One Who Created All* would listen to these humans who did not obey any of the rules taught in the village or were not willing to undergo the purification techniques that required inner peace, patience and mental fortitude.

He had studied them when he went with Nayan to the beach or to buy groceries. A frenetic rhythm overpowered them all the time, directing them to small, insipid activities; an almost intentional unwillingness to find the blessed, quiet space where *One Who Created All* could meet them and open their eyes and heart to *His* power.

"Let's confront the shop owner," Nayan persisted, still not giving up the fight on finding another solution to their problem.

"There is nothing we can prove, my son," Bart replied paternally. "He would say that it was a bad batch, apologize and offer us a free supply for the rest of the year, but he would never admit to any wrong doing." The scholar looked at the bookshelves, giving the impression that he was trying to decide which books to take on the trip, then continued, "Whining won't change their minds. We have to conform to the Council's decision. It's up to you if you want to join us in Korobat. You can stay behind to take care of the house and sort through the notes until we get settled over there."

Nayan finally understood that they were powerless against such political decisions. He dropped himself on the couch, defeated. "I don't think that I want to come with you now," the apprentice declared in a wretched tone. His own world was falling apart; Bart was the only one he had. Master had never explained truthfully why he had chosen him from all the parentless children crowding the orphanage, but he had his theory: Bart wanted someone as physically odd as he was. Someone who needed a special environment to fit in and be accepted. Bart had no idea at that time if Nayan would be smart or well behaved, he just counted on his experience and strong belief that a child could be molded into whatever the molder wanted. And master succeeded, turning him into a fine young thinker who, someday, could become the city's greatest scientific authority.

"You know, you can change your mind any time before the end of next week. I won't force you to come against your will. Both Rakash and I will need you in Korobat, no matter the outcome," Bart tried to soften his protégé's rushed decision.

Rakash came out of his thoughtful silence. "I will cooperate with the people in Korobat, so everyone can achieve the *state of bliss.* If *One Who Created All* wants me to do it, I'll do it." A powerful image of himself dedicating his life for the betterment of others filled his mind and heart, solidifying his belief that everything around him happened for a reason.

It was a statement that Bart wanted to hear, confirming the willingness in the villager's heart not to spurn a gift, potentially offered to everyone by *One Who Created All.*

Their faith was sealed for the next little while.

CHAPTER 7

The honeycomb of your mind should be filled with love for Thee all the time.

From the book *We Are One* – Chapter 7

HANDO MARTINEZ WAS VISITING A construction site in the north-west district of Korobat–the last undeveloped plot of land within the existing city boundaries–when he received news from Laeta. It was good news and would postpone the need for investigations for Plan B. His strategy had worked. He decided to call an emergency council meeting to inform everyone about the new developments and get confirmation on next steps.

He hurried back to the office, changed into a pair of maroon pants and a bluish short sleeve shirt with white floral patterns. He combed his hair again, gathering it into a ponytail, and mentally reviewed his speech for the meeting.

All four members responded promptly to Hando's request.

"The plan I put into motion several weeks ago achieved successful results," Martinez started the meeting without any other introduction. "The boy and his master couldn't deliver significant results, so our bid to get them transferred here to Korobat was unanimously approved by their board."

"Congratulations," said everyone.

"I'm expecting them to arrive in about one to two weeks. We need to get ready immediately."

"What do you suggest?" Mirena Vande asked.

"We'll house them on one of the large apartments in the building across from Orlando's company, to cut on travel time. Huidan, please have your team committed to this project. I don't want to interfere with technical decisions, but in terms of who is managing this newly formed group, you and Orlando have equal say. You work well together, so I don't expect anything less this time."

Martinez had put a lot of thought on how to approach this initiative without upsetting anyone. A neutral lab owned by neither Artilla nor Huidan would have been the obvious choice, but he wanted to show them that he trusted their business experience, mutual interest, and above all, their intention of doing good work for Korobat and its people.

"We both looked at the material you gave us, and to be honest, I personally didn't understand much. I don't have a clue what could generate this *state of bliss*," Banaar declared. His grayish moustache, recently groomed, looked sharp, its ends painted light green.

"The strategy is to give them several days to adjust to the environment," Martinez explained. "Blackwood is familiar with the city, but a lot has changed since his last visit. All will be new for Rakash–the name of the villager child. I'll ask the scholar to share any notes with us that he has put together since he started working with the boy. It might take us two to three days to go over these and be able to have a knowledgeable conversation. Understanding how far they went down this path is important." He started to play with his ponytail, wondering if he missed anything. "Rakash was kept pretty much in a bubble, no contact with more than a handful of people. They let him outside now and then, but his interaction with anyone else in Laeta was limited. We'll try to do the opposite, even if Blackwood protests. Slowly, I want to separate them, give the child a taste of his own independence."

"You just said Blackwood might be against it," Elenadore Tam reminded him.

"He is also a scientist characterized by an inquisitive mind and lots of curiosity. When the time comes, I want you to show him the main labs at Orlando and Huidan's headquarters. Let him ask questions, mingle with the staff; visit the Scholars Academy so he can witness the upgrades and realize what he missed out on by turning down our offer. Get to know him closely," Hando said seriously. "You are both adults, single, maybe you can change his mind so he won't go back to Laeta."

"You want me to seduce him?" The woman leaned forward in her seat and the shoulders of her leather jacket went up, enhancing her seriousness in getting the answer she was looking for. Her eyes didn't flinch, but followed Hando's movement around the room.

"Not at all," Martinez replied jokingly. "Be yourself and see if you enjoy each other's company. I want to take his mind away from his failure and from Rakash."

Tam didn't like the idea. Everyone in the Council knew about her lacking an amorous life. They took every opportunity to encourage her applying the same boldness used in her daily activities to finding the right mate. She was slimmer these days, always wearing pants and a leather jacket over an elegant blouse or an ordinary T-shirt. She never commented on why the jacket was so special, but somehow, it gave her added confidence when acting on the city's behalf.

"Ok," she agreed, smiling unconvincingly, but if he gets the wrong impression and jumps on me, I'll break his healthy leg."

They all laughed, knowing she would do it.

"What plans do you have for Rakash?" Huidan asked, recognizing that what he heard was only half of the plot.

"Yes, of course. The boy is the most important piece. His enticement has to be so potent that not even his bond with Blackwood could make him leave."

"Wow, you really want to keep him in Korobat," Mirena Vande remarked.

Hando looked at her, hinting that she would be the subject of the next announcement.

"Mirena, I want you to take care of him."

The request was as unexpected for her as the request for Elenadore was minutes before.

"You know how busy I am with all the programs and new activities ...."

Hando raised his hand and closed his eyes briefly, hinting that she should stop before the list of excuses could grow any longer.

"We all appreciate the effort you put in, especially while having a family, but that's why you're the right person. You have a young son, you spend a lot of time with kids in schools and know how to handle them. He needs a motherly figure to become attached to. That's the only way we can break him from Bart." He paused, waiting for a reaction. He picked up a small red apple from the bowl on the table, brought by Elenadore from the first crop of one of the miniature gardens dotting the city. He bit into it. There was no taste of known chemicals, just a bit sour. He was done in three bites.

Mirena said nothing. For a moment, her dark blue eyes seemed a nuance darker from concentration on what her answer should be, and she bought a little more time by playing with the lobe of her left ear. No one interrupted the stillness.

She finally broke the silence. "You want me to trick him, and fake a potential deep bond that could emotionally affect him long term," she said in a low voice.

"I'm giving you the motive, so you can understand what's at stake. He's a kid. You'll get attached to him and he will reply in kind," Martinez justified himself. "I've never asked any of you before to do something so radical. In case our research time runs out, I want to be sure that at least Rakash stays behind of his own will as stipulated in the contract. If we don't succeed, having Rakash here will give us more time to succeed."

Artilla and Huidan nodded with admiration. This convoluted plan was more complex than most of the business decisions they made on a daily basis.

"Isn't it in Laeta's best interest to leave Rakash with us until we develop a workable technology?" Mirena asked, still looking for a motive to back out of the forced maternal position the leader had put her in.

Hando knew that they were all intrigued by this strategy and none of them would go against it. Unanimity was key to their successful track record.

"The only reason I've accepted the one year deal and not fought for more is because I have confidence in our ability to develop the required technology. Blackwood is old school; he couldn't advance much without an improved scientific approach and equipment to monitor the kid. I'm not sure if Laeta's president accepted our offer because he really believes we can deliver or just to scare and motivate Bart to produce results much faster after his homecoming," Hando confessed. "My goal to bring Rakash over has been achieved. Now, in parallel with the research, we need to facilitate the conditions of a voluntary stay. Laeta can't force him to return."

He stood up and walked around the room, unsure if he should keep pressing the big picture into their heads or just give them until tomorrow to let their thoughts sink in.

"Each of us has a role to play," he went on. "We trust each other, and there are delicate tasks that can't be handled by outsiders. When this is over, we'll own part of a device that will be desired by hundreds of thousands, in cities all around us. Don't forget that, with my plan, Laeta can use it exclusively for only five years, after which we can sell it or trade it directly with the rest of the world."

No more comments or questions followed as they finally understood the long-term strategy Hando had designed for their future prosperity. The long silence confirmed their agreement to the plan, so Martinez decided to adjourn the meeting. A knock on the door made all of them turn, hoping it was not an official matter that would keep them longer.

Soheila ushered in Commander Tonio Clapel, Chief of the Maintain Order Unit (MOU), charged with maintaining peace in the city and whose structure was mainly composed of volunteers. He only met the entire board twice a year for his report on the status of the safety and security of the city. Clapel would usually ask for an appointment with Hando, and never came unannounced unless there was an emergency.

The commander was tall and slim, his body showing the countless hours of training he went through. His face had a squared jaw and an untamed lock of hair scythed across one eye.

"Hello, everyone. Sorry to bust in, but I couldn't wait until the end of the month. The Tanas brothers gang is very active again on the western fringes. They attacked what they thought was a drug shipment to Laeta. It was a White Tiger transport and several White Tigers were injured and killed on site; four of them, were taken by the Tanas for their sweat shops."

The board knew Tonio wasn't afraid of facing the local Tanas gang, but he was looking for approval to either retaliate or find some middle ground.

"Since when are they after such shipments?" Martinez asked. "I thought that the route between most of the cities in the east and Laeta was under the protection of the White Tiger gang and the smaller players like the Tanas were all aware of it. Their boldness is troubling."

Martinez's street skills had helped him a lot while campaigning for the main position in the city. He was not in Tanas' pocket financially since no money had ever exchanged hands, but he had struck a deal with their elders to let him rebuild Korobat. A broken city with poor people wouldn't be able to buy drugs, no matter how affordable.

Always a realist, Hando understood the challenges of creating a gang-free city, an impossibility given the times they were living in. Instead, he aimed for a balanced relationship. Conscious of its frailty, the leader compromised, thinking of the overall benefits for the citizens.

The Tanas's lair on the western edges of the city had no distinct differences from the rest of the new districts except that it was completely run by them, like a family business. For infrastructure and medical emergencies, access was allowed anytime, but the Tanas' lieutenants, if any, dealt with major disturbances, internally. No physical barriers such as fences or brick walls delineated the boundaries; but everyone knew where Tanas's territory started and ended. Gang members could move freely between other districts, so long as they followed the strict rules of being in small numbers, carrying no weapons, and not attempting to sell drugs. The buyers would usually come to them.

"My informant told me that the Tanas are planning to infiltrate Laeta, where all the action is. Their tourist numbers almost doubled last year, triggering an increase in the consumption of quality powder. What the Tanas produce is raw; it causes unexpected reactions, most of the time opposite to pleasure, getting their local consumers in real trouble," Tonio explained, knowing that not all board members were aware of this hidden warfare. "I've also heard that they are inquiring about talented chemistry graduates that can help refine their drugs or even develop new ones. The hospital reported cases where even small doses of the drugs that the Tanas sell resulted in a coma and then death. Soon, no one will buy from them even if they give it away."

"But why do they want to inflame the White Tiger? They can start a pretty nasty fight. We aren't ready for that," Hando said.

"The transport lacked a proper security detail because no such attack has occurred for such a long time," Tonio said. "The next ones will be a different story. The Tanas know that the only way to Laeta is through Korobat since the marshes are impractical. It is their way of sending a message to the White Tiger about the tax they have to pay in exchange for safe passage. The White Tiger was never interested in our small market, hence, the Tanas' new leaders decided to capitalize on that fact."

"What should we expect?" Banaar intervened, worried that not only businesses might be impacted, but personal safety too.

"I doubt that the White Tiger would agree to pay any type of tax to the Tanas," said Clapel. "They will come to Korobat, extinguish them and lay their label on whoever wants to join them, so there is no more local gang. No one will stop their delivery to Laeta. It's an important part of their revenue." He eyed the apples on the table. Martinez nodded, encouraging him to take one, then asked Clapel, "Do you think we can convince Tanas to apologize and stand down before the killing starts?"

Clapel, mouth still full of apple, responded, "Not bad, a bit too sour for my taste.... The Tanas have grown in numbers recently and think they are invincible. They even went after several businesses in the western district for a protection tax, breaking our agreement."

Hando didn't like the gang going out of control. The brothers were getting greedy and restless, looking for trouble. Wiser and less ruthless, the elders had built a gang mentality that never hurt the community they were apart of; a mentality that their offspring were ready to trash. Staying friendly with the White Tiger also brought the elders some perks from time to time in the form of fair sized quantities of refined drugs that sold in Laeta and in most cities in the far East. Nevertheless, he still thought that he should exercise some influence on them as he preferred them to the White Tiger with whom he had never interacted.

"The two main gangs in Laeta have strict rules, they don't mix their territories," said Clapel. "They would even unite against an outsider who wanted in. This is the only reason not even the White Tiger was able to become the direct seller in that market. They kept Laeta as a steady client, which was more important than fighting a long bloody battle for twenty percent more profit. The White Tiger makes tons of money from selling in volume anyway."

"So which one of you is going to bring the Tanas to their senses?" Elenadore Tam said, pushing for immediate action before scores of White Tiger fighters filled the city ready to spill blood. Her eye twitch was bothering her and she kept massaging her cheek to unwind the tension.

Tonio trashed the apple core then sat down, since the discussion was taking longer than he had anticipated. "The MOU doesn't have enough manpower to face the Tanas; it would leave the other districts completely unprotected. They used to be very practical and smart, so I don't know why they generated this challenge."

There was a level of worry in his voice. Half of his squads had volunteered to keep the city safe and orderly from small incidents like thefts, brawls and domestic quarrels; but they hadn't signed up to give up their lives to face unscrupulous criminals.

"Can the informant gather more info before we firm up a strategy?" Hando asked.

"Hard to say. It might not be fast enough. I expect retaliation from White Tiger very soon."

"What exactly were they delivering to Laeta?" Martinez pressed the commander.

"Mainly sex toys for high-end brothels and hotels, and a small quantity of drugs. The loss is more moral than financial."

The city had to be protected at any cost against a potential gang war. Years of hard work could vanish as quickly as a line of drugs up an addict's nostril. The Tanas had started to consume their trashy drugs themselves, making them unstable and untrustworthy. Martinez had a bad feeling about the whole situation; he had little confidence that a new arrangement with the gang could be struck to avoid any escalation to the situation. And even if the Tanas could understand the mistake they'd made by poking at the beehive that was the White Tiger, he felt uneasy that the latter would pay any attention to his guarantees that the Tanas would remain peaceful.

Hando and Tonio working together was the only option, while the other board members would have to focus on the matter involving the guests from Laeta.

"Do you have electro-shockers for all your men?" Hando asked. The device constituted the only advantage they had in one-to-one street fights against the swords, knives and maces garnished with metal spikes, which were the preferred weapons for most gangs. Martinez had to twist some arms when the owners of Spark Industries, the manufacturers of the electro-shockers, approached him with their invention several years back. They offered it to the city's law enforcement for a promotional price just to get their foot in the door and brag about an important client. He understood immediately that if the device got into the hands of gang members, they would become abrasive and wouldn't fear any law. Keeping it off the streets was paramount and he had to think strategically to keep everyone happy.

At that time, his relationship with Banaar and Artilla was in an incipient phase, and only his registration for the mayor position convinced them that he was serious about the betterment of the city. So, they both endorsed him during the campaign, providing funds that tipped the balance in his favour. And Hando had kept all his promises. He enticed Spark Industries to accept an investor and convinced the businessmen to buy a considerable chunk of the company at a bargain price. The most important clause of the sale was still valid to that day: the electro-shocker wouldn't be sold to any private individual or company, except to law enforcement departments run by cities or towns. That way they had a captive market with little risk that the thugs could level the playing field of defense.

"We expect a shipment of twenty units within the next few days. We should be okay controlling the situation at a smaller scale."

* * *

THE TRIP TO KOROBAT WAS UNEVENTFUL. Barren land interrupted by patches of tall, thick trees, remnants of what was once an impenetrable forest, became for Bart an amalgamation of images, a continuous blur of colors through the windows of the car that took them to their forced home. His body hurt from the thought of leaving Nayan behind, even if he had received the president's guarantee that he would be taken care of financially to maintain the house. Arrangements were made for Panette and her mother to visit weekly, to check on the food supply and spend time with the boy. Bart didn't want the house to turn into a burden for Nayan. His preoccupation should be to finish high-school while reading and understanding the pile of books left for him with specific instructions on what details he had to identify and log as part of their research on the villagers.

Bart hoped this way to keep Nayan's mind active; perhaps Nayan could find details that would help increase Rakash's capabilities upon their return from Korobat. The scholar's confidence was unshakable that not even the experienced technical people that produced so may technologies they used on a daily basis, would be able to translate the *state of bliss* into an automated body-mind reaction.

"You can't stop meditating," Bart advised his disciple before leaving. "Meditate for longer periods, focusing on the name of *One Who Created All.* Write me about any images you see during sessions, or changes in the way you perceive the world around you. Without Rakash and me here, you might think that there is no motivation to remain on the same stringent schedule. In fact, your will to reach the *One Who Created All* should be even greater. Let's prove to all the nay-sayers that they were wrong, that the *state of bliss* is real, and that the *One Who Created All* listens to other humans' prayers, not just to the villagers."

That was all he could say to Nayan whose gaze didn't leave the ground for the entire duration of this talk. Bart hugged him lovingly, but got no reaction in return.

The car transporting them to Korobat was a new generation, larger, with better cushions for the seats and an improved design of rounded shapes, as explained by the gregarious driver, Karitan, a fifty-plus year old dark skinned man with long dread locks dyed red, yellow and black. Karitan's squared off beard elongated his enormous head even more, giving Bart a jolt every time the driver turned towards them to share a joke or facts about how wonderful life in Korobat had become.

Blackwood could only nod his head at the small talk; words had dried out, leaving his mind void of anything that could have had meaning. Beside him, Rakash was equally silent, understanding only bits of Karitan's heavy speech, imbued with slang. The novelty of the landscape kept him glued to the window. His eyes would follow a flock of birds taking off to the sky or scared animals retreating from the barren openness. Then they would focus again on the straight smooth path stretching out in front of them.

The sadness of leaving Nayan by himself covered Rakash in a thick layer of anxiety, blurring the barely opened energy channel to the *Supreme Creator*. Just recently while meditating, an old forgotten teaching passed onto him by Otan, surfaced noisily into his mind.

'*Think at the One Who Created All even when doing the daily chores. Even when sleeping, your subconscious should pray to Him, praise Him, so your subtle energy and spiritual connection with our Father is permanent. Practice it daily, aware of the love you are offering and receiving in return, and in time, this communication will deepen so much that your consciousness will be in everlasting awe.*'

This was a divine passage whose guidance Rakash now relied on, away from the home he knew and lacking any other spiritual guidance. Nayan would surely visit them soon, after realizing that he was missing out on a unique experience in a city which Master had mentioned so many times in their discussions about his forming years. Rakash hoped that through meditation, his friend's mind clouded by the notion that Master had not invested enough effort on keeping them in Laeta, would generate an abundant positive vibration, making him understand that stubbornness and selfishness would only prevent smooth sailing on the ocean of consciousness towards the all-encompassing *Spirit*.

'*Renouncing oneself onto Him, into His open infinity, was so natural in the village,*' Rakash thought staring at the road. '*Our way of living is so ... natural, so involved with every creation and creature One Who Created All blew life into. Will these humans ever be able to understand what is being asked of them to experience the most powerful and celestial link known to any being?'*

"We are gettin' closer, man," Karitan informed them.

Several buses carrying visitors to Laeta passed them, travelling in the opposite direction, and the road suddenly became more crowded.

"Thez's a bit of panic in the city thiz' days. The local gang exceeded its power limitations by attacking the wrooong people and now everyone is talkin' about potential repercussions," the driver explained theatrically, this time keeping his eyes on the road.

Bart wanted to pull himself out of slumber, so starting a conversation on a newsworthy topic seemed to be the right opportunity. "Are the Tanas going through one of their egotistical phases again?"

Karitan didn't look surprised that a Laetian had such knowledge, even if the gang had kept a low profile until recently.

"Yes, indeed," the driver confirmed, adding no other details.

Blackwood realized that he had to pay more attention to the information willingly offered by Karitan. He decided on using the slang too, keeping Rakash completely out of the conversation.

"Have the offsprin' took over the buzness?" he insisted.

No vocal confirmation, just a nod of his big, colourful head. A refusal from the jovial driver on providing specifics. Unexpectedly, Bart felt as if he were in front of a paralyzed man who could only communicate by blinking his eyes or nodding his head.

"Do the young Tanas want more power?" he asked.

The nod followed.

"Are the Tanas still the only gang in town?"

Nod.

"Are they trying to bring more people under their brand?"

Pause, then nod.

"Have they upset an outside gang?"

Nod.

The scholar hadn't heard of any trouble in Laeta recently, so he assumed that the conflict involved other parties.

"Are we talking about the crazy-proud, quality-obsessed gangs in the east?"

Nod.

"In my inexperienced opinion, the Tanas are close to becoming an extinct species. With their elders gone, there is no one who could apologize and negotiate a truce on their behalf."

Rakash noticed the strange dialogue his master was having with the driver, and turned his focus to it, hoping to catch its meaning.

"Did anyone figure out yet why the Tanas planned such a move?"

No nod.

The scholar had backed himself into a corner, but he was not ready to give up.

"Now MOU has two options: either join the Tanas against the outside gang or admonish them, offering an example for the city to be left alone."

It was more of a statement than a question, but the nod followed.

"Not a good time to visit Korobat," Bart concluded, addressing Rakash, who was still trying to understand why Master was pursuing this monologue.

The landscape changed to small, colourful houses, three-storey buildings and side streets, forming the city's suburbs. Leaving his questions unanswered, Blackwood switched his attention to his surroundings, which he hadn't seen in a long time. He rolled down the window and pushed his head out, taking in the pulse of the city. The bustling sidewalks in front of restaurants and cafes, indicated that not everyone knew or worried about this gang war. He smelled the mix of spicy foods that were so popular in the east, the fresh dough of bread and the sweet aroma emanating from the cluster of bakeries at the end of one of the streets they passed. His taste buds tickled with desire, and he turned to Rakash who was observing the other side, and said: "After we settle in, I'll initiate you in some fine gastronomy. Some of the brands we have in Laeta are just lousy copycats."

The boy forced a smile, but didn't say anything.

The official car they were travelling in got swallowed by a wave of oncoming bicycle riders leaving work during rush hour. It was the cheapest and the most reliable mode of transportation, affordable by most of the people.

Karitan slowed down to avoid any hurried rider that switched lanes without paying attention. Obvious city improvements made Bart think, that in spite of the circumstances, their stay might be quite enjoyable. He could breathe the air fully and even distinguish the farthest ends of the now smog-free streets. Clusters of tall buildings appeared in the distance, their exterior glass sparkling in the reflected sunlight.

"Those might be part of the business districts I've heard so much about," Blackwood said.

The city had become a well-organized hive where the inhabitants seemed instinctively guided on their activities by an invisible energy. This was still chaos through Bart's eyes.

The car took several turns towards the center of the city, aiming for the municipality building where Karitan was instructed to drop off his passengers.

In front of the entrance Hando Martinez was pacing slowly, like he was trying to avoid any insect that crossed his path. He noticed the car approaching, descended the stairs, and opened the car door for Bart as soon as Karitan came to a full stop.

"Welcome back to Korobat," Hando said jovially, extending his hand toward the scholar, who shook it and moved aside, letting Rakash get out as well. This was Bart's third encounter with the leader; the first time took place years ago in Laeta when the Board officially introduced Martinez as one who would deliver amazing technologies to their city in return for fresh food. Blackwood, as the assigned scholar, had a say in evaluating the technologies brought forward, before the Committee started any contractual negotiations.

This time Hando would be Bart's main contact while in Korobat.

"Where is your apprentice, Nayan?" Hando asked. "We were expecting him as well."

"We decided that he would stay behind to finish high school. He'll visit or we will, based on how busy we will be here." The scholar was not in the mood to dwell on the depressing thoughts he carried all the way to Korobat.

Martinez sensed the scholar's pushback in offering more details on the subject. He didn't expect a joyous attitude from Bart considering that he was visiting Korobat against his will.

Nevertheless, the leader kept his aplomb having trained himself to show no sign of discomfort in the scholar's presence, and had instructed the entire Board to do the same; he even trickled the message down to the technical team that would work with Bart.

"Your luggage will be taken to your apartment which is not far from here, then Karitan will come back and wait for you," Hando explained while waving to the driver that he could leave.

After that he focused on Rakash, dressed as any other behaved child in Laeta: dark pants, tight on his legs, a white plain shirt and a blue vest buttoned all the way up. His hair had grown long, so that it touched his shoulders, and only the orange triangles on his cheeks and his penetrating orange eyes made him look different. The child's appearance would not have made any impact on anyone else, except to those who understood his potential which could be turned into another golden business opportunity for Korobat.

Hando's intuition had paid off handsomely since he had become Korobat's leader. The plan he had put in motion weeks ago had unraveled without a hitch. The only bother, the irrational behaviour of the Tanas, should not distract him for too long if taken care of promptly before its ramifications spread like a plague.

"Hello, Rakash. My name is Hando Martinez, the person in charge of Korobat. Thank you for deciding to visit us with your master."

Martinez spoke slowly as he would to a much younger child as he wasn't sure of the extent of the boy's vocabulary.

"Hello to you, too. It is my understanding that we are not here for a simple 'visit', as the meaning of that word is a temporary departure followed by a return home," Rakash replied with an even tone, looking Hando in the eyes. "But if we can help create a more direct way for everybody to experience the levels of consciousness I've recently enjoyed, my master and I will happily cooperate."

Martinez swallowed what he had prepared to say as they no longer fit for this mature youth. Bart had no intention of intervening since he was equally upset with the situation. Turning Rakash into a diplomatic orator never crossed the scholar's mind. He preferred Rakash to speak his mind.

"I hope you had a smooth trip. Karitan is a good driver, but sometimes he pays more attention to what comes out of his mouth than to the road." Hando didn't expect a reply to his pleasantry, so he continued detailing the schedule for the day, while pushing both towards the building's entrance. "Now you will meet Korobat's decision makers, a kind of welcoming committee. They are the ones who supported this initiative from the beginning. They've never met anyone like you and, to be honest, they are more than willing to volunteer to test any device we develop," Hando said conspiratorially. "After that, Karitan will take you to your apartment so you can rest," the leader concluded.

He then led them to the side of the building where a glass box was sliding down, hanging from thick cables that originated on the roof and attached to pulleys on the ground. It came to a stop when they got closer. Waiting outside the glass box stood three middle-aged women who knew each other based on their animated chatter.

A short, heavy man, wearing a green T-shirt and a green hat, both embossed with the city's name and logo, hurried to slide open the metal grille that replaced a regular door. A woman and her daughter stepped out, and the city employee waved his hand for the new group to get in.

"Only six at a time, please," he said, stopping the count behind Hando, who nodded his head to him.

"Push the button for the floor you want to visit and slide the grille on the other side of the cabin," he instructed those who happened to visit the building for the first time.

"This is our *box in the sky* invention," Martinez whispered to Bart as the space was tight and the women's conversation only grew in intensity as they entered the cabin. "Still a bit rudimentary, but it gives us the option of building vertically and saving essential land."

Bart was impressed. He thought of the time he last visited when the highest point in Laeta was no more than four stories. The box stopped at the fifth floor for the women to take their noise into one of the law offices listed on the wall.

"This is a technology we still have to develop further," Hando continued as soon as they started moving upwards again.

"Works for me at the stage it's in; otherwise, you would have had to carry me up the stairs," Bart joked, startling his host for a second with this little known side of his personality.

He looked up at the purplish sky that was herding clouds on invisible windy corridors. From their vantage point, the scholar had an unobstructed view of the straight streets and their hypnotic traffic. He noticed green spots of vegetation speckling multiple roofs on some of the lower buildings.

"What are they growing on those roofs?" he asked, pointing down below.

"Miniature gardens. A new experiment that we are encouraging people to try. It instills in them the motivation of care, affection, and satisfaction for a plant that, like a human, goes through its own life cycle. It's part of another social program one of our board members came up with."

Martinez had no intention of revealing the long-term sustainability plan. He provided enough information to display candidness and diminish Bart's interest in the topic. The leader opened the metal grille at the tenth floor and steered them to the boardroom.

The other four board members stood up when the guests walked in, the women, of course, showing more interest in Rakash, but without visibly ignoring Bart.

Hando started with introductions. "Everyone, this is Bart Blackwood and this is Rakash, the reason we are all here today." He bowed to each then continued," Elenadore Tam is in charge of our social programs. She had the idea of the roof top gardens that you saw earlier."

Elenadore vigorously shook Bart's hand, smiled and welcomed him in her own way, keeping in mind the task assigned to her. She was wearing a dark blue skirt for the occasion, a white blouse and her second skin, the leather jacket. She addressed Bart, "When you are free from reading or watching your protégé light up his triangles, let me know and I'll show you around town."

"Thank you," Bart replied instinctively, straightening up his back and forgetting to turn his damaged skull the opposite way. The woman didn't flinch when she looked at him.

Martinez swept an arm to the next member. "This is Mirena Vande. She is the great-great-great-grand daughter of the Scholars Academy's founder, hence education runs in her blood. What other better position for her than overseeing the educational programs and permanent interaction with the children."

"Good to have you both here," she said exuberantly. "I have a similar offer like the one from Elenadore, for Rakash. Our kids would love to meet someone as special as you, if Mr. Blackwood will allow it." Mirena addressed the boy directly, but her hands gesture included Bart as well.

The scholar nodded his head, amazed to notice that not even the second woman had issues looking at him.

"And these two gentlemen are the ones who lead the team that you will be working with. Orlando Artilla and Huidan Banaar are the most successful business people in Korobat and have offered their precious time in an official position. The brightest engineers from both companies came together for this unique opportunity."

Artilla took the initiative. "Our resources are at your disposal, Mr. Blackwood. It's a welcome challenge for us. We did a little bit of work on brain implants, nothing complicated or perfected enough to put on display. We can't wait for more details on what you are trying to achieve."

Bart realized that the man was ugly, and if asked to choose between his appearance or Artilla's, he would have stuck to his rather than the disproportionally fat body on top of which was stacked a double chinned head.

"I'm anxious too. Joining a team of experts in various fields is something I've missed. Our local scholar community has a narrow vision and they were not willing to help, afraid of a potential failure," the scholar quickly improvised an answer that was not far from the truth.

None of his peers had felt the same enthusiasm as Bart, after they fully understood the Committee's intentions with Rakash. Professional suicide, they muttered, and walked away from the additional incentives dangled as bait.

"Also, if you have any other project that you wanted to work on, but lacked a well-equipped facility, please don't hesitate to ask," Banaar added.

With introductions concluded, Martinez encouraged the boy to help himself to any of the refreshments prepared on a side table. Knowing his habits, various seeds had been procured. Blackwood noticed this and while he couldn't trust Korobat's intentions completely, it didn't make any sense to poison Rakash again. The countless assurances from Laetas' officials that their sickness, if it was indeed real, was just a coincidence never washed this doubt away. Bart couldn't convince them that what they went through was not artificially induced.

"You all did a great job with the city," the scholar tried to repay some compliments. "The clean air and streets are impressive."

"Our people deserve it," Hando replied with a humble tone, then continued, "Karitan should be back any minute now to take you to your accommodations, but we just briefly want to suggest our next steps and see if you agree or not."

"Go ahead," Bart said.

"Our knowledge about the *state of bliss* is limited to the three or four books we read, and our research is non-existent. We heavily rely on your notes from your interaction with Rakash. We might need several days to go through them while you visit the town, rest and enjoy yourselves. After we have a better understanding of what was achieved, we will attend one of his meditation sessions. The real monitoring will start a bit later after a medical examination. We won't rush him in any way. You tell us to stop when necessary, and it will happen. We understand the connection you two have, and we appreciate it."

Blackwood thought it was a well-thought out plan. "I'm totally in agreement with what you said. I can provide my research tomorrow morning to whomever comes to pick us up."

"Great. This is a good start, everyone." Hando started towards the door trailed by Rakash, who was holding a bunch of seeds, and his master.

Everyone behaved exceptionally well, following the script that they had agreed upon. Hando could also sense an authentic interest from his colleagues on getting to know the boy better, and a genuine intrigue that a versed scholar like Bart had such strong beliefs in a mythical jungle story. Blackwood had witnessed something illusory, for which, jeopardizing his status was worthwhile.

Martinez's gamble mirrored Bart's blind faith in his own intuition. What would life be without taking a chance every now and then?

* * *

THE NEXT DAY, the scholar woke up with no outside help. There was only silence surrounding him, as the noises of the city coming to life didn't have enough strength to reach their location high up in the building.

Initially, Bart worried about how fast his body would adjust to the new environment and how soon he could expect a good night's sleep. To his astonishment, he had a dreamless sleep, and felt recharged. A positive energy invaded his being, erasing old and recent anguishes, freeing up his mind from shackles of insignificant but persistent mental habits. He had to regain his clarity of thought by removing his nagging thoughts about Nayan, push them to a deeper consciousness level temporarily, just to be sure that his mind was sharp enough for the intricacies of this unexpected venture.

Their apartment was on the tenth floor of an office building, designed to offer accommodations to business people traveling to Korobat. Both bedrooms were spacious, filled with natural light flooding through the floor-to-ceiling windows. The view of the city at dusk, when lights were still on everywhere, gave Bart the impression that he was a bird surveying unknown territory, gasping at the marvelous amber pattern of the lights, traced on the grayish background. The city was alive, and much more vibrant than he remembered. However, his lifestyle and professional preoccupation made him consider all the noise and trivial activities an unnecessary waste of time, unlikely to pay off at an intellectual level.

He thought about his physical shortcomings that had built psychological barriers, from behind which, he rarely came out. His intermittent outings were only to confirm that he hadn't missed any earth-shattering political news that could have affected him directly. Maybe now, breaking his own rules, he would take advantage of Korobat's generous offer to enjoy the new version of the city.

He took a shower, then put on a pair of brown cotton pants and a white shirt lined with beige embroidery on its chest. He set about to arrange his research files on the glass table in the common room, ready to explain to Hando the proper reading order and what areas to focus on. Rakash was still in his room, trying on the clothing he found in the closet, which were a perfect fit for him. There were a couple of pairs of pants made of thin, soft, grayish leather, used for special occasions, and several cotton and silk shirts that he could wear daily. Bart also received a black suit whose tunic matched his figure perfectly. Korobat had prepared for them exceptionally well, trying hard to prove that they took their role as hosts seriously. Gifts that were not ostentatious, but mindful, considering that they had only packed a few items of their wardrobe for the trip.

The scholar prepared an omelette of four eggs for both of them, a mixture of greens, mushrooms and cheese. Rakash's half was still steaming on the plate. Bart ate his slowly, watching the city below follow its cycle of waking up. In the beginning, there were only a few people and bicycles, a trickle of several tributaries that would turn into a small river as time passed. A flux of human energy would start pounding the pavement, channeled by the narrow avenues. When viewed from street level, the entire movement had no beauty, no mathematical equivalent that could be used to create a pattern.

There was a knock on the door and, a moment later, Bart let Martinez in.

"Good morning. Oh, I see that you already had breakfast. I wanted to take you to a place famous for their bacon and eggs... the spices and butter they use are delicious. Some other time then." The leader's mood was upbeat as usual; in his philosophy any worries would cloud his judgment, affecting his actions. This was a lesson learnt many years ago from his father: *'Stay and think in the moment, because the so-called future can only be changed by your present actions.'*

"Would you like me to prepare something for you?" Bart offered.

"No, thanks. I'll grab a quick bite after I drop your research off at the lab. Let's do this!" Martinez couldn't believe that he finally had in his grasp a well-documented interaction with a villager.

"There it is," Blackwood pointed to the two piles of folders and notebooks. "Each separate year details physical, mental and psychological transformations. Challenges he had in learning a new language, new customs, and interacting with us. Recently added are the observations on meditation techniques we used; what worked and what didn't; key words that triggered certain behaviours, and also confirmation of some of the details published so far about their community. Most of what was published is fiction. Rakash helped us identify the phenomena he personally experienced. Don't forget that he is still young, even by the villagers' standards, and was exposed only to a bit of the ancient knowledge they've accumulated over the centuries. And we noticed that memories are resurfacing each year. This work has barely started."

Hando realized the merits of the strong bond the scholar had with Rakash to gather this valuable data. He had no intention of altering his plan of dividing the two, no matter how well things went with the boy.

"Let me bring Karitan in. He's helping me carry this to the lab," Martinez said and opened the door for the driver, who was waiting patiently and holding a cardboard box.

"Good morning," he addressed the scholar, and followed his boss's lead towards the table.

"All these folders have to be delivered to either Artilla or Banaar on the seventh floor across the street. I'll be there shortly myself," the leader instructed.

Karitan understood the importance of the documents he was looking at, so he placed them with great care into the box, picked it up and left quietly.

Rakash came out of his bedroom proudly wearing one of his new shirts, but with the same pants from the previous day.

"Mr. Hando, good morning," the boy said happily.

It looked like the oppressing disposition that had followed them since they left Laeta had lifted inexplicably. All their emotional baggage was magically removed, rooted out completely, and suddenly replaced by a higher level of awareness.

"I don't like formalities. Just call me Martinez or Hando, either one works for me," the leader said, displaying once again the loose relationship he had with everyone, compared to the rigid formalities imposed by Laeta's president. "By the way, you look great in that shirt."

Rakash's smile widened, as he was not aware of subtleties that could inflate an ego.

"You should eat your breakfast. It's getting cold," Bart intervened. He didn't want to stop the dialogue between the two, he was just concerned that the boy would eat a lukewarm omelette.

"One more thing," Bart turned to Hando, who was about to leave. "We need a meditation area in the lab. We brought a couple of items to make it homey, but we need a wooden screen or a type of divider for more intimacy. A room within a room is even better. Quiet surroundings are an important element to the process. He is not advanced enough to withdraw his senses within entirely, and become oblivious to everything else."

"It will be in place before the first session," Hando assured. "When you are ready, Victoria Tam will be waiting for you downstairs for the tour she offered. Don't rush it. There is plenty of time for you to become accustomed with the city again." Martinez turned around as he remembered something else. "Do you want to meet with any of your old university colleagues? We can trace them down."

The scholar didn't have many fond memories of his university life, so he couldn't think of what he would talk about with strangers he hadn't seen in thirty years. "I'll think about it. I doubt many of them are still in town. The two who moved to Laeta are involved with private corporations and we never met."

"Very well," said Hando then left.

Bart sat down, observing the boy swallowing equally cut omelette pieces. He was playing with his food again, while his mind was busy sorting thoughts, impressions and questions pertaining to the new stage of his human journey.

"Master, is our work thorough enough, such that they will grasp the meaning of *state of bliss*?"

Bart didn't answer right away. He picked up a fat seed and used it to trace the lines on the tablecloth. He wanted to offer a straightforward answer. Inducing a fictitious façade to the whole situation would only portray him as weak, incapable of sharing feelings that sooner or later would emerge, affecting their relationship.

"You taught me that the connection each of you has with *One Who Created All* is personal. Your life's goal is to free yourself through the *state of bliss*, if *One Who Created All* deems you worthy of returning back to *His* domain. This basis, the secular foundation of your community believes in this higher purpose that you are all one, but at the same time, necessary individual parts of the whole." The scholar stopped playing with the seed and looked Rakash in the eyes. "I do believe that our research has enough physical evidence so their engineers could rationalize the overall concept; nevertheless, no technology could replace your deeply ingrained love, gratitude and acceptance in *One Who Created All*."

Rakash was done eating, ready to inquire more of his master. "But do they think that they can somehow replicate it, otherwise, why are we here?"

"Yes, but the right word is *fake it*. Understanding and accepting *One Who Created All* takes time. The result of that could grow into faith, then devotion. What Korobat told Laeta's leaders is that they can turn everyone into *forged believers* by pressing a button. And, instantaneously, they will face *One Who Created All*, who would disseminate a dogma easily understood even by neophytes. Upon their return from the world within, they will be changed forever."

"*He* would not accept them," the boy raised his voice at the sacrilege explained by his master.

"That's a possibility. But let's assume that the induced *state of bliss* would change these people positively. Maybe they would discern the corrosive existence they were having and reverse it. Only *One Who Created All*, in *His* kindness and wisdom, might shower blessing upon these newly adopted children."

"Master, are you saying that even a fabricated *state of bliss* could be accepted if it produces positive results?"

Blackwood nodded his head. His stiff principles could be bent if, in the end, Laeta's slogan changed to the '*City of Bliss*', transforming human sludge into something that even the *Supreme Entity* could be proud of.

CHAPTER 8

In the calmness of his mind the wise devotee will cast a net of conscious thoughts into the infinite sea of wisdom of One Who Created All, waiting patiently to catch precious nuggets of knowledge, which will smoothen the path to self-realization.

From the book *We Are One* – Chapter 8

TABER BROUGHT HER FOUR PUPILS TO their favourite spot, a small opening on the jungle floor, not too far from the village, and off the main path. Filtered by the canopy above, the light embraced the children protectively for another day of learning. The humidity pushed the wet fabric of their clothes against their skin, turning them into grayish statues frozen in a meditation pose.

All around them were smashed papayas and bananas, thrown down by restless monkeys, that had turned into a maronish paste mixed with the leaves of mopane trees and palm. The spicy smell it released helped the kids breathe easier, opening their lungs to more air, which allowed them to hold their inhalation longer. Red ants and beetles scurried around carrying heavy loads over twigs and pebbles, on a path pheromoned with amazing precision.

The children, Janka, Makori, Indah and Danish, encircled their elephant teacher in a semicircle, the *Book* resting on their knees. It was a precious gift handed to each of them three cycles after birth, when the awareness of their surroundings was slowly starting to make sense to them. The community had developed around the *Book*'s commands, written down by those who had heard the words of *One Who Created All* for the first time. Faith and dedication pushed generation after generation of villagers to travail on multiplying the *Book* relentlessly, so the knowledge wouldn't perish. The copies left behind in good condition by successfully transitioned souls were painstakingly restored and added to the library, along with the owner's name and his or her achievements.

Taber was on all fours, trunk resting flat on the ground, right in front of her, like a dead snake turned gray and wrinkled, decomposing. Her blank stare went beyond the children she had to focus on, seeing nothing but Nagoti's smiling face before heading out to the walls. A void that Danish was trying hard to fill through kind words, extensive hours of study and questions that kept her attention away from the tragedy. Her mind, bruised from the pain, could barely communicate properly with the children. Only fragments of disparate thoughts propagated over the short distance.

The entire herd was troubled by the loss that would be etched into the common memory to be accessed and passed on as a warning. Taber's uncontrollable internal agony was not only hers to bear. Morinda, her six-cycle old daughter, perceived it the most, absorbing the shock of pain with tremendous intensity, unlike anything else she had experienced before. Its ripples touched and altered her own perception of life, and that of her own pupil, Valdina, of the Builder caste, and part of the Council.

Taber sent a mental signal and waited patiently for the kids to come out of their first daily meditation session that would connect them with the environment. It was a necessary link that needed to be established before starting a new lesson, confirming that they were part of a whole, single breathing organism brought to life by *One Who Created All.*

"It's good to see that your focus has increased and you can go deeper and deeper, searching for yourself and for *One Who Created All* at the same time," she said.

The thick layer of steamy leaves she was sitting on made her hot, so she waved her shredded ears back and forth several times to cool down.

Drops of perspiration rolled down the children's faces since they had no equivalent method to dissipate the heat.

Indah spoke first. "This time I've focused on our physical world's limitations. Do we create these limits ourselves or are they imposed on us by the *Supreme Being* just to observe our reactions?" She had a round face with black eyes that contrasted her white skin, and a reddish scar on her forehead from a fall by the river.

"And?" Taber encouraged her.

"I think that finding and identifying ourselves within the body is the answer to this question. Being aware of who we really are, spiritual entities, would bring the clarity we chase. The alternative is the unbounded, infinite realm of dreams. Its dimension, in the actual bondage to the body, can't be phantom by our minds while awake. It's a fluid environment in which any idea or reflection becomes real, and us, the main characters." Thoughts and words alternated in Indah's conversation. She tried to face her shyness by talking first whenever given the opportunity.

"What if we, ourselves, are dreamt by someone else and we can't tell the difference?" Taber pushed their limits of thinking. "What do you think, Makori?" she asked one of the boys.

Makori stopped pushing away the ants that approached his knees with his energy field and answered, "Anything is possible. I assume you are hinting at us being *One Who Created All*'s dream. This entire world could be his dream."

"Are you saying that *One Who Created All* teases us by giving us a sample of what we are capable of achieving spiritually, and whispers that more marvels expect us when reaching *Him*?" Danish intervened, puzzled by the possibility.

"We could be one of the many dreams *One Who Created All* has. Why would such a high, pure *Spirit* have only one reverie turned into matter?" Makori voiced his reply.

"But we are mentioned in the *Book*: the children and the elephants. That should mean something," Danish insisted. "We are special and under *His* protection."

Taber gently pushed a thought towards Janka, the only boy who hadn't participated yet.

The wind shifted the leaves above lightly and a thin sunray found its way onto Janka's face, forcing him to close his eyes.

"I tend to agree with Makori. Yes, we are special in this world just as Danish said, but only in this world. If *One Who Created All* birthed multiple dreams, *He* did it with a purpose known only to *Him*. We can only guess the motivation behind such action. Our fantasies remain just that, fantasies, as we lack *His* primordial power of organizing matter. Maybe we have been sent out to *His* other dream-worlds so our souls could be exposed to more experiences, but, in the end, this is the dream in which we should attain the *state of bliss*."

Unexpectedly, a papaya smashed on the top of Janka's head, fruit and juice sliding down his abrupt forehead, following the blunt tip of his nose, falling on the ground in front of him. Everyone burst into laughter, releasing the strain of the argument. Even Taber smiled and snorted delightedly. Janka used his long sleeve to clean his face. Some orange remains still coloured the side of his nose.

The She-elephant sent forth another thought to the girl. "Indah, I know you have more to add."

Indah recollected herself from the welcome break. "Numerous dreams equal a similar number of worlds, and my guess is that *One Who Created All* populated them with characters that don't resemble us. Why multiply us over and over again? If we believe that, it means that *He* has only one recurrent dream. Is *One Who Created All*'s imagination so limited? I dare say, no."

No other comments followed and Taber continued, "Remember that you are all born with dormant qualities, which you have accumulated through the cycles of incarnation. Our duty as teachers is to blow life into smoldering coals of this knowledge and ignite it, until its flames engulf you completely. When the energy rises in you like a hot, unstoppable river, you'll know that your inner spiritual potential was dug out from the shackles of ignorance. And when that energy reaches the wisdom eye, you are one step away from entirely merging with our *Maker*. *He* blessed each of you with the volition to move through the challenges of each incarnation, but wherever *He* is, *He* wants you to succeed."

They all sat quietly in serene calm, mentally filtering the essence of the words Taber had just spoken; their minds almost re-creating the feeling and intensity of the energy wave that would jolt their bodies in the eventually of a successful awakening.

"It's free will that powers every move, thought and action. And only free will and volition can strengthen your desire to reach the *state of bliss*, which could become a permanent way of being while still existing on this physical plane. Reaching this elevated state of consciousness will mark your awakening and the realization that this world is indeed a dream," Taber loaded her thoughts with passion, remnants of pain and a desperate desire to see them bathe in *His* eminent blessing and love.

The children all crawled toward her at once, covering her body with their tiny faces rested gently on her large ears, which were folded backwards, hands bringing comfort to a hurt soul committed to them by *One Who Created All*'s command. A mutual consolation; vibration, love and compassion exchanged as one, singular entity.

A wailing tremor built inside Taber and shook her frame violently. Agony hammered out through her pores, then tears gushed out on her rumpled sheath.

The children were crying too, holding her tight, pretending that they had the strength to stop Taber's shaking and offer her comfort. She made no other sounds, but the reverberation of such torment couldn't be hidden from the herd. Involuntarily, her hooves sent a signal through the ground as a natural way of communication.

Trumpets of different intensity awakened the jungle, an almost instantaneous reaction from the anguish of the family. Fearful birds took flight to the open sky, disturbed colobus monkeys swung to higher branches and groups of capybana scurried to their holes. Taber and the children held each other for a little while, waiting for the signs of weakness to parch away.

"*One Who Created All* guides us to display courage in such moments. I'm sorry that I'm not living *His* teachings. I have faith that wherever Nagoti is, *He* is taking care of her, preparing her for another journey through the *Trees*."

The children let go of Taber and picked up their books sprawled on the ground. The elephant pulled herself up and sent one more instruction, "Read book two on meditation, chapters eight and nine. Practice sustaining a longer introspective period without being distracted by externalities."

The lesson was over. They all paced back to the village in silence. Taber joined the herd of cows leaving in search for food. The *Commoners* found their way to their daily chores, repeating mantras in the back of their minds, knowing that *One Who Created All* smiles fatherly at their sustained effort towards enlightenment.

* * *

DARK SPOTS FORMED ON the open spaces in the village from the grayish clouds bumping into each other, obstructing the sun right above it.

Ruffled leaves pulled by the wind, fluttered with more intensity, now and then overpowering the call of the wild. The signs of rapidly changing weather disturbed agitated insects, mammals and birds. The downpour had no scheduled arrival, either then or several sunrises later, but *One Who Created All*, in *His* kindness, was alerting their natural senses. The rainy season was upon them, a welcomed richness that would revive the landscape, refill the watering holes and would send the animals' mating instincts into a frenzy.

After the morning lessons had finished, the herd moved out for their long afternoon stroll that sometimes would stretch late into the night, despite not wanting to leave the children by themselves too much.

Altan, Bagham and the other bulls turned west, splitting away from the cows led by Brinka, whose slow walk would give everyone, even the youngsters, ample time to look for juicy acacia trees or low hanging bananas. The matriarch's belly throbbed with life, a calf that was supposed to be born at any moment.

Inside the compound, the *Commoners* had split their chores between the kitchen, library and garden. It was physical labour that kept them occupied, although mentally, their thoughts were comprehensively focused on *One Who Created All.* Their unobstructed adherence to specific teachings went beyond time spent with the teachers, a measure of their continuous refinement of the spiritual link to the *Supreme Being.*

Piles of bamboo canes covered most of the ground outside the workshops area, where Nukua, helped by Danish, was stripping the fibers lengthwise down the stem and creating a separate pile close to two pots made out of smoke-blackened stone. Each pot was large enough to hide an elephant calf.

The pots rested on a clay mound, embedded with flat stones on the sides to sustain the weight above. Inside the mound, a fire burned lazily. Water and bamboo fibers stewed together into boiling mulch, three palms below the upper edge of the clay pots.

A low supply of bamboo paper emboldened Nukua to take his turn at making more and put to use what Manash, his teacher, had taught him. Blisters were forming at the ends of his fingers and any new pull brought a small twinge of pain that, by the time the piles would be finished, would become significant.

"With practice, your skin will harden into a bearable numbness," Manash told him in his first lesson on how to produce such paper.

Beside him, Danish kept the discussion alive, not muttering a single complaint about the hard work. He had offered to help as soon as he heard Nukua inquiring. "I was curious if there was a special formula regarding the paper quality," said Danish. "I've noticed that in some books it's not as smooth as it should be."

"Like anything else we learn during our existence, it's a process passed from generation to generation," said Nukua, without stopping his peeling of the fibers. "Carefully balanced steps are required in selecting the right canes and the correct boiling temperature. I'm not saying that the final steps are less important, but you asked me about the quality. Sometimes we also experiment with different types of canes and less mincing for obtaining a thicker volume. We mainly use the resulting paper for drawings or paintings since the colors won't bleed through. Or we just store it for emergencies."

In the *Writer* caste dominated Council, Nukua was one of three; the other two were girls, Akila and Fenila. Nukua's short stories and poems were noticed by the entire community and adored so much that any new work he created had several *Commoners* busy producing handwritten copies.

Words of exhilarating energy and wisdom blessed by *One Who Created All* infused everyone with additional motivation and made them search deeper for new layers of joy and love. Piercing the veils of the omnipresent *maya* was the main challenge of their itinerant life, an obstacle that this bottomless and profound love should melt away in the unbounded consciousness. Nukua's creations were a statement of his spiritual level, moving closer and closer to the final step before his acceptance by the *Supreme Being* into the realm of eternal purity.

The *Writer* noticed that the fire was dying down. He picked up a thick stick, polished by its many immersions in the melting pot, and checked the density of the boiling paste. He moved the stick slowly in large circles, feeling its resistance. Then, he turned to Danish to share more of what he knew were signs of a ready mixture. "Up until five cycles ago I needed a more experienced *Writer* or one of the teachers to check it for me. I almost ruined one batch because I added too much water. The elephants know it by smell, but we have to rely on intuition and physical touch."

Danish came closer and looked inside the pot, careful to avoid the steam and any drops of hot liquid bursting up. "May I?" he asked Nukua shyly.

The *Writer* handed him the stick, a little puzzled by the request since the *Commoners* usually stuck to their daily chores and didn't show much interest in the creation process, only caring and appreciating the end results; a book, a painting, a new hut design. He found Danish different. Nukua let his helper check the status of the second pot.

"It feels the same to me. We can pour out the content of both pots any time now."

Nukua tested it for himself and nodded in agreement.

The next step required their full attention to avoid any sizzling paste from coming into contact with their skin as they scooped out the paste and laid it on a large flat wooden surface, stained by so many previous uses. Its surface had several holes so the excess water could drip through. After the bamboo fibers were spread evenly, the boys started to mince them with mahogany sticks. Drops of the paste flew everywhere, some landing on the boys' clothing staining them. They didn't care, and persistently continued the chore. With the clouds spread thin by high winds, the sun fiercely beat upon their tan necks. They had to hurry if they wanted this batch screened, pressed and dried before sunset.

"Everyone is enthralled with your writings," Danish said without breaking his flow of pounding the bamboo. "How do you do it? There are *Writers* and *Artists* that end their cycle void of energy and inspiration, empty shells that feel sorry for themselves. They barely conceive an outcome worthy to be recorded in village's history. But you're so consistent." He used a tone of awe and admiration in his voice, one he used to break any caste barrier and gain trust.

Around them, noises vanished as most of the children retired for their afternoon meditation. Parrots, cicadas and monkeys were the only ones left to keep the jungle bursting with noise. The two of them were left alone, rhythmically hitting the wooden board with merciless thuds.

"I'm blessed by *One Who Created All* with a constant river of inspiration. I look around me, at the plants, the elephants, the ants, the rain and the sun, and I see *Him*. An urge builds inside me after each contemplation of *His* creation, to craft words that would caress *Him*, and display my devotion and deep love for what I experience. It's written in the *Book* for us to understand that each new sunrise is a miracle. It's a miracle to have such wonderful teachers for guidance; it's a miracle to share my existence with all of you, my brothers and sisters, which indirectly, empower my creativity. We feed on each other's love and compassion. It is in the *Book* that we will perish and wither away if our connection with the common knowledge and *His* energy is broken."

Danish absorbed the reply, moved around the corner of the wooden surface, then posed another question. "Do you think that each and every writing or artwork has already been created before, and the only thing *One Who Created All* has to do is to select one that fits a specific villager at a particular time? Did *He* craft them the moment *He* materialized this world as one of *His* dreams?"

Nukua stopped the beating, cleaned his right hand on the back of his pants, scratched his sweaty dark skinned forehead, and, with great care, as if he was afraid of divulging an important secret, said: "I've heard this theory and I've even discussed it with Manash. Yes, the elephants also believe that the content of the *Supreme Being's* library was written by *Him* shortly after *He* forged this world by freezing *His* thoughts into matter. Our purity of prayer and intensity of craving *His* love attracts the proper creation."

The *Commoner* kept silent for a bit, weighing the risks of mentioning an aspect of their life he had never heard mentioned either among themselves or with the teachers. "Has anyone remembered previous incarnations in which they belong to a different caste?"

Nukua used his sleeve to wipe the perspiration drops from his face, and looked up to see how much longer before the tall eucalyptus bordering the fence would block the sun, then he focused on Danish who waited for an answer. "I personally don't remember mine. Your comments about how popular my books are, enforce my conviction that this is the existence during which my soul will awake and merge with the Spirit of *One Who Created All.* Very soon I'll pass my Council responsibilities to the next in line as my meditation sessions become longer. My consciousness will search deeper into the labyrinth of infinite wisdom looking for *Him.* I'll not get lost in there as the love and devotion I mentioned earlier will trace the convoluted way, keeping me safe from any temptation lurking outside the path of divine light."

This was not the answer Danish expected. So he offered more of his thoughts. "The awakened incarnations are mentioned in several older books I found in the library. More as a theory than a fact. Do you think it's possible?"

"We know it's possible for the *Orange Souls.* They are special emissaries sent by *One Who Created All* with messages for us, who still struggle on the spiritual path. I didn't hear anyone in the village openly talking about such personal recollections. Why do you ask?" Nukua queried, starting to pay more attention to Danish's questions.

Aware that he was entering a slippery slope of their discussion, the *Commoner* tried to diminish the wealth of information he had planned on sharing. He couldn't determine yet if he trusted Nukua enough to keep his confession to himself. A seed planted now in the Council member's mind might help Danish very soon when he was ready to unveil his secret. "From time to time," he began, "images of me working on bamboo frames, weavings and miniature paintings, rapidly pass my dreams. These aren't lasting thoughts. I'm not sure if my subconscious works based on my interaction with the *Artists* or if it's indeed a personal memory fighting to reveal itself from the layers of my memory."

Never before had another brother or sister asked Nukua for advice since the teachers were the main source of comfort and wisdom. He felt obliged to offer something in return, even if it was conventional. "It would be a joyous moment for all of us if you start experiencing real memories. Some internal blockages are coming down, withered from the positive blow of meditation and teachings. Now more than ever, your awareness is the necessary tool to assess what's been released from behind your mental gates. It could be a flood of knowledge that might help you transition sooner, or just unrelated snippets of life events. It is you who should decide its importance, and discuss it with Taber."

This was what Danish wanted to hear; he pushed forward a final question whose answer might express the attitude of the entire Council on this matter. "Should I try replicating these flash dreams? I would like to get some sense of what's involved in the creation process. It will give me more purpose than you think." Emotions filled the *Commoner*'s voice. He desperately needed formal consent to justify and continue his secluded artistic activities. He felt that revealing who he thought he really was, an *Artist*, to the entire community just became much easier, and emboldened by this perception, he didn't care if Nukua shared their discussion.

The *Writer* realized that Danish had touched a sensitive spot by mentioning 'purpose' as one of the main motivations of their lives.

"The creation process is a beautiful, fulfilling state of being. As you said, it gives one a purpose and, at the same time, a justification for why we create. We are serving the community and the *Supreme Being*. The bond with our teachers is something else that brings purpose to us."

A wave of energy moved through Danish, loosening up his stiff muscles and focusing his mind. His body had the weight of a feather and even though his feet were sitting firmly on the ground, his attention, relieved from the strain of the discussion, escaped briefly into a plane of joy and love that was so familiar during his meditation sessions. There was hope in him coming forward. Claiming that he belonged to the *Artists*' caste would be a shattering event, and a positive one, that would mark his name in history.

Silence engulfed them both while they applied the dye and spread the paste on a meshed screen for one final step.

"Great job, thank you," Nukua beamed a thought to his helper, who nodded in return. "I'm confident that very soon, with aid from *One Who Created All*, a clear path will be disclosed on the purpose of your dreams. There is nothing random in our existence."

Danish's effort had paid off. Nukua's support in the council would influence the other caste members in his favour. He had to wait for the safe arrival of the *Orange Soul* before all the pieces of his plan could move forward. His heart was light and his soul floated with creativity.

They walked the short path between the library and the main eating area towards the huts in silence, holding in their minds warm thoughts about each other's life purpose. The *Commoner* smiled and nodded at Nukua, grateful for the meaningful conversation, then they parted ways. Danish strolled closer to his hut, but then, forgetting about the sweat streaming down his back and spoiled clothing, he changed direction towards the garden for another assessment of his artwork. He felt himself an *Artist* in every cell of his body, despite the colour of his hands.

* * *

THE MATRIARCH LED THE HERD of cows on a new path through the bush, leaving behind a trail of fresh dung and broken trees. Huddled in the middle of the group of older cows, the young calves fed on the leaves and fruits brought down by forceful and experienced trunks.

Morinda stopped in front of an acacia tree and challenged herself to rip off its bark with a stick firmly held in her trunk as a tool. Her mother, Taber, showed no interest in the rich bounty Brinka had led them into. Instead, she started digging absent-mindedly for salt, keeping the weight of her body on her toes since the distressed attitude she displayed earlier was still trailing her.

The approaching rainy season would stir her natural instincts and make her a desirable target for the bulls in *musth*. She saw the signs in a couple of them already, and even Altan had started to ooze sticky fluid from the side of his face. Due to his status in the herd, she was expecting him to be the first to chase her, before any younger bulls even dared.

A ramble from Brinka made everyone freeze for a moment, then a quick separation began within the herd as the hierarchy fell into place as she was about to give birth. Two of the older cows, Taber and Nadira, approached her, the remaining ones stayed alert to protect the youngsters.

The matriarch released the contents of her bowels noisily, urine squirting her back legs. She moved back and forth agitatedly, ears flapping quickly to cool herself down. Her stomach produced more rumbling as if sending instructions to the cows who would observe her travail. More liquid came out, this time with a different colour and a sour smell. She squatted to ease the calf's way out. Her breathing intensified and she remained as still as possible. She pushed hard, the pain bringing tears down her crumpled skin.

Its hind legs were out of the womb. Brinka's effort and agitation affected the herd too, the older cows stomping around and purring in low tones. Another push, then another, and the newborn fell on the ground, stuck in a sticky, protective sack. Brinka turned around to look at her baby. It was a healthy little cow, disoriented but already determined to stand up and make her mother proud.

Using her trunk gently, the mother removed the remains of the sack still hanging on baby's back and legs, then she focused on helping her keep her vertical balance.

Through purrs and bellows, Brinka started to pass on the first survival lesson about traveling with the herd. The cows, who waited aside came closer to greet the new addition to their family. One by one, they touched baby's trunk, which was hanging limp, introducing themselves.

"The children will call her Nara," Brinka said.

They couldn't move on before the newborn had a healthy sip of milk.

Brinka pushed Nara towards her chest where her nipples were heavy. She felt Nara's teeth, then the calf's lips lock unto this source of energy. While watching her daughter getting strength, the matriarch started eating the afterbirth remains, which contained vitamins and nutritious hormones.

The wind shifted direction and an unfamiliar scent of rancid, wet fur, reached them. In an instant, the herd's calmness changed into a standoff attitude, their ears became flat against their heads and tails firmly stretched out. Nara vanished under Brinka's belly, fully protected against any attempts of being snatched away. The mature cows got in position, ready to defend the calves.

Attracted by the smell of blood, and lack of any other easy prey nearby, the *dapanees* approached the herd swiftly, their treading muffled by the tall grass. There were three of them, all young males with short, thin horns sticking out of their thick foreheads. Their dark brown fur seemed black in the dim light, and their red, phosphorescent eyes stared at the elephants in a miserable attempt to hypnotize them. Their power was useless against their only worthy opponents, just as the mental force of the elephants could not take over the *dapanees*' brains, which was protected by an impenetrable skull and adapted with an additional neuronal layer that repelled invasive brainwaves.

Brute force was the only means of settling their confrontation. Brinka signaled to Taber and Nadira that she would not be able to engage. Her main concern was Nara's safety. Eight cows huddled together in one compact line, facing the quadrupeds, one third of their size, and keeping everyone else secure behind them.

The cows raised their left feet and stomped on the ground forcefully to intimidate the young *dapanees*. The shockwave would reach the bulls, who would find a way to make their presence known.

Moving slowly from one side to the other, the *dapanees* looked for a weak spot to attack as the rumbling amoung the cows grew more intense. The elephants swung their trunks in front of them, trying to keep the hungry beasts at a safe distance. One of the *dapanees* shifted to the right attempting to charge from the side and distract the tight, intimidating barricade of tensed muscles. The two cows that noticed the sly tactic, trumpeted loudly and changed the angle of their enormous bodies towards the daring *dapanee*, forcing him back. Feeling overpowered, the furious beasts howled for reinforcements, a sharp, penetrating sound that made the calves shiver with fear. It was that moment when Brinka produced a resounding snort. Then, the cows charged forward unexpectedly, catching the dapanees on the wrong foot while changing direction. Trunks uncurled violently into their bodies, hitting their softer sides and heads. Bones cracked at impact like dry, feeble branches, and the furred bodies flew in the air several yards from the cows, landing with a thud. One of the cows barked a sharp shriek, letting everyone know that she was hurt. The fight was not over. The cows were wrathful and ready to attack again.

In the distance, a chorus of trumpets replied to the call for help. Alerted, the bulls were on their way to help squash the enemy. Scared and hurt, two of the dapanees vanished quickly into the tall grass, leaving behind one, which was badly hurt. Nadira reached him first. Blood was dripping from a hole on the tip of her trunk. One of the horns had impaled her muscles on impact. She towered over the fallen body, which was trying to drag itself to safety. She lifted her right foot, then dropped it on its head, smashing it with a noisy clunk. Several more stomps followed. The remains of the fearless beast, mixed with dust and grass, were unrecognizable. The other cows watched Nadira release her fury, keeping alert to any new dangers lurking in the night.

Brinka barked in a low tone, beckoning a return to the safety of the village. She already registered in the common memory Nara's birthplace, attached to the perils of the new path. Nadira had rolled in her trunk to prevent more blood loss.

The cows sent continuous sound waves through their toes to the bulls, orienting them to their position. The pace was quick in spite of Nara's visible exhaustion and distress from the events she had just witnessed.

"We are almost home," Brinka signaled to her as encouragement, understanding the trauma her daughter was going through. "You will recover in the peaceful sanctuary that we and the children have created. They will take care of you, and soon, you will become their teacher. You have so much to learn."

The *Commoners* on duty opened the gates, letting them in. Once inside, one by one, the elephants wrapped their trunks together in a loving greeting, and also touching the inside of Brinka's and Altan's mouths, confirming their respect, submission and dedication to the herd. It was a trying moment that brought forward such explicit gestures rarely used by all of them at the same time.

Nara was in the middle of it, still scared in spite of so many reassurances. She hid under Brinka's belly when the children approached her. She felt their thoughts touch her mind, and more panic overran her. They had to step back and give her space and time to comprehend their role in her life.

Akila, the *Writer* Council girl, broke down in tears when she saw the wound on Nadira's trunk. She and a *Commoner* cleaned the crust of blood around the hole, poured a powder made from wild mushrooms and acacia bark, then wrapped it tight in two layers of acacia leaves. Focusing on positive energy, she moved her hands along the damaged muscles, mentally shifting a golden light up and down to release some of the pain.

"Keep it dry for at least four sunrises," advised Akila who would have shared her teacher's torment if possible. "The horn didn't pierce completely. You can still hold water, but lifting the trunk might be painful."

Torches spiked the dark all around the village. Every caste was on the move, bringing food and water for the elephants, calming the restless emotions of the calves or removing thorns stuck in the thick skin during the insane run.

Only a few of the advanced children, sitting by the *Trees*, maintained an undisturbed pose throughout the night's disruptions. They were the ones for whom *One Who Created All* had opened the doors to *His* infinite kingdom cycles ago. They were caught in a web of sensations beyond human comprehension, their bodies just shells left behind in the lotus position, taken care of by their brothers and sisters. Even if present in both mind and body to the whole drama that alighted the village, they would have been completely detached from it due to the newfound knowledge and meaning that all was an illusion. They were beyond any of *maya's* deceptive tricks and life scenarios that seemed so real to an untrained mind.

For the last five sunrises, two *Commoners* and Fenuku, the Builder boy who led the Council, had not returned from their internal, magical journey. They sat on holy ground, facing the *Trees of Life*, in an unseen vibratory conversation with *One Who Created All.* Awake by sustained efforts and unrelenting faith, their souls dipped cautiously first into the boundless knowledge of *Supreme Being.* That shy dip broke down all the internal mind barriers, setting them free. They had no yearning to come back to their physical form, not even for a moment to say their goodbyes and thanks to those who had helped them reach enlightenment. They were part of the universal cycle. They had become the cycle themselves, fluttering energy moving willingly.

Their physical bodies would soon wither and loosen the pose. A sign for the children and the elephants that the time had come to let them go, and be happy for their accomplished souls. They would finally bury them by the *Trees.*

It was a cycle of birth and rebirth, performed by *One Who Created All* with his materialized frozen thoughts. There was no concept of death; only that of a transition into a realm to appropriately reflect on a life whose outcome hadn't been completely fulfilled, that is to say, hadn't reached *the state of bliss.*

Rays of morning light chased the shadows away, exposing the night's drama. Huddled in their area of the village, the elephants were calm now. The young ones slept, their trunks still attached to their mothers for assurance.

Acacia and bamboo leaves were spread in disarray over the ground. Most of the children made it to the huts for a quick nap, while others, too tired to move, sat down and leaned their heads against the library's wall, falling asleep immediately.

Altan and Brinka felt drained after sending thoughts relentlessly to anyone who needed consolation or just direction on how to help. The bull missed Fenuku's clear mind and concise guidance of the children. Fenuku's spiritual development had shown real progress recently, punctuated by longer and deeper meditation sessions. Altan had nothing else to teach him as contact with *One Who Created All* had opened the boy's energy channels, releasing his soul into a new dimension of understanding of who he really was. During last night's crisis, Altan had tried unsuccessfully to reach out to Fenuku whose consciousness had left his body, deciding not to return to its physical form.

So the bull was surprised and relieved when he saw Fenuku approach him, helped by one of the *Commoners.* His walk was wobbly due to his extensive immobility, but his body had a glowing aura around it. Altan realized that if it hadn't been for his desperate attempts to contact him, Fenuku wouldn't have come back.

"It was selfish of me to try to bring you back." Altan's thought was apologetic, since he was aware of the effort and focus it took to achieve enlightenment.

The boy sat on the steps in front of the workshops and smiled happily, no trace of castigation against his teacher. His recent astral experience had moved him beyond any usual reaction.

"I have to thank you for reminding me that I still have responsibilities to our community," said Fenuku. "The transition to my successor in the Council is not done yet, and if I go now, you'll bear the entire burden."

Altan touched his pupil's face with the tip of his trunk in a gesture of appreciation for his concern. He would miss his bright and dedicated student, with whom he had a strong bond from the beginning.

"The *Orange Soul* should arrive any moment now, and we discussed including him in the Council when he comes of age," said Fenuku. "We should consider assigning my position to Nukua, who, I believe, will follow me into the astral plane in no more than two cycles."

Altan didn't respond immediately. Then he finally said, "You are right. He shows signs of leadership and his writings display a mature view of *One Who Created All's* creation. He would have his name recorded as one who rose to the *Supreme Being* in this existence. When do you want to make the announcement?"

"Tomorrow should be fine. I want to go back. I can't wait to feel *His* persistent love and warmth again. You are my family, but *He* is my spiritual *Father*, my *Creator.*"

A statement that Altan understood completely.

This was their private farewell. Fenuku stood up and leaned his forehead on the elephant's left flank. His palms touched the rough skin with tenderness and increased emotion, transferring his deep feeling and knowledge into the common memory of whose guardian was Altan. Tears burst on his cheeks, and he sensed Altan's trunk encircling his waist, returning the hug.

The boy realized that spending time in the astral didn't burn away all of his attachments to this world, and going back was a priority. He untangled himself from his teacher and started towards the kitchen for a light meal. He would have to prepare Nukua for the official nomination.

* * *

THE DAY WAS COMING TO an end when the elephants waiting for their pupils to be born felt a sudden jolt of pain. A final *call*, more intense than the previous ones. The peapods were ready to be brought down and release the newborns into their incarnations. Everyone gathered around the *Trees of Life*. There was excitement among the children and the calves that had never before witnessed the ceremony. The council members, wearing white ceremonial tunics and pants painted with their specific caste sign, stood waiting for Fenuku to clarify the meaning of this ancient custom.

"We are blessed with the arrival of new souls sent to us by *One Who Created All*. They are the ones that decided they were ready for another attempt to reach enlightenment. It is everyone's sacred duty to help them achieve this. As the *Book* says, '*any self-realization touches all of us in a positive way, bringing joy and a smile onto our Spiritual Father's face*'.

Fenuku shifted his field of view, encompassing the entire crowd. And, as he did many times when he spoke in front of the community, he pushed his right hand backwards, to touch Altan's trunk for additional comfort and strength. "Aside from everything we are celebrating today, this is also a special moment for me, because I am ready to transition and meet our *Creator*!"

They all kept quiet, but sent thoughts of encouragement. He felt their warmth and thanked them.

"I have not been told yet if my stay in the astral plane will be indefinite or if I will return to you as an *Orange Soul* or even be sent to a different world for a new experience as an elevated energy being. In the meantime, Nukua will be the new council leader. He is aware of his responsibilities, and Altan will be around if any advice is required. Now let the ceremony begin."

Several children from each caste squatted down in a semicircle, leaving enough room between them and the *Trees* for the elephants to detach the peapods. They started chanting in a low tone while striking each other with bamboo sticks held in both hands. It had a gloomy rhythm, punctuated with high vibration notes, and almost synchronized with the pulsating light coming from the unborn.

It was the vibration of the land, nature and everyone included in it; it was the harmonic sound played by the *Supreme Being* during the creation process. A reminder that they were all *One*, part of a cycle that only enlightenment could temporarily put on hold.

The elephants added their squeaks and purrs to the medley, while the first in line approached the *Trees*, and with extreme care used his trunk to snap the stem of one of the blue pods, which he carried to a grassy area where the *Commoners* were waiting to perform their part.

One after another, all eleven peapods were placed on the ground, heads facing east. The chanting increased in tempo, a language of music and sound communicating with the infants that allowed natural adjustments to their new environment, enhanced their brain stimulation, and, at the same time, activated a dormant history.

Emerging from the dark behind the standing *Commoners*, Alanda, an elder *Artist* girl, started to sing a lullaby in a high pitch. The added vibration made the pods translucent, exposing the curled, little bodies inside. Awakened, they moved slowly, pushing fragile limbs into the flexible walls. Alanda kept her voice strong, above the chanting and the bamboo beating. A moment later she was the only one left singing. She pushed the sound a note higher, her neck muscles strained with effort.

The peapods all burst at once, drops of the liquid inside splashing. The *Commoners* picked up the newborns. They wrapped them in white pieces of cloth and used it to clean their faces of any trace of the colourful liquid. No cry disturbed the silence, only guttural sounds of baby talk, confirming that they had all arrived safely, with no trace of trauma. More *Commoners* approached the peapods and scooped up the liquid, high in nutrients, into wooden jars to be stored as food for the newborns for the next several sunrises, until they grew strong enough for solid food.

Extending their trunks towards the infants, the elephants caressed them with maternal tenderness: an exchange of chemical signals, scents, and a quick mental connection, a non-invasive touch. This was the first physical contact between pupils and teachers that never lost its powerful impact over the centuries.

Fenuku moved aside, encouraging Nukua to step forward for the next phase of the ceremony.

Initially, Nukua's voice lacked the energy of his predecessor, but a nudge from Manash, his teacher, emboldened him. "We thank *One Who Created All* for sending new brothers and sisters, whose spiritual growth was entrusted to us. Awakening the wisdom within them is a cherished gift that, together, we'll be able to see them achieve." Then, he picked up the book *We Are One*, to read a prayer before the *Commoners* would take the newborns to the huts specifically prepared for them. "*Supreme Being*, purify them, so they can knock at the doors of *Your* awareness, devoid of evil thoughts and temptations. Guide them on the path of their fulfillment to reach *You*, and melt into *Your* omnipotent wisdom."

Only the children and elephants assigned to assist with burying the empty shells stayed behind. In a muttering tone, this time intentional, as the custom requested, Nukua murmured an incantation addressed to the *Trees of Life*. He let them know that the lives they brought forward were safe, and that the holy ground could absorb the peapods, concluding the cycle. The ground shifted and opened up a chasm. The villagers picked up the eleven shells, now devoid of life and dropped them into the dark wound that closed on top of them as soon as the leader recited the incantation one more time.

Altan and Manash had one more task to accomplish, witnessed by Fenuku and Nukua. The bulls leaned their heads against the *Trees* separately, sensing the happiness and energy flowing through the portals. They signaled to the *Trees* that the ceremony was over so the valuable seeds could be released for safekeeping. The *Trees'* bark parted in the middle and the kernels to create a new generation of portals were released into the elephants' trunks. The bulls dropped the seeds into a small bag held by Fenuku and then Altan took it and disappeared with Manash into the darkness to find a safekeeping place for them.

After a long stillness, Fenuku stirred and embraced Nukua, saying goodbye.

The former leader sat down beside the bodies of the two *Commoners* that were still deep in *state of bliss*, and called *One Who Created All*, assuring him that there was nothing else worth coming back to the village; all matters were settled. He closed his eyes and fell into deep concentration, his *soul* ascending with unimaginable speed to a luminous level where weight and his sense of orientation vanished. He was finally home.

* * *

ANY DISPLAY OF the *Trees of Life's* potency was a powerful demonstration of the *Creator*'s unlimited imagination, and each time, it brought Bagham to tears. Last night was no different. And with Fenuku transitioning to the astral level, the event carried even more significance. Nukua became the village's history keeper, and the arrival of so many new *souls* would be his first entry on a fresh thirty-second volume. Bagham's anticipation about the birth of his pupil, an *Orange Soul*, should come to an end soon, since his attraction to the scorched tree had increased to an almost unbearable intensity. He stayed nearby just in case the jolt of pain indicating the imminent birth hit him unexpectedly, but also to protect the pod against hungry predators. The children and the elephants on the council were also ready to drop everything they were doing and rush to the edge of the jungle to welcome the special birth, at the portal chosen by *One Who Created All.*

Since the miraculous appearance of the orange peapod from the barren wood, Bagham had confirmation that indeed, if impregnated by the potent desires of the *Supreme Being*, any of *His* creations could carry the seed of life. He endlessly praised the *Creator* for this honour and asked for the right balance in teaching the distinct soul.

Aside from being the one chosen to care for the new *Orange Soul*, Bagham was trying to find an explanation for the quick arrival of such an entity, only ten cycles after the birth of the now departed, Rakash. The thought kept nagging him so he asked Altan, who also couldn't provide a reasonable answer to his query.

"I asked Fenuku several sunrises ago what will be the name of the *Orange Soul*," said Altan. "He said that the children would call him Herven. So maybe *One Who Created All* had a plan for Rakash and that plan stopped when he disappeared. Herven might continue it or just go ahead with new duties ingrained by the *Creator*. We have to wait and see."

"We still can't be sure that both Rakash and Otan are dead. Could this wise *soul* be the beacon to bring them back home?" Bagham asked his elder.

Altan didn't answer. Deep down, he wanted Bagham to be right about their lost brothers.

The punishment of dense rain began after an endless parade of grayish clouds moved relentlessly by a moody wind. The layer of puffy, but menacing sources of precipitation and thunder, kept everyone tense to how devastating the deluge might be. Suddenly, Bagham felt the impulse of the newborn ready to arrive and he stomped the ground with both feet, letting the council know that the time had come. Then, from the safety of the jungle's edge, he charged towards the gnarled wood from which the peapod was hanging.

He could see dim orange light pulsing through the wall of rain. The shell was hanging in a vertical position against the twisted, upright wood. He grabbed the stem, snapped it and placed the peapod on the muddy ground. The thirsty land would swallow the water for a while, but not for long, thus everyone had to hurry for a much quicker ceremony. The auspices of this birth revealed abundance. Nevertheless, the storming sky could have been interpreted differently.

The council arrived, elephants in the front, followed by the children who were using them as shields against the intense rain. Thick mud tried to hold onto their legs and prevent them from their sacred duty. Words were useless and the chanting was covered by celestial noises. It seemed that *One Who Created All* was throwing a natural obstacle to see how determined they were to follow the ritual of such an important event.

Nukua took the initiative. He told the elephants to raise their trunks and get closer together until they touched each other, forming a roof under which the rain was less invasive, allowing the children a better chance at chanting. They started the rhythm of the bamboo sticks again until it reached the right note, then, step by step, they all gathered strength to focus only on the sound they produced. When the vibration fell into place, Alanda performed her part, and the peapod burst open, releasing its precious content.

Nakila snatched Herven, covering him with an already wet cloth and placed him in a large bamboo basket, a *Commoner* emptied the orange liquid into a bowl, then Bagham grabbed the shell to take back to the village, and bury it by the *Trees.*

He felt empowered and elated, determined to contribute to the community by guiding Herven and learning from him at the same time.

CHAPTER 9

If you can't find time to bring One Who Created All in your heart, He will not find the time for you either.

From the book *We Are One* – Chapter 9

THE VILLAGE WAS QUIET this early in the morning; just the normal brush of wind against the huts' roofs and the bamboo leaves left on the ground by the elephants. It was swirling through each tight space, changing its tone from hurling to screaming, then pausing again to catch its breath.

The moisture in the air was thick and imbued with the fragrances of a thousand flowers and trees, happy to be alive one more day.

The children were not awake yet, nor their teachers. Only he was conscious, the old scholar from Laeta, wisdom eye wide open, sitting outside the library, measuring his breaths in and out, the way the elders taught him.

Bart could feel the vibrations of every single form of life surrounding him, sending wave after wave of energy towards him as though trying to empower the weakened body that had lasted way past that of any other human in the village.

The elephants, after much deliberation, decided that the spot by the library could be spared for the old scholar to spend the rest of whatever days One Who Created All had given him. Food and water were brought twice a day. He couldn't remember the last time he walked. His legs, depleted of energy, broke the ground underneath him, turning into roots that connected him to the village, the jungle, and to each and every particle reverberating with One Who Created All's blessings.

He consumed his days with prayer and meditation, declaring his love for the Supreme Being that he encountered so late in life.

Rakash, after taking his rightful place in the Council, hadn't been visiting him more than once a week. A coldness inserted into a relationship that was once utterly strong.

The wind abruptly slapped his left cheek. The blow, while vigorous, was diminished in strength by the thick, tangled beard that covered his face. It was punishment for forbidden thoughts about a time when Rakash was lost among strangers and forced to reveal secrets so well guarded up to that moment.

Bart, or whatever was left of his identity, had experienced enough flickers of the state of bliss to comprehend the vastness and beauty of the world within, which made up the entire life's purpose of the village community.

He would transition peacefully, prepared, and for the first time in his existence, convinced that he was immortal and the cycleable rules of this land applied to him as well. In fact, the rules applied to every human being in Laeta and Korobat, east and west, but they didn't know. They were too busy wasting energy on foolish, ephemeral gratifications.

While the wind played with his beard and his ragged clothing, a question rose in his mind: are they going to bury him among the Trees of Life or, right here? The ground will absorb the physical me, bit by bit, until my open eye migrates to the top of my head for one last sight of the sky...

He would take that memory down with him, so he could pass it onto the grass, the worms and the insects that would feast on his decomposing body.

But he didn't care about perishing physically since the other journey, of the soul, was what fascinated him for years. He felt being swept by the wetness of the ground, the roughness of buried rocks and sticks brushing his skin, tearing it apart, as the body was pulled deeper and deeper. He was still aware of his physical form, but he shouldn't be, and realized that his soul wasn't lifted to the astral but to its opposite, evil location.

The scholar woke up, shivering and sweaty.

Drops of perspiration streamed down his forehead, falling onto his eyes, stinging them. A vivid dream that revealed a lost thought he had once fantasized about: living in the village. He imagined Rakash asking the elephants for permission to join them as a trusted family member, so Bart could observe their customs and, after many tests, to be initiated in the esoteric *state of bliss*.

The dream revealed what could have happened if he had walked that path. A more proper end than spending his remaining years in Laeta. Bart got up slowly and headed for the bathroom. A cold shower would freshen him up and ready him for a new day in the lab, where a team of engineers and psychologists were studying Rakash.

The boy woke up shortly after his master and went to the kitchen to prepare breakfast for both of them. Lunch was always provided on site, and for dinner, when they were too exhausted to think about food, a cooked meal would be waiting for them at the apartment, steaming and smelling delicious, care of a chef hired by the city.

They ate in silence. A bowl of dried fruits and oatmeal on top of which they poured warm milk.

The first week had passed surrounded by new faces, whose names would have to be remembered again. Short introductions and many scientific discussions preceded the work they faced. Unfamiliar thoughts tangled with unfamiliar feelings that would not yet settle to form an unyielding impression on how genuine Korobat's intention was.

Each of them reflected differently on what was happening to them. Rakash, being more introspective, asked *One Who Created All* for answers on how to best communicate with the new breed of humans he was living amongst, and how to apply the concepts of life's meaning that was taught in the village. Bart, in spite of the flawless reception and continuous signs of respect from others, was not convinced that the disruption of their lives would pay off as everyone else hoped.

They were done eating, and, followed by the same stillness of words, crossed the street where the lab was set up.

Rakash held up quite well considering the barrage of questions these people constantly fired at him. Hando kept his promise about the meditation room being ready for the first session. It was just big enough to fit a small bed and a night table with sufficient space left on the floor for the woollen meditation carpet. One of the walls had a glass opening, so the team could monitor the boy, while wires connected between the equipment and the sensors applied to Rakash ran through a hole at the bottom of the wall.

The team consisted today of ten members and four were women.

"The number will fluctuate based on the additional skills required along the way," Hando told them.

Most of the researchers were in their mid-thirties, hungry to prove themselves by stamping their initials on new innovative technologies. Artilla, Banaar and Hando, who Bart had met at the introductory meeting, influenced the attitude of the researchers so they held back on showing too much enthusiasm. '*Bosses always inhibit workers, no matter the environment,*' Bart thought.

They still reported to the businessmen, so despite Martinez's words of encouragement about a 'no stifling rules' approach, nothing would loosen up with them there. While Bart understood the potential limitations that the hierarchy could generate during the research, he had no intention of interfering in any way with their process and wouldn't indicate any flaw whose reparation would accomplish faster results. His fundamental objective was to protect Rakash and display an unlimited desire for cooperation; positive feedback would reach the Committee back home.

On the first day in the lab, after the introductions and pleasantries were dealt with, the real conversation began.

"Sorry, that it took us longer than we thought to read your material," Hando opened the floor, "but we wanted the entire team not only to read your research, but to come up with questions and potential suggestions on how to approach this work. It also gave you more time to explore the city."

"So what do you think of the results of two years of grunt work?" Bart inquired. Deep inside, his ego was restlessly fighting to surface for recognition from his peers. No one in Laeta openly offered any praise for his previous achievements.

The man introduced as the team leader, Prakit, started first. He had a tall, thin frame that widened at the shoulders, making him tower over his colleagues who were sitting. A plain yellowish T-shirt was stretched on his body, through which his well-formed biceps showed nicely. A couple of moles on his right cheek, just above his beard, gave the impression that he had just finished a paint job and drops of the brownish colour had hardened on his skin with no hope of being removed. He looked intensely at a piece of paper with notes and questions, probably a summary of everyone's input. "Sir, this is really impressive work ..."

Blackwood raised his hand, stopping him, even if the words, as expected, soothed his ears. "Just to be clear, I am Bart to all of you. Don't forget that I'm used to your less formal way of addressing each other: I went to university here in Korobat. Please go on."

Prakit pushed his thick lensed eyeglasses up on his nose, gently patted his trimmed beard, and then continued, "The fact that you've been able to confirm what's real from most of the published material saves us a lot of time. We can discard all the garbage, the assumptions and the imaginary stories built around the few confirmed facts."

Bart nodded. That was an achievement that only a minority could understand its critical role, when combined with the research data, in generating a meaningful interpretation.

"We were also amazed at the evidence that we thought was fake but proved real. We're referring to the odd locations chosen as birthplaces for the *Orange Souls*. The *Trees of Life* are the most fascinating birthplaces and that's why it's so hard to comprehend that such awkward portals exist. Even the notion of an energetic corridor between our world and an ethereal one is mind boggling, and we, as researchers, are all fascinated by it." He looked down at the notes, searching for the next point on the list. "Your records regarding the spiritual celebration of *One Who Created All* that takes place outside the jungle is much more comprehensive than the details presented in any of the books we've read. We assumed that they were partially true."

The academic side of Bart began to itch, ready to engage at the intellectual level with someone who was not his equal, but had a similar background and enough knowledge about the villagers to challenge his atrophied appetite for debate. He stretched his shorter leg in front of him to ease a sudden muscle spasm, and he jumped in without waiting for any invitation to talk.

"It's a unique celebration, in fact, the only one that takes place outside the settlement," Bart said. "I couldn't find any record of this community previously interacting with the exterior world, hence their gifts are offered out in the open to *One Who Created All* with the belief that *He* is taking them away. Beautiful artwork, bamboo weavings, small paintings, delicately bound books displaying daily scenes from the village. Each year, these children put their heart and devotion into creating tokens of faith to reaffirm their gratitude towards the *Supreme Being* for another chance at reaching the *state of bliss.*"

The scholar couldn't sit any longer and, in spite of the pain, he stood and took several wobbly steps, still keeping a hand on the edge of the table for additional support. Excitement emboldened him to lose his usual cold attitude that he preferred when dealing with Laeta's officials. The audience in the room was ripe to hear the passionate story behind the dry written words. His mind envisioned the young researchers as well behaved children that were shown candies and toys to be rewarded with if they listened quietly to their teacher.

"Based on what Rakash has told us, it's the only time of the year when the community leaves the safety of the jungle," he said and looked towards the villager, giving him the proper credit for the useful information. "Imagine that only through sheer luck, a bunch of lost merchants from Laeta found this treasure laying in the sun, and no one around to claim it. It looked like junk to most of them, but there's always one who's smarter than the rest who picked it up, and, upon their safe return to the city after weeks of wandering around, he sold the entire lot for more than he expected."

Rakash kept silent, internally happy to see his master regaining his energy and determination. Watching all these people exhibit so much interest in the story of his brothers and sisters, and in all their customs, made him joyful. Sharing the teachings of the *One Who Created All*, at least the ones he remembered, brought an elated feeling upon him, a well-deserved tranquility that balanced the craziness of the last few days. He would let master lead the spectacle, intuitively sensing that he needed the attention, even if only for a short while.

'Humbleness can restrain the ego; if left unchecked, ego will ruin one's internal peace,' the *We Are One* book stated.

The boy understood that only by living by example and by applying the teachings, he could change these people, and make them believe that gratitude, love and forgiveness, are essential ingredients for *One Who Created All*'s attention.

"There are certain details that I left out," Bart said, laughing. "But it will be included in a book that I intend to write upon my return to Laeta. I'll have a draft ready while here, but I want to incorporate the results of our combined research. Your names will be listed in the Acknowledgements. So, let me finish my story. The merchant went again the following year to the same spot, driven by greed, but also on a personal quest as his curiosity was above the norm. Hidden behind a boulder, he saw the procession of children and elephants, and the offering ritual. He didn't intervene, but waited for them to leave before it was safe to pick up the items offered to the *Supreme Being* and left in a hurry. This is how our Committee found out that the villagers mentioned in several fantasy books are, in fact, real. They decided that kidnapping a child could potentially generate money. The president has entrusted me with Rakash ever since."

The women gasped at Bart's last statement, as they never knew the official circumstances that brought the boy to Laeta. Only one or two in the group were parents who comprehended the psychological schism that could trigger in a kid's mind when yanked from his family and a recognizable environment.

"Have any other expeditions been organized since?" The woman who asked the question was sitting next to Prakit, her legs hanging off the high chair. Her long blond hair fell straight down on her face, exposing just her narrow brown eyes, thin-bridged pointy nose and mouth with full, red lips as if she was ashamed of her ears and most of her face; skin that might have relayed a dark secret about her. Naranta was introduced as the brain specialist.

"No. No one in Laeta went back to the village," Bart reassured everyone, still holding onto the edge of the table. Standing gave him a controlling position within the group. "We assumed the elephants would be prepared in case another party showed up, and the outcome might be different. We didn't want them to track us back to Rakash. Heated debate took place between Laeta's Committee members and several advisers, myself included," the scholar continued his report of the events, "regarding the effectiveness of another trip to the jungle to capture another villager. Hopefully, this time, one who would generate faster results. But my conviction was that Rakash would open up if given enough time, so I voted against it."

Even to this day, he didn't regret his decision. Another reason for his veto ran much deeper than anyone would have guessed, and had to do with his assumption that the community the boy left behind had been highly disturbed by his disappearance. He felt responsible for Rakash being snatched away from his family as he fed the committee sacrosanct details about the mysterious village. He looked at Rakash who was sitting on the other side of him, munching on seeds, and a warm feeling spiked through his aged body, giving him goosebumps. The boy's agile glance told Bart that he was well aware of the discussion even if, to everyone else, he seemed detached. Meeting new faces always brought him joy, and Bart had to admit that keeping Rakash secluded most of the time, didn't improve the boy's disposition.

Bart went on, "In his book published almost one hundred years ago, Magusti mentioned for the first time of a wanderer who wore a strangely coloured sign on his cheeks. This strange character chose markets and other public places in Laeta for his loud orations spoken in a language that no one could understand. People laughed at him and ridiculed him for becoming no more than a madman consumed by dark dreams that were eating him from inside."

The pain in Bart's leg spiked profusely and he had to sit again to continue. "It was Magusti who heard the babbling of the odd foreigner and one day decided to feed him to have a closer look. Magusti describes this encounter in detail. Yehuda was his name. His hands shook profusely and deep wrinkled channels that gave the impression that his flesh would fall off any time, crossed his face. Squalid rags covered his withered physique and his pestilential odor kept the odd passersby at a distance. Magusti took pity on him and hosted him for several months, extracting, with excruciating patience, the information he later made available to all of us."

"Have you brought this book with you?" Naranta interrupted, her hands drumming on her tights. She gave the impression that either her tolerance for listening to the story was running low or she needed to be somewhere else more important.

"Unfortunately not," Bart replied. "It's one of the few copies of a the first edition. I'm not aware of any reprints, so maybe that's why you are not familiar with it." He shifted his weight on the chair, trying to minimize the persistent throbbing. "Yehuda's deteriorating health concerned Magusti so much that he brought in one of the best doctors in Laeta, who concluded that the man was dying of old age. Magusti couldn't reconcile that information with what Yehuda told him, that he was only thirty-nine years old. How could someone be so young and old at the same time, he wondered? Soon after that Yehuda passed away leaving behind several crumbled pages with drawings and notes in an unintelligible language."

"Are the drawings about the places we mentioned earlier?" Prakit asked. Almost unnoticeably, he brushed his hand on Naranta's generous left hip. She did not react, like she was accustomed to such a gesture by him.

"Affirmative," said Bart. "Each new publication suffered alterations with little or no other content from the first edition, hence Magnus' is my point of reference."

Hando handed the scholar a glass of water, as his voice got a little harsh.

"Thank you." He gulped quickly, thinking what else was worth mentioning. "Rakash helped confirm the following: the villagers grow old much faster than us. If they don't reach the *state of bliss* in their prime, they will phase out physically. The jungle is located in the direction Yehuda kept pointing at, south of Laeta. The elephants and the more evolved children possess an extraordinary mental power that is used as their main defense tool. Their focused mind generates energy fields large enough to protect the village against any intruders. Power of thought and intention of spoken word are concepts totally new for us. I can barely wrap my mind around it, but witnessing Rakash's steady evolution, nothing amazes me anymore. The overall message Yehuda tried to convey was about an invisible, yet powerful force that created all of us, observing our every action and thought to this day. Every other story in the book is fluff crafted by Magusti, but attributed to Yehuda."

"Have you been able to rationalize why Yehuda left his village?" Orlando Artilla asked while munching on a pretzel.

"Common sense dictates to spread the word about *One Who Created All.* Yehuda felt his end near and, while he understood the power of the *Supreme Being* without experiencing *Him*, concluded that everyone should be aware of a path that will bring happiness from within himself. The harsh treatment he received from our society might have accelerated the aging process. Doubly disappointing."

Prakit dropped the notes on a desk and looked at his team members.

"Any other questions?"

Merlaya, a tall, skinny woman, with small breasts hidden underneath a hollow blouse, broke the silence: "I saw a note dated no more than four months ago about your own meditation sessions. Anything you want to add to it?" Her deep voice startled Bart, and it took him a moment to conjure the right statement, as he knew it would go on record. She had short hair, dyed in various nuances of red, and a pierced nose. Yellow and red flames of a tattoo hidden underneath her blouse covered her thin neck. She could have fit perfectly in Laeta's Entertainment District. Here, she was an electrical engineer with a keen interest in electronics, complementing Prakit, who was the brain behind complex automated designs.

"I've learnt in life that one of the most rewarding accomplishments is to experience for yourself what other people have also experienced and describe to be amazing. Helping Rakash reach the *state of bliss* and not trying to understand it myself, would just be hypocrisy on my part. Why does it seem so unachievable? It's because of our lifestyle. Most of us will not consider changing our life style to give up innocent pleasures that, in our minds, are an unworthy sacrifice. I started by cutting back on meat and wine. Others must give up smoking, drugs and anything that pollutes their bodies and minds. Thinking like a villager, like Rakash, needs a different mental wiring towards empathy, inclusion and nature. The concept they use in the village is to 'love yourself', and, if mentioned in the presence of the wrong entourage, would trigger a disparate connotation altogether. If viewed within the big concept spawned by *One Who Created All*, its meaning is radically changed to a gentle, more encompassing aspect of loving everyone.

"One can't start meditating tomorrow, without any preparation and expect miraculous results. If nothing happens soon, disappointment and discouragement will settle in, the initial determination vanishes, and the person is back to their old habits, while spreading the word that this *state of bliss* and meditation thing is a waste of time," the scholar shared reflections that no one in Laeta was interested in. "The committee only wants results with no patience for the tiring details," he said.

He noticed Naranta fidgeting again, her hair waving left and right each time she moved her head like a field of wheat disturbed by a reckless wind. The others were taking notes. The lab was devoid of human noise. Only an intermittent beeping from the equipment could be heard. Bart felt sweat crawling down between the valley of his shoulder blades and he welcomed the tickle as a signal that he needed to remove his coat. The elation of people paying attention to him made him burning hot.

"Taking the time to prepare yourself mentally and physically will increase your chances of success. I've had to make changes that were, in my opinion, not drastic enough; but working on my self-improvement continues even now in Korobat. I'm not giving up." Bart received a sudden burst of confidence that pulled these words involuntarily out of his mouth. It felt good to be confident and inspire others to do the same.

"Do I sense encouragement in that we should become the object of our own research?" Merlaya asked like she was eager to start right away.

Silence again.

"You should try it. Nayan and master did it. It's fun."

It was an unexpected intervention from Rakash. All eyes shifted to him, anticipating additional words of wisdom. Bart gave him a nod of reassurance.

"I've noticed a certain level of anger and puzzlement when master told you about the events that led to my arrival in Laeta. It was a word that triggered a reaction in women, proving that they are more empathetic than men: kidnapped."

Everyone forced a gentle smile, realizing how right the boy was.

"I didn't know about Yehuda until master revealed the book to me and read me the story. I think only the elephants might remember him as all the brothers and sisters of that time are long gone. Maybe, like Yehuda, I walked out of the jungle under *One Who Created All's* guidance for a second attempt to spark a divine light in all humanity. I must succeed myself first. But if *One Who Created All* lets me reach thus far, I believe *He* wants you to succeed as well. So maybe, in the end, this kidnapping will benefit us all."

They kept staring at him, numerous questions churning in their minds.

"Do I miss my family? Yes, even if master embraced me like a son. Will I ever go back to them? Only the *Supreme Being* knows. *His* plans for me have not been revealed yet ... but that time will come."

Everyone's facial expression was changing at each new revelation. Outrage, surprise, bewilderment. A mature child was giving them a lecture on self-betterment and spiritual development. Even the meaning of 'spiritual' had not completely sunken into the team's vocabulary.

Rakash looked around the lab at all the working desks full of blinking boxes and asked no one in particular, "Do you expect to find an answer for the *state of bliss* by using all these?"

Hando sensed the conundrum the team was in, and offered an answer. "Yes, the equipment was developed by them and interprets the results of your monitoring while in meditation, which could lead to the precise method. The equipment will tell the team the story of your vital signs so they could understand how to help you advance on your path."

The boy assessed the response, got up and started walking towards the meditation room. "Instead of expecting positive results, have faith that you will achieve them. Deep, deep faith." Then he closed the door behind him.

* * *

THAT FIRST INTERACTION of the team with Bart and Rakash had shifted attitudes in a visible way. What they initially thought to be a frightened child dropped into an unknown world, turned out to be a source of unbelievable wisdom, guided in his search for enlightenment by a patient, caring, and at the same time, a very different teacher that had no resemblance to Otan, Bart.

It was the moment when the team of experts understood, based on Bart's latest research notes, that only through meditation could Rakash have changed so radically.

Slowly, most of the team members became fond of the boy; except Naranta, who in fact, didn't show any signs of affection for anyone around her. Not even to Prakit, with whom, Bart thought, she had a romantic relationship. She displayed all the signs of a drug addict, the assumption being that only her specialized skills kept her in the game. The governing bodies of each of the self-run cities were busy working on programs for improving the standard of living of their citizens, and were not preoccupied with creating legislation to restrict the distribution and consumption of harmful substances.

Merlaya and Prakit unofficially signed on to try meditation on their own, following a short list of rules put together by Bart. Giving up desires and enticements craved by their egos and senses, seemed an almost insurmountable task. To enjoy an evening with friends became a defiance against everyone around them who was smoking, drinking or drugging, in their ambition for an enhanced life experience.

Clear minds and clean bodies were pre-requisites for the long and arduous journey to enlightenment; Merlaya and Prakit were setting an example, intrigued that their brain could change its patterns, learn new tricks and pull them into inconceivable depths of thinking, only to bring them back to conscious life more mature, adaptable and sensitive.

At least this was their understanding of the expected outcome based on Blackwood's notes.

"Let's check your personal results three weeks from now. By then Rakash will be familiar with his routine and might not need that much attention from you. We'll decide then if we'll build another meditation room from which we can monitor you," Bart addressed the researchers that had signed up for the meditation trial, thinking that setting up firm deadlines would motivate them even more.

"How are we supposed to focus on a non-physical entity which we aren't even sure will listen to our calling?" Merlaya inquired.

"I believe that *knowing* an image of *One Who Created All* is secondary. The intensity of the feeling is more important. Our brain creates permanent visual stimuli at an amazing rate, deceiving us from the inner peace that is mandatory for preparing ourselves for the journey. Whatever surrogate persona gets formed in your mind's eye, keep it steady, lock it in with your full attention, so that no other thought sneaks in. Build around it a wall of mental strength that will firm up over time, and be able to withstand the permanent knocks of human temptations. Switching to deep feeling helped Rakash with his progress. I felt some improvements as well, but they weren't too significant to mention."

This was all that Bart could deliver as encouragement. He wanted to lend as much support as possible to the volunteers, and hoped that more would join, adding weight and, potentially, more substance to the project. The greater the wannabe number, the noisier the reverberations of the expected failure.

Since she was single, Merlaya had no restrictions on what she could try and for how long. Bart only wished that her enthusiasm wouldn't diminish before it became contagious and spread like a curiosity worth trying.

"When you make notes in your diary don't leave out any details, no matter how insignificant. We'll discuss it and discard later," the scholar advised seriously, because despite the final outcome, he was still obsessed with gathering any piece of information that would tweak his future interactions with Rakash.

"Create a meditation space in your home, fill it with your own vibration and don't bring anyone close to it. Also meditate at the same hour every day. A steady schedule is important as your brain will expect to calm down and body will slow its activities in correlation with lesser signals from the brain."

His promise of including the team members' names in his book was another incentive for them to follow his lead.

Bart's eagerness to hear the results of Korobat's brain research was building up inside him; nevertheless, the question should come out very casual, as a logical continuation of their discussion he thought and formed his next words carefully. "Let Rakash meditate on his own for the next several days. His body and mind will need readjustment to the vibration of the lab and all of us here. He will tell us when he is ready. What about your amazing results in this field? What can you share?" he asked.

Naranta took the lead without waiting for anyone's approval. She took control of her shaking hands by cramming them in her pants' pockets.

"The Scholar's Academy decided to create the Brain Research department sixty years ago, after a couple of professors realized that a high percentage of the mess each of us is in during our existence originates in the brain. At one point or another, we do something stupid enough, or someone else is doing it to us, that our neurons become inhibited and go berserk, confusing the normal release of our neurotransmitters, hence distorting a natural process that very rarely becomes undone. They initially delved into people affected by air pollution or exposed to the chemicals used by the tanneries. The data was inconsistent because the body was fighting back a major attack from various diseases; the artificial stimuli induced to the brain couldn't be separated from the natural ones, sent out in defense."

Naranta put her hands under her tights, a sure way of controlling them. She was talking with an even tone, giving Bart the impression of a memorized lecture. Everyone else kept quiet, listening to an over familiar story.

"The next phase started when they established a new set of rules: healthy bodies, screwed up minds. Suddenly, the number of available samples diminished to the point that they couldn't gather a critical mass of data. They had to become creative, and, I don't know if this is still a classified case or not, lured in drug addicts from Laeta."

Bart didn't flinch. No more than a simple nod of his head confirmed his awareness of such an initiative. In fact, he had been surprised to find out about the various covert activities Korobat was running in his city.

"The enhanced substances had a direct correlation with brain activity, leaving most of the other organs alone as long as the daily dose was kept under control. Two decades of research generated a map of stimuli and the respective affected brain areas," she went on with the background story.

"What type of stimuli have been used and on what age ranges?" Bart asked, pulling a small notepad out of his pocket ready to take notes.

Naranta stopped for a second to push her hair sideways, revealing round cheeks void of any scars from childhood diseases as Bart had thought.

"There were three groups, each exposed to a different stimulant: rhythmic light, sound combinations, including known frequencies between 4Hz and 10Hz, and images of artificial and natural objects. The age group was the same all across the board, twenty five to forty years old, both men and women. We'll provide you with an updated copy of the report," she nodded to Bart. "We've been adding to it since our team took over several years ago. We increased the range of frequencies and image variation with very little disparity in the results. The use of light flashes allowed us to measure brain activity not only on the visual areas, but on the whole cortex. To be honest, we weren't quite sure what we were looking for."

The woman inhaled profusely and started again with a changed tone, energized, like her first script ended, and a new, more dynamic, one began. "The founders' goal was noble: to heal people from the clutches of their internal demons; nevertheless, their hard work didn't pay off as quickly as expected. The trial patients were not getting better and the results were inconclusive. The funding dwindled for a while, so new ideas were thrown in the hat, with one significant winner: plant medicine or hallucinogens, as they are called in the east. An induced state of consciousness, easier to control than any drug found on the market, and above all, non-addictive."

Gently, not to disturb the conversation, Prakit left his chair to check on Rakash. Sitting in the lotus position, facing the internal window, the boy's breathing was calm, barely noticeable. Prakit looked away to the middle of the room where Naranta's scientific tirade had caught the guest in a web of alluring fantasy. He was proud of his girlfriend and how she'd succeeded in maintaining her professional status in spite of a ravaging addiction that affected her health and their relationship. Nevertheless, somehow she had to get better, quench the urge of the stimuli her brain was still yearning for, and apply her experience in healing other addicts.

This type of research was their ticket to fame in the scientific community, maybe in obtaining a place on the board of one of the important local companies or even a teaching position at the Scholar's Academy.

"We continued on this path, cataloguing and experimenting with six varieties of similar plants that generated indisputable proof in terms of brain health benefits. We also noticed an expansion of the brain's neuronal learning patterns."

Blackwood raised his hand, stopping Naranta from continuing. It just dawned on him that every generation of researchers took more or less a similar approach, using external stimulation then recording the results. They should have tried the opposite, but they didn't have Rakash ... until now.

"I know what we will be doing different this time," he said. "Rakash doesn't need external stimulation. He will use the key words I've already mentioned to meditate. We just have to monitor the activated areas in his brain, and document any physical sensation he reports. The *state of bliss* comes from within. Also, don't forget that he has a natural monitoring device embedded within him, which is better at keeping track of his internal state than any piece of equipment in your lab: the orange birthmarks. Their intensity increases when his consciousness enters a higher level. This is what will confirm the readings of the equipment."

The scholar paused to gather his breath, everyone focused their attention on him. "And there is something else we have to keep in mind. The *state of bliss* is not a medical condition we have to identify and treat. It's part of, let's say, our psychology. It's part of the villagers' psychology too."

Naranta stepped down off the chair and started to pace around the room, mulling over what the Laetian had just said. Her hands were tucked deep into her front pockets, keeping their tremor under control.

"I assume we can call this Phase IV of our research," she said, looking at Bart with renewed respect. "Today and tomorrow we'll do a quick inventory of the equipment to decide if we are missing anything, now that we know exactly what we are monitoring." She got excited at the thought of how different Rakash was from all the other people they had studied.

Naranta moved her head towards Prakit, delivering another message that would put things in motion even further. "If we start monitoring you and Merlaya, and potentially, many more, we must build spare equipment, and fast!"

Prakit nodded.

"We have technicians on standby to work on it, two weeks tops." But right away she asked a rhetorical question. "Where and how are we going to monitor you, guys? We need you to oversee most of the experiment."

Bart found it impressive how seriously this team of relatively young scientists was immersing itself in an unfamiliar direction with no fear of failure or second thoughts. For the first time since arriving in Korobat, he felt like he was in the right place. Where his intellectual potential could be utilized and recognized. He let thoughts play out in his mind's cage about what would happen if he reconsidered the offer that was always open for him at the Scholars Academy. So many outcomes to choose from. He ignored the chatter around him, closed his eyes and enjoyed the fuzzy feeling of an alternate existence.

CHAPTER 10

Through consistent meditation and deep love for One Who Created All, one's life meaning will unravel from the mists of ignorance, elevating the soul to untapped peaks of happiness and fulfillment.

From the book *We Are One* – Chapter 10

IT HAD BEEN POURING DOWN uninterrupted for the third sunrise in a row, not giving anyone, animals, humans or nature, a break from the monotonous rapping of water on every surface. In the gardens the plants were half submerged and even the small openings at the base of the bamboo fence could barely keep the water level below the huts' entrances. The strong smell of dishes cooked with turmeric and herbs coming from the kitchen were overpowered by the damp, oozing out from every wet surface.

All the children gathered for their lessons inside the main hall while the elephants remained at the mercy of the rain, keeping a mental connection with their pupils. So far, the repairs that strengthened the roofs were holding against the relentless pounding. The natural noise kept most of the newborns awake, and concealed their cry from everyone else. In the end, the exhaustion and the soft chanting of the caretakers calmed them down. They were only one week old, but the color of the birthmarks on their hands, for the *Commoners*, and cheeks, for the other castes, were visible. They all had safely arrived through the portals and the entire community was in high spirits after the dramatic event of losing Nagoti had disturbed their way of life. The bad weather prevented the welcoming ceremony from occurring. This allowed the children of all castes that were at least four cycles old, the opportunity to prepare a gift for the *Orange Soul.*

Alanda and Baqar, the elder *Artists* that received Bagham's acceptance to become the caretakers of his unusual pupil, couldn't be happier. The honour bestowed upon them emboldened a new meaning into their remaining sunrises in the village, before the *Supreme Being*'s call for their return in the astral plane. It was a unique chance to show kindness and dedication to a soul that encompassed the experience of countless incarnations, and whose ultimate reward for his unwavering faith and love during all these lives was the *state of bliss*.

Caring for the little one felt like compensation for their lack of creativity. Also, deep inside, they both hoped to still be alive when Herven would be able to show gratitude by sharing teachings and advice that could help them achieve better results on their next trip to the village.

The two huts reserved for the newborns had only ten beds each, smaller than the ones in the other huts. This allowed enough space beside it for a table and a chair. The *Artists* were supposed to take turns, especially during the night, but their dedication reached a limit that not even they thought possible, and only seldom was one away to bring food or clean themselves. The babies gathered strength and clarity in their new environment as they recuperated from the pods on nectar and sleep. Because of the weather, none of them could be taken outside for a closer encounter with their teachers, so the side shutters had to be opened for the elephants to reach in with their trunks and touch the offspring. The link between them established during the creation process, had to be further intensified, both physically and mentally, so that customs of the village and knowledge of their world could slowly surface into the newborns' minds.

While excited about being chosen to guide an *Orange Soul*, Bagham knew he had to be patient working with Herven. The elephant understood some of his responsibilities, but had to connect to the herd's consciousness for finer details. Herven's arrival so close after Rakash had a meaning that Bagham couldn't yet comprehend, and not even Altan could answer that question when asked.

"Is he eating properly?" Bagham inquired the *Artist* pair while, with the tip of his trunk, he was touching the boy's left hand.

"He's fine. He takes the nectar well. No cramps." Alanda sent back her thought.

"Don't worry, we're capable of handling him," Baqar added.

"I know, I know," replied the elephant, confirming his level of confidence in them. His head filled the entire opening, adding darkness to the room. "I still can't believe the twist on my path. *One Who Created All* is so generous with me. There are other, more mature elephants who could have been his teacher," Bagham continued his thought. He moved his touch to the boy's head, gently inhaling his fresh scent.

"The *Supreme Being* gives each of us chores that challenge us. This is what I've learnt from my failures," the woman encouraged Bagham. "But sometimes, even if we are destined to end our existence like a piece of land scorched by unbearable heat, *He* still keeps us in *His* heart and watches us closely. Baqar, tell Bagham what happened to you."

The *Artist* smiled, straightening his back, proud of what he was about to confess. The skin of his face and hands looked so much like the elephant's hide, rumpled and grayish, an unmistakably sign of old age. Only his eyes had a twinkle of hope.

"Since I heard that there was a slight possibility that an *Orange Soul* would arrive while I'm still in this physical plane, I sensed a tremendous amount of energy through my body. Creativity overcame me. I felt like a real *Artist* that is not done yet. A piece of artwork materialized in my mind's eye, and, later on, I made it. It's my gift for Herven," Baqar concluded his thought.

"That's amazing! I really hope Herven becomes an inspiration to many children," Bagham sent his thought and curled his trunk, exposing his enthusiasm.

"Imagine if an entire generation were motivated by his wisdom, achieving its caste goal, and transitioning to *One Who Created All*," Alanda said out loud.

Bagham snorted softly at the idea and played along. "You want us to be left alone with no one to care for but ourselves? Waiting for more children to arrive would be painful. We need each other," he replied.

"Oh ... I didn't mean it like that," Alanda said covering her mouth to stop another word that could embarrass her.

"The rain should stop soon. I'll see all three of you at sunrise,"

Bagham said. He moved out slowly, leaving the *Artists* to marvel at the little *Orange Soul* who, in his sleep, pulled his hands over his chest, in a praying position.

* * *

THE VILLAGE WOKE to a clear sky and a burning sun. Thick mud, left behind by the drained water, made everyone's walk slow and slippery. After spending the night in the jungle, the bulls returned, carrying bamboo canes and large palm leaves for the cows that stayed closer to the children.

Nukua, newly in charge of the village's responsibilities, attended to the *Commoners*, pointing out that food had to be prepared and the newborns taken outside for a sunbath and fresh air. Then, he went to the gardens to assess any damage. There was nothing that a couple of energy sessions couldn't restore. He moved closer to the *Trees of Life*, looking for Fenuku's and the other two *Commoners*' bodies left behind by their accomplished souls. He found them fallen on one side, but still maintaining the lotus position, their faces displaying a peaceful smile. Their garments were wet and partially covered with twigs and leaves carried by the deluge.

'*The burial ceremony should not be delayed, now that the weather has cleared,*' he thought and looked around for anything else that needed his attention. On the west side of the garden, by the bamboo fence, he noticed Danish, gazing down and muttering to himself words that Nukua couldn't decipher. He wanted to call the *Commoner* to help him reposition the bodies, but he changed his mind. Danish seemed very focused. In an act of desperation he covered his face with his palms and fell to his knees on the wet ground. The tip of his shaved head was still visible from where Nukua was standing.

Excitement and responsibility were tugging at each other inside of the new Council leader, trying to overwhelm his calm nature. He closed his eyes for a moment, interrupting his visual senses, then covered his ears and started a breathing exercise, exhaling worries, doubts and feelings that didn't belong. Shortly after, he felt whole again, loving and loved, ready to face challenges brought upon the village as a way of making them stronger. He will connect with Danish later to understand what caused the distress. Now, sightedness he had more pressing tasks to take care of.

Without their precious load of souls, the *Trees* seemed almost regular, only their blue and purple leaves and spots on the bark, gave away their noble descent. The grass around them displayed no sign of where the empty shells were buried.

"The scars of the ground heal so fast. Those done to our souls, we carry for many incarnations," Nukua said out loud addressing the *Trees*, and waiting for a reaction. Then he continued his monologue with the portals. "Thank you for your blessings, for the seeds and for the *Orange Soul*, you entrusted us with. There are so dear to all of us." He directed his gaze upwards, praying to *One Who Created All*. "The unborn loving *Father*, enshrine your devotional children in *Thy* protective vibration, thus harm evade them, and fill them with undivided attention to *Thee*."

An eruption of protrusive inner warmth followed each time he addressed the *Supreme Being*. Like a rooted blaze that needed a soft, holy blow to reignite his awareness of such connection. He bowed respectfully, then turned his cognizance to the immediate duties that still required his attention. He generated a thought to Altan and to his teacher, Manash, asking them if the elephants were ready to participate in the burial ceremony. Confirmation came back that the herd would not leave the village tonight, so everyone would be present to say their goodbyes.

Returning to the main hall, Nukua chose six *Commoners* to recover the stiff bodies laying in front of the *Trees*, wash them and garb them in fresh clothes, a step that was part of the rite. He encouraged everyone to finish their chores early and get ready. Gifts and best wishes were customary in the presence of an *Orange Soul*. Then he walked to the *Writers*' hut to prepare himself.

Dusk approached the land calmly like a kiss of a wild bee on a flower. Torches were lit and the community gathered by the *Trees*, void now of the glowing peapod lights that gave them their magical appearance. Children and elephants took their places, whose choreography had been repeated thousands of times since the village's existence: the council members and their teachers with their backs to the *Trees*, faced everyone else. The three bodies whose souls had transitioned into the omnipresent consciousness, laid on the ground, waiting to be swallowed by the insatiable land. Their faces had rigid features now, giving the impression of a tormented slumber.

Nukua didn't have to copy any of Fenuku's gestures as the new Council leader, and he had enough confidence on his ability to follow the rituals. "Let's start with thanks to our *Spiritual Father*," he said. "We come to *You* tonight, humbled by *Your* majestic greatness visible all around us. We ask again and again for *Your* love that we will never be able to match, and for *Your* forgiveness when we, in our weakest moments, forget *Your* teachings."

The words, repeated by a chorus of voices, echoed through the village, imbuing the space with a positive vibration. "Receive these shells of the departed and bless all who join us with messages from *You* for our betterment," he continued, feeling, for the first time, the full responsibility and weight that the words carried.

Holding short bamboo sticks in both hands, four *Commoners* stepped closer to the bodies and started a low incantation while hitting the sticks against each other gently to maintain the grave tempo. More children added their voices for a little longer until an underground rumble could be heard.

Beneath the lifeless physical shells of Fenuku and the *Commoners* the ground softened, gradually ingesting them and taking back the discarded matter as nutritious food for the *Trees of Life*. The chanting stopped, concluding the first part of the ceremony.

"Few of us have had the privilege of meeting an *Orange Soul* sibling in person. We've all read stories and marveled at their spiritual skills, and, above all, the burning desire of returning among us as a flare of knowledge. But to encounter two such souls born so close one after another is something that has never happened before. Herven is his name and Bagham is his teacher," Nukua announced happily and stepped sideways to let Alanda, who was holding the boy, come forward. Bagham watched closely from behind.

Alanda raised the newborn above her head so everyone could see the orange birthmarks. His teacher curled his trunk outward, signaling his elation silently. Herven, still in Alanda's hands, squeaked noisily, his body wrapped tight in a white cloth. His eyes were searching through the crowd like two amber charcoals that came to life by a powerful blow. Motivated by Nukua's speech, the villagers began another chant, more animated. They praised the *Trees*, their community life and the one who made everything possible: the *Supreme Being*.

"You can offer your gifts now," the leader said when the chant died down.

The Council members went first. Akila and Fenila, the *Writer* caste girls, each brought one of their stories, the cover encrusted with acacia bark and the title woven with thick blades of tall grass found two days away from the village. *Valdina*, the Builder caste girl, followed, offering a structure composed of three miniature huts, connected by fragile bridges and swing ropes, all glued to a thick rectangle of bamboo paper.

Nukua was last. He bowed in front of Herven, who was still in Alanda's arms, and said, "I wrote this poem for you, *Divine* incarnation. My wish is for us to meet in the astral as well and sing prayers to our *Spiritual Father*." Then he placed his gift on the ground and joined the girls of the Council.

One by one, the remaining members of each caste came forward presenting food dishes, artwork or even just well wishes. Holding onto his decision to wait longer before publicly declaring that he considered himself an *Artist*, Danish presented a bowl of coconut balls dipped in wild honey.

Baqar planned his turn last, so everyone would notice his gift and the blessing that was brought upon him. "Dear *One*, my battered physical form was ready to leave this existence, when the news of your arrival fluttered by my ears. My spirit rekindled and burst with energy that I thought was lost. This is the gift of my regained creation consciousness," he said and presented the artwork given to him by Danish. The old *Artist* felt Herven's gaze fixing him intensely, so a bit intimidated, he turned towards his brothers and sisters for a more dramatic statement.

"You can all see now the impact such an arrival had on me. If it happens to you, come forward and share it with us. I personally feel that before my transition, more artwork will be forged out of these wrinkled hands and tired mind, emboldened by the permanent touch of this wonderful *Orange Soul*," he concluded.

Several elders hugged him gleefully.

"This is an amazing feat for our dear Baqar. It seems that Herven couldn't have had a better caretaker," Nukua said loudly. "Our teachers have decided that in three cycles, when Herven becomes completely aware of his incarnation, he will join the Council as its fifth member." He recited the first part of the opening prayers again. The gifts of food were left on the grass for spirits and critters, but everything else was brought inside the hut where Herven was taken care of.

* * *

THE END OF THE SEVERAL rainy sunrises brought a much needed respite from the overwhelming humidity and the omnipresent mud that made a mess of the villagers' clothing and bamboo sandals. Whatever was salvaged from the gardens was either immediately cooked or dried out for consumption later. The area where the elephants rested looked like an enormous pothole from the pounding of their feet. It still held water and made a perfect replacement for a miniature waterhole where the calves could splash themselves.

Danish stepped out of his hut and instead of heading to the main hall for the evening meal, he hurried down the path to the hut where he knew he would find Baqar. The *Commoner* walked onto the porch and shook his legs to remove some of the mud stuck to his bare feet, then snuck in, looking for the *Artist.* Baqar was alone by Herven's bed. Only two other caretakers were on the far side of the hut, busy with their own chores.

"How are you holding up?" Danish asked in a lower voice, still not sure if Baqar was enjoying this responsibility or putting up a good pretense.

The *Artist* smiled at him, his thin lips almost indistinguishable on the rumpled face. Danish noticed the sparkle in the elder's eyes and the straight posture, a significant improvement of his attitude since their first encounter in the garden. Otherwise he didn't look any bit younger.

"I'm being spoiled by Alanda," Baqar replied while letting his pinkie finger twirl in Herven's tiny hands as distraction. "She's so happy that I've chosen her as my pair that there is nothing she won't do for me. Now she's out to get food." Baqar glanced at the baby. "And this little guy has been good, too. He doesn't sleep much but he's quiet; he gets more agitated when Bagham visits. Mentally, he's active. Sometimes I get a brush of a solitary thought, innocent and peaceful. I don't reply to it, I just assent to it like a fresh breeze on my old soul."

Danish saw a wooden box on the shelf beside the bed and pulled it down to look inside.

"What are you looking for?" the *Artist* asked.

The boy rummaged in it until he found the artwork he had given Baqar to present as his: a bamboo framed yellowish leaf, which had ancient markings painted on it. "Aha! Got it," he said as he held it up for another glance. 'The rain came down so fast that I didn't have the chance to seal the hole where I keep all of my creations. Most of them are damaged, so I have to replace some of the frames and the painted leaves. I want to replicate this one for myself," he explained.

"When are you going to help me create my own piece?" Baqar asked.

"Soon. Let the ground dry for several sunrises, then we'll gather supplies." The *Commoner* turned his attention to Herven whose orange eyes were fixed on him. "Here is my blue hand to play with," he said and let the newborn touch him. Danish felt a faint wave of energy that made his arm shiver, a pleasant tickling that, for a moment, he thought Herven was trying to connect with him. "Why is the color of the triangles on his cheeks so intense? Is that normal?" he asked Baqar.

The *Artist* prickled the skin on his head in an effort to gather his thoughts before answering.

"I asked Bagham about it since it seemed odd to me too. He said it's not normal for his age, but the *Orange Souls* are so different from the rest of us that Herven becoming aware of his surroundings sooner than three cycles shouldn't surprise anyone."

Alanda came in carrying two bowls with salad, one for her and one for Baqar. She didn't want him to eat alone.

"Nice to see you, Danish," she greeted the boy. "Herven is impressive, isn't he?" Alanda was proud of being chosen as a caretaker, and totally dedicated herself to the high responsibility task. Danish couldn't see any visible signs of physical improvement in her, except for her upbeat attitude. The sagging around her eyes and protruded cheeks were even more pronounced, an impending warning of a potential transition.

"You both show him unconditional love and he feels it. His blessings will make the goal of your next incarnation more easily achievable," Danish replied with the right words.

Alanda chuckled and her face reddened with warm emotions.

"I have to go back to my chores," the *Commoner* said, and walked out quickly. He liked the positive changes in Baqar and his unwavering determination to go along with the initial plan. Even if the rain ruined his stashed art pieces, Danish didn't lament much; he decided to bounce back with more intricate designs. While Baqar's announcement made known the rebirth of talent once thought lost, Danish's had to happen differently. With Fenuku's transition, he was left with only one ally in the Council, Nukua. Nevertheless, the reception of Baqar's disclosure from the other brothers and sisters gave him the confidence that his would be met with the same effusion.

Most of the herd was ready to leave for the nocturnal stroll, and Danish caught up with Taber by the main gate. "Taber, I need to confide in you about a marvelous sensitivity that has developed in me, and, until I heard Baqar mention the influence the *Orange Soul* had on him, I didn't dare to share it with anyone else, not even with you," he said humbly.

The elephant sent back a gentle thought of encouragement for him to continue.

"When meditating, there are moments when I feel like an *Artist.* Vivid images of me creating large paintings, depicting the history of our community over hundreds of cycles. In these visions I used strange symbols that I couldn't find in any of the books we study. It began right after Bagham started to respond to the call from the roots where Herven was born. Do you think it's possible I was an *Artist* in a different incarnation?" the boy asked hesitantly.

Taber flapped her ears several times, stomped her right leg and then touched Danish's shaved head with the tip of her trunk as though she were trying to extract more thoughts out of him. Suddenly she seemed nervous.

Danish didn't expect such a reaction. The physical contact could have told Taber more than he really wanted to reveal. His practice of hiding unwanted beliefs deep in the caves of his mind, proved useful now.

There was no reply from the elephant, so he pushed further.

"It creates a duality within me, which is troublesome. My concentration shivers, preventing me from finding the calmness and the blessings of *One Who Created All.* I'm even able to reproduce some of the designs from my visions, but at a smaller scale."

Taber curled her trunk in and looked towards the gate. The cows were outside, waiting for her. "Our common consciousness has no record of anyone coming forward with such a claim. But if the vibratory energy had such impact on Baqar, it might have affected you as well. It's a sign that I don't know how to interpret yet. We'll talk about it tomorrow during the morning lesson," she sent out her conclusion, then turned around and slowly joined the herd.

Left behind, Danish smiled, reassured that his plan of being publicly recognized as an *Artist* would succeed.

The next sunrise Taber summoned him ahead of the other *Commoners.* They met in front of the main hall and this time Danish sensed that his teacher was calmer than the night before.

"I've shared with Altan what you told me about your dream perceptions. He said it is possible, but least expected to happen to a *Commoner.* It's a step backwards for an *Artist* soul if this is really happening."

Danish processed the statement, and while his stomach clenched, preparing for bad news, he kept his face void of any visible reaction and his thoughts hidden, waiting for the rest of Taber's entire feedback.

"We're going to help you clarify if this is the experience of the same soul or if it's a random occurrence that we can't explain. But do you have any intention of using this knowledge?" the teacher pressed another question onto him.

The boy discerned a level of concern emanating from her. He arranged the *Book* under his arm, waved his hand at a storm of mosquitos flying around Taber's trunk then cautiously replied, "Proving how powerful the Orange Soul's energy is on some of us should be appreciated by the whole community. It brought purpose to Baqar's last days among us and to the other elders that, as creativity-famished souls, thought that everything is lost. I want you and Altan to see the results of my dreams and decide if you will change my caste no matter the colour of my hands. If I can create a meaningful piece of art I deserve to be an *Artist*."

Determination in deepening the wisdom of the *Book* and of the other teachings passed down from the common consciousness was encouraged by each and every teacher, but something in Danish's attitude bothered Taber. She had the feeling that he was more interested in the trivial task of validating the potential existence of an *Artist* than redirecting all that energy into a more profound relationship with *One Who Created All*. "How does declaring yourself an *Artist* help you achieve the *state of bliss*?" the elephant asked.

"It might not help me much in this life time, but my name will be recorded in the village's history as the one who, without being an *Orange Soul*, remembered a previous life. Also it might help me return as an *Artist* and accomplish my destiny next time," the boy replied, his last words extending into a large smile.

Taber finally grasped the flaw in her pupil's behaviour: his ego was still housed in the material form of his body and mind, feeding him grandiose delusions of a maya-based reality. The shallowness of his misunderstanding of everything he had learnt so far came forward unobstructed by any protective veil. She felt weak and helpless, and, at the same time, responsible for his short-sightedness. "Let me talk to Altan again. If he agrees, he might ask you to hold onto the announcement until Herven becomes a fully aware *Orange Soul*. Having his blessing would add even more weight to the revelation and to the written record," Taber suggested in a firm voice.

Danish wanted to oppose the idea. He couldn't wait two or three more cycles. He craved the recognition and felt entitled, but he also had to admit that his teacher's recommendation had merit. "You're right," he concluded and touched Taber's forehead as a thank you.

"In the meantime, no one is preventing you from forging future artistic visions. Keep them to yourself until the time comes," the elephant said.

She was sad that she had to use Herven as an excuse. She hoped that the *Orange Soul*'s awakening would clarify the *Commoner*'s murky judgment. She raised her trunk and purred loudly, welcoming the other pupils who approached for the morning lesson.

The group moved slowly out of the village towards their favourite spot in the jungle.

CHAPTER 11

Become one with the tides of life as that of a humble leaf riding on the currents of a river and flow through time with a clear sense of direction and determination. All the while, avoid the rocks that break the surface of this river and disturb the natural ebb. These rocks, though seemingly random, are obstacles carefully interspersed by The One Who Created All to test your faith in Him when it would be so easy to simply latch on to one for fear of drowning.

From the book *We Are One* – Chapter 11

NARANTA OWNED A ONE-BEDROOM APARTMENT on the fifth floor of one of the newest buildings in the district west of Banaar's headquarters. Although she had moved in with Prakit two years ago, she had decided to keep the apartment for herself. She did this not out of fear that their relationship would suddenly cease and she would be left homeless, but because from time to time she desired a place of solitude. A place to exist without any external interference. And now, after Bart's recent regime, a place to meditate.

She didn't do this to intentionally avoid Prakit. Naranta loved him and it was this love that drove her to secret away the parts of her that she despised. The parts she did not want to expose Prakit to and potentially corrupt him.

While larger than her apartment, Prakit's own home was just big enough to turn one corner of the living room into a makeshift office by mounting a shelf full of specialty books on top of a desk buried under piles of thick folders and crumpled pieces of paper.

Its size also served to bring them closer together, but at the same time, she yearned for space. Maybe it was naïve to keep the apartment. While she presently strove to better herself in its confines, it also presented freedom and a means to revert to old habits. At least in Prakit's apartment, they were constantly in close quarters so she would have no opportunity to get high without Prakit's knowledge of it. Though, this same advantage had adverse side effects on her mental health.

She became increasingly self-conscious with Prakit around her so frequently. While it was not in his kind nature, and despite being unfair to accuse him of this, Naranta could not shake the feeling that he was judging her. Constantly and relentlessly scrutinizing her every thought and action, which set her nerves on edge and made it that much harder to stay clean. All she wanted to do was dull the pins and needles that seemed to make up every surface in Prakit's apartment.

Her apartment was not completely barren. Some of her personal effects had remained behind since they weren't important enough to justify cluttering their new living quarters. Some items were left behind intentionally, such as the mattress that lay on the floor, for when she broke and needed a place to mend. Some clothes still hung in the closet, covered in plastic to save them from an invasion of dust. However, the rest of the apartment wasn't so lucky.

Several metal rings that linked the translucent curtains in the living room to the curtain rod were missing and the material sagged in places, letting light permeate the room and exposing a thick layer of dust on any surface it found.

Ironically, the ineffectiveness of the curtain allowed Naranta to better navigate the shards of broken glass littering the kitchen floor. It was a sort of twisted beauty that made the dangerous debris glitter so magnificently. She unconsciously thought her own shortcomings might actually make her dazzle more brilliantly as well, but she quickly pushed the thought out of her head. She rushed through the fragments towards the broom and felt embarrassed at her own lack of self-control. The glass was not there as decoration; they were the remains of several glasses she had smashed during her last visit two days ago.

The outburst had occurred when she decided to quiet her ego in an attempt to meditate. Sitting in the lotus position brought excruciating pain to her legs after only several minutes, undermining any effort to focus on the point between her eyebrows. She shuffled left and right, uneasy, as if she were sitting on termites biting into her flesh. Frustration got the best of her, giving her a splitting headache that generated the smashing as a desirable release.

She was too irritated to clean up the glass at the time. Careful to pick up every last shard of glass, she swept it to the trashcan in the corner of the kitchen only to find it overflowing with empty food containers that she kept saying she would throw away. Eventually.

With an audible sigh, Naranta left the pile of glass by the trash and moved into the living room.

She sat down in the corner of the room, the spot she frequented the most and also the cleanest area in the entire apartment. It was almost as if an invisible energy kept all impurities at bay since the spot was devoid of dust, but it was actually all her doing, a sign of respect to the *Supreme Being.*

The entire space was simply comprised of a square, burgundy woolen carpet that she now sat on and a low table right in front of her. Upon the table a small vase held violets and a half-burnt scented candle. Stuck on the wall opposite her at approximately eye level was a piece of paper containing motivational remarks from Bart outlining the necessity of meditation and cheering her on. She rolled her eyes.

She didn't approve of Bart all that much, but Prakit and the other scientists all held him in such high esteem. She almost felt as if it was her duty to remain rebellious against Bart because someone had to be the antagonist of the group and hold opposing opinions. She was already unpopular among the others due to her past drug problems so she had no problem shouldering the responsibility of the pariah. She had Prakit at least. He had convinced her to listen to Bart, as least as far as the meditation was concerned.

Prakit and Merlaya publicly acknowledged their intention of meditating, but she wanted to do it on her own terms, and not be forced to display results, if, in the end, she couldn't produce any. They didn't have the addiction that had haunted her for the last several years. What started as a treatable medical problem for a visible and painful spasm of her thigh muscles, generated by a concussion during a hiking trip, ended with surgery to release the pressure on nerves that were pinched down to the bone. The torment, before and after the intervention, hollowed her out, turning her into a screaming ghost as her body shrunk and borrowed an unhealthy pallor. Nothing could keep the scorching throbbing at bearable levels except for powerful drugs that hospitals were allowed to use in small quantities and as a temporary palliative. But the determination not to miss any university classes made her rely on increased quantities before realizing that she couldn't control the craving anymore.

She turned her focus to the present moment, thinking that she still couldn't completely grasp the concept explained by Bart and she needed extensive practice to hone it. And patience was not on her side, especially when her disgruntled brain couldn't stop sending a litany of signals about missing stimuli that her deprived body had to somehow produce using the scarcity of its own resources.

Naranta had to stay clean because the alternative was a bleak existence in Laeta, pleasuring others, and where the payment in drugs would have prolonged her addiction to the end of her days. None of Korobat's drug-free policy companies would offer her a job if Banaar had any suspicion that she was consuming again. Losing this job would mean losing everything. Even Prakit might turn his back on her if past excesses would resurface with the same intensity.

The woman tightened her feet in the lotus position, shook her head vigorously, sending any unwanted thoughts away, then fervently started reciting the affirmations and praying to *One Who Created All* for help.

* * *

HANDO DECIDED THAT THE MEETING with Tonio Clapel would take place in a more relaxed environment, at his home. This lowered any tension recently built around everyone close to them. He invited him over with his wife, so both women could have some quality time while they discussed how to handle one of the most delicate city crises in a long time. Sophia's cooking was superb. It was nothing ostentatious–food that she and Hando would eat on a regular basis–but deliciously prepared and amazingly presented.

The well-done salmon was marinated in a mixture of white wine, thyme and rosemary herbs, while the potatoes received a pinch of turmeric and cayenne. A dressing made of wild honey, garlic and more herbs was served on the side. A homemade cake of cacao and strawberries from Laeta concluded a relaxing dinner.

There was nothing else more important on the men's minds since the attack on the White Tiger transport other than finding a less painful solution to the city's problem.

"I ran some budget numbers to see if arming more volunteers would make any sense," said Hando, sipping from a glass of white wine, after the men retired to his office. "We don't have enough funds. Even if we convince Spark Industries to advance us more electro-shockers, we have nothing to offer in return. I could talk to both Banaar and Artilla as they are still the major shareholders of the company. Self-preservation is the only reason that we could obtain leniency in acquiring the additional devices." Tonio completely filled the armchair he was sitting on. He put the empty glass down on the table beside him and presented his point of view.

"It doesn't matter if we get the electro-shockers for free or not, we don't have enough volunteers ready to risk their lives. At least no one local. We might be able to find a handful of mercenaries in Laeta, desperate for cash to go against White Tiger. But they will be very unreliable and unpredictable. It might give more confidence to the existing ranks. But as you said, there is no budget left for this."

"I can convince the council to shift funds from one department to another if this is the only solution available to us," Hando said, and pulled his right leg on top of the other. He sounded encouraging, knowing he held sway with his colleagues. "But to be honest," he continued, "helping the Tanas gives me an uneasy feeling. They broke too many handshakes in just days. Being on their side would only reassure them that future mistakes would have no repercussions. *Bolder and bolder* would become their motto."

"So do you prefer a seat on the White Tiger's side? A much safer bet if you ask me," Tonio voiced what Hando had in mind.

Martinez straightened himself in the armchair, grabbed the bottle of wine from the table and filled both glasses. "If we go that route, it stays between you and me, and no one else. You heard the council–we have full support in whatever we decide to do." Hando knew that such a strategy had to be done in a more subtle way than just officially backing the gang in the east against the Tanas. "Let's pay our friends a visit, show our concern about their actions and see if they'll continue this irresponsible tactic of pissing everyone off."

Clapel nodded in agreement, but added his thoughts too. "They won't stop, especially after they've tasted an easy victory. I expect them to ask us to join forces in case there is retaliation."

"And we have to play the charade of being upset because of the danger they put the whole city in. After that, get your bags ready for the trip east. Our safety depends on your power of persuasion. I'll call a council meeting as soon as you're back."

They dried their glasses and joined their wives' conversation about the tomato crops they had obtained from their miniature gardens.

* * *

"ENTITLEMENT. THIS IS HOW the Tanas behave. They told us that they feel entitled to a protection fee for any drug transport crossing city lands. The thin layer of diplomacy the elders had has vanished along with their deaths. Tonio and I saw it again first hand," Martinez declared loudly, gesticulating his hands while doing his back-and-forth in the council room.

As promised, he had called an emergency council meeting as soon as Tonio Clapel was back safe from meeting the White Tiger leaders.

"Both brothers were high, and even sniffed a line or two in front of us to give themselves more courage. There is no way that either us or White Tiger can reason with them," Hando continued, drops of saliva gathering at the corners of his mouth. "At least they were considerate enough to share ten percent with the city as a sign of good faith. It's crazy. They think that we are as corrupt as they are," he said sardonically.

The city leader was quite upset with the attitude of the brothers, the sneers on their faces when mentioning that moving forward they would make the rules, still haunted him. Sending Clapel to negotiate an alliance with the White Tiger proved to be the right decision that would save lives in the city and its long-term peace.

"Those audacious scum bags don't care about the rest of us if a gang war starts in the city. We are just a liability to them," Martinez continued his tirade, looking at the worried faces in front of him.

Mirena Vande stopped him and asked what everyone else wanted to ask. "What's the solution to push them back into the previous limits of common sense? Why involve the White Tiger?"

The leader pushed his eyeglasses up his nose again, checked the positioning of the jack on the back of his skull, then divulged the plot they'd been working on. "No matter how we look at the Tanas's erratic behaviour, they've become a liability. A noticeable one that can't be trusted anymore. On the other hand, the White Tiger is all business; according to Tonio's discreet research, they keep their agreements."

Clapel knew it was his turn to intervene and provide more details. "There is no doubt in our minds that the Tanas wouldn't accept the old terms Hando had in place or any new ones that would restrict their version of additional power and wealth. We have to eliminate them completely. And when I say "we", I mean helping the White Tiger do that for us."

The council remained quiet, in expectation of potentially more evidence that would make the agreement to such a drastic measure easier. The MOU's chief crossed his enormous palms behind his freshly shaved head and continued. "My mission was to convince them that we're serious and honest on getting rid of our city gang. I explained the reason openly and in the end I put forward our offer. It didn't take long for them to deliberate. I have the feeling that their spies infiltrated the city after the attack, confirming everything I said."

"And how are you planning on doing it?" inquired Artilla in a voice that suggested relief at some action.

"Another White Tiger transport will leave for Laeta in four days. Information will be leaked about its contents, high-quality powder, a jackpot for the Tanas, who already received the official rejection of the protection fee. So they are pissed and ready to attack again."

Clapel grabbed a pen and a piece of paper and started to scribble on it how everything would fall into place.

"This is the city." He drew a circle. "And here is the swamp and the highway to Laeta." He added a wiggly area north of the circle and a straight line to the left of it. It was sketchy, but good enough to serve as a battle map.

"The transport will stop two miles outside of the city, beside the swamp. Flat tire, engine issues, something that will look real and supposedly keep the White Tiger's goons preoccupied. Nevertheless, they will expect the Tanas' attack. There won't be any drugs in those vehicles, just warriors."

"Why would the Tanas attack?" Elenadore Tam asked.

Tonio smiled and let Hando answer, as it was his plan. As usual, Hando was efficient and diabolical. "Because we'll tell them to do it, pointing at the fact that White Tigers are sitting ducks. There is more to the plan then what Tonio has already shared."

He asked for the pen and kept adding to the drawing.

"We'll tell Tanas to split their force and send half of it north behind the hills, right where the transport will stop. Hypothetically, the White Tiger will be in the middle with no chance of survival, being attacked from both the south and the north. We decided that a complete eradication is required, so we took extreme measures to be sure that none of the Tanas survive. Tonio's unit will stay behind to identify and kill any warrior that somehow escapes the bloodbath and tries to sneak south. In fact we want our volunteers to be safe and not exposed to the battle in any way."

Hando looked around to be sure that he got their full attention, then continued. "Tonight and tomorrow, three buses carrying warriors, disguised as tourists heading to Laeta, will arrive in town. We've already arranged for replacements to continue the trip so no suspicion will be raised. These warriors will attack the Tanas' main force from behind, while another group will hide up the road."

Martinez completed the battle plan with the White Tiger locations, giving everyone the full picture of how the local gang would be smashed in between experienced fighters, with no chance of survival.

"Impressive!" exclaimed Artilla, still a little skeptical of the level of synchronization required.

"If everything goes well, all the bodies can be dumped into the swamp. The White Tiger has agreed to take care of it. This is the scenario we've rehearsed. Of course, only the people in this room know what's really going to happen," concluded Hando, proud that he made them speechless once again.

"You still haven't told us what we offer in return," Banaar asked.

"Yes, our offer." Hando played with his ponytail for a moment and took off his eyeglasses as part of his ritual to gather his thoughts. "Intuition told me that the White Tiger might be interested in diversifying outside the drug trade to create additional sources of revenue. I was right. We offered them a couple of things. One, Tanas' existing manufacturing site. They will bring a limited number of workers and update the equipment. The main mandate of this location is to supply Laeta and several other cities to the south. It saves them transportation costs and there'll be no more opposition to stand against them. Second, I gave them exclusive rights to the east region to the *bliss technology* we are working on. Their distribution networks in that part of the world is impressive and strengthens our business relations."

He sat down. There was nothing else to share.

"Are you mad?" Mirena Vande's reaction took everyone by surprise. "What if we can't deliver on this technology?" She understood the challenges faced by the technical team. Her fingers clenched in fists on the table were void of blood, her lips pursed tight, demanding an answer.

Hando didn't panic, but calmly removed a piece of white thread off his pants, held the woman's fiery gaze and replied. "Mirena, your concern is valid and also covered in our agreement with the White Tiger. If the *bliss* device is not functional within the next twenty-four months, they will accept an improvement of one of the technologies they use today, under the same terms."

Martinez felt drowsy and dropped his head in his palms, searching his thoughts for any other detail he might have missed.

"I'll share the contract with you shortly, so there are no more assumptions and worries about what was agreed upon." He turned from Mirena to the rest. "We are under a lot of pressure these days, but we have to keep it together and push forward. We are facing a terrible crisis. I am aware that things could go wrong and all our efforts might go down the drain, but the only option available to us will unfold at the end of next week."

Martinez's energy had almost run out. He felt like lying down for a deep sleep from which he would wake up after the Tanas were dealt with so he bared no responsibility for the attack. He would have rather talked about the positive, less aggressive events developing in Korobat. "Speaking of our progress ... how are we making out with Rakash?" he asked Banaar.

Without hesitation, the businessman started his impromptu report in a concise business-like tone. "The boy is being monitored four hours daily, two hours of meditation in the morning and two in the early evening. He spends the remaining time in a gifted children's class under Mirena's close supervision. Prakit and Merlaya have their own meditation schedule, and next week Bart and the team will have the opportunity to read the notes highlighting any behavioural changes. Nothing else unusual."

Hando turned to Mirena and nodded for her update.

"I did what you asked me," she responded, "and, integrated him with kids his age. They have above average intellect and he fits right in. He stays there for half a day and I can see it on his face that he enjoys it. The boy misses that type of interaction. Initially, the others were a bit unsettled around him, but that phase has passed. This learning curve might positively impact how he feels while meditating. It's obvious that his attitude and morale have improved. I'll keep you informed on any further developments."

Elenadore Tam was next. "I can report the same conclusive changes in Bart's demeanor. Do you remember how he was trying to cover his damaged head? Not anymore or at least less often. Acceptance of how he looks is an important step forward. He doesn't feel estranged anymore. And no, we didn't fall in love with each other, in case you were wondering,'" she rolled her eyes in the leader's direction.

Everyone laughed.

"As you suggested, I showed him around the city. We went to the library, the Scholars Academy and several labs. He was excited. While Rakash is at school, he is at the library reading or researching. There is visible progress on him too."

'At least this part of the plan is moving as intended,' thought Martinez. He said out loud: "Thank you all for sticking to our arrangement. Let's try to keep everyone safe for the next several days until we sort out this Tanas issue."

The gathering dispersed quietly, affected by the gruesome decisions they tacitly concurred with. Killing their own people was a heavy burden.

Bart's research and the books he read on the villagers made Hando aware that *One Who Created All* would condemn his plan. It was a violation of the principles Rakash and the *Supreme Being* stood for: love, compassion and forgiveness. What would these thugs do if they had to choose between death or shifting their consciousness to an elevated level devoid of any memory of revenge, destruction and violence? He wouldn't find out since they were all going to die soon.

* * *

SEVERAL CONSECUTIVE, SUCCESSFUL meditation sessions raised the team's morale in finding a way to induce the same feelings that Rakash experienced. Fascination over the orange triangles that brightened during the boy's trances, caught everyone's imagination, already playing similar pleasurable scenarios in their minds. They were likely witnessing the most important scientific event of their professional lives. Whoever had doubts about the existence of *One Who Created All* and *His* communication with Rakash, couldn't muster a word of reluctance any longer. They turned into believers, ready to join the ranks of those who had enrolled for the preparatory stage before proceeding with the meditation sessions on their own. Great enthusiasm and energy webbed them together, like turning an estranged family into a tightly knit one that realized the advantages of united efforts.

Even the council members appeared one day at the lab to observe how one of the initiatives that began as a pilot with a very low chance of success, was taking shape vigorously into a well-defined project. There was no more guessing involved; it was a structured process, scientifically applied so the end results could be backed up by conclusive data. Bart's unexplained faith in a story became the unlikely alternative for regaining the unconditional respect of his peers away from home.

Aside from periods when the entire team was watching the oscilloscopes and monitors while Rakash meditated on pre-determined words or mantras, the after session discussions were the trophy no one wanted to miss. The boy, turned storyteller and aroused their imagination with his revived ancient memories and sensations.

"I can say with certainty that the messages I receive from *One Who Created All* are related to the word or mantra I focus on. This time I felt the love of all the other souls resting in the astral plane. A protective blanket wrapped my body like a cocoon in which I could find the means for enhancing my own love for them. A reciprocal exchange that elevated my soul," explained Rakash at the end of one session.

"Next I thought about compassion. I almost lost my breath under an unsettled heaviness. There is so much suffering in this world and so little compassion. It's difficult for me to explain faith and compassion. You need to feel them in your heart, a burning desire up and down your body, like the wave on that monitor." Rakash felt disappointed that he had no other way to convey the amazing transformations his mind witnessed in a state of awareness.

"We focus a lot on the brain's reactions, but is the physical body going through a similar metamorphosis?" Merlaya asked, interested in monitoring her own body for known signs.

Rakash pulled a shawl over his shoulders to warm himself.

"I'm more interested in the spiritual experience of the mind," said Rakash. "I'm convinced that positive changes are taking place at a cellular level. I don't know how they can be measured."

He grabbed several walnuts to regain his vigor. Everyone was waiting for more insight.

"Master, do you remember that time I felt vibrations inside my body?" the villager asked Bart. "Lately, the intensity and clarity have increased. There are specific sounds that come and go if I move my focus from one internal location to another. It's like each organ has its own vibratory language that I want to understand. In these instances my body seems hollow, just an acoustic shell housing a beautiful harmony of sounds."

Then he turned to Merlaya to address her previous question. "Maybe this resonance, in a pure, high frequency, is what would improve the organs' functionality and the only visible sign would be a positive attitude through joy, happiness and love, concepts we keep coming back to."

"It's still a challenge for me to quiet my mind, let alone identify such subtle markers, but this is something to be conscious of as I progress," she said, making a note in her journal.

"You're right. I'm a long way from such finesse," added Prakit, trying not to give any false hope to the audience.

"Don't say that," said Rakash. "*One Who Created All* is listening to you now and if your faith wavers, *He* will stay away, withholding any encouragement that he was ready to offer. I told you before that faith, intention and intensity is what attracts *Him* to us, *His* spiritual children. Don't make yourself less valuable in *His* eyes. Fight for *His* love and attention."

Prakit fell silent, absorbing the unexpected lesson. He'd noticed changes in his overall behaviour. He was much calmer and less reactive to the daily craziness. All noted in his diary to be shared with everyone else soon.

Bart was enjoying the spectator role, watching a new bond develop between the boy and this extremely talented young team. They were treating him with respect and no condescendence. The sincerity of this contribution broke down the age barrier and any other deep, embedded, generational blockage. They unconditionally accepted Rakash as a source of knowledge from which they could learn for years to come. Discretely, the scholar looked at Naranta, whose changed brashness intrigued him the most. For the first time since he met her, her entire face was visible, hair pulled behind her ears. She had smooth skin that needed more sun exposure. Her hands had a less pronounced tremor and she didn't have to shove them in her pockets all the time. She hadn't enlisted for private meditations, so he wasn't sure what had caused the change.

A radiant Rakash was in the middle of a mature crowd, explaining the principles of sharing as imbued into his being by the countless experiences of the *Orange Souls* that preceded him.

"I also believe that the internal change would reflect our own perception now. It's like they never existed before. Our brain's neural network, as you, Naranta, explained to me, can re-wire itself to accommodate and adapt to the stimulus uncovered in the silence of meditation."

"So in other words, I should observe how my existing habits will evolve in a direction I had never previously thought of," Merlaya reflected out loud.

They were all anticipating the boy's reaction since they sensed that the conversation could be extended to everyone's delight.

"An innate intelligence inhabits our body. *One Who Created All* is beaming life into us, temporarily lending our souls *His* own intelligence as a sign of reinforcement for the daunting task of enlightenment. But it's up to us to push forward and develop our brains with the correct messages," Rakash explained in a grave tone to enhance the notion.

During one of her short meditation sessions, Naranta had admitted that her demons had to be conquered with relentless effort. There were too many questions she never knew she needed answers for. "What happens to our personality when the *state of bliss* becomes preponderant in our daily life?" she asked.

A daring question, and a new challenge for Rakash since no one else knew how to attempt answering except him. He didn't rush into it. He mentally asked for help from the encompassing wisdom of *One Who Created All.* He looked intently for any manifestation of energy in his mind. A smile broadened on his face. The boy put his palms together and bowed his head, thanking *Him* for the guidance.

They all observed the delicate communication, an indisputable exchange between the physical world and an intangible, omnipresent *Spirit*. *'In time, would they be able to open similar channels?'* a thought sparked in the boy's mind.

"A strong-willed person might not accept what I'm about to say; however, once on this path, we have to surrender to *His* greatness. Our ego holds us back, whispering deceptive words into a weakened ear by the elusive *maya*. But once destroyed, the fight is over. What we call personality would melt in the sea of universal consciousness, becoming wave and sea at the same time."

It was an enticing perspective that even Naranta would enjoy: relinquishing the struggles of an elusive betterment. An equal opportunity for all of *His* children, villagers or not, to escape the ephemeral realm they were assigned to.

"One can channel the vitality used to maintain their strong ego into ways of breaking away from bad habits and enslaving thoughts. Once we realize the narrow scope of the ego and consciously detach from it, it will be an easier decision to let it go," added Rakash, standing up, a sign that he was done for the day.

Bart, who had been observing the crowd, wanted a quick summary of the week's achievements. "We have a pretty good idea which areas of the brain respond to love and compassion. Moving forward, we will change the words and repeat the process. Anything interesting to report from your end?" he addressed Merlaya and Prakit.

The two looked at each other, and the woman went first. "I've been following your instructions, and keeping the meditation schedule the same length, a minimum of one hour per session. Edgy thoughts still crowd my mind at the beginning, but as I keep steady, I usually manage to calm down, empty my mind and enter a relative state of emptiness. Your advice on setting up initial expectations was invaluable. Before I start, I repeat this to myself as a reminder: *long-term benefits*. I'm done with short-term gratification. That's pretty much everything. We can go into more details next week."

Bart nodded, pleased, and waited for Prakit.

"I'm going through the same baseline process. Only by being constant can we begin to generate irrefutable data. I've also noticed that I'm calmer now. I can categorically link it with the meditation sessions. We all know that Naranta isn't the calmest person on the team and most of the time her anxiety and panic attacks affect me involuntarily. Not so much anymore. In fact, I've found her less restless as well. Maybe the influence has reversed tide and my state touches her."

That this relationship was finally mentioned publicly took Bart by surprise. He didn't notice an angry reaction from Naranta, solidifying his theory that a certain transformation was taking place inside her. In private, he had started his own observation log on these volunteers, so he set a mental reminder for himself to add Naranta's name to it, intrigued by her improved demeanor.

"Thank you, everyone," Bart said.

The discussion was over. The team flocked to a corner for a quick chat of their own before dispersing for the day.

"Wait for me in the hallway," said the scholar when Rakash approached him so they could both return to their apartment together. "I need to finalize my scribbling in the observation log. There are certain aspects we'll talk about later."

In the last couple of days, during their private and extended discussions, Bart had noticed that Rakash had become aware of the feeling of inclusion that was so predominant in the village. A properly created milieu, suitable to meditation, had improved his development radically in a very short time. The higher frequencies moving through the boy's body worked in a strange way, making his physical form less dense and more energetic. Intuitively, he knew that this was a good sign on the path of conscious transition. The scholar watched his protégé leave the room and the door closing behind him. He turned his attention to his notes.

In the hallway, Rakash went to the window and leaned his head on the warm surface. The sun's fiery rays were more bearable behind the protective screen. He felt a tap on his shoulder. Happy and radiant as always, Hando greeted him.

"If you are looking for master, he will be out any moment now," said Rakash and tried to turn his gaze back to the outside world that fascinated him so much.

The leader told the boy that he received constant reports from his colleagues on any activity that took place in the lab. It was all positive news, so Rakash wasn't sure why he kept coming himself to check on them. "I've heard the good news regarding your progress. It's very encouraging."

Rakash smiled, not knowing if any comments were expected of him.

"I hope you don't mind, but I have to ask you a question that bothered me after your master explained to us how you ended up in Laeta." Hando gently grabbed the boy by the elbow, moving closer to the glass box and away from the lab's door. "Why didn't your teacher or anyone else from the village come looking for you? You're a special soul that's very important to your community."

It was an unexpected occasion for Martinez to start drawing a wedge between the two. With a gang war on their doorstep, this might be the only chance to plant the seed of doubt for the next while.

Rakash felt his calm rattled by such a simple inquiry. "I have no memory of what the elephants would do if one of us ever went missing," he said, his mind searching a bit deeper for any trace of such evidence.

"Don't you feel betrayed that they gave up on you so easily?" pushed Hando. "They're your family. We fight to keep our families together and protect those we care about. It shouldn't be different with yours."

Rakash sensed that the leader had touched a sensitive spot in his psyche. He had always accepted the lack of a search party for him as a normal reaction embedded into the village's millennia-long way of living. Why would he feel doubt now? He was speechless and stared blankly at Martinez who said goodbye and went inside the lab to also greet Bart.

* * *

"WE'VE CLOSED THE SOUTH AND EAST exists to the highway and we've received confirmation from Laeta that no tourists are leaving town for Korobat," Clapel informed Hando, who joined the gang's leaders earlier to monitor the situation personally. "They've come up with an impromptu

Parade Day to keep them busy. The White Tiger warriors are getting ready, waiting for a signal as soon as the Tanas have moved out to attack."

Hando had just returned from a quick tour of several locations to be sure that the announcement to stay indoors had reached everyone. The city was almost deserted, only the downtown area had some life left to it.

The MOU force consisted of sixty men, all in official gear and equipped with electro-shockers. They were given firm instructions to stay behind and secure the Tanas' retreat if necessary. Not a word about the understanding between the city's officials and the White Tiger was breathed, in case any sympathizers had infiltrated their ranks.

Part of the Tanas gang was already stationed behind the low hills covered in knee-high grass by the road, with the remaining majority led by the brothers, hidden inside two dilapidated buildings near the highway from where they could monitor the incoming traffic. They were supposed to advance as soon as the White Tiger's trucks passed the hills, squeezing them in between.

It wasn't even mid-day when the vehicles appeared in the distance as four small black dots on the road. The gang members fretted, anticipating the excitement of spilling blood. Most of them were already high, their artificial empowerment giving them the illusion of invincibility.

At the meeting with the White Tiger, it was suggested that the transport pass early in the day while the sun was still up, not to give any surviving Tanas the opportunity of hiding in the marshes.

The dots grew larger, passing the hills and suddenly stopped as Hando expected. Black smoke billowed from under the hood of the first vehicle. This was the sign Clapel was waiting for to embolden the attack. He approached the Tanas brothers, two stocky men that were laughing uncontrollably, and pointed at the White Tiger's stupidity of sending out an important transport using faulty vehicles. Tonio didn't fear them, but seeing their broken and rotten teeth again, their callous look and the thick curvy 'T' tattooed on their necks, reminded him why they had to perform such radical measures. They needed to be eliminated; otherwise their sick inclinations and unruly characters would affect the entire city.

"It can't get sillier than that," Clapel said, playing their tune. "They're sitting ducks. What do you think about advancing immediately? This should be a quick win for you."

By asking first, the chief gave the brothers the opportunity to take credit for initiating the charge.

"Yeah, yeah. Get on the buses, let's show these fuckers a warm local welcome," Zirin, the older of the two, yelled orders. His hairy arms poked the air feverishly, imagining that he was already cutting down the wayward warriors that encumbered on their territory. "They don't pay, they don't pass. That's the rule."

Several thugs hurried to open the rusty doors of the hideout, while the others started loading themselves onto the two old model buses that were discontinued in Laeta a while ago, but were still reliable enough to travel short distances. The doors and most of the windows were gone, but the paint was relatively fresh, displaying the malefic curvy T. They moved out slowly, then picked up speed when they reached the highway's shoulder. They drove in parallel, blocking any potential escape of the White Tiger vehicles stuck behind the one in smoke. It was a stupid move on the Tanas' part, thought Tonio, giving away their intention before getting close, another sign of egotistic behaviour.

The distances between the gangs shortened. Two of the White Tiger vehicles maneuvered onto the incoming lane, driving towards the Tanas' buses in a defying move. Martinez and Clapel, along with the MOU unit, watched the action unfolding from a distance.

Zirin blew a horn several times, signaling the group behind the hills to attack.

Clapel noticed, as per the discussed plan, how one of the White Tiger trucks sped up, taking a lead position in the middle of the road. The steep hills on the left, and the deep ravine edging the marshes on the right, left the Tanas with no option to retreat except to push ahead into the oncoming vehicle that revealed no sign of slowing down. Tonio could even distinguish a painted smiley face on the front grille of White Tiger truck that was gaining even more speed, an ultimate affront to the egotistic brothers that had no idea they were living their last moments. Suddenly, the second White Tiger truck slowed down to an almost complete stop in a choreographed move, waiting for the impact ahead.

Then metal hit metal, Tanas gaining ground on impact for just a few moments before the hundred liters of gas placed in the sacrificial vehicle ignited, and flew through the missing windows, turning Korobat's thugs into burning torches. Another explosion followed, the engines blew over, spreading charred body parts on the road. After the initial shock, the screaming started, the men sitting at the back of the bus, and protected by the people in front of them, jumped out with lacerations on their heads and hands, dizzy and completely unaware of the eighty White Tiger warriors approaching them from behind to finish the job, with more coming out of the second truck that stopped before the blow.

The highway grew black with thick smoke, whirling higher and higher by winds curious about the scuffle. Tonio squinted his eyes to assess the height of the dark column, then his gaze went back to the battlefield.

The remaining Tanas climbed down from the hills, saw the carnage and froze. In a desperate attempt of revenge they charged what they thought was a handful of warriors left around the disabled truck, only to be surrounded by a third group, who, as instructed, had no intention of sparing anyone's life. In less than fifteen minutes, the job was done. Then, the clean up started. Dead bodies were thrown or pushed down the ravine, piling up at the edge of the marshes. In the end, the only visible signs of the gruesome fight were pools of blood drying in the sun and the burning buses.

Thick metal cables were hooked to the metal skeletons and dragged off the road, back to the buildings where they'd come from.

Clapel's unit of volunteers looked horrified at the ferocity and fighting discipline of the White Tiger warriors, and was even more scared the moment bodies were dumped into the marshes, thinking that they were next. They were ready to turn and run, but both Tonio and Martinez stood firm, explaining that everything was planned.

"The White Tiger are here to help us not kill us," said Tonio to put his unit at ease. "The Tanas had gotten out of control and were planning to attack any new transport crossing Korobat. There would have been an open war with potential civilian casualties."

"What if they betray the agreement?" asked one of the volunteers.

"The White Tiger know that we are not professional fighters that stand a chance against their numbers. They will honour the agreement as they have no interest in taking over and running a city. It's too much work for them."

Clapel sensed the panic subside, so he exposed a little bit more of what the parties had agreed upon. "Most of the district controlled by the Tanas will be ours again to take care of. The White Tiger only wants two or three buildings to run their operations. Nothing else."

"Will the bodies be left where they are?" inquired another unit member.

Tonio looked at Hando, asking for help.

"There are too many of them to dig graves, and honestly, I don't want the thugs to be buried in town. I suggest we go down to the ravine and push them further into the swamp, otherwise we might have a scene on our hands, with tourists stopping by and looking at the putrefying corpses. Not a good way of promoting the city."

Hando had decided on this radical measure after his investigation on the gang members concluded that only a few fathered children, and, based on their erratic behaviour, the dead wouldn't be missed.

"Let's go. I want to identify the Tanas brothers among the dead and do whatever clean up is left. The city is secure now, this is what you have to remember. Our families are safer," he concluded and moved out towards the marshes, followed by the entire unit.

* * *

"BART'S DEAD!" a disheveled Hando yelled, busting open Banaar's office door. He approached the businessman's desk as if in a trance, propped his hands on the edge and said it again. "He's dead!"

Hando's face was very pale and Huitan Banaar had never seen him so frightened and panicked before, not even when handling the Tanas massacre. Blood stained both his shirt and pants, and his hair had escaped the orderly arrangement of his ponytail. A small cut on his left cheek was still bleeding.

He sank into a chair, unable to shake off the agitation that convulsed his body.

"What happened?" Huidan asked.

Almost sobbing, Martinez gathered his breath and cleared his voice. "I took him to the west district to show him the Tanas' lair. He was curious to see what was left behind. We drove around for a while, inspected the dilapidated buildings by the highway, then we stopped for a bite at Julie's. The patio had only several customers. We weren't in a rush, so we took our time. Suddenly two teenagers walking by jumped at us with knives. Just before making their move I saw the Tanas 'T' tattooed on their necks. Bart had no chance to react since they took him from behind. One guy stabbed him, the other one came after me. I stumbled backwards on my chair, evading his knife. That gave Karitan, who was waiting by the car, enough time to knock him out. When we checked on Bart it was too late. He died of multiple stab wounds. What're we going to tell Rakash?"

"Where is Bart now?" Banaar asked, clearly shaken by this turn of events.

"A medical team took him to the nearby hospital. He needs to be washed before Rakash sees him. Blood was everywhere. It was nasty."

"You'll need to clean up too. I'll round up the council. You get ready and come up with a plan to possibly mitigate this crisis."

Martinez couldn't comprehend what the businessman had just said; his mind fixed on the tragic events that had almost cost his life.

Banaar had to come around his desk to help a stunned Hando stand.

"Get yourself together, man! We'll find a solution for this mess."

There was no vitality left in Martinez's body. He was standing, but couldn't move his legs. The enormity of the guilt he had been carrying for the last couple of weeks since the Tanas incident, raged fiercely, knocking him down psychologically. A remnant of what he thought was exterminated had come back from the dead to collect unpaid debts. Only now could he fully understand another of Rakash's unfamiliar concepts that "every action generates a reaction." The city had created the punishment itself as backlash to the slaughter of the Tanas.

'Why didn't the Supreme Being stop the killing or present me an alternative?' a foggy thought formed in Martinez's already confused mind.

Banaar pushed him out of his office and let Karitan take over.

* * *

THERE WERE REAL CONCERNS from members of the council about the many emergency meetings called lately. They thought that the Tanas incident was behind them and the city's life would continue smoothly. Martinez's disheveled appearance didn't give them confidence that this time his capacity for problem-solving would save them. The council would have to step in.

Clapel joined the meeting as soon as he heard the horrible news and had his team already scouring every block, searching for the second assailant who fled after stabbing Bart. Interrogating the youngster that attacked Hando didn't shed any light on the whereabouts of Bart's killer as the Tanas' code of honour forbade snitching over one's personal safety.

"I thought we were assured that all the Tanas were accounted for in the attack. What happened?" Elenadore Tam inquired.

Council members becoming targets in similar acts of revenge had a high probability and she didn't want a live to watching over her shoulder.

"These are teenagers who were in Laeta having fun during the events. Their fathers died that day, so the only way of grieving they know is retribution," Tonio justified the mishap.

"We could start a fund to support the families left behind that have at least one minor child and no other income. They won't be removed from the apartments they're living in, thus we might build some confidence that any resentment is curtailed," Mirena Vande suggested.

Desperation made them come up with ideas that, several weeks, ago were off the table.

"And create a special training program for those looking for a job," she continued.

"I'm telling you, these guys are an exception. There is a sight of relief now that the gang is gone, and we are seeing support from those living in that section of town to reintegrate with the city," Clapel assured in a pitched voice as if he couldn't control his tonality anymore. The chief's determination to infuse confidence in the group didn't impress them. They wanted more guarantees.

"We'll leave several patrols on the streets for the next three or four weeks. This should quench further potential incidents," he said when he got no reaction to his first statement. "But I'm telling you, what happened was an exception."

They all nodded in agreement, feeling that any preventive measure could bring back some of the lost self-reliance in the city's protective force.

Now they had to deal with Martinez, whose gaze had gotten some clarity back, meaning that he was thinking deeply.

"What are we going to handle next?" Artilla asked him.

"We have to let Rakash know about his master. His reaction might determine how to approach Laeta, but as it stands right now, the boy has to return if their Committee says so. Death was not part of my plan; it was not included in the contract. I've asked Karitan to bring Rakash here."

He then went to the door, opened it and let the villager in.

Rakash walked in silently, observing the uneasiness on all of their faces. Mirena Vande had tears in her eyes, and he knew something was amiss, especially since master was always present when the boy's presence was required.

Hando offered him a chair beside his then he also sat, putting his hand over Rakash's.

"I spent my entire morning with your master, getting to know each other better since he really enjoyed the changes Korobat went through from when he visited last time. He even said that remaining with us longer was something he would consider." He stopped for a moment, gazing at the other council members, looking for approval to continue. They were expecting to hear more. He knew that empathy was the only way to the boy's heart. "While talking, we were attacked by two gang teenagers. They didn't have the time to hurt me, but master wasn't so lucky. He died immediately."

Hando lost his poise and brought the story to an abrupt end, no matter how painful for Rakash.

Silence blanketed them all, eyes focused on the boy who had just lost the second family he ever had. A high price demanded by *One Who Created All* from such a blooming disciple.

Hando retracted his hand, as he had no other words of comfort.

"Where is master now?" Rakash had an immovable voice that sounded a bit authoritarian.

"His body is at the hospital. We'll make arrangements for him to be transported to Laeta tomorrow. I'll go with him. I have to personally inform the committee. Do you want to come as well?" Martinez's mouth voiced that last sentence before his mind could fully process the damage it would cause, in case Rakash answered affirmatively. His unconscious intuition asked the question, knowing that such an invitation needed to be put forward.

"I won't go. We have unfinished work at the lab."

This was his way of saying that by the time they would reach Laeta, the pain of losing Bart would surface profusely, making him appear weak in front of the committee. He would rather show weakness in front of the people which whom he have build a relationship and who would understand his pain, because loosing Bart would be their pain as well.

"Your friend, Nayan, will be hurting too. It might be good for both of you to spend time together," Hando suggested. "I can bring him back with me."

Rakash concealed his face with his right arm in an attempt to stifle tears. "We left Nayan very upset. That's why he didn't want to come and never replied to our letters. He'll stay with master until the end. Ask him if he wants me to return."

Intense pain started piercing holes in his impenetrable calm, disturbing an internal balance that he'd built with so much effort. He suddenly felt like he was standing on the edge of an abyss from which meditation and positive thinking about *One Who Created All* supposedly kept him away.

'There was nothing safe and certain in this world anymore, just the constant pain generated by irrational decisions of small-minded individuals. What would happen to me now, pushed constantly on the river of life like the Book said about the leaves?

Restlessly moving from stone to stone, used and turned up side down by the cold, insensible water, following a rut carved with force, and numb to the continued degradation of the leaves that happened to fall into the current. Leaves lingering around a stone could also mean attachment, and his pain just proved that his was still profound and not easily removed. Otan came again to his mind as someone who could help him escalate the ladder of consciousness to the next level. A necessary ascension to shed his remaining bad habits and haunting thoughts. Remnants of human life that prevented him from lifting closer to his spiritual Father. The village was lost. Now master. The journey chosen for him by One Who Created All he deemed to be a lousy alternative, which, had he the power, would've gladly stopped instantly. Was the work in the lab so important to deserve this sacrifice?'

Thoughts swirled unchecked, usurping the orderly intuitive guidance that had been slowly forming as part of who he was becoming. An insensible death had shattered some of his insatiable desire for liberation.

"Yes, ask Nayan what he wants me to do," Rakash repeated while standing and heading to the door. "I want to say goodbye to master now."

CHAPTER 12

One's murky water of consciousness needs purification through the daily filter of prayer and meditation. Let your superconciousness become crisp like the morning air as my name is called continuously with relentless faith.

From the book *We Are One* – Chapter 12

THERE WAS AN EERIE SILENCE in the room, as if the wood-paneled walls had the power to absorb words before they were spoken. The four members of Laeta's committee were staring at each other, incapable of initiating a desirable conversation after Hando had dropped at their feet Bart Blackwood's coffin. When writing the contract with Korobat, they had considered many scenarios, but death wasn't one of them.

Stunned by the enormity of the situation, they listened to Hando's verbal hemorrhage. He first apologized profusely and then explained the events leading up to the fatal incident. They paid attention when the leader asked for permission to keep Rakash for the duration of the contract. Everyone in Korobat was so excited about the tangible data gathered in the last two months that it would have been a mistake not to continue.

"Stopping now won't help either party," Hando pleaded, hoping that the committee would consider the betterment of the city over an unfortunate accident, which would only affect a handful of people.

It was a cold business decision that, in his opinion, was simply common sense.

"We have developed a smooth process and we are able to progress without Bart. I'm not lessening what could have been his invaluable contribution moving forward, but here we are. We can't delve too much in the past."

Kravis Kanar, the president, kept silent, increasing pressure on Martinez.

"I also have a message for Nayan from Rakash," Martinez added, refusing to let their silence govern the outcome of the meeting.

But no one was interested in what the message was. At least not yet, as they still couldn't believe the ineptitude of the situation. Kanar dismissed his guest coldly, adjourning until the next day for their verdict.

"This is a disaster," Victoria Kaft broke the silence. "They were responsible for Blackwood's well being. They can't just claim that there's no specific contractual clause that refers to it. What if this was intentional? They have all the research and the boy, and they've left us with nothing."

For the first time in many years, the committee doubted its decision to rely on Korobat for the next phase of their future.

"We can't prove any of your concerns," said the president pushing his elbows further on to the table, a sign that he was upset and focused on getting his ideas across to the other members. "What if Bart's initial claim that Korobat poisoned them to prevent any local success with Rakash was true? Could his death be part of the plan?" He looked around, waiting for feedback that would confirm his suspicions.

"Why did we agree to go ahead with the project when Martinez sold us the idea?" Gerald Misk asked rhetorically. "Because we all thought Korobat was capable of delivering on its promises. They might still be able to, but with Bart gone we have no other means of knowing when the technology will be finalized."

Laeta had already captured most of what the imagination could dream in terms of sex, drugs and partying; they felt a desperate need to raise the threshold of sensual pleasures.

"In the end Martinez might want a contract renegotiation, claiming that they did all the work with little input from Bart," said Orgil Nurkan, raising his own concerns.

The harsh reality gave them pause, and they individually acknowledged that they should have given the scholar more credit and support. Their impatience cost him his life. But these were weak thoughts that couldn't be exteriorized openly. Hando's update on the excitement generated by the visit of Bart and Rakash in Korobat and the small, but increasing fellowship buying into the *One Who Created All*'s existence, had shocked them. Hando had witnessed the energy flowing through the orange triangles on Rakash's cheeks, an experience they missed because of their inflated egos and distrust in one of the most valuable assets the city had.

"We need to get Rakash back," Kraft demanded, crossing her arms over her generous breasts. "I don't trust them anymore."

As usual, Kanar preferred diplomacy to confrontation. "What if we give Korobat the same deal we gave Bart. Two months to finish their research, after which the boy is returned to us. Meanwhile we'll decide how he can generate revenue while we are waiting for the device to be ready. What do you think?"

"It's a good idea. By giving them notice, we are still within the contractual terms," Nurkan confirmed sulkily. "I also think that we have to find ways to generate revenue off the boy."

Unanimity prevailed.

"Bring Nayan over so we can deliver the news. We have to convince him that going to Korobat for the next two months is of the upmost importance, and that his friend needs his help and consolation," the president concluded.

* * *

"MASTER IS DEAD, master is dead, master is dead." Sitting by himself in the library with his head between his knees, Nayan repeated the words unceasingly in an attempt to dissipate their morbid meaning. "Master is dead, master is dead, master is dead..."

Life was throwing blow after blow at him, impeding his way, each one more forceful than the last, unabatedly testing his psychological strength and new beliefs. Long meditation sessions that kept the torment of Bart's and Rakash's departure at bay, resumed once again with the fatidic news of irreparable loss. His face had a swarthy expression that not even Panette's charm could remove. Ever since they had left he matured more than he could have thought possible. Even his physical appearance had changed: his hair had grown unruly and a timid beard shadowed his face.

Resentment towards the council and warm memories of master collided inside his head in a fight between good and evil, obstructing him from making a decision.

It did make sense to join Rakash in Korobat, especially if the resounding success of the meditation steps he had helped create, was indeed real and not a mortal trap like the one Bart had unconsciously stepped into. Rakash needed him, but because of his self-imposed silence, Nayan wasn't sure how to initiate the first stride.

It seemed to Nayan that his friend's spiritual path had a crisp clarity that also embraced human qualities such as empathy and forgiveness. Rakash would be willing to forgive his stubbornness and fixation on matters of the past, and prepared to accept a reconciliation of hearts in the wake of the devastation that affected both of them. If Korobat's leadership-sickened minds would have him killed, at least he would see his friend one last time. He would pray that *One Who Created All* would appreciate his sacrifice and send him back for another try. Maybe he would wake up in the village this time.

That thought put a shy smile on his face, but just for a moment. He would let the committee know of his decision immediately then pack for the trip.

He stood up and shook his body several times to gather more energy. Panette would be in charge of the house until their return. No one should touch the books and the latest notes he had generated.

Beyond layers of grief, his innate scientific curiosity pushed its head upwards, eager to absorb the results achieved in Korobat, and use it in tweaking and improving his own attempts. Stepping in master's shoes wouldn't be possible at his age, but he was the only one left who had witnessed every single step of Rakash's development, therefore, maybe later on, he might be asked to join the team in Korobat. No matter the future plans, Rakash had to return safely, bringing with him as much information as possible.

* * *

THIS TIME, during the long drive from Laeta, Karitan subdued his vocal exuberance; he'd been informed who he was transporting, an apprentice grieving his master, who was better left alone with his own thoughts. The driver parked in front of the building, then took Nayan upstairs, carrying his only luggage of several items of clothing.

The boys ran at each other, melting their pain in an extended hug. Tears followed. Neither falsity nor pretense could enter their relationship of compulsory brothers in a tense world that *One Who Created All* would not make easier for them yet. Words followed, words bleeding of remorse, heavy with untold confessions that Nayan's mind created.

"I'm so sorry I didn't come with you from the beginning," Nayan lamented, still holding Rakash's hands.

The time spent by himself after the incident allowed the villager to assess what could happen to him next. He faced master's death with a strong will and considered it another sign of his soul's convoluted journey.

"You couldn't have changed anything. Master and I had our regrets too. Leaving you behind upset and tormented was difficult." Rakash paused, looking straight into Nayan's eyes as if he were preparing for an important confession. "Coming to Korobat was a worthy change for both of us. Master found the respect he deserved from a generation of researchers who understood and appreciated his experience and effort of the last two years. He came back to life, fuelled by an energy that even he thought he didn't have anymore. The enthusiasm of these young people affected on him. In Laeta he was poised for unfulfilling years. Now he will be remembered and revered as the scholar who turned a story no one believed in into a potentially world-changing technology."

The letter Nayan had received painted a similar picture, but hearing it directly from his friend had far more impact. Tears followed again. "How did it affect you?" Nayan asked after the sobbing subsided.

"All the pressure built in Laeta vanished. Real or not, Korobat's hospitality proved beneficial for us. We didn't talk about it; nevertheless, we both felt relieved after only spending several days here. It took master a while to start trusting the council. They offered him a permanent position. You'll see that their research facilities are amazing. We've achieved so much."

Rakash eyed Nayan more closely and noticed the subtler changes of his physiognomy marked by the responsibilities of being on his own. He had even grown a little bit taller. "Are you here to take me back?"

Nayan nodded his triangle-shaped head.

"Kanar wants you in Laeta in two months. In his opinion it will give us enough time to tie up any work left hanging, assuming that the research data gathered up to this point is enough to create the *bliss* device. They also told me to bring back any material that belongs to master."

"We'll do whatever they ask."

"How confident are you that the team knows what it needs to make it happen?"

Rakash didn't reply immediately. He had asked himself this question several times, even when Bart was still alive. "They could have everything they need or only a fraction. In the end it's up to the *Supreme Being*'s will if this technology should appear in our lives or not. If it serves a higher purpose, *He* would allow it. If not, it will materialize when this world is ready for it."

Nayan listened intensely to his friend's encrypted message.

"When meditating, my communication with *Him* is so vivid. It isn't the *state of bliss*, but it's still an elevated thought dialogue that we used with the elephants. I get answers almost every time. And this peaceful turbulence lights up the orange marks on my cheeks, showing any doubter *His* might." Rakash smiled, confident in the authority and power he was carrying inside of him. "We wrote you about the researchers that agreed to become part of the experiment. They have all shown behavioural and health improvements. It's amazing."

Then he suddenly remembered something important. "Master mentioned that he would write a book containing the entire research and give the team credit as well. We should continue this work in Laeta. I'll take you to the lab tomorrow. You'll like it. Tell me what's new back home."

Left behind, Nayan had disobeyed most of the advice Bart had tried to impose on him. He attended high-school as a necessary distraction and made notes on a couple of books identified by the scholar as essential. His meditation sessions lacked a rigorous schedule, his way of rebelling against the decision of not pursuing and challenging the committee's announcement.

"Ego took me over like black ink absorbed by soft paper. I lied to myself that, mentally, I was strong enough and meditation was not required. You were my bearing, my motivation. Please help me get back into it," he pleaded.

There was no need for confirmation. Rakash's loving gaze was enough for Nayan.

* * *

VARGAS AND HIS OTHER two business partners stepped into Laeta's committee room for the first time, proving that confidentiality was required for whatever had to be shared. President Kanar occupied the head of the long table, while the remaining members, Victoria Kaft, Orgil Nurkan and Gerald Misk, were facing their guests.

"Do you know what's on the walls?" the president pointed to the dried, colour-faded frames of paintings and other indescribable items brought from the jungle.

The men looked at the objects with curiosity, not fully understanding the question.

Vargas shook his head in surrender. None of the other two muttered a word.

"These are artwork we recovered from the south along with a child villager. It happened almost three years ago. Since then, we've been studying him, trying to replicate the *state of bliss* that was so popular at one time among the city's elite."

Vargas smiled condescendingly. "Do you really believe in that non-sense?"

The president's back stiffened, but he kept his temper in check. "It's our mandate to identify new ways of pleasuring tourists. We understand that you are content with what you are offering in terms of drugs and sex, therefore you think additional stimulants are not required. Maybe not today or one year from now, but we strongly consider that the threshold of what is seen as pleasure will increase drastically. And more of the same won't be enough because it will kill them. Their bodies will not cope with the higher doses. We can't kill our clients. They are the ones bringing in all this wonderful revenue. Something harmless, but potent should be the replacement."

He gave them a moment to fully comprehend the committee's point of view.

"What do you suggest?" Vargas inquired.

"The city has always given you three the right of first refusal on any new mind-enhancing or psychedelic products brought by outsiders. This time we are not yet sure if such expertise would be developed based on the research achieved on *state of bliss*, so we have to change the strategy." Kanar nodded at Orgil Nurkan, ready with a much more detailed explanation.

"We know that a significant percentage of your business comes from fetishism and sex with deformed people," said Nurkan grinning his teeth. "The villager is seven-years old and the only odd thing about him are orange triangles on his cheeks. These birthmarks are supposed to light up by an internal energy, which at maximum intensity, translates into the *state of bliss*."

Vargas couldn't fill the depth of the chair due to some pain in his short legs, and felt uncomfortable. The green nuance of his hair matched the colour of the long shirt hanging just above his knees. "Would this *state of bliss* take away pain? And I mean permanently. Even high quality powder can't achieve this."

Kanar's initial description of a threshold that goes higher related to either pain or pleasure, resonated with him. He could confirm that any dosage increase would make him functional for a number of days, but in the end he had to snuff more ... and more ... and more. He was falling apart.

"Supposedly. Nevertheless, we can't perceive it in the same way the villager does. We are missing, fuck knows what, and the guys in Korobat are working on it."

Nurkan's annoyance that he still didn't have a tangible device to sell was noticeable. The revenue generated from the transaction he was about to offer would only be a fraction of its true potential. "We want you to lease the villager from the city for a monthly flat fee. There are certain conditions that need to be followed, since he needs to last for at least several years. You'll turn a nice profit by using aggressive promotion to a selective clientele. C'mon, I don't have to teach you how to package him in a real mind-blowing story. In fact you can create any story you want."

"Is physical contact allowed?" Vargas wanted more upfront clarification before committing to a deal that might not bring the profit Nurkan suggested it would.

"Yes. He has to be physically functional at the end of, let's say, five years. In the beginning, you can simply ask the boy to enter the state that brings the birthmarks to life. Create the impression that you value what he's doing. Show enthusiasm. If that doesn't generate enough cash, take it up a notch."

"When do you need an answer?" Vargas asked, acting as a spoke person for the other two dealers.

"In twenty four hours."

After the three men left the room, Victoria Kaft, who kept silent until then, addressed Nurkan and Kanar.

"Have any of you thought of an alternative? I don't like selling the boy just like any other piece of merchandise. At least, not without his consent."

"No, Victoria, there are no other options to make money off him unless the device is built soon," said Nurkan, raising his tone, not liking his judgment questioned. "I wouldn't have him in Korobat even if they would be willing to pay a fee. We have to show some determination in protecting our assets."

The president showed his agreement with Nurkan's statement by keeping silent. After a while, he spoke slowly, looking for the right words as justification. "Bart is gone. He was the only one who could have opposed us raucously and shamed us. We've treated Rakash well, but now it's his turn to contribute to the city that's been his home for the last two years. We all make sacrifices from time to time."

"What are we going to tell Nayan?" Misk inquired.

"A story that, long-term, has to stick. Let's say that Korobat begged for his return for three or four months for a prototype testing. Nayan can write to him. We would control the flow of letters. This will buy us some time. For now, let the boys be together and reconnect," Nurkan suggested. "If he doesn't believe us, he might have a little overdose accident."

* * *

RAKASH WAS BACK in Laeta after an intense two months of endless meditation sessions and tiring discussions with the team in Korobat, whose members had opened up even more after the announcement of his imminent departure became public. Nothing had changed in Laeta since he had left; only the house seemed smaller and darker, as though clogged with memories that had become part of his life experience.

Thinking retrospectively, even if the scholar's death occurred under Hando's watch, Rakash didn't blame him or the circumstances that brought them to Korobat. He somehow found peace in daily work as a natural continuation of what Bart would have wanted him to do: finish the job and give everyone a chance to uplift themselves. Returning to Laeta's dull life was more of a self-imposed punishment than a sincere desire. Nayan needed his moral support more than the other way around. The research team gave Rakash the energy, the joy and the stimulation he yearned for. The committee's ultimatum for his return didn't allow for any compromise and going against it would only generate unnecessary ruckus between the two cities.

Hando, who broke the news to the team, had a hard time pushing back on the yelling, anger and displeasure because he had agreed to 'the surrender'. Rakash was theirs for the next several months, no matter what dramatic occurrence made the terms of the contract nil. The boy had appreciated the fondness shown by all of them, and he intervened. "It's my understanding that this relationship between Laeta and Korobat is based on mutual trust and long-term business interest, so it's not Hando's fault that I have to return. He's being asked to respect the contractual terms."

They calmed down, but didn't hide their discontent. Ideas on how to circumvent the request bounced around loudly, in a cacophony that made Rakash tired. He spoke again. "I promise that if you have a device ready and want to test it, I'll convince the committee to let me come back for a while. Continue the meditation sessions and don't stop sharing results with the team. Nayan will help me answer your letters."

Naranta took advantage of the silence following Rakash's statement to express feelings that only such a hastened departure and a real internal change could have brought forward. "I now understand the meaning of controlling yourself. I finally see that a sustained meditative effort is what we are missing in our daily life as an antidote to all the external stimuli we are exposed to. I've been meditating since Prakit and Merlaya started, but I kept silent because of the addiction I had to battle. I'm gaining ground against it. And even if the *state of bliss* is a remote experience for me, just holding my condition in check is a major success. Thank you."

The boy bowed to her, love and warmth lighting up his face. He could have ignited their internal fire himself, liberating them from the clutches of failure, if only he had the power and if they were ready, but neither conditions were met. Until recently he housed similar fears that the orange triangles were just accidental birthmarks with no spiritual meaning as master had thought. Faith had created the spark for the first fire in the lower part of his body that had smoldered for days, slowly purifying harmful subconscious thoughts and unfulfilling desires from previous incarnations that could have prevented him from ceaseless devotion of *One Who Created All.* Then the blaze spread upwards along his spine releasing a fragrance of papaya and cinnamon. It triggered in his mind's eye the jungle sheltered by an energy field, banishing him from entering and finding the nourishment that, once bestowed on him, would allow the cleansing to go even higher, and reach his *wisdom eye.*

"Are you taking Bart's notes with you? We hope that the book he was talking about will be written," Prakit brought up a subject that was on everyone's mind.

Rakash took his time to answer, remembering the committee's request conveyed through Nayan. "Yes. If you don't mind I want to sort them out, and add any unfinished comments then present them to you in a concise form so you can attach the research. It will be a nice way to honour master."

The blockage was palpable around his heart; no meditative ecstasy could soar pass that point, and he intuitively knew that only a teacher like Otan could unlatch it. His self-discovery had reached a plateau.

A question Hando had asked him echoed in his mind. *'Why was no one from the village looking for me? Will I be allowed to return?'*

There was nothing else keeping him in the Entertainment City. The committee should let him decide his own path from now on. Only Nayan would come with him, as his calling for *One Who Created All* was sincere and necessary to be attained. He couldn't see any other vested interests in either Laeta or in Korobat that would justify an extended stay.

As a welcoming gesture Panette and her mom prepared a delicious dish of grilled chicken and green salad mixed with Rakash's favourites seeds for them. Both women had personally tasted the food to prevent another unfortunate incident of food poisoning.

"Thank you for taking care of the house ... and of Nayan," he addressed them.

They bowed their heads and stayed like that for several seconds, returning the appreciation and silently offering their condolences.

"We would like you to keep working for us."

He knew that Nayan wouldn't say no to having Panette around. The heaviness built recently inside his friend would tremble near the exultant young woman, releasing its gnarled claws from around his boastful heart. A happy Nayan could be easier redirected on the spiritual path and away from delusive afflictions. Working together with master's legacy would rekindle a friendship that they both thought was lost.

He was home in Laeta at last and sorrow, shame, rage and despair were percolating to the surface of his being, an eruption of rubbish feelings that had no place in the holy house of *One Who Created All.* Tiredness and hurtling emotions enveloped him like a waterlily closing its petals at dusk, catching the insects fouled by its aromatic scent. There was no escape from that tight embrace and his breath paused, horrible grunts echoing from inside him. His subconscious was sending out the remnants of gross manifestations of human behaviour. A purge triggered by the familiar sight of Bart's belongings and a whiff of his body. Rakash's mind stumbled, faced with this eruption of unfamiliar feelings, and flashes of duties he had to perform for the committee attached themselves as additional worries to his already exhausted mind.

"I'm all right," he assured everyone when Nayan and Panette jumped forward to offer support. "Just tired from the latest work we did in Korobat. Now I have enough time to rest."

Rakash thanked the women again, and after they went to the kitchen, he addressed Nayan. "Tomorrow we have to face the committee, describe everything that occurred in Korobat and handover master's research. Keep the copies in a safe place. We'll start organizing them soon."

The villager realized that the committee had no expertise in using all of the entire research and couldn't add any value to it. By holding onto it as the main keeper of knowledge, they thought it would give them some advantage over Hando and his team in case contractual terms had to be bargained again. It was an illusory strategy, but Kanar didn't care. During the last two years while Rakash was in Laeta under Bart's supervision, the president's only interest amounted to no more than a couple of questions each time he met the scholar: do you have any results? And when are you going to produce something tangible?

Inwardly, Rakash remained hopeful that even without his presence, the Korobat team's determination would prevail, maybe not immediately, but before the decadence of these humans reached the point of no return.

Based on his experience in Korobat, the boy had proof that if anyone who started on the spiritual path persevered, both internal and external changes would be significant and visible. The key ingredient was persistence against a well-embedded mentality of easy-to-obtain achievements and the understanding that *One Who Created All*, even if *He* loves *His* children, is a demanding *Father* that can't be persuaded to grant access to the astral level by tears of helplessness.

The next day, feeling more light-hearted, Rakash climbed the stairs inside the municipality building accompanied by Nayan. They were both ready for a meeting that Bart always loathed due to a lack of visible results that could be brought forward. Rakash mentally rehearsed his main discussion points in case they let him speak before answering any questions. He carefully crafted a timeline of events since they had left Laeta, enriching it with details that would have made a professional storyteller proud. Rakash honestly thought that describing the scientific steps to reach the *state of bliss* would engage the committee well beyond the financial gains they were after.

Waiting for them in the dimly lit lobby was a visibly bored doorman, a new addition to the municipality's staff, which stood up from the chair positioned by the door, and guided the boys upstairs to the meeting room. "The council will join you soon," he said and left them there.

This gave them time to browse their surroundings, as they were not sure at what end of the long table they should sit. Rakash's gaze fell immediately on the village's artifacts. It felt like a foggy memory that would bring clarity to his eyes the more he focused on them. Filtered by the coloured glass that made up the top right side of the windows in the high room, the sunrays lend a surreal aura to the items hanging on the wall.

"These artworks were brought back along with you," Nayan said, in an attempt to refresh his friend's memory. "We had them at home for a while, but Master couldn't convince the committee to leave them with us longer. He thought that interacting with them would trigger some of your buried memories."

"I remember these paintings," Rakash replied as he got closer to the wall displaying the artwork.

He wanted to step on a chair, extend his hand and feel their texture, but he would still be too short to reach. He hoped a quick touch would ignite in him spells, teachings and vibrations, encased in them by their makers as part of the creation process.

'So many stories I could potentially unlock with a simple touch unless One Who Created All had already extracted the essence of the message that was meant to be

conveyed to Him,' Rakash thought.

He gazed around the room, looking for any other items from the village, but only portraits of the existing and previous city management team hung on the walls of the room: a variety of faces, mostly men, devoid of smiles or emphatic looks. A collection of razor-thin lips, protruded cheekbones, straight chins, merged eyebrows, and tunics of every possible dignity-enhancing colour. It was an austere room where no one could add his or her personal touch and make it more welcoming. It borrowed something from the rigidity and steeliness of the acting committee members that, at times, seemed like they had no space inside of them for basic human emotions.

A side door opened and the president strolled in followed by his peers. A forced smile elongated Kanar's lips in preparation for delivering a sober message that would express his sorrow for Bart's death, and release them from any responsibility that could be attached to their early decision of sending the pair to Korobat.

The president gestured for the boys to sit, while the city's decision makers spread along one side of the table. Kanar took the power seat, his usual spot, facing the door.

Nayan froze standing, his hands holding the back of one of the chairs. Bart's leather bag hung heavy on his shoulder, filled with the documentation requested by the officials. The boy had never met the assembly in its full composition and just from looking at them now, he understood why his master had prepared for each meeting so carefully. He couldn't decide which one had the meanest look and seemed that not even a tragedy of such proportions would move their needle of internal empathy. Nayan pulled back the chair, sat down and placed the bag at his feet. He squinted his black eyes at the people in front of him, an involuntary reaction to the pain they had caused and for which they were parading a no-guilt attitude.

Rakash kept his back straight and his palms clasped under the table, waiting for the elder of the group to speak. He was wearing one of the outfits given to him in Korobat, grayish leather pants, a light blue silk shirt and on top, a silk vest, its colour a nuance darker than the shirt. The villager noticed the impression his clothing made on the adults since in

Laeta he was only provided with plain-coloured items of the cheapest quality. Dressing him lavishly, it seemed, was an unnecessary expense from the council's point of view.

"We are pleased that both of you have come back safely. We just can't imagine the ordeal you went through, Rakash, after Blackwood perished," Kanar said emphasizing the 'we'. "You and your master made us proud with all the achievements mentioned by Martinez. It's a pity that Bart won't be around to test the device."

The president's voice was even as if it was below his dignity to get excited under any circumstances.

"Why did you want me back in Laeta?" Rakash wanted some clarification early in the discussion. He would be respectful, but he wanted to ask questions that would show him their intention. Kravis Kanar stretched his lips again into a large, thin line, annoyed that he had to answer before his entire speech was over.

"There are certain contractual terms that have been activated upon Bart's death. We also thought that you would be safer here, now that a new gang has installed itself in Korobat."

"Really!" Nayan who sensed the hypocrisy burst out. He didn't have anything to lose, especially after Bart's will explicitly stated that the house was left to Nayan, along with a generous amount of life insurance, enough to cover necessary living expenses for at least ten years. He was willing to forgive those he held responsible for his master's death if they had shown sincere remorse and not just dishonest platitudes.

Kanar frowned, but he let the outburst slide. They all had to swallow their egos because antagonizing Nayan and responding to his provocations would affect their already jeopardized relationship with Rakash.

"Did Martinez mention the research component related to the team members that followed the same process I was going through?" the villager asked.

"Yes, he did," replied Nurkan, trying to relieve the president of some pressure. His round shaped face had sagging cheeks, a wide nose dotted with blackheads, and small round eyes so alive that they seemed to lack eyelids. His hair was cut very short, exposing several bald spots on the sides of his head. "He gave us the details about the interest built around your meditation sessions and their beneficial impact," Nurkan continued.

"Do you think people in Laeta would be interested in trying it?" Rakash asked, thinking of ways to positively contribute to the city's turnaround towards *One Who Created All.*

"Those guys in Korobat are researchers," replied Nurkan. "They'd try anything odd. It's kind of difficult to apply the same approach here. Can't imagine having too much fun either waiting for you to light up your triangles or staying immovable in an attempt to talk to an imaginary energy," Nurkan ended almost laughing and drawing smiles from Victoria Kaft and Gerald Misk.

Only the president kept quiet, evaluating a potential tip that could work in their favour. "We might have some people interested in practicing with you. Give us a couple of days to make the arrangements," he said, and gestured to Nurkan that he could put forward any other comments.

The villager was not done yet. "The work I initiated in Korobat is only the beginning. The team still needs guidance while they advance on their own spiritual path. There is no one they can turn to," Rakash explained, looking into Kanar's sunken brown eyes, aware that any final decision sat with him. "I would like to return after the situation settles and my safety isn't a concern anymore," he proposed.

The president saw another unexpected lifeline that could be exploited, and replied without having any second thoughts. "We've already agreed with Martinez that you'll be available when a device is ready for testing."

"Thank you," the boy said and turned towards Nayan to share this pleasant surprise with him.

Borrowing from Bart's untrusting attitude, Nayan's mood was still somber.

"Boys, the energy and sacrifice we all put forth towards this goal needs to pay off, therefore we'll do whatever is necessary to see it through," Kanar added.

Encouraged by the positivity of the discussion, Rakash pushed forward. "When can I go back to the village?"

It was a terrifying question that neither Bart nor Nayan were able to answer months ago. And the committee had no intention of attaching a tangible date to it.

"It will have to wait until a prototype is ready. Once started, the work of *One Who Created All* can't stop," the president replied. It became so natural to deliver deceiving statements that would gain the boy's trust. Even mentioning the name of the *Supreme Being* felt familiar and convincing.

"I'll remind you about this request when the conditions are met," Rakash said formally.

"Have you brought the documents?"

Nayan pulled out several folders in which the research was structured based on Bart's analytical mind. Most of the results achieved in Korobat were included except for the latest feedback from Merlaya and Prakit. The act of holding back information was more of a rebellious stroke against the committee and also to prevent them from acquiring personal information of the Korobatians. The boys could have bet their lives that none of the people in front of them would have the slightest interest in browsing the research, let alone reading it for a better understanding of what was already accomplished.

'*The book, whenever ready, would have to be published in Korobat, out of reach of such a controlling bunch*,' Rakash thought, losing for a moment the focus of the discussion. Master's presence was so pervasive in his daily thinking; sometimes interrupting his dialogues in the middle of a statement, giving the other party the impression that he was short of words and needed time to find more meaningful ones.

"This is the information given to Korobat on the first day we arrived," said Rakash, pointing to two thick folders in the pile. "And the other ones contain the latest results, which is the effort of both teams."

Nayan pushed them across the table towards Kanar, who nodded to Gerald Misk, the designated keeper.

"If there is nothing else to report, this meeting is over," Kanar concluded.

The boys stood up, but Rakash pointed to the familiar artifacts hanging on the wall and in an almost demanding voice, said: "I would like to have the small painting of the map of my village. It belongs to me anyways."

The committee members looked up, then at the president, waiting for his reaction. The older man tensed the skin of his narrow forehead several times, processing the request, saw the determination on the boy's face and decided to end the meeting with a conciliatory gesture.

"Of course you can have it," came the confirmation. "Not too many people can see it in here. It's better for you to hold onto it. I'll have it delivered tomorrow." After which, he produced a real smile, a self-reward for doing a good deed.

* * *

RAKASH WAS HOPEFUL ABOUT the next chapter of his life in Laeta after all the reassurances regarding a possible return to Korobat, and then, if everything went well exposing the masses to the *state of bliss*, a return home to his brothers and sisters who likely thought him dead. His life's mission directed by *One Who Created All* could become more than just lifting some humans from their stupor of useless endeavours. He thought of himself as bridge between two worlds that seemed to have nothing in common. The story of his disappearance and survival should convince the elephants that some of humans could be trusted. Rakash understood that the sanctity of the village and of the relationship between the children and the elephants must prevail; therefore, a gentle and patient interaction was necessary. He would achieve that which no other *Orange Soul* before him had.

Kanar kept his word and several days later the boy received the message that a car would pick him up for a meeting with a group of *state of bliss* enthusiasts. Nayan was not allowed to come along, since these people wanted their identities protected.

Rakash agreed and he was sitting now in front of three men, in a windowless room, whose only furniture were three couches, several chairs and a table loaded with seeds, nuts and fruits.

The boy brought his meditation rug that he kept rolled up on his lap, waiting to be shown where to place it. A man with green hair and a large body addressed him first.

"We've explained to the president that certain people we know are interested in learning more about the process that brings one closer to the *state of bliss*. We would like to observe such a session before reaching out to them."

Vargas had to weigh his words carefully so as not to raise any suspicion in the child that was more mature than he looked.

"Do you prefer this room? If not, you can choose another one," and he pointed to the doors on the opposite wall.

Used to a more confined space, Rakash, still holding the rug, stood up and took Vargas up on his offer. The first door opened into a room that seemed small due to the size of the bed encrusted all around with erotic scenes. On two corners it had super sized wooded phalluses like a permanent sexual provocation for those entering this stimulating territory. Natural light slipped through the white curtains, playing with the colours of the silk pillows that covered the bed. Various sized paintings of naked women hung on the red walls, giving the impression that a crowd was looking at him. Several brownish fluffy furs were laid on the floor with no apparent use or intention of complimenting the colour of the other items in the room.

Rakash stepped back, left the door open and tried the second room. It had the same arrangement of furniture and accessories, only the walls were different, being light blue. He turned around to face the men who were expecting his verdict. "Either room is fine with me as long as the furs are removed. I'll use my rug instead," he said and sat back on the couch. "I'll start my session in there and everyone who waits in this room has to keep quiet. They can take turns watching me meditate. I was told that the moment my birthmarks come alive is quite unique."

He placed the rug beside him and stood up, aiming for the bowl of seeds. He chewed on some and enjoyed the familiar taste. "I'm sure you bought them from the same store we buy ours. There's no better store in town."

Vargas smiled sheepishly. "You're right. No one can beat Vargas' Seeds and Nuts. Always fresh," replied the merchant, elbowing the closest man to him.

"Not always. I got really sick once from these nuts. It was a bad batch," the boy said, helping himself to another bowl.

"Not possible! I know the owner. He personally checks everything he buys!" Vargas was suddenly upset that his undisputable reputation had a blemish from a kid who didn't even know that he was the owner.

"I didn't expect that either, but Nayan, master and I, all got a fever and vomited profusely. It happens," Rakash concluded with a 'no-hard feelings' tone.

The merchant recognized Nayan's name and everything clicked in his mind. The prank he was asked to go along with had, indirectly, affected this child as well. Maybe that was why Nayan never returned to his store.

"I see you came prepared for the meditation session," said one of Vargas' associates, speaking for the first time.

He was a thin man with a receding jaw, an elongated curved nose and locks of black hair covering his hunched shoulders. His frail body continuously trembled underneath the clothing hanging on his frame.

Rakash looked at him and silently thanked *One Who Created All* for giving him the gift of not judging anyone by appearances alone; even the soul of such a poor looking fellow could yearn for spiritual uplifting, leaving behind a life scorched by material desires.

In Korobat he created a habit of welcoming all those whose souls gave a hint of potential awakening either in a subconscious dream or in other ways. He wanted to believe that he could recognize the signs of readiness for pouring forth one's heart to a higher goal.

Rakash finished chewing on the seeds and, without a word, he walked back to the couch, picked up his meditation rug and spread it over the thick carpet covering the floor.

"If it's only the three of you, I won't bother using the room," he said while squatting in the lotus position and fiddling for a comfortable position. He closed his eyes and started the mental stages he'd developed so well, focusing on the point between his eyebrows, and on his breathing exercises at the same time.

A white light manifested at the fringes of his mind's eye, timid and transparent like fog on a humid morning in the jungle. It reached a certain clarity when his prayer intensified, then he could see it gathering in a shape of the crisp white-bordered circle surrounded by an all encompassing blue that quieted the last of the buzzing on his mind. He knew that at the end of this step the orange triangles were alive, energy pulsing through them at half the intensity grasped at the final stage.

A jeering laugh pierced his concentration, dissolving the peaceful white and blue of the inner world. It pulled him back brutally to the room where the men were talking to each other, excited by what they'd just experienced, with zero comprehension of how such silly behaviour could impact Rakash.

The third man was talking with a shrill voice. He looked almost as though he were a replica of the other thin man, but bald and with pronounced ridges dropping from the corners of his mouth. They could have been brothers.

Rakash didn't move, just stared of them, sensing the omnipresent greed in their animated conversation. Bringing these humans down the right path would be a challenge even for an evolved *Orange Soul.* He would try anyway. His lips felt dry and he licked them a couple of times. The chattering stopped and he was ready to reprimand them for their insensitive demeanor, but he knew better.

"Meditation requires one to be calm and find an inner balance. That's why I need a separate space and the people attending to be quiet," the boy explained calmly.

"We're sorry," Vargas apologized, vaguely bowing his head, feeling equally guilty for the disturbance. "When can you start?"

"In two days. And don't bring more than six people," Rakash replied, then he stood, rolling up his rug and starting towards the door.

The men followed him, all largely smiling, revealing their yellowish teeth wedged on sickly-looking gums.

"The car is downstairs waiting to drive you back home. See you soon," they said as they shut the door behind him.

* * *

RAKASH RETURNED TO DEER'S HEIGHTS two days later, mentally prepared to guide Laeta's people out of ignorance and into the invisible omnipresent ocean of love *One Who Created All* spread everywhere like a magic powder, and for one to see it, one had to recalibrate his senses. His mission would continue in a more familiar environment, but as he learnt by now from his Korobat experience, the message and the sincerity of its delivery was more significant than where it was conveyed. He hoped that his hosts would carefully select individuals adorned with innate curiosity to find a meaningful purpose in life, a question that he doubted the crowds visiting Laeta or the locals, posed to themselves.

Rakash knew that he had to convert the initial awe of energy-enhanced orange triangles into personal motivation for each of them, promising the evanescence of bad habits and a holistic overhaul of their soul. Having the *Supreme Being* on his side, the most desirable teacher of all, Rakash felt rewarded for his solitary life away from the village and the hurdles dotting his spiritual path. He'd found shelter in loving and adoring *One Who Created All* to ease the toughness of the last three years spent in a world so foreign to him.

While climbing up the stairs to the fourth floor, the discussion they had in Korobat about Yehuda, permeated his thoughts revealing a subtle association between the two of them, but one hundred years apart. He now understood his brother's frustration in not being able to spread the teachings of *One Who Created All* outside the hallowed village. Rakash didn't know if *He* forbade the sharing of knowledge since the time was not right or an overwhelmed Yehuda couldn't calibrate himself to the vibration that would have opened him to the subtle communication channel with the *Spiritual Father*.

The path Rakash had followed so far was much more smooth not only because of his arduous faith, but because for some unexplained reasons, *One Who Created All*'s support was palpable and encouraging.

The boy stopped in front of the door, took several deep breaths to calm himself, and then knocked. Vargas opened it. His fat, saggy face was shiny from sweat and his hair had a new coat of red and blue on the sides, and a dark purple in the middle where the colours were supposed to mix.

He moved aside so Rakash could step into the bustling of a small, but excited crowd. Immediately, Vargas raised his voice to draw everyone's attention.

"I need you to be quiet for a moment, please," and the clatter dimmed to a whisper between the two thin men, Vargas' partners.

"Here is Rakash, the reason for today's gathering. He's from the jungles of the south, but he spent the last three years commuting between Laeta and Korobat trying to develop a technology that can induce a *state of bliss.*"

They all raised their glasses in the air and cheered for him like he was their savior who was about to offer an unexpected repentance for their numerous sins. Rakash wasn't sure if it was their way of showing respect or just a normal reaction to a potential new experience. The participants, both men and women, six in total, in addition to the hosts, took their excitement further and began embracing him as a newfound brother. Drops of wine spilled on the boy's shoulders from the precariously held glasses, and Vargas had to extract him by gently pushing aside a couple of guests.

"Let's settle down now. Rakash, thank you for your enthusiasm. I've already explained you, people, what the process is. Let's stick to it. The boy will answer your questions. Please sit!" Vargas said.

The men spread out on the couches, and even though there was enough room for them as well, the only two women preferred to squat on the floor beside each other, staring at Rakash, and based on how the hosts promoted the encounter, anticipating him to perform a miracle any second now.

Rakash remained standing in front of them, holding his meditation rug. Silly smiles were plastered on most of their faces, a sign that alcohol had taken over before any reformation work could be done. He glanced at the docile crowd whose understanding of his teachings would be forgotten as soon as their soberness was reinstated.

"Pursuing the *state of bliss* is a serious matter. How do you suppose to discern what's happening in front of you when your mind is artificially altered?" he admonished them firmly, empowered by the respect he had gained in Korobat.

The group fell completely silent since none of them expected to be reprimanded by a child.

“You need a clear head, an open mind and a heart full of love, otherwise this is just a waste of time,” he continued with the same tone.

The smiles vanished and, for once, their glasses were left untouched.

“What questions do you have?” Rakash asked.

One of the women raised her hand halfway then, understanding that she was the only one willing to satisfy her curiosity, said, “Can you summarize the main steps and how long the whole process would take?”

In the question, the villager sensed the same urgency in reaching enlightenment. Like with any other activity performed, instant gratification was the main reward. They were actions devoid of any spiritual meaning or consideration for a higher purpose. He pitied them for such decay. This was an almost insurmountable task weighing heavy on his shoulders enshrouded in a garb of holiness offered by *One Who Created All.* Rakash felt *Him* close, and that sensation of support made him stronger and determined to bring to life the belief for which Bart had lost his. If he considered everyone his brother and sister, as per the *Supreme Being*’s teachings, this undertaking was not a sacrifice, but the moral duty of any *Orange Soul.*

Selecting his words with considerable care, Rakash offered the details put together in Korobat. His voice became passionate when he mentioned *One Who Created All* and *His* unlimited forgiveness and understanding for those willing to attune themselves to a higher vibration, leaving behind a complacent existence, malnourished by any spiritual touch.

“What you will see radiating on my face,” he said as he touched the triangle on his left cheek, “is proof of *His* acceptance of my unrelenting desire to return to a realm that I’ve already had a glimpse of. But my calling in this world has only begun as is your journey today. When will it end? Only you and the *Father* know that. Forsake bad habits and a goalless life. Don’t be oblivious to *His* dispensing of love and care that you’ve never sensed before because you had no one to open your eyes to it; mend this priceless relationship, repent, and *He* will forgive you and welcome you back into *His* celestial home."

Rakash didn't wait for their reactions. He turned around and strolled across the room to the only door that was open. The furs were gone and the bed was pushed to the right, creating more space for his meditation rug, and, even if he didn't request it, the paintings were also removed, leaving behind rectangles of darker blue on the faded walls exposed to daily light. He placed the rug on the floor and sat down in the lotus position, initiating his breathing exercises.

"Is he mad?" whispered one of the guests. "What are we getting into? You said we'd have fun," he said pointing at Vargas, who was also taken aback by Rakash's ardent speech.

"You're going to enjoy it, just sit and watch," he advised.

"Yes, Derek, let's wait. We already paid the fee anyways," one of the women amended.

They all pulled their chairs closer to the room's door so they could all see the boy. His back was straight, eyes closed and palms pointed upwards, resting on his thighs.

From behind his guests Vargas leaned forward to reach as many ears as possible and reminded them very softly, "No cheers, laughing or any disturbing noises when you see the orange light. Just hold tight until he's done."

Then he sat in the third row. They didn't have to wait long. It came as a flicker at first, then the light insinuated itself underneath the boy's skin, while his chest movement was barely visible. The women opened their mouths in awe of the spectacle, but made no sound. They turned towards Vargas smiling in appreciation, their glowing faces confirming the uniqueness of what they were witnessing. The men were harder to impress since sitting in one place and focusing on an immobile child was far from enticing.

Fifteen minutes later Rakash started the reverse process, coming out of the deep meditation. The four men invited to the performance had no more patience left now that they were allowed to move around. They voiced their disappointment to Vargas and his associates, and only after they extracted the promise of a free pass to an exclusive party later that day, did they calm down and leave. It wasn't the outcome the hosts had expected, but they focused on the women whose excitement was visible and who had more questions for Rakash.

"Very impressive," said the younger of the two, a petite blonde, her hair gathered in an intricate bun on the top of her head. Her upper body revealed a tattooed sequence of bizarre signs and letters covered by a T-shirt barely larger than the size of her bra. There was nothing appealing about her round, flat face and her unusual bulky brown eyes, but a different kind of beauty Rakash sensed, deeply embedded inside of her, made him listen.

"I want that skill."

She had frivolous behaviour, but who didn't in this city of sin?

While thinking of an encouraging answer, the boy noticed the worry on Vargas' face that he might have scared the remaining customers of a spectacle too elaborate for them. Rakash only now understood, from the snippets of the earlier conversation Vargas had with the men, that they had all paid a hefty fee to watch the freaky villager. Keeping the women interested and retained for another session would please his hosts.

"Anyone can attain an inner enlightenment, and, as I explained already, you have to convince yourself that no hurdle can stop this decision. There's nothing easy about it. You are asking *One Who Created All* for the redemption of your lost soul," he chose to reply.

The meaning of his words didn't penetrate her mind completely, but she smiled and nodded her head. The other woman also looked hopeful that *One Who Created All* would listen to her request and grant her wish.

"Come back tomorrow sober," he said and dropped on one of the couches, waiting for the room to clear.

He presumed Vargas would provide some feedback, but he didn't care too much anymore, as the striking truth hit his reality again about the deceitful arrangement between the committee and the people running that place. The corroding of senses-bound humans was a disease eating them alive, purging them of any feelings that made them human and leaving behind empty shells that were easily broken. He feared that the spiritually forgotten people of the entire world gathered in that city and he would have no one to infuse divine qualities into through meditation and exposure to *One Who Created All.*

"Not bad for the first trial. The ladies will be back tomorrow." Vargas sounded confident; his eyes avoided Rakash's, a sure sign that he foresaw a higher retention for the following day.

'Maybe even Vargas overestimated what would qualify as an eccentric encounter, and maybe the device the president mentioned is the key to a new level of entertainment and pleasure,' thought the boy.

"This isn't the right place for the teachings of the *Supreme Being.* I don't feel a good vibration," the villager declared, wishing for a certain level of understanding and empathy from Vargas who could have arranged for a more suitable location. The man pulled a chair in front of Rakash so he could deliver an honest assessment of the session.

"What's happening here can't be shared with anyone else, not even with your friend, Nayan. We have to handle it with extreme sensitivity while each of us pursues his own goal. More people eager for new sensations equals more money in my pocket, and, at the same time, plenty of people to choose from for your great master. I need you here everyday, do your gig with passion, go home, and repeat it the next day. There's no other option. At least not for now, we've just barely started."

It was a sober statement framing a dull future in Laeta for Rakash who wanted nothing more than to serve other humans while keeping a humble profile. The thought provoked a thick lethargy that overtook his body, disconnecting his brain from sending any signal that would allow movement. He stared, immobile, at Vargas, blinking several times in acknowledgement.

"Good. I'll see you here tomorrow," Vargas dismissed him. "I have more guests arriving in ten minutes ..."

Then he walked over to his partners.

* * *

RAKASH SHARED WITH NAYAN ONLY the positives of his first session in Vargas' lair, leaving out all the dirty details that might disturb his friend.

He exaggerated the participants' excitement in witnessing the power of *One Who Created All,* and, in the following days, the number of devotees that kept coming back for their own inward experience. The two women that had shown initial interest lasted only five days, after which the inescapable gnarling of neglected bad habits roared back furiously. Rakash found himself again in the blue room, facing a weird audience each time. Mixed physical bodies of various shapes and sizes, unsure of their own direction in life and unaware of a meaningful goal, stared at him coldly, still unsure of what to expect from the young lad.

The daily grind of exposing himself to strangers with no comprehension of the concepts he was describing numbed his noble desire to spread goodness and ancient teachings. He was ashamed of his growing impatience and realized that his hard-fought inner peace was easily being swept away by the crowd's tidal wave of low-vibrational cravings.

Deer's Heights' fourth floor had a different dynamic that day. Rakash was forced several times to avoid colliding with heavy men carrying fresh supplies to Vargas' apartment. Alcohol, fruits, and pots of cooked food, left behind a trail of a tingling scent of spices. It seemed that the businessman might have invited a bigger crowd than usual. The boy dragged himself upstairs, loathing the thought of mingling with more newcomers and explaining the rules and purpose of the sessions once again.

The apartment's door was open and he found Vargas directing where each item had to be placed.

"Hey, here you are. The guests should arrive any minute. Do you want to eat or drink anything?" he asked.

"No, I'm fine."

Vargas made a sinister chuckle, his eyes brighter than what Rakash had noticed before.

"Are you okay? What's going on?"

The man chuckled again like he was ready to deliver a joke that he had already told others and was still giggling at their reactions.

"I'm expecting a special guest. He's extremely rich and needs the best of everything. Don't worry, he and his entourage will use the opposite rooms. As long as they stay inside you won't hear a peep. Just recite your speech, start the session and try hooking two or three suckers," he said, head jolting backwards in a high-pitched laugh.

'Could be drugs,' Rakash said to himself, even if he never saw the man take any in his presence.

He entered the blue room to escape for a moment from the bustling outside. For a brief moment the noise faded completely. Then, the narrow stairs echoed loud with voices of a merry group looking for a welcoming place. Moments later, a mixture of men and women burst into the main room. A short man shook Vargas' hand, giving him a thick envelope. He wore thick-soled shoes that put his head at the same level as Vargas' shoulder. His lean body sustained a disproportionately large head. He looked around the room and Rakash could see his face, half wrinkled, half smooth, and his mean eyes, round and green on the left, oblique and dark on the right. A silk cape embroidered with dragons and multicoloured birds that Rakash had never seen before, covered his shoulders.

Vargas bowed to him slightly, which was very unusual for his inflated ego, and, together, they moved towards the room reserved for the party. From where he was seated, the boy recognized partially exposed elephant and tiger heads tattooed on the backs of the two women that were part of the group. The wide band of their bras covered the hypnotic eyes, so walking behind them would be safe.

Moments later, people enticed to watch Rakash's performance arrived and began to fill the chairs in the main room. The group was predominantly composed of women who knew each other judging by their vivid conversations. Vargas' partners asked them to quiet down, and Rakash, dressed in silk orange pants and collarless shirt, a gift from his hosts to match the colour of his eyes and birthmarks, gathered his wits to take him to the end of another session. He looked through them, tired of assessing potential 'suckers' as Vargas called them. He knew better. They were all children of *One Who Created All,* who surrendered their will to a manipulative force that incinerated any trace back to a spiritual path by feeding them false signals of material desires. His own soul felt bruised and destitute from so much indifference. For a moment, Otan's shape appeared in front of him out of a dispersing cloud and he asked himself again why no one from the village was looking for him. People in the audience giggled when the details of what they were supposed to see were revealed. He didn't reprimand them this time, it would only scare or make them angry.

He squatted on the rug, ready for the show.

He would go deep inside himself, break new boundaries of personal exploration and forget about these fake creatures that wouldn't expect any final comments from him; the orange lights on his cheeks should be enough to complete the performance. Hopefully, they would get bored soon and let him be. He needed to dive where no eternal sound could reach him; a complete physical shutdown of his body. Then he merged with the shimmering hue of his consciousness, descending, descending, descending. A soothing calmness embraced him in a celestial garment fit for those fighting in *His* name with endless determination. His battered soul thanked him for the recharging incursion in the energy field. There was no outside world anymore, no worry, just floating in the ocean of consciousness, aware that he was only a drop in it.

But a high-pitched scream penetrated all of his shields, shaking his balance. He was tackled to the ground, his hands held tight and clothes ripped off. Drowsy from his inward journey, Rakash barely opened his eyes to see a large shaved head attached to giant shoulders crossed by blackened scars. He stayed glued, face down and incapable of resisting the brutal force.

"Let's see what a jungle ass looks like!"

It was an arrogant voice that spoke, and a rumple-skinned face bent over close to his as if the character was looking for Rakash's approval to check his bottom. Rakash could barely open his eyes halfway from the pressure generated by the enormous hand keeping his head pinned to the carpet, but he recognized the features of Vargas' esteemed guest. From the odd angle he could see his audience and the entourage of the hideous man that Vargas had so ceremoniously welcomed mingle together, some of them completely naked, their senses in disarray. His vision blurred again, the reek of spilled alcohol choked his senses.

The women with the animal tattoos on their backs hovered close. A black man with long, entangled locks of hair caressed them both. Rakash tried to scream for help, but all he did was gnash his teeth painfully, no sound escaping his mouth.

He was hopeful for an instant, noticing as the women stopped for a moment and looked in his direction when the same voice gave an assessment of the boy's ass. "Guys, this ass looks just like ours, only fresher and with no hair. Maybe it's different on the inside. I'm going in to find out!" the man with the distorted face announced loudly.

Everyone laughed and cheered. Stumbling on a fallen body, Vargas approached the door for a closer look. He was also naked, his belly hung over his exposed genitals, and he could barely keep his balance.

Rakash's eyes welled with tears, understanding that no one would stop whatever was going to happen to him. The drunken brute collapsed on top of him and pulled his legs part. Sudden pain flamed through him as if a metal jagged edge was grinding his insides. The pain was like nothing he had ever experienced before. He groaned and hissed, sounds that only a wounded animal in the jungle would make. For a brief moment, the excruciating pain heightened his senses and he took in the filthy smell of sweaty bodies, the belching, the farting. All the odors conspiring to punish him through asphyxiation. He felt lower than a wounded animal .... Lower ... Lower.

'Why does One Who Created All want me to feel so much pain?' he thought before passing out in a pool of blood.

CHAPTER 13

Dear Father, beam Your light onto my spiritual path so that I will not get lost in the dense entanglement of my delirious thoughts.

From the book *We Are One* – Chapter 13

TANDAR AND MARIAM WERE THE first to come to their senses and witness the devastation generated by what everyone would refer to as 'a party to remember'. Naked bodies lay strewn on the couches and on the floor, some of them frozen in painful positions, numbed by the excessive use of drugs and alcohol. The women were also naked. They moved to the room where everything started, avoiding spots of vomit and shards of glass from shattered bottles. After a quick search, they found their skirts and bras tossed in a corner and put them on, ready to disappear before anyone else woke up.

Vargas' client, Tafaran, as he had introduced himself, had really messed up the place with his appetite for high consumption. Mariam walked closer to the other side of the main room as she had a recollection that something significant took place over there. Vargas' thick body was blocking the entrance to the room on the right side so she had to step over him. His head rested on the floor, saliva dripping down from the corner of his mouth. He had several bruises on his left arm and thigh from his friendly wrestling match with Tafaran who didn't comply with any rules, and had kicked Vargas repeatedly with his heavy shoes until the businessman's legs gave out from under him.

"Tandar, come here!" Mariam called her friend in a shrill voice.

The woman with the elephant tattooed on her back pushed her head in, not wanting to step over Vargas. "What happened?"

"Isn't this the kid we saw at the beach? The one Martinez told us to keep an eye on?" Mariam pointed to a body sprawled on its belly with blood all around it.

"Turn his head towards me," Tandar said, still not moving from the doorframe.

Mariam bent down and gently turned Rakash's head in the opposite direction where more light was coming through the windows. They both noticed the orange signs on his cheeks at the same time.

"It's him! Poor thing. Tafaran did him last night," Mariam clarified.

There was dried blood on the boy's back and a larger dark crust around his anus. She then noticed Tafaran laying in bed, almost completely buried under several women that were not part of their initial group. The wrinkled side of his face was easily distinguishable from the smooth skin of the young bodies he slept with. Mariam held back the urge to kick him for what he did to Rakash, but she only swore at him. The life the women were living didn't involve a high level of human decency, but one paramount rule they always obeyed was not to involve children in any of the twisted requirements their clients had. Many children had perished, including some of their friends, in Korobat over the last twenty years due to the contamination hazards, creating a sensibility in them.

"Help me cover the boy. He's cold," Mariam called to her friend.

Tandar, who just wanted to leave the apartment, hesitated for a moment, then stepped over Vargas. Mariam was already holding a bed sheet to wrap Rakash with.

"Turn him slowly towards me. I'll pick him up. Perfect. Now grab those pillows and put them by the window. We'll lay him down on them so he is out of the way when Tafaran wakes," she instructed Tandar.

They were almost done when Vargas suddenly groaned and tried to shift from the doorframe. He was too heavy and only with considerable help would he be able to move from that awkward position. The women froze and waited for him to doze off again.

Rakash hung inert in Mariam's arms and made no sound when placed on the soft cushions.

"How did he end up like this?" Tandar wondered with heavy remorse in her voice.

"Let's go now. I'll tell you whatever I remember," Mariam whispered.

They shut the apartment door behind them and hurried down the stairs.

When they emerged into the anonymous safety of the street, Miriam gave her summary: "Tafaran demanded that everyone in our group keep up with him on drugs and booze. We did for a while, but then he snorted from the elephant's trunk. We thought it would slow him down, but it had a reverse effect on him. Then Vargas tried, then all the others and, suddenly, the room seemed suffocating and we all spilled out to where the other group was watching Rakash. Tafaran shared some synthetic with them and then walked towards the boy. I had no idea what was going to happen. I was paralyzed anyways." Mariam grabbed Tandar's arm. "We have to tell Martinez, even if he's not interested in the boy anymore. Maybe we can do a good deed. The damage is already done!"

Tandar nodded, but her usual smile was absent, wiped out by the jarring image of Rakash's battered body. It was the first time since they became Vargas' 'exclusives' that remorse entered their minds.

* * *

TANDAR AND MARIAM WERE ENJOYING a warm afternoon in Laeta at their favourite terrace close to Vargas' shop one week after the incident. It was the same place the businessman used to deliver the details for the women's nightly encounters with high profile clients, mainly held at Deer's Heights. The plan to help Rakash escape Vargas' insatiable greed was put in motion as soon as the women received, through a White Tiger messenger, detailed instructions from Martinez. "Help the team extract him immediately. Pack all of your belongings, you are not returning to Laeta." This was quite radical compared to all the previous messages from Korobat's leader.

"I didn't know that the kid was so important," Mariam said, sipping a coffee.

Since the incident with Rakash a week ago, they loathed going back to the crime scene. The boy was still there, staring blankly. His abuse had become routine, but they couldn't do anything to stop it. Even talking to Vargas was painfully difficult, knowing that he was consciously taking advantage of a traumatized child veering on a path of no return. They recognized that an unfortunate accident had happened that night, and expected not to see Rakash in that building again. But Vargas, contractually in control of the boy, assessed his options and informed the committee of the incident. Defiling a villager proved to be much more profitable than anyone expected, and even if Vargas left out the financial reward that Tafaran, his wealthy client, paid for the experience, his smiling eyes and the tremor of his hanging chin at the thought of the amount, gave the committee a pretty good idea. "The boy won't be able to do his show for a while now," Vargas concluded. "His gaze is hollow. His mind maybe already looking for *One Who Created All*," he said and a laugh shook the fat covering his body. The unanimous decision that the defilement should carry on was immediately put into practice, and only three days later, the waiting list was two pages long.

"The dysfunctional piece of shit", as they started calling him, didn't wait for Rakash's wounds to heal and for his pain to recede, but instead continued the show since certain clients liked young meat.

"We'll have to give up all this," Tandar replied, gesturing to the surroundings. "We had a good time, saved some money and kept our families safe," she concluded, pleased with the brief summary of their achievements in Laeta.

They had both developed a nice tan from the time spent on the beach by themselves or with various clients. One of Vargas' employees, a tall, thin youngster with long hair and a squished face, ran towards them and handed Mariam a piece of paper.

"The boss is busy right now, so he sent me instead," he stated the obvious. "He said he won't come tonight, the apartment is all yours," he added then he turned around and was swallowed by the crowd.

Mariam opened the note and her face lit up. "This client wants Rakash and us together. The boy will be brought upstairs. This is the opportunity we've been waiting for. We wouldn't have accepted this job anyways." She turned halfway to her right, still pretending to address

Tandar, but the two heavy built men at the table beside theirs, knew that it was meant for them. "Tonight at 8:00 pm at Deer's Heights, fourth floor. We don't expect more than one guard to be present as Vargas won't be there. Let's try not to hurt anyone. Meet us thirty minutes earlier at our place so we can load up our stuff," Mariam said still looking at the note.

The men didn't say a word. They finished their drinks and left. They were both wearing long sleeve shirts and black scarfs around their necks, the only way to cover their White Tiger identification tattoos. No one in Laeta would connect the gang to the rescue mission.

* * *

BUTTERFLIES FLUTTERED INSENSIBLY in their stomachs while they climbed the stairs to the fourth floor at Deer's Heights, aware that this would be their last night in Laeta. They would never be able to come back, at least not until Vargas was dead or their identities forgotten or both. They were about to divest the businessman of an important source of revenue, and the city of the only jungle boy ever captured. The climb seemed harder than ever, each step tugging at their feet like an invisible creature feeding on their energy, trying to drain it all before they reached the top. They were perpetrators this time, but they couldn't display any sign of weakness if they wanted to liberate Rakash from his ordeal.

"Hello, ladies!"

Belanar had already brought the boy to the apartment and was now guarding it. Tandar and Mariam smiled back at him as he opened the door for them. He was one head taller than Vargas and heavier, more of an intimidator than anything else.

"The clients should arrive soon," Tandar said touching Belanar gently on the arm.

The door closed behind them and instead of getting ready for the client, they went to Rakash's room, the same one in which the orgy had taken place.

Rakash didn't see them, in fact, he didn't see anyone anymore. He was fed, bathed, and clothed by hired hands, then brought upstairs almost daily to satisfy the carnal desires of deranged individuals that had reached the limit of mundane experiences and were looking for flickers of originality.

The women talked to him, mainly for their own comfort since repeating the plan out loud gave them more confidence in its success. Rakash wore a blue silk robe and, as expected, nothing else underneath. They had mentioned to Hando that appropriate clothing was required and the White Tiger were supposed to bring it with them.

Tandar helped the boy stand and, together, they went to the main room while Mariam looked around for any items that belonged to him. She took the stained meditation rug, the blood couldn't be removed completely, and a small painting on the wall above the bed, that she had learnt belonged to Rakash. She unhooked it and hurried after Tandar.

The butterflies still moved relentlessly in their bellies, adding to the torment of restless thoughts about a potentially failed extraction.

The door opened and the two White Tiger warriors from the cafe walked in backwards, dragging Belanar by his hands. They dropped him in one of the rooms, out of sight. A third man was waiting in the hallway, watching for unanticipated visitors. Clothing for Rakash was handed to Mariam so the women began to disrobe the boy, then dress him again.

"He's ready," Tandar announced and they all moved out. On top of the stairs the women's hands were tied and their mouths gagged. Then they were lifted on to the warriors' shoulders, a pretense that they were taken against their will. Rakash was also lifted in the arms of one of the men. The climb down was fast and the party stopped at the reception desk for several moments, just enough for the young girl on duty to witness what was happening. She was tied to her chair and watched by a fourth warrior that smiled at her, as they passed then left himself.

Outside, the warriors put the women down and untie them. Then, they all followed the narrow street between the buildings, turning left and right several times, towards the fringes of the Entertainment District where cars used to transport drugs to Laeta were waiting. No passerby paid any attention since parties were about to start and everyone was in a hurry. They reached their destination safely.

It was a new beginning for the women.

* * *

FACILITATING RAKASH'S RETURN TO LAETA without the approval of the council, had been a daring undertaking that Martinez took on his own. Even if his colleagues had seen Rakash' abuse through the same lenses of understanding as his, sanctioning the rescue and antagonizing an important client of their technologies, such as Laeta, was out of the question, no matter how many arguments Hando could have presented. But for the leader, it was an act of compassion, a way of searching for leniency when his turn for *One Who Created All's* judgment came.

While alive, Bart had explained the meaning of judgment, and, at that time, it sounded odd to Martinez: but if, somehow, this judgment lifted the current heaviness off his chest, he wouldn't care about any repercussions.

Asking the White Tiger for a favour was the obvious choice in helping with Rakash's extraction. To keep him safe and away from prying eyes, Hando had also arranged for the boy to stay in an apartment inside the gang's building where only Clapel and himself were allowed in.

It resembled the previous residence Rakash and Bart lived in, but only one bedroom was used this time. A replica of the lab's meditation environment was also recreated in one corner of the living room, facing the large windows to the east.

Several familiar objects, such as the painting recovered from Laeta, a couple of books about the villagers, left behind when Rakash departed, and a new rug, were integral parts of the recuperation process that Hando had been monitoring on his own. Nothing had changed in the boy's behaviour since the escape. He displayed the same inertia and dependency on outside help for basic needs, such as dressing, washing and feeding. The leader couldn't present a broken Rakash to the team, knowing that the enthusiasm of building a life-shifting device still resonated with everyone involved in this venture. The image of a battered human being that they revered only a short time ago would crash their wit and potentially create discord in a team that was getting along so well. Martinez could only imagine the pain, the dissolution and the anguish Rakash experienced at the hands of lascivious and utterly sick adults.

The leader hoped that patience and loving care would snap Rakash back from behind the protective mental fields he had created for himself. At least, this was his uneducated guess. He expected that, deep inside, among crumbled beliefs and bitter feelings, the spark of the boy still flickered, waiting for the right chance to light and flare up with even greater ferocity. He knew that the knowledge and help that he could provide were limited, and would only generate constraints that would elongate Rakash's recovery. Therefore, keeping his involvement with Rakash to a minimum was the best course of action, but it did not help to ease his growing feelings of guilt and uselessness. Martinez would have to play the charade of not knowing what happened to the boy and send updates to Korobat's committee on the development of the device every now and then. He expected Laeta to maintain the pretense that everything was alright and that Rakash was available to assess the device when ready. It was a strategic balance that he didn't want to disturb, at least not until the boy came out of his inner 'hiding', a process that Hando had no idea how long it might take. Suddenly, Nayan had become an important element in his shaky strategy, and maybe the only person whose love for Rakash could melt his self-imposed consciousness freeze. Convincing Nayan that his friend was badly hurt would be a less daunting task, only if Nayan could travel to Korobat under a false pretense, and be faced with a reality that no words could describe.

* * *

"PEOPLE FROM KOROBAT PICKED UP RAKASH today in a hurry. They have a prototype they want Rakash to test," Nayan remembered being informed by a note sent by Kanar about his friend's abrupt departure from Laeta. "Rakash will write to you if time allows him. You might be able to visit him as soon as we get confirmation from Korobat's officials that such visit is appropriate, the note went. Nayan felt elated that, finally, the sustained effort of the last three years could materialize in a physical device that would bring everyone closer to *One Who Created All*, and even change perceptions and lifestyles.

Nayan somehow swallowed the president's explanation that the Korobatians that had come to pick him up couldn't wait a minute longer, but he hadn't heard from Rakash in four weeks so he was now at city hall waiting patiently outside Kanar's office. No one besides the president had updates about his friend.

"How much longer?" he asked the secretary, a middle-aged woman wearing large rimmed-glasses that distorted her pupils.

She raised her head from the papers she was shuffling and smiled condescendingly as if she were saying '*Be a good boy and stop bothering me. The president will see you when he's ready.*'

"I understand he's busy, but I need to know that Rakash is well. I haven't received any letters yet. He promised he would write me every week," he pushed harder, hoping that raising his voice would attract some attention.

The woman was ready to admonish him, but the door to the president's office opened and Kanar stepped out. "Walk with me, Nayan," he said jovially and moved quickly towards the stairs.

The boy followed, barely keeping pace with him. "Do you have any news? You promised that you'd send a messenger to Korobat," Nayan asked.

"Yes, I did. All is well. Rakash was meditating and couldn't be disturbed. We should get a reply from him next week. Maybe he'll ask for you to join him," Kanar said and laughed suddenly as if he were hearing a good joke. "There is no reason for you to worry. We all agreed that he would return to Korobat if necessary. And it seems that it was necessary," he concluded.

Nayan reached the bottom of the stairs safely and moved in front of Kanar, blocking his path. They were almost the same height so the boy didn't feel intimidated in any way. "Don't you find it suspicious that Korobat found a solution so fast?"

"Not at all. Maybe their research was indeed as strong as they claimed it to be," Kanar said, justifying his sudden abundance of trust in Martinez and his team. Then walked around Nayan, continued onto the street.

The boy didn't chase him. He sensed the evasiveness in the elder's behaviour and tone.

Nayan went home, filled a small backpack with some snacks and a change of clothes, left a note for Panette saying not to worry about him for the next couple of days, and then hurried to catch the first bus to Korobat. He refused to abandon his friend again.

He let himself be lulled by the engine's humming, his thoughts drifting to happier memories of the past when both master and Rakash were well, and surrounded him with love and care. He was not sure anymore if the path opened by his benefactor, and sustained with so much effort, was worth the personal sacrifices that had affected their lives. Now that he was left by himself, Nayan, once again, comprehended the impact master had had on his upbringing by creating the warm atmosphere of a family, even without a woman's presence. Sleep took him over unannounced.

Three hours later, he was waiting in another antechamber, this time for Martinez.

When Martinez received the message that Nayan was in Korobat, he couldn't believe his luck, and, out of a newfound respect for *One Who Created All*, he looked towards the sky and sent a quick mental 'thank you', just in case his name was on the 'special list' of those who had direct access to the *Supreme Being.*

"I want to see Rakash right away!" came the demand as soon as Hando stepped into his office where the boy was waiting.

The leader disregarded the boy's tone and hugged him fondly like an old friend he hadn't seen in a long time. "I'm so glad you came," Hando replied after freeing Nayan from his arms. "I didn't know if it was wise to reach out to you in case the committee was monitoring your moves," he said, taking a seat in front of the boy.

"Why would they monitor me? I don't understand. I spoke with Kanar today about Rakash. He said my friend was here, helping you validate the device, the prototype. But I didn't believe him completely. Something is off," Nayan blurted out.

Hando went through the ritual of touching his ponytail and removing his eyeglasses to massage the base of his nose, then put them back on and said, “Rakash is here with us, but no one else knows about it, except for Clapel. Kanar was improvising, as he really doesn’t know where Rakash is. He might think he’s here, but he has no proof. I don’t want to lie to you so I need your word that I can trust you.”

Nayan nodded and pushed his body forward to catch every word Martinez was about to share.

“My concern was that if I had told you in Laeta what really happened to Rakash you wouldn’t believe me unless you saw it for yourself.”

Hando took his time telling Nayan the abominable story of the rape, but left out the obscene details that Tandar and Mariam had described to him first hand. If he wanted Nayan’s cooperation, he had to be honest with the boy. He watched Nayan’s face change, distorted by burning rage, tears bursting down his cheeks. Then, his entire body cringed with pain and his internal pressure exploded into a long yell that turned into more sobbing.

Soheila came in, alarmed by the noise, but Hando waved his hand at her to leave. “I’ll take you to him now. He needs you. Mentally, he’s in a lot of pain,” the leader said after Nayan showed signs of recollecting himself.

“I won’t let Kanar and Vargas go unpunished,” the hurting boy said, clenching his teeth, giving the impression that he was already thinking of ways to torture them.

Hando grabbed his shoulders making Nayan look him in the eyes.

“We can only help Rakash now by pretending that we believe in their game. Let’s keep the illusion up until our friend is back from the dark recesses of his locked memory,” the leader said emphatically as he had no other words of encouragement.

A car was waiting for them outside. No words were exchanged during the short ride, each of them mulling over what should be done next and what could be an efficient strategy of getting Rakash alive again.

Hando’s car was let in through the main gates by the White Tiger, and then they used the ‘box in the sky’ to reach the floor where the villager was hidden.

"I'll wait outside," said Hando in front of the apartment. "If he doesn't recognize you, don't push it. We have plenty of time for rehabilitation."

Nayan went in.

He saw Rakash from behind, sitting on a chair and gazing out the only window at a reddish flare in the sky, left behind by the sun that was retiring for the day. Nayan moved closer in smaller steps, careful not to disturb his friend's reverie.

"Rakash," he called gently, expecting, in spite of Hando's warning, to see a perceptible reaction to his voice.

He stepped in front of Rakash, blocking his view, waiting for some feedback this time. The villager barely blinked, and sustained his blank stare without seeing anything. There could have very well been a wall in front of him and it wouldn't have made a difference.

Nayan hugged the inert body and muttered more for himself than for Rakash.

"We both lost master. Let's not lose each other. Even if you have *One Who Created All* and all the brothers and sisters back in the village, I have no one else. I'll take care of you, but please, please, come back to me."

He came out fifteen minutes later, his eyes red from crying and displaying a somber face.

"You alerted me to his condition, but honestly, I thought you were exaggerating. He didn't react at all when I talked to him." Nayan leaned with his back against the wall and squatted over the carpet. "What can I do to help him?"

Martinez sat beside him, not sure how his suggestion would be received. "You can leave Laeta and move in with Rakash. There is no one else more suited to take care of him."

Nayan looked at Hando a little bit puzzled by the proposal and asked. "Drop school and give up the house just like that? No attachments?"

"Exactly. I think you should go back and pack all of the books and any material saved from the committee's clutches. Everything else is replaceable."

The boy rose to his feet with a profound exhale. An existence with a clear path until three years ago had been exciting after Rakash joined their family, only to turn now into an entanglement of deaths, conspiracies and high degree of pain, dragging Rakash and himself further away from the *Spiritual Father* that was patiently waiting for them. Perceiving this new reality in a positive way required much more than just unconditional faith in the finite vibratory energy surrounding them. It required a focused mind capable of assimilating and understanding the enriched thoughts and sensations that he had never experienced before; a mind engrossed in a perennial love that would shed frightening tendencies and reflections, which were adapting quickly to any new mental blockages he was creating and restlessly pounding at his inner peace.

"Karitan will drive you back to Laeta in the morning and drop you off at its fringes. You can't be seen together. He'll come by after it's dark to pick you up. Get whatever else might resonate with Rakash. Do you think you can manage in there for the night?" Hando asked and pointed to the apartment.

Without a word, Nayan stood up and went inside to face his silent friend once again.

* * *

AROUND HIM, the light vanished in an instant sucked by a malefic force to which his body reacted with a shortage of breath. Dense darkness engulfed Rakash's surroundings, preventing his senses from readjusting and finding their way back to the light.

He started praying to One Who Created All, but even if the silence was deafening, he couldn't hear his thoughts. He wasn't aware that his message was even ascending to its chosen destination. The thickness held him frozen, preventing the connectivity with the Supreme Being, so he felt lonely, forgotten and incapable of adapting to this newfound blindness. His head shrieked with pain every time he tried to conceive a thought, as though a threshold of punishment was linked to his brain.

He stopped fighting the awkward sensation of immobility while his body melted with whatever substance he was floating into. Time lost its meaning for him, perfidiously hiding any hint of reality that could have indicated his whereabouts. He sensed no panic or fear in the space around him, just an impersonal nothingness that avoided any contact, and, somehow, kept him alive for an unknown purpose. From time to time a breeze entered this hermetic space as he felt its cajoling and gentle brush against his cheeks, making him wonder if he could use the same opening to escape to the light and to a world from which he only remembered insignificant fragments.

He dwelt no longer on where and why he was; he conceded himself to One Who Created All, the only entity he still had a vague memory of. Germinating coherent thoughts was challenging. Lucid moments were longer now or at least he thought that was the case, because each time he accessed his consciousness, the dark surrounding him had a lighter nuance. It gave him hope that his efforts to stay awake would, in the end, implode the darkness and release his memory back to him. Lately, even muffled sounds were finding cracks in this protective layer, and all his energy was focused on filtering a potential message on how to escape his existing limitations.

He had an unceasing desire to peer through the dissipating twilight, deeper and deeper, knocking at its thickness until pure light basked his face and melted any other restrictions of his consciousness. Several words kept swirling in his mind, even if he didn't understand their meaning.

"One Who Created All, save me. Bring me back to my path."

He mentally repeated it over, and over again; a mute howl for help that might pierce the blockade that held him prisoner. There was no echo or answer. Rakash clutched at faith, which was another meaningless concept emerging from the reduced awareness around him.

"Faith ....faith ... faith"

* * *

A BLONDE BEARD, denser and sturdier than the hair on his head, but still thin and fluffy, rounded Nayan's angled chin giving the impression of a permanent aura. Grayish bags hung underneath his eyes that were happy in spite of the tiredness revealed by his hunched shoulders.

He was sitting beside Rakash on a bench in the courtyard of the White Tiger's compound in Korobat, hidden from unwelcome eyes. It had been three years, following Martinez's advice, since he left everything behind in Laeta and assumed the exhausting task of taking care of his friend. Rakash was still completely inwardly immersed. Occasionally, Nayan marveled at the villager's facial features that almost seemed frozen in time since he had slipped into the self-induced mental coma. He was a bit taller now, his hair kept at shoulder length, and his eyes a darker nuance of orange, lacking the sparkle that used to be an emotional indicator of his interest in daily activities. It was still difficult to stir emotions, feelings and memories that could have snapped him back from his existing vegetative state.

Once in Korobat, Nayan's life radically changed to fit into a strict schedule of watching Rakash's reactions to daily-imposed activities with the hope of noticing positive signs of recovery.

At the beginning, it felt odd for Nayan to express every single movement he was doing out loud, but he understood the rationale, and, after several days, it became natural. The long monologues he held in front of Rakash were quite good for his own psyche; talking to a mute audience that couldn't reply. From the steps of preparing breakfast to reading passages from the added research data that Martinez kept bringing him as soon as the team, still lead by Prakit, made it available, Nayan consistently turned all into stories. Most of the time he embellished with unnecessary elements that made no difference to his friend, but Nayan would mention them anyway, trusting that Rakash's stupor would filter only the necessary information and discard the rest.

Martinez paid them weekly visits, and, once a month, after Nayan disguised himself properly, he would take the teenager on a long drive with a stop for a tasty dinner at a less frequented 'hole in the wall' in the west district. It was a treat that helped Nayan unwind from worries built up inside him while in the compound.

All his efforts to stimulate Rakash seemed futile until two weeks ago when the mention of sky, clouds and the sun, drew a sensible movement of his eyes upwards. Nayan continued with words representing elements naturally ingrained in everyone's mind like the ground, trees, birds and body parts. Rakash's eyesight searched and identified all of them except for the trees. There were none in the paved courtyard.

"How is he today?" Hando asked, coming out from the building's shadow, and stepping into the warm embrace of the sun.

Nayan kept his eyes closed and without turning around, replied, "He's acknowledging the environment. I ran out of words that he could associate with. There is nothing else in here that might be familiar."

Hando sat on the bench on the other side of Rakash and touched his hand, not expecting a reaction. "We're not giving up on you, boy" he said, then addressed Nayan. "What do you want me to do?"

The Laetian didn't answer right away. He let the heat soak into his lean body a little longer.

"I think it's time we take him to the lab, and before you object, let me finish,'" he said, still not looking at the leader. "We can limit the number of people entering the lab only to those you can trust. It's been long enough since Rakash and I have disappeared from Laeta. No one else should be looking for us. He needs interaction with more people than just me."

Martinez removed his eyeglasses, wiped the perspiration coming down his nose, then put them back on so he could reply.

"If I do this, the committee might find out. I'll lose their trust."

"I'm not saying to move him into the lab permanently. We'll bring him late in the day so he can spend two or three days with a small team, and then we'll bring him back here. At the beginning, twice a month. The committee doesn't have to know yet. At least, not until Rakash is Rakash again," Nayan pleaded.

Martinez stood up, patted the villager on the head and said in a non-committal tone: "Give me a week to find the right moment to approach Prakit. He will be shocked to find out that Rakash was here all this time. I might need his help to give the news to the girls so there isn't a lot of commotion." Then he walked away.

Exactly a week later Martinez returned, beaming his usual optimism and bringing good news. "Prakit, Merlaya and Naranta are on board. It wasn't easy to convince them that I was serious when I said that Rakash has been in Korobat for the last three years. All this time I've deflected their questions about the boy's whereabouts and only now has it made sense to them."

"That's really encouraging," Nayan replied and embraced the leader with gratitude.

"However, the story I gave them is significantly less macabre. While in deep meditation in front of a crowd in Laeta, one of the guests, too drunk and bored, hit Rakash in the head with a bottle and the boy hasn't recovered since. Let's keep it that way," Hando added, revealing the delicate balance he had reached with both sides. "Only this reduced team knows the plan and will be allowed to interact with Rakash. While he's in the lab, the other members will be given tasks at different locations. We'll come in and out after dark," Martinez shared the rules.

On the decided day, all three of them snuck into the building and took the stairs since no city employee was on duty that late to handle the 'box in the sky'. The lights were dim and the blinds pulled in the lab. Prakit, Merlaya and Naranta formed black silhouettes against the white wall, but they could clearly see the faces of those entering the room. It was a quiet welcoming, full of meaningful hugging and sorrowful patting of Rakash, who stayed impassive and didn't react in any way. They talked in low voices even if no one else was around to hear them.

"We haven't used Rakash's room too much since he left. We've all continued our practice at home," Prakit clarified the situation for Nayan. "The best approach would be to stimulate his brain areas in reverse to what we did when he was around. We'll keep the sessions two hours long, pause for a couple of hours, and then continue," the research team leader explained.

They decided not to dwell on questions as to what happened to their friend, and instead immediately started using familiar steps that Rakash's brain might recognize as hidden patterns. All they had to do was, through signal repetition, rebuild those patterns, which were broken by a powerful emotional trauma.

The unusual circumstances of Rakash re-entering their lives didn't diminish their determination to find a remedy to his stupor; instead, it emboldened them even more. Their stale research could only advance further with the boy's help, which required him to be in a fully conscious state. The team only wished that Hando's decision to bring the boy to them, could have happened sooner.

Prakit led Rakash to the room built especially for him, sat him on the rug and tried to arrange his legs in the lotus position as best as he could.

Behind him, Naranta was busy with the wiring that had to be attached to the boy's head. On the other side of the window, Merlaya was selecting signals for the brain areas excited by the word 'love', the one with the highest feedback on the initial tests. Nayan and Martinez watched the preparation in silence, knowing that there was nothing they could help with. They were just facilitators of another type of experiment.

"Look at this!" Naranta exclaimed after everyone gathered back in the main room, waiting for the thrust of the information to take effect.

"His brain is very much alive and active," she continued, pointing out the intense colored areas pulsating in and out on the screen. "It's an activity bottled up inside him that can't be expressed. His brain is not damaged. It's sealed itself from the outside world as a protective measure. All we have to do is to tell it that there is no danger anymore, and that it's safe to release its jams."

"It sounds so simple," Hando said. "Will it need more than just the familiarity of the key words?" he asked.

None of the team members ventured with a quick answer, but in the end, Merlaya shared her opinion. "I believe we can bring him back. A trained brain like Rakash's is easier to reactivate than one without similar experiences. Another factor we have to consider is his heart's intuition."

"Heart's intuition?" Nayan repeated words asking for meaning.

Merlaya hugged herself as if she were trying to warm from a sudden shiver, then provided the details. "Recently, we came up with a theory that there might be a connection between the heart and the brain. It's a type of subtle communication that we stumbled upon by chance. Someone in the team compared the heartbeat charts with the one for Rakash's brain activity. No doubt, there is correlation between initiation and response and there is also a time delay but not initiated by the brain as we thought. It's the heart that dictates the brain's reaction."

"Are you saying that we have to unlock his heart, too?" Martinez asked, visibly concerned.

Merlaya nodded her head, and then continued. "The newly developed concept is based on the fact that the heart has its own *'thinking mechanism'* and has added sensibility compared to the brain. It has the *'feel'* that the brain lacks, turning the latter into an action tool. Though it's just a hunch that still needs to be tested. Each of us will take turns talking to his heart during the breaks. It's so crazy that it just might work."

"Good luck to all of us," the leader said. "I'll be back in the morning. Lock the door behind me." Then he left.

"How are we going to do it?" Nayan inquired, his hope suddenly sunk by the news of additional effort.

"We'll talk to him the same way you did, but we'll apply some physical contact. Our hand, when touching his chest, should be able to transfer our emotions and positive intentions. When that signal synchronizes with the brain, the unlocking mechanism should initiate," Merlaya explained.

"Can we start now or does he need rest?" Naranta interjected.

"He can't tell the difference between night and day anymore. When he's tired, he'll just close his eyes," Nayan provided another detail characterizing his friend's behaviour.

Abruptly, the goal of reaching the *state of bliss* became secondary, taken over by bringing clarity to Rakash's mind. Losing Bart was hard for everyone. Failing the villager as well would have been devastating. In that state, the boy couldn't add any value or issue an opinion. His special faculties aside, they still desired to call him friend, and reconnect with him like in the days he was living in Korobat.

The clandestine work that started in the dead of night continued over the next several weeks, Hando being especially careful that his repeated visits to the White Tiger compound wouldn't raise suspicions.

Each week, Rakash's reaction to new stimuli improved, his eyes recognizing objects once so familiar. Even an updated chart of his heart's behaviour indicated a more frequent communication with the brain, like a dam that was preventing a constant flow had just been removed. Before each session they all prayed to *One Who Created All* for strength and clarity on how to handle Rakash, and they also asked the *Supreme Being* for forgiveness on the boy's part for actions that had brought such a tragedy upon him.

* * *

SOMEONE WAS POKING from the outside at the shell surrounding him and he tried yelling several times just to let them know that he was alive and wanted out. But the walls that, over time, turned from black to gray muffled the words. He had the feeling that he could sense his cells pulsating with energy, happily talking to each other after an extended separation. He could acknowledge now that he had a body with its own weight, the impression of being suspended and immobile, slowly vanishing. He now knew that once he had an identity, a name, and people that were close to him that, somehow, he had lost the moment he entered the darkness.

An image came forward from the labyrinthine depths of his mind, a pair of beautifully colored trees in between which a child with orange eyes was sitting calmly, staring at him. He conveyed a message, and then the image dissolved: "You are not alone. I'll arrive soon".

The change in energy was palpable and predictable, sizzling inside him and sprouting buds of hope that his freedom was near. Thoughts of what brought him in this tight space raised in his mind a wave of constant doubts and heavy feelings that he had no memory of.

* * *

TIREDNESS OVERCAME THE ENTIRE TEAM after several intense hours of monitoring Rakash, whose recent inner activity on the monitors was almost identical to readings taken during his first trip to Korobat. They all fell asleep either on the couch or directly on the carpet, forgetting to unhook the boy from the sensory stimulation so he could also rest. The slumber hit them instantaneously; thus none of them witnessed the villager's resurrection from his three-year blackout.

Rakash sluggishly opened his eyes and looked around without moving his head. He noticed the window in front of him, the wires squeezing through the wall and a flickering light reflected on the glass, but he didn't want to formulate a conclusion. His mind could still be playing a macabre game of an illusory reality, tricking him back into the dimness.

The next test would definitely convince him of the difference between dream and reality so he moved his hands to the side. There was no pain or uncomfortable feeling. He could sense their weight. He grabbed his right hand with his left and the touch of firm flesh discharged some of the pressure built inside of him with a deep exhale. Once parameters such as volume and awareness were established, he shifted his body forward, trying to bring his legs underneath him for a push upwards. The action was interrupted half way, pulled back by the wires still connected to his head. He smiled, elated to receive another hint of his awakening in a recognizable environment. He slowly detached the sensors, dropped them on the floor, and stood firmly on his feet while his head fought for several moments with a light dizziness. In two steps he reached the door, and stepped into the lab, which was dim and quiet, where he identified Nayan and some of the other team members, fast asleep.

Hunger clasped his stomach, growling desperately, but his attention was directed to the windows. A final verification of his reality was needed, so he pulled the blinds aside just in time to observe the sunrise. Never had he witnessed a more dazzling scene, light radiating gloriously, dispersing the dusk and, at the same time, chasing away the gloom that he had been immersed in for such a long time. Warmth penetrated the window, touching his face, and gently reminding him of *One Who Created All*'s power.

Strength emanated from the sunrays, replenishing his exhausted reserves so he froze in that position to absorb every new sensation.

Behind him, disturbed by the light, Nayan fretted on the couch and raised his arm to block the intrusion. "Naranta, please, pull the blinds down. We need more rest," he said, associating the height of the person sitting by the window with that of the woman.

Then he glimpsed her laying on the opposite couch, still asleep. "Rakash?" he asked loudly, standing up to check for himself. He approached swiftly, incredulous that his friend's torment was over and it was really him by the window, basking in the sun. "Rakash!" This time he yelled the name, waking up everyone else.

The villager turned around and let himself be hugged and kissed by Nayan, who was overcome with excitement.

"I knew that if we kept pushing, you'd come back," he said, overwhelmed with gratitude.

Merlaya, Naranta and Prakit, still drowsy, dragged themselves closer for a better look. They embraced him as well, roaring with sudden enthusiasm. They realized that this was the only significant achievement that they could be proud of since working with Rakash.

"I'm hungry," the boy said to answer the commotion generated by his awakening.

The wave of gratitude that permeated his being while watching the sunrise vanished from his heart, extinguished by a vivid memory of what had happened to him in Laeta. He felt an unbearable pressure on his head and an eviscerating burn of his entrails as if a spontaneous, phantom fire combusted inside of him. Shrieking laughter pierced his mind, increasing the strain on his fragile equilibrium, and for a moment, he had the impression that the abyss from where he had just returned was prepared to swallow him whole once again, this time for good. '*Let's see what a villager's ass looks like,*' were words that flared in his consciousness. He covered his forehead with his arms, preventing a potential fracturing of bone that seemed so fragile at the mercy of the pressure built underneath. There was no inner peace anymore; instead, an awareness of a smoldering fire that kept him tense. Rakash stumbled and arms caught him before he fell.

They carried him to the large conference table that was used for all purposes, worried that they were optimistic too soon.

"Are you all right?" Nayan and Merlaya asked at the same time, bending over Rakash's shoulders and offering a glass of water.

Rakash shook his head slightly, giving an unconvincing confirmation, then he said: "Just a moment of weakness after so much inactivity. I'm fine now ... and hungry," he reiterated his initial request.

The rest of the team scrambled for their shoes and slippers. The women rushed outside the lab to freshen up in the bathroom while Nayan and Prakit cleared all the books and loose pages into one big pile and dropped it on the floor. Then, promptly, spread several bowls of nuts, seeds and fruits on the table that were always on hand for such a joyous occasion.

Cheese, ham, butter, and bread were also added to the early feasting, as they were famished as well.

Naranta returned first and Rakash immediately noticed a significant change. Her hair was longer and caught in a ponytail, and her body posture straight, lacking its previous tremors. She casually kissed Prakit, then sat on a chair fixing Rakash with intensity. "I just can't imagine what was going through your head all this time," she said in her direct style and then she picked up a piece of cheese and started nibbling at it.

"Hey, don't start without me!" Merlaya cried out from the door and hastily sat beside Naranta. "I've asked Karitan to bring Martinez over."

She marveled at Rakash as a miracle, a recovery they had barely thought possible. It was a reset of their initiative, strengthened by the boy's experience gathered from his internal reality. Confidence engulfed the team once more. Without a firm direction from either Bart or Rakash, they had struggled to establish factual steps generated from their personal achievements in meditation that could be followed by anyone.

In theory, there were a couple of sensible approaches that none of them were able to translate into a technical solution for the *state of bliss.*

"Why am I in Korobat?" Rakash asked looking around the table. "Only you three are left?"

"You suffered an accident in Laeta so Hando arranged for you to be moved here," Nayan, the only one who wasn't eating, explained. "It's been three years since the incident and we finally managed to appeal to your locked psyche." Nayan's eyes urged his friend to eat, then added. "Only we four and Hando know that you're here. We didn't want anyone else to see you in that state. Bad for morale."

"What type of accident?" Rakash asked, probing what they really knew about what had happened to him, now that some memories were resurfacing. Slowly, he occupied himself with the food, waiting for the answer.

Nayan didn't delve into details, but stated the same story Hando and he agreed to relate to the team.

"You were supposed to teach, whoever was willing to listen to you, the necessary steps to reach the *state of bliss.* During one of those meditation sessions, while you were deep in trance, one of the guests, too drunk and bored, hit you. No one could explain what prevented your consciousness from returning. Kanar kept this incident hidden and told me that you were in Korobat, testing the technology, while justifying your lack of appearance as indisposition, in front of Korobat. In the end, Hando found out about your situation and extracted you."

Rakash, hunched over the bowl of seeds on top of which he dropped several cubs of cheese, kept munching.

"What's next?" he asked after a while.

Prakit glanced at Naranta with a puzzled look on his face, knowing that they were pretty much out of options.

"We all went through positive internal transformations, which are most visible in me," Naranta took the lead again. "My destructive urges are gone and the same goes for my awful behaviour. The question of how to convert what we've learnt into a physical device still eludes us. There is a missing link that we can't seem to grasp."

Rakash perceived the explanation of the lack of significant results as a burden passed back to him after three years of living in a blur of darkness, in which he himself was lost. '*How could he ward off a responsibility that was left with the team to move forward?*' He felt mentally tormented and pressured by hidden obsessions and tainted thoughts that had infiltrated his weakened fences. *One Who Created All* couldn't help in this personal battle with the remnants of obsolete human cravings such of envy and ego entitlement, encouraged to return by his lack of meditation and prayer to the *Supreme Being.*

"I need Otan," he blurted out, unsure of why he said it.

No one reacted, waiting to see if he understood the circumstances. Prakit spoke up finally, "Otan isn't here and there is no way to bring him over. Why would he come anyways?"

The boy bought himself time, pretending to chew on seeds, then said, "I've stagnated on my spiritual path and only my teacher can help me grow further. There is no more harmonious vibration running through this physical shell."

He could sense the researchers' disappointment at such a somber attitude from him. Somehow, they wanted him to elate them back to the level of fervour from his first days in Korobat. They needed positive reinforcement and comfort to clear the fog from the path that they had all started together. It was selfishness and a lack of compassion on their part to ask for any kind of contentment from him: a boy who had only gotten his identity back only minutes ago.

"Maybe Martinez has a solution," declared Prakit, trying to hide his disillusionment that help from Rakash might not be so easily forthcoming.

The natural light in the room dimmed from a passing cloud, and they all noticed the intensity of the orange colour on Rakash's cheeks. Usually it vanished the moment the boy was out of deep meditation. But not this time.

A moment later, someone knocked at the door, and they could all hear a faint, "It's me."

Martinez had gotten the message and hurried over. Nayan let him in, and, in a theatrical way, he pointed his hands towards Rakash, announcing, "We delivered!"

The villager accepted the leader's hug, full of honest empathy and care.

"Congratulations, everyone!" he shouted, displaying his satisfaction with the team. "What's the next step?" he asked, and they all laughed, remembering that Rakash has asked the same question earlier.

Naranta brought him up to speed with the boy's request. Martinez didn't flinch, but, instead looked at Rakash and asked for more details. "How exactly could Otan help you?"

It took the boy little time to understand the trouble Hando had gone through to save him from Laeta. It might have been out of compassion or pity or just a burning ambition to deliver on his promises, but, nevertheless, Hando's actions had ensured Rakash's safety. So the villager instantly decided to push the boundaries, forge new rules for the group, and create an urgency he could exploit.

A stillness inside him had replaced the warm feeling of love he'd had for other humans, hence, the ease in his decision to ask for more and more. Everyone had pretended to be his friend and he had believed them.

"My link to *One Who Created All* is broken. I'm not worthy anymore. I believe Otan can guide me back to the righteous path and obtain clemency for my soul. I'm lost right now."

Martinez thought for a moment then asked. "Why are your orange triangles lit up?"

Rakash involuntarily touched his cheeks, but they didn't feel any different. He stood up and went to the window of the meditation room to glance at his reflection. Indeed, they looked like two burning wounds that needed time to heal.

"This is not from *Him*. It's a distinctive energy inside me that I can't explain. I need Otan," he reinforced the initial request, staring at the team's reflection in the glass.

"I can't promise anything, but planning and preparing for such an adventure won't hurt anyone," Martinez conceded. "We have to know more about Otan. We'll also need volunteers. Clapel can take care of that. I'll talk to the council only after the entire plan you design in here is agreed upon. Nothing in the existing schedule changes: Rakash and Nayan come in and out at night, and that door stays locked. You can continue your work if you want or focus entirely on this strategy," the leader addressed the researchers.

Rakash returned quietly to his seat. "There is something else Otan could help all of us with". Then, almost afraid that *One Who Created All* might hear his confession, the boy whispered. "He knows where the *Trees of Life*'s seeds are hidden. If you can't succeed in creating the *state of bliss* inducing device, the battle to be uplifted is lost. I need more of my brothers and sisters. We can plant the seeds and wait for the gates to open to bring children forth. You and I might not be around to experience this, but Otan will or someone else from the herd. Born in this world of decadence, would make the children understand better than I how to activate a permanent connection with our *Spiritual Father* and ascend to *Him*."

"Are you referring to the drawings from the books? The coloured *Trees* that you consider to be portals to *One Who Created All*?" Martinez asked.

The boy nodded, pleased that he had gotten their attention. Logic and fact was what the leader used to make most of his decisions.

"Why don't you just convince the members of the existing community to help you? Otan should understand your arguments and support such a request in front of the elder elephants."

A knot formed in the villager's stomach, urging him to yell at Hando and put him in his place. The leader had no right to question his demands that were beyond human understanding. Rakash swallowed several times to quell his rage, then explained, "The village is a pristine environment in a perfect inward and outward balance. Exposed to anything other than returned souls through the holy portals by *One Who Created All*'s decision, the community would be tainted and overcome by the magnitude of malefic thoughts of your people. Birthing souls here is an experiment that might fail, but, at least, the sacred world in the jungle will remain untarnished," he replied, hoping that the answer would persuade Hando to move forward.

Which he did. "Will the children bring other tangible financial benefits? My colleagues will ask about a long-term monetary value that would justify the initial cost."

"*Of course, it's all about material gain,*" Rakash thought and quickly searched for a plausible skill that his new, depraved family could profit from. "We can mend illnesses with energy borrowed from *One Who Created All.* We are *His* healing vessels. I saw my brothers reenergizing dying plants and trees. It's a gift we cherish."

Martinez was impressed and pleased with himself for the outburst he had forced. He walked towards Rakash and hugged him one more time. "I'll send Tonio over tomorrow to start planning the trip. Include every possible scenario, so nothing surprises us," he said as a closing remark.

CHAPTER 14

Deep Love for One Who Created All is the only requirement to taste from the bottomless well of infinite knowledge, joy, and happiness.

From the book *We Are One* – Chapter 14

"SLOW DOWN. AT THE NEXT CURVE turn left. We'll go off the road and continue south," Clapel said, standing next to the driver of the bus.

He traced a path with his finger on a map spread out on the dashboard, saved by Blackwood from the leader of the group that had kidnapped Rakash years ago. From that point on it lacked details; the main references were odd rock formations and gatherings of dead trees. Based on other crumbs of data gathered from the scholar's notes, all they had to do was to keep going south until they reached the jungle.

"Don't rush. Watch for holes and boulders. If you can't go around, stop and we'll clear the way," he added and sat in the first row of seats beside Rakash. "Excited?" Tonio asked the boy who hadn't talked much in the last six days since they had left Korobat.

Rakash kept staring at their desolated surroundings, trying to recall any memory of his first trip away from the jungle. It bothered him that he could remember no trace of it. An event so important to his life was erased completely. "Yes," he replied unconvincingly. "Just worried about Otan's reaction when he senses me. If he even does sense me. It's been a long time."

He only hoped that the party was approaching the jungle closer to the location where the village made its offerings to *One Who Created All*, since not far from there was the spot that he and Otan had once used for their lengthy and challenging mental discussions. Intuitively, he knew that even without him, his teacher would always be there, guiding a new generation of souls.

"Why don't you want to remain with your kind?" Clapel asked.

Rakash looked at him and smiled sadly. "It took you a while to ask such a straight forward question. I thought Hando would be the one asking that."

"We didn't want to upset you during preparations, but now we are in the middle of the operation. There's no reason to hold back."

Several answers crowded the boy's mind, eager to spill out. He shuffled them briefly and chose a display of fake humility, a trick he had learnt from these humans that he knew would touch their sensitive side that was still hidden inside them. "Shame. I'm ashamed because of my failure and shortcomings in maintaining my spiritual channel with *One Who Created All.* Facing the community as an unaccomplished *Commoner* or *Artist* is different than declaring myself a failed *Orange Soul.* My kind is supposed to carry some of the awakened knowledge of our community, and be an example of wisdom and determination. Even the elephants hold us in high regard. I've spoiled thousands of cycles of rituals, so I can only face Otan. He understands me and if he forgives me and helps me become who I supposed to be, the community will take me back."

Tonio eyed the invisible road ahead, and the boy realized that he was filtering everything he had just said. The bus bounced on the rough ground and everyone bounced along in their seats. They had long since left behind the main highway and were entering unknown territory. A dozen volunteers under Clapel's command, Nayan, Merlaya and a young doctor hungry for adventure, made up their entire party.

A truck behind the bus carried a metal cage, constructed to specifications provided by Rakash. No one had seen a real elephant before, just a faded drawing in one of the books Bart had rescued from a soiled pile in front of an antique store, but they could have never imagined its sheer size. The bars were thick enough to sustain hits from within; nevertheless, if Otan's force, when enraged, was close to what Rakash predicted, he could push the truck on its side and crash it. The boy's mental control over his teacher was their only chance to bring him back safely to Korobat and avoid using electro-shockers on him.

"If Otan loves you as much as you love him, he will follow you," said Tonio with the conviction of a converted person. "It's important that the message we all agreed upon is conveyed from the beginning: we need redemption even if most of us are not aware of it. The lack of understanding and belief in a higher, omnipresent intelligent energy is what prevents us from advancing on the path you revealed to us."

Rakash observed how, during the last several months of preparations after Martinez had obtained the council's approval for the trip, the MOU's leader spent a lot of time with the team, ironing out the smallest wrinkles that could have derailed another delicate extraction. He became immersed not only on the operational aspects, but also on the spiritual concepts that expanded the villagers' consciousness and their relentless faith in *One Who Created All.*

Witnessing the discussions between team members about new feelings, visions, and energy levels resulting from their meditation, was unavoidable; so Tonio started to pay more attention to the suggestions that they made to each other.

His first meditation session followed naturally. It was short, restless, and as he would find out later, it shadowed the pattern everyone else went through until the mind and body's vibration synchronized in a welcome calmness he had never thought possible.

Hesitantly at the beginning, Tonio asked a lot of common sense questions for which the team always had answers. Soon, with growing interest, he became active in the discussions. Rakash noted the interaction with no intention of intervening. He, somehow, felt that he was in Bart's position before he passed, a quiet observer of people gelling together based on common interests.

"Otan doesn't know anything about your world. Our ancient records mention that it is a terrifying place and we should stay away," Rakash offered another piece of information that recently resurfaced from his diluted memory. "This subtle connection that has lasted since the *Supreme Being* created us, could be extinguished by the fiery lust of human decadence. Our fragile balance doesn't stand a chance against dreadful waves of negative thoughts and material desires. We never learnt how to overcome such intrusions. *One Who Created All* hasn't prepared us for more than just the world of the jungle where everyone has their own place and meaning."

Clapel didn't know what else to say. Only recently had he understood how misguided his life was and how far it was from its true meaning. Extremely clear was that purpose now, despoiled of falsity and flattery. A naked truth that, from now on, would prevent him from any devotional infidelity against his newfound *Spiritual Father.*

Once awakened in him, the resonance of love alerted Tonio's consciousness to a deeper meaning of his daily existence. The longevity of this hidden community intrigued him, and this new inner experience changed his perception of the operation he was leading.

The bus ran over another hole, sending everyone flying up from their seats. The driver swore loudly and checked Clapel's reaction in the mirror. The leader raised his fist in the air, warning the driver to pay more attention. There was no draft from the open windows in the early evening. The inside of the bus felt like a boiling pot. By their calculations, it would take four more days in this heated oven before they reached the jungle. Four days of crystal sky, shimmering horizon, unbearable heat and plenty of time for introspection.

Why disturb the balance between the children and elephants by removing Otan, yet another significant part of the symbiosis? Clapel would have let Rakash return to his natural home, and leave the community untouched. But the villager had other plans, in spite of the fact that he had always had this desire.

The alternation of night and day passed uneventfully, even the dust and the continuous shaking of the bus became routine. The cooler nights helped ease their sleep only to let the melting heat punish them again during the day.

"Check out that mound!" the driver yelled, trying to get Clapel's attention, from where he was resting on one of the back seats.

He pulled himself up and approached the driver, holding the support bars tightly.

"I think that's the last landmark on the map before we hit the jungle," the chubby, grayed-hair man driving the bus, said with a raspy voice.

They were heading straight towards it. It laid like a natural wall protecting an invaluable treasure behind it. Its left side was made up of an amalgamation of rocks half the size of the cage they were carrying, while the right was only a pile of dirt accumulated over thousands of years, on which barely any vegetation had grown. They slowed down to assess the terrain and find a way around it. Everyone picked a seat by the window, taking in the beauty of the naked rock, rough in some places, polished by the wind in others. They observed a miniature world of cracks, angles, and deceiving shadows, moving, and changing with the speed of the bus. Ahead, the ground had an inclination that forced them towards the rocky side of the mound, as though a concealed rope was stealthily attached to the bus, luring them to an imminent crash.

"Stop," Clapel demanded and he jumped out before the vehicle could come to a complete halt.

He walked over to the truck driver who had also stopped, had a quick exchange, and then came back.

"The inclination is a bit too steep for the truck. The weight of the cage might topple it. We'll pull the bus in parallel and anchor the cage onto it. The counter-balance should keep the truck straight," he explained. "Also, you all have to sit on the right side of the bus."

Half an hour later the hook-up was in place and, thick cables held the two vehicles together in a stable balance. The pace had slowed so much that several volunteers were able to keep up by walking.

"There is an opening ahead," the driver said, pointing.

As they got closer to the rocks, they could see the reflection of the sky through the asymmetric arch protruding from the wall and revealing an unexpected path. The ground evened out again, but they went under the arch with the vehicles still tied together, not knowing what to expect on the other side. Only a few meters in and their angle of observation changed once again, revealing in the distance what the wall was trying to protect all along: the jungle. On the horizon, a thin line of green vegetation broke the monotonous brownish color that had followed them for most of the trip.

"We'll stop here for the night," Clapel ordered and everyone busied themselves with their designated duties. "We'll approach the jungle early in the morning so we can prepare the cage. Rakash, please refrain from making any contact. We don't know if your thoughts could reach Otan from this distance."

They spent the night in dark and silence, using hushed words only when necessary. Everyone understood the importance of the task that was assigned to them.

While the volunteers laid down on the benches inside the bus, Clapel, Rakash, Merlaya, and Nayan gathered in a small circle on a flat rock just beside the camp for their nightly meditation. They wanted to express to the *One Who Created All* their commitment to the practice and ask for strength and luck when facing Otan, whose mind was much more spiritually evolved than theirs. Rakash had explained that the thought power of his teacher could make them dizzy, giving him the opportunity to either attack or disappear back into the jungle.

Silence engulfed them and the darkness froze them in the lotus position. They were trying to open a channel to the *Supreme Being* through arduous prayer. This newfound faith had brought them closer to the source of wisdom that had also transferred many spiritual nuggets to the villagers over millennia.

Shrill tones of scared birds ripped the thick quietness, but no one moved. Their minds clutched the meaningful affirmations that would bestow on them the energy of a positive outcome tomorrow.

Sleep didn't touch many of them. The dissipation of the dark provided the excuse of preparing breakfast or finding a vantage point to admire the most amazing sunrise they'd ever witnessed.

They were still in the shade of the arch when Clapel called everyone around him for a quick reinforcement of the rules that had to be followed in the worst case scenario.

"Stay alert so that no one can approach this location from another direction without being spotted. If Otan destroys the truck and kills me, you go back to Korobat right away. Even from this distance you should be able to figure out what's going on."

It was an emotionless farewell that suited his personality. He couldn't risk anyone else's life in this attempt to bait the elephant with fond memories and mental persuasion. Merlaya and Nayan took turns hugging Rakash and saying their own goodbyes in case Otan decided to drag their friend back to the village.

"Let's go," Clapel said in a hoarse voice that complemented the rough look of his unshaved face.

When the dust settled after their departure, the truck was no more than a moving green dot, spitting a trail of grime in the distance. The bus driver turned the vehicle around, facing the direction they had come from. They loaded the bags, getting ready for a brisk escape if necessary.

"Are you afraid?" Tonio asked Rakash while approaching the edge of the jungle.

The boy just nodded his head. He had a leery feeling that suddenly weakened his confidence in the plan he had proposed and which everyone had agreed upon. '*How much influence do I still have over Otan?*' he thought. '*I don't want to return to the village. Not yet.*'

Clapel slowed down as he wanted to avoid unnecessary noise and vibration.

"We should stop here," Rakash said, noticing a pile of items similar to the ones from Laeta's council meeting room.

Tonio drove the truck around the stack of dried leaves, bamboo frames, and fruits, positioning the entrance of the cage facing the jungle. They both stepped down and, together, pulled out the metal ramp from under the truck. Then Rakash climbed in and sat down at the far end of the enclosure. Tied to one side was a large plastic canteen filled with a mixture of water and tranquilizer. Clapel took its lid off. They only wanted to make Otan sluggish and more docile during the trip back.

"You can start sending the signal. I'll wait in the cabin. Good luck."

Rakash closed his eyes, focusing his thoughts on his teacher. "I'm here my friend. This is not an illusion. I am alive. Come to me, I am at the offering site."

He felt the vibration intensifying in his body, the energy emerging into an invisible intelligent stream that spread in search of a matching pattern that could unlock his message. If still alive, Otan should react with the passion of a parent that had found his lost child, refraining from assigning blame for the long silence.

A forceful reply hit his mind, hungry for answers. His teacher and friend frantically responded with doubled emotion and hurried towards him.

"He's coming," Rakash yelled at Clapel through the open window.

A hundred meters away, the wall of vegetation parted by the elephant's body in motion. Rakash saw him run for several more moments still sensing his thoughts, but then he stopped abruptly when he finally distinguished the strange object in front of him. The elephant held his ears out intimidatingly, hoping that this thing would release Rakash voluntarily.

The boy stood up and advanced to the entrance of the cage.

"My dear teacher, you didn't forget me," he sent out another thought. "How much I missed you!"

Otan was frozen in place, unsure of whether to move closer to Rakash even though the thought he received was warm, sincere, and lacked fear.

"Don't be afraid. I'm here because I need you, now more than ever before."

Rakash stretched out his hand towards the elephant, an invitation for physical contact that he yearned for.

Otan took two more steps forward, but stopped again, sensing more thoughts, different from Rakash's. "There is someone else with you!"

"Yes. He's a friend from the other world of humans. He brought me here," the boy explained.

"Why did you leave?" Otan asked, still not moving.

"I was taken away. All this time I lived with them," and he pointed over his shoulder, "never having the chance to return. I always remembered you and the siblings I had."

From inside the cabin, Clapel observed in his side mirror the body language of the teacher and pupil during the invisible dialogue.

"I learnt their language, customs and observed their barbaric behaviour. They hold no spiritual belief or any other similar values." Rakash broke his confession for a moment, encouraging Otan to approach him. "But I continued my meditation sessions and my communication with *One Who Created All.* Some of their wise people knew about us and they showed me books in which I saw the *Trees of Life.*

The elephant became agitated again.

"They know about the *Trees!* And you led them back to us," he said and stomped nervously.

"No need to worry. The people I came with believe in our *Spiritual Father* and in *His* power of talking to them. They witnessed my own interaction with *Him* and I saw their internal evolution by practicing meditation and prayer. *He* can touch anyone who believes, not only our community."

"How is that possible? We are the chosen ones for *One Who Created All's* full attention," Otan replied incredulously and moved closer to the cage.

"It's true. Come with me to see for yourself. Together we can help them '*live*' the *state of bliss.* These humans are far from perfect, but they deserve a chance. Our community is safe here. We'll return with stories to fill many books."

The elephant touched the edge of the platform with his trunk, looking for hints of unexpected danger. Only now could Rakash see the signs of aging. Otan's hips and shoulders were more pronounced, and the temporal region just under his forehead was sunken in. He realized that his teacher might have just enough physical strength left for a one-way trip.

"This is how they travel for long distances. There is nothing to be afraid of," Rakash encouraged Otan, aware that more elephants could arrive at any moment. "I have so many things to tell you. All my experiences in this new world, my interaction with *One Who Created All.* Let me share it with you," the boy passionately tried one more time to engage his teacher.

Otan took another step forward onto the ramp. Listening to what the *Supreme Being* had communicated with an *Orange Soul* itched his curiosity. His responsibility to the community and his pupils became secondary now that his beloved Rakash had come back asking for help.

All the suffering of this loss that lingered in him for many sunrises and was still buried inside, shifted into a positive warmth, electrifying his body, and pushing his legs forward onto the ramp, closer, and closer to Rakash until their foreheads touched. The hands that could once barely reach the edges of his ears, affectionately embraced Otan's enormous head. Tears gushed out in a display of powerful love so overwhelming that Otan didn't notice Clapel who, silently, closed the cage door and locked it. Motivated by the thought of what would happen if more of these beasts showed up from the jungle, Tonio found the strength to lift the ramp by himself and pushed it back in. It was the noise of metal on metal that broke the human-elephant entanglement.

Otan looked around disoriented, but couldn't kick the metal bars with his legs since there was not enough space for a vigorous swing.

"It's all right. They'll let us out as soon as we get further away. I knew you would understand me," Rakash reassured Otan.

The boy broke eye contact with Otan for a moment to watch Tonio jump in the cabin, start the engine and drive away, relieved that he was still alive and pleased to have listened to his instincts when planning the strategy. In that short moment, Rakash read on Clapel's face how impressed he was by the amazing creature he was seeing for the first time and also witnessing the connection between the two of them on consciousness level. It finally gave him appreciation for the intricacies that the community had with *One Who Created All.*

The truck kept a steady speed to prevent the cage from shaking and creating unnecessary panic.

In the cabin, sweat protruded from every inch of Clapel's clothes, gluing him to the leather seat, but he felt animated and motivated to continue on the spiritual path now that one of the many stories was proven real, and was unfolding on the back of the truck.

The safety of the rocky arch was near. Clapel could see the bus and most of the faces inside, waiting for his signal to move out and put more distance between them and the jungle. He turned the headlights on and off several times. Soon, they all arrived at the inclined plane, but using the cable again made no sense as Otan's weight could easily topple both vehicles on their sides.

Clapel stopped the truck and climbed down. He finally dared to properly look at the elephant and he found himself staring at its magnificent size.

Otan's trunk reached out through the bars, trying to touch Tonio who jumped back, almost falling.

"He's not going to hurt you," Rakash said. "Why did we stop?"

"Otan has to come out and walk until we pass the steep portion of the road. It's too dangerous to keep him inside. I hope he won't run back," the man explained, getting ready to extend the ramp and unlock the cage again.

"He won't. But everyone has to stay in the bus. He needs time to accept a new environment and so many strangers." Then, Rakash addressed his friend. "Drink some water and splash it on yourself. We'll go on foot for a while."

Otan listened and slurped from the canteen with incredible force. He not only spread it on himself, but on Rakash too, who giggled with pleasure and pushed the trunk away. An innocent gesture that was so common earlier in their lives. After the playing was over, Otan bent his left knee and let the boy climb onto his back.

For the next three hours, Rakash, on top of Otan's neck, walked his teacher, reforging a relationship so dear to them. The vehicles gave them room, crawling behind in the unbearable heat.

"Altan will be worried. I remember how much everyone suffered when you disappeared. It took me a while to recover," Otan confessed. A slight drowsiness was impairing his thinking so some thoughts stumbled on their way to Rakash. "An *Orange Soul* who vanishes so quickly is always a tragedy. After much debate, we consoled ourselves that maybe *One Who Created All* had other plans for you," he continued and curled his trunk upwards to touch the boy's head.

"And you were right in your assumption," came the reply.

Rakash tenderly kissed the rough and wrinkled skin, then caressed it more by holding it tight, infusing love, and receiving a vibrating energy that no one outside the village could offer. It gave him the confidence that with Otan's added support, finding a way to induce the *state of bliss* at will, would become much easier.

"My path in the last ten cycles was challenging. I learnt and lived states of mind, sensations, and situations that are so foreign to us. The village is an immaculate environment that I never want changed. Even if *One Who Created All* chose the other humans as an experiment, I strongly believe that it is we who are closer to *Him*. The customs and teachings we inherited are meant to liberate our souls from the smallest material clutches that may still reside from previous incarnations. This is what makes us tenacious in reaching this goal."

The elephant only listened, void of any answers.

"When I thought that everything in my life was calm and settled, I was pushed in extreme directions. In those moments, the *Supreme Being* challenged me the most and watched my reaction," Rakash said and released Otan's trunk.

The elephant shook his head slightly, visibly struggling to select the most appropriate statement from the many battling inside his head.

"You know I couldn't leave the herd to come search for you. None of us have done it in the past. None of us were told by *One Who Created All* that survival of such a venture was possible. We have always had to keep to ourselves and protect the village before any personal demands or dilemmas."

His thoughts were pushed out slowly like the first heavy drops of rain pouring down at the beginning of the rainy season. One after another, grinding at the rift that ten cycles of separation had created between the two of them.

"Helplessness that I couldn't reach you in any way incapacitated me for uncountable sunrises. But I knew that our paths would cross again through the kindness of our *Maker*," then the elephant snorted, delighted by the thought of such an incredible opportunity.

They reached the point where the ground was even and where the truck could bear Otan's weight again.

Using Otan's leg and trunk, the boy climbed down and, gently, guided him up the ramp.

"We'll cover the cage only when we approach the highway. We'll drive mostly during the night, anyways" Clapel told Rakash after the door was secured. "Let me know if you need anything else."

"Before we move on, please tell Nayan and Merlaya to come outside," the villager instructed.

Tonio nodded and hurried towards the bus. Moments later, the two of them approached the cage hesitantly.

"Otan, these people are Nayan and Merlaya. Nayan has been my friend since the day I arrived at his master's home. He took care of me and, in return, I taught him how to practice meditation."

The elephant swung his trunk left and right. It was his way of thanking the Laetian for the care he had given his pupil.

"And Merlaya is one of the people working on obtaining the *state of bliss*. She's also following a daily meditation practice aimed at connecting with *One Who Created All*. Tonio, the person who ..."

But Otan didn't hear Rakash's next introduction. His legs buckled underneath him and he dropped on one side in a pleasant sleep.

* * *

DUE TO OTAN'S WEIGHT and added concerns of being spotted with the odd load, the trip back took longer, stretching everyone's patience. Subdued by tranquilizer, the elephant behaved well like a docile pet that would wake up only to eat and drink, then go back into a deep sleep.

The stench of Otan's urine and feces concerned the team; it was the only factor that could give away their unusual cargo. Clapel's volunteers took turns cleaning the cage. It was a tedious job of using brooms and the little water reserves they still had to push out the smelly mixture while Otan lay on the floor. They had all gathered the courage to get closer, but only because of the semi-conscious state the elephant was in.

Now that the first stage of their plan had succeeded, Nayan and Merlaya conversed at length on what to do next after Otan's acclimatization to his new home. The Laetian, isolated from the home he always knew, felt welcomed by Korobat and the tiny family of researchers he was now a part of. Even if the assurance of being accepted filled his being with warmth, he still couldn't shake completely the metaphor of a meager brook trying desperately to find its own channel to the tributary of a larger body of water. His age and experience didn't qualify him for a permanent role based on accomplishments, but only on his exposure to Bart and Rakash. Regardless of how he was perceived by the group, he had to be seen as a potential leader moving forward.

Before they left Korobat, Hando had put together a small team of labourers brought from the east to finalize the renovations on another dilapidated building in the old Tanar fiefdom. These labourers were paid a premium for such a small job that, in other circumstances, could have been done by the local residents. Secrecy was paramount, and, as usual, Hando didn't want to take any unnecessary risks. He even kept the White Tiger in the dark to prevent turning Otan into a spectacle.

Based on Rakash's advice, providing the elephant with a significant natural outdoor range would diminish the awkward feeling of being removed from his habitat and would assure him of their positive intentions.

The team knew that sharing Rakash's real whereabouts with the council lifted a hefty pressure off Hando's psyche, and allowed him the liberty of acting more openly, at least in front of his colleagues in preparing an adequate home for Otan.

"You heard what Rakash said: Otan is too drowsy to discern anymore information about our world. What he was provided with in the first day was just enough to calm him down and confirm that Rakash was in no imminent danger," Nayan raised his voice when talking to Merlaya, a bit annoyed that she didn't understand such an obvious reason. "An overwhelming influx of data will happen in Korobat. Let's not rush it," he continued. The boy used his last traces of calm to keep the conversation decent. No one had had a shower in days. Their clothes and the air surrounding the vehicles were filled with Otan's heavy smell, bringing them to the brink of their sanity. The challenges of the return trip threw them off their regular meditation schedule, adding to their overall irritability.

"All I want is a more concise strategy that we can present to Prakit and Naranta. That's why we are here: to observe and analyze Otan, and prepare a viable plan," the woman replied, miffed by the youngster's attitude.

Nayan used his hand to wipe the perspiration caught in his unruly beard. He was leaning against the window, feet up on the bench, staring at an equally disheveled Merlaya, his mind frantically looking for a conciliatory statement. Walking on eggshells around the woman would not smooth his path within the group. "We've trusted Rakash thus far and he hasn't let us down. Who else knows Otan better?" he said in a calmer tone. "Let's just enjoy this victory for now. Both Naranta and Prakit will understand that we had to adapt to the situation."

Across from him, Merlaya cupped her thin neck in her hands, covering the colourful flames of her tattoo, almost in an attempt of diminishing the omnipresent heat. She refused to answer.

"We'll be home in two days. Better decisions will be made when everyone is rested, clean, and properly fed," Nayan added, and tried a smile that barely pushed the corners of his mouth upwards, his dried and cracked lips would not surrender to another facial effort.

Merlaya bowed her head slightly in agreement.

* * *

THEY TIMED THEIR ARRIVAL IN KOROBAT for late in the evening. Both vehicles sneaked quickly off the highway into the courtyard of the new location, protected by high metal fences. Two volunteers removed the tarp covering the cage and pulled out the ramp, but didn't unlock the door yet, as per Clapel's order.

The commander gathered all his people inside the building for one last, vigorous reminder that the covert operation they had just concluded never happened. After that, he let them go. He returned outside where the reunited research team and Hando were marveling at Otan. Their first reaction was one of awe, forgetting for a moment the stench of the thick layer of feces formed in the last day since they had stopped cleaning the cage due to too much traffic on and around the highway.

"It's just unbelievable," Hando exclaimed after shaking Tonio's hand and hugging Rakash, Nayan and Merlaya. "You look exhausted, but it was worth it. Look at him! What an amazing creature." He couldn't hide his excitement. "Can you let him out?" he asked, like a kid begging to be allowed to play with a new toy.

The elephant was standing since the tranquilizer had worn off, making him more conscious of his surroundings.

Rakash approached the door and engaged Otan. "This will be our home for a while. I'll let you out now, but you have to keep within these limits." He pointed to the fence that in the dusk was barely distinguishable. "Only a few people know about you so any noises like loud trumpets, snorts or barks could attract attention. I know I'm asking a lot, but it's just temporary."

The boy removed the lock and Otan stepped backwards until he felt the grass under his toes. He shook his entire body and raised his trunk, happy to be out of the enclosure.

"Tell him that there is a shed to the left where he can keep out of the sun during the day and another area prepared inside of the building. It's a garage that we removed the doors of, so it's open all the time," Martinez addressed Rakash.

"Can you read their thoughts?" the boy asked the elephant instead.

Otan closed his eyes and froze in place, his consciousness expanding outwards in search of known vibrations so easily identifiable in the village. He mainly gathered unreadable noise and only several fragments of positive reflections from the women. "Nothing meaningful. Their channels are clogged, their minds troubled by matters I don't understand," the elephant gave his conclusion.

Rakash patted his friend's side with added tenderness. "I need to clean myself and get some sleep. Would you mind if you stay by yourself tonight?"

Otan put his trunk around the boy's waist displaying his unconditional love. "I need rest too. We'll start the lessons after sunrise. *One Who Created All* be with you," the teacher said and disappeared into the dark towards the shed.

"You all did a wonderful job," Hando congratulated everyone. "Take the next two or three days off and rest properly. It'll give Rakash and Otan the chance to reconnect after such a long separation," the leader said encouragingly.

"Prakit and I will be around in case you need anything," Naranta said to Rakash. "We've put together a couple of new tests, but what matters the most is to see how Otan influences you while meditating. If that output improves, then we are on the right path," she continued, excited by the success of the trip.

"When do you think we can touch him?" Prakit said, looking inquisitively at Rakash.

"Maybe in a day or two. The breakup from the herd's consciousness will be hard on him. We'll have to keep his mind busy, and focused on me and on our goal," Rakash answered.

Tiredness, added to the emotion of getting his spiritual teacher back, consumed the boy physically. He looked thinner, almost transparent in his dirty, white covers and with his shaved head. Having Otan lethargic on the way back allowed him to relax his guard on his thoughts. The mental blockages he had taught himself were useful in dealing with potentially less developed spiritual people like those on the research team, but they would stand no chance against Otan. The hate, the delusion, and all the other negative feelings he had involuntarily acquired since his time among these humans he kept hidden from Otan. But the sum of all of this was still weak enough not to completely overpower the positiveness he was born into. Nevertheless, they were nibbling at the core of his goodness, silently raising questions about the logic of unfolding events for which he had no answers.

Engaging Otan's ancestral knowledge was the villager's assignment since no one else on the team had reached a consistent level of awareness to be able to communicate with him, and also because the elephant would never trust these humans with records of the well-preserved history of their jungle community. "Otan can be stubborn sometimes and bringing him out of that state will be a time-consuming endeavour. It's better to take small steps. I'll handle him carefully while we rediscover each other," Rakash said and started walking towards the building.

"What are we going to do about the smell?" Nayan asked when no one else brought it up.

He was leaning against Clapel's arm as a last resort to keep himself vertical. The energy drained from his body the moment they had safely entered the courtyard, and now he desperately wanted to lay down and sleep for whatever length of time he could.

"We'll clean up daily and throw everything into the swamp. I'll check with the park committee to see if we can relocate some of mature dogwood and cherry trees. They can overpower the stench," Martinez suggested. "If you think of anything else, let me know."

The group dispersed with Hando and Clapel being the only ones to leave the compound.

* * *

"SO YOU HAVEN'T LIVED HERE the entire time since you left the village?" Otan interrupted Rakash's story.

"No. Only for the last four cycles. I've been working with this team to create a '*thing*' that can induce an artificial *state of bliss*," he replied.

There were many new words and concepts that Rakash had to slowly explain to his teacher for their conversation to make sense. It had been hours since the boy initiated the detailing of his disappearance with no significant headway in their discussion. Even when visualizing in his mind's eye what he wanted to convey, the elephant still had issues comprehending it. Otan's brain was void of any '*polluted*' thoughts or notions. His being was immersed in the jungle, a micro-cosmos imagined by *One Who Created All* and in which children and elephants considered themselves the primordial components.

Rakash had never before connected his inability to achieve the last step on the path of enlightenment, the *state of bliss*, with the accumulation of all the toxic information and lethal vibrations that had inundated his psyche from the moment he'd arrived in Laeta. Even if the Korobat people's attitude were more positive and less aggressive, transcending their consciousness to a higher state was an unfamiliar concept and missing from their grocery list of self-betterment.

Trying to describe the realities of this other world to Otan, made Rakash understand how much he had changed. How, in time, his perception had molded around this new life, diminishing the sensitivity he was born with. '*This dullness can't overcome Otan,*' the boy thought deep inside, careful to keep some of this introspection away from his teacher's reach.

"I don't know how I'm going to define my experience to you," Rakash said, but almost immediately he answered his own inquiry. "Maybe through pictures. For tomorrow, I'll gather all of the books I can find that have visuals of what I want you to understand."

They were sitting in the narrow shadow created by the building after several hours of baking in the sun. No one else bothered them in the courtyard. The team was working inside, giving them the space they had asked for. A pile of acacia tree branches and large oval leaves brought in the morning by the volunteers from the trip lay close to the shed. It was enough to last Otan two, maybe three days.

Rakash had observed the lack of appetite in his teacher, but wasn't overly concerned. It could simply be related to the change in environment and other necessary adjustments. Keeping Otan constrained to the limited area of the courtyard didn't help either. His legs were used to long walks over uneven terrain, foraging high grasses, and relishing freedom and happiness that no other creature of the jungle had. Rakash had to keep him motivated to reach their goal, drain him of as much knowledge as possible, and in the end, if necessary, discard him to these humans to use as a pet. Or they could find another manner to generate money off him.

The boy's body jolted the moment that wicked thought dispersed from his mind, a delayed reaction that would have never germinated in a pristine inner habitat like his. It was a deliberate separation from the principles of love, joy, and empathy that he tried to preach most of his life.

"Is everything okay?" the elephant asked, and Rakash sensed Otan's surprise in being unable to read what had caused the jolt.

The boy knew that Otan was used to everyone's openness in the village and any blockage from his side would tell the elephant that either his mental capabilities were lessening away from the herd, or that Rakash had built his own defense system, involuntarily spawned by exposure to the new world. The villager didn't want to worry his teacher too much, but to have his *Orange Soul's* mighty potential reignited, meant to give Otan the chance to communicate with him at a deeper level. He had to be careful.

'*That's why I went back for Otan after so many cycles, and it was his duty, entrusted by One Who Created All, to continue with me the holy teachings, even in a remote place that had no resemblance to his dear home*,' Rakash thought.

Otan walked a short distance to a basin full of water, sucked it in, and splashed it over his body. It was more of a habit ingrained by countless generations than to cool down from an excessive temperature. His instincts kicked in, demanding a mud bath by the water hole, but there was nothing like that in the paltry green space with barely any natural shade.

Forgetting that he was not covered in a thick crust of mud that needed to dry, he stepped into the burning sunrays, only to step right back under the building's cover. He looked aloof at the food again. Lately, the pain provoked by chewing made him aware of how gradually weakness had infiltrated his body. If his count was correct, he was using his last set of teeth, which were almost worn out. He couldn't tell Rakash this detail about his frailty and unnecessarily worry him.

The feeling of hunger stung Otan's stomach, bringing back vividly the memory of what the boy had mentioned to him upon their reunion at the edge of the jungle: something about his own unusual path led by *One Who Created All*. Would Rakash's path apply to him as well?

His decision to follow Rakash and leave behind an accomplished life as a teacher and knowledge holder came as a radical impulse. Maybe it was the *Supreme Being's* whispering in his ear that had eased his judgment and emboldened him on such a bizarre journey into a world that ancient records warned of its perils. Or maybe it was his personal ego that still yearned to be close to an *Orange Soul*, an honour taken away from him, but now rectified.

"It's just some bad memories haunting me from time to time," the boy replied after a long pause, as if he had almost forgotten the elephant's question. "I've had my share of unpleasant incidents while here," he explained further.

"So why didn't you come back home?" Otan asked, still unsure of the real reasons that held Rakash back and kept his soul unbalanced.

The villager looked over the elephant's head at the clear sky, imagining for a moment that he was sitting in a jungle clearing, feeling the wind brush against his skin, and listening to the monkeys quarrelling over scarce papaya fruits. "I followed the path laid down in front of me by *One Who Created All.* I have no other explanation. I can't tell you yet if it was the right decision. I just did it. I let myself be guided," Rakash said mindlessly. "It could be our destiny that, far away from home, we bring comfort to such a decadent crowd. There is no time to teach them even a tiny portion of what we know, as they want everything in their lives to happen quickly. Resting their thoughts and building a harmonious inner space is just not possible for the vast majority. The members of the research team are different. They practice it and they believe it."

Otan knelt down, trunk flat on the ground, ready to hear more.

"Will you teach me how to activate the healing energy encased inside of me?" Rakash asked and sat on the bench, legs pulled under him.

That question proved to Otan how much of a negative impact these humans had exacted on his pupil. An *Orange Soul* should have remembered all the innate properties of his mind and soul by now, even without a teacher. It worried Otan, but he protected that thought from the boy. "This is an amazing gift from *One Who Created All,*" the elephant said instead. "We have to be careful with who to share it so that they won't abuse it. Not everyone is worthy."

"Why do you say that?" Rakash adjusted his lotus position, appearing ready to go into his meditation session at any time.

"How would you feel if one of these humans were to be healed, but show no appreciation for it? To not even offer a bow or a sincere thank you to the *Supreme Being.* We can't let that happen," Otan explained forcefully.

"I understand," Rakash said, intuitively acknowledging that only a handful of Laetians and Korobatians would be indebted for such blessings.

"It should come naturally to you. Visualize the sick person as being healthy. You are in control of this process by channeling the energy given to you *by One Who Created All,*" the elephant said. "Do you remember the older children in the village attending to the late-blooming vegetables?"

"Vaguely," Rakash replied, but he made no effort to remember such an event from his distant past.

Otan encouraged Rakash to pursue a simple plan before experimenting on humans. "You'll practice on plants first. Their higher sensitivity will instantaneously reflect the accumulated energy. It's quite a visible process. You should ask Hando to plant flowers and legumes on a small patch beside the gate where there is more sun exposure. They wanted to plant trees anyways, so it won't make much of a difference."

The boy nodded his head firmly, but Otan saw the lost look in his eyes, reflecting an inner emptiness and dissatisfaction. The teacher realized that the thirty sunrises since their reunion were not enough to rebuild their bond after ten cycles of separation. He would give Rakash more time to open up, remove his protective energy layers, and let him help with his own healing, before he could heal others.

"You need to effuse love, my boy," Otan continued. "If you don't feel love and compassion for the person in front of you, you might deepen their suffering rather than sooth it."

Rakash didn't say or beam any reaction to his teacher. He just closed his eyes.

"This is the reason we all have to purge attachments, impure thoughts, and atrocious intentions, whose heaviness will hold our soul's vibration back. Overcome all of this and you'll be able to reveal your full potential," instructed the elephant. "At least, this is what I taught the children from other castes."

"Should I be able to remember previous incarnations?" the boy asked, keeping his eyes closed.

"Yes," came the reply as a soft wave of energy.

"So why don't I recall such experiences and wisdom?" Rakash asked this question out loud, his edgy tone making the orange triangles on his cheeks flare. "You told me that we are special souls that have purpose to return through the *Trees of Life*. What's mine?" he yielded to his despair and frustration, angry that not even this interaction with Otan could bring clarity to his path.

"I thought that you had come to terms with bringing the *state of bliss* to these humans as your path, your assignment from *One Who Created All.* I allowed my path to change because of your request. What has changed?" the teacher asked, trying to calm his pupil.

Rakash put his feet on the ground. His upper body leaned forward, as if he was ready to leave without answering the question. "I feel that tangible results are far away, evading me. Both personal results transposed in recalling all of the spiritual footprints that led me to be born as an *Orange Soul*, and the team's results, related to the *state of bliss*. None of it is falling into place," the boy said, respecting his teacher by staying and providing an answer.

"I've to remind you of the first lesson that I ever gave you. And this same lesson is repeated again and again every time one of the children become restless about what they call *'stagnant progress'*," Otan said.

"I think I remember it now because it was then I realized how big you were compared to my tiny body," Rakash interjected, a bit calmer now.

The elephant started to walk the perimeter of the courtyard. He turned his head towards the boy, flapped his ears several times, and then distributed the last part of the lesson. "Apply patience to everything you do. Don't let yourself be influenced by the trivial habits of these humans. How can they continue to follow you if you turn into them?"

"I've been patient for a long time. I wanted to help all of them and share the knowledge about the infinite beauty we have inside us. But they hurt me," Rakash said again in a harsh tone.

At that moment, Nayan came out of the building to bring each of them an apple. He opened his hand, waiting for Otan to pick it up with the tip of this trunk. Which he did. Then, he waited to be thanked with a gentle touch on his head.

Days after arriving at the compound, Rakash had introduced the research team members to Otan. His warm references to how each of them had helped him integrate into the new world established a familiar relationship with the elephant except for Hando who was away most of the time. There was no more fear on their part to approach him with offers of fruits or vegetables or just to talk to him. In return, as a thank you for the tasty snack, they hoped to sense his mental strength probing their own mind to prove that humans were as special as the villagers, that their brains could become sensitive to foreign brainwaves, and teach themselves this speechless language.

"How is he feeling?" Nayan asked his friend after Otan started another walk.

"Other than his appetite, he's fine," Rakash replied, standing up, and shaking his legs. He passed his right hand through his hair that was growing back again; he didn't care to shave it anymore.

"What about you? You look upset," Nayan persisted.

"How would you feel if you were locked in a place from where you could leave only at night for two or three hours at a time? I've been in hiding for almost four years. It's crazy!" the villager snapped at his friend, only to realize that, in fact, Nayan was in the same situation, and they had both suffered the same constraints together.

Rakash was aware of his own moods lately. The resentment that he'd been trying to keep under control bubbled up from the potential failure in finding a suitable approach for the technology. His self-control was losing its grip on his mind. Working with Otan hadn't made an effective impact on his overall emotional state as he had initially thought. It was as if an invisible force had wiped out most of the elephant's powers after crossing an imaginary line outside the jungle.

"You know that everyone is working on it. We had all hoped to see a spike in your brain activity since Otan joined us. Don't get me wrong, maybe he needs more time to adjust," Nayan added right away, as he didn't want his comment to be misinterpreted.

Recently, the Laetian made it a habit to observe from the second floor the interaction between teacher and pupil and learn as much as possible from the tacit exchange. Their mental communication translated into gestures and actions that seemed to have a flawless connection as the two of them had finally re-established a lost synchronicity. Only seldom the mute dialogue was marked by Rakash's spoken words. Their body language was so unique that Nayan had started to jot down such reactions that could later be translated into common human behaviour and integrated into the book that still had to be finished. Actions like the swinging of Otan's head and trunk from left to right didn't frighten Rakash, but only told him in a physical manner to try whatever exercise he was working on once again.

This was the type of research Nayan enjoyed the most instead of looking at images displayed on monitors that didn't always make sense to him. Research through observation, the same tactic his master had used during his career as Laeta's scholar. Nayan's avid perception of details, sharpened by continuous exposure to his protector's polishing remarks, infused confidence that his long-term professional path would, somehow, be attached to Korobat's effervescent technological creativity. The rigor of the researchers' minds needed a harmonious balance through his softer and more flexible approach of visually perceiving human cues that no equipment was capable of.

"We need to get him out in the open. We might find our balance if these walls and fences are removed. They involuntarily create boundaries for our free souls," Rakash said, letting his friend's statement slide by as if it wasn't important.

Nayan didn't want to argue a topic that was brought up several times already so he replied conciliatorily. "I'll talk to Martinez again, maybe he can find a solution." Then, he gave Rakash a quick hug as consolation for his misery, and went back inside.

CHAPTER 15

I sense that my journey in this physical plane is coming to an end. I've already glanced through the veils of maya at the magnificence that waits for me on the other side. I yearn to become pure energy, moving around by the power of my thought. Endless travel, piercing countless universes and skins of time.

From the book *We Are One* – Chapter 15

IT WAS POURING RAIN FOR the second day in a row. Furious and soundless flashes of energy cut the sky's grayish canvas. The water quickly pooled in the dried ruts made in the courtyard by Otan's endless walks, and covered the whole area with a layer of water several centimeters high. Close to the elephant's outdoor shed, the water in all directions was eroding a pile of yellowish leaves.

'*This weather would have been perfect for Otan to enjoy, to get on his belly and roll several times, mixing under his weight the soft soil with water and turning it into mud,*' thought Rakash, standing under the building's door overhang and out of the wetness. He noticed the pronounced rust on the fence, washed by the rain, its colour just a bit darker than the orange of his birthmarks. The metal was shiny when the team had moved in four years ago. "Even Otan was much healthier back then," he continued his thought, and started walking along the building towards the indoor garage, transformed into the elephant's accommodations during cold weather.

The opening from the removal of the door couldn't clear away completely the stench of Otan's feces that were only cleaned up once a day. The boy stepped in and approached his teacher who was laying down on a thick layer of hay with his eyes closed and trunk curled in. Faint breathing moved his voluminous side up and down. Vegetables and fruits that had started to rot were spread on the floor within the elephant's reach, but he had no more teeth he could use for chewing food. Rakash was the first to remark a year ago on Otan's loss of weight and the fact that the fresh leaves brought to him daily were left almost untouched. Out of respect, he asked his teacher about it. Unexpectedly, the answer came back instantly. The elephant was on his last set of teeth, strength draining out, impairing his ability to walk and his mental accuracy.

Alerted immediately, the team brainstormed for alternative solutions. They began blending fruits and leaves that were cut into very small pieces, and mashed into a paste that could be easily swallowed. In fact, this was the only approach, but it proved unsustainable due to the large quantities required to bolster the elephant's energy. He also refused to be fed that way. It was against the natural cycle of birth and transition, a cycle created and given to the community by *One Who Created All.* He just couldn't cheat the rhythm of nature that was instinctively telling him that the time to join his ancestors was near.

Rakash understood Otan's decision. Shreds of memories of agonizing deaths of elephant teachers revealed to him in deep meditation, gave him a glimpse of what Otan would go through soon. The boy pulled a wooden stool from the right side of the garage closer to Otan and sat down looking coldly at how helpless and void of any desire to live his teacher was. His hand almost moved forward to touch him and bring some relief, but he held back, remembering Otan's denial to teach him further after he had asked, over a year ago, about the seeds of the *Trees of Life.*

From that moment on, the elephant shut off all communication with the boy and tried to force his way several times through the fence in an attempt to escape. He had dented the metal, but couldn't break through. There wasn't enough vigor left in him.

Rakash had recognized his sacrilege by inquiring about the community's most precious treasure, which was guarded so well by the herd, but he desperately wanted to create an alternate option for the potential enlightenment of these people. He also needed to keep his word in return for the help Hando had provided in getting Otan out of the jungle.

"Imagine growing the Trees in this part of the world and allowing more of our

brothers and sisters come through," the boy had pleaded with his teacher at that time, right after his energy healing skills had improved.

"Why do we need that to happen?" Otan asked incredulously.

"Their souls need mending. I told you about who they are and how they behave. You have to believe me!" Rakash shot back his arguments. "You and I alone can't overcome so much resistance to love, compassion, and positiveness. More of us can change them, make them accept One Who Created All as the only creator and universal energy," the boy continued.

Otan shook his head and tried to walk away, but the Orange Soul stepped in front of him.

"What really happened to you? What changed you so much?" the elephant asked.

He was furiously forcing his thoughts on Rakash, expecting a prompt answer.

"People in Laeta hurt master and I badly. They shouldn't be allowed to force their decadence upon others. We have to liberate them."

"It's not possible, child, to grow the Trees here. Who would take care of the newborns? These people? They would change them the same way they've changed you. Who would teach the children? This is not a place for our community to thrive. They have such a heavy vibration. Do you think that any elephant would willingly come here?" Otan challenged his pupil and flapped his large ears aggressively as though facing a menacing enemy. He also stomped his left foot to reinforce that he didn't want to discuss the subject anymore.

Rakash thought for a moment, still facing the infuriated beast.

"I'll pray to One Who Created All to bless a new colony of children and elephants. He is the one everyone will listen to," said Rakash.

"Not even He would put us in such danger. What do you expect from these non-believers? A miracle?" replied Otan. He gently pushed the boy aside with his trunk and started his circular walk along the courtyard perimeter. Then, he hurled another thought that should have put an end to the discussion. "Even if we plant the seeds now, we'll be long gone before the Trees fully mature and turn into viable portals. Don't mention this again!"

"But how would we trigger the state of bliss within them without bringing more of us here?" the boy persisted.

"Why do you ask this? Have you lost your faith, too?' Otan sent one last thought to his pupil, then stormed off to the furthest corner of the enclosure.

That was the last exchange between them until two months ago. Sensing the feebleness of his body, the elephant had reached out to Rakash.

"Keep these people away from the jungle. If that happens, the records will say that you and I destroyed a balance that has lasted for generations. Don't shame me in front of the Supreme Being," he pleaded with his pupil.

But Rakash wasn't ready to promise anything yet. He recognized that, somehow, his heart had hardened. Words that had once created potent vibrations were hollow of any meaning, and, slowly, the energy channel meant as a link to *One Who Created All* was getting clogged. And now, not even Otan would help.

He heard steps behind him. It was Nayan, also checking on the elephant's state.

"Any change?" Nayan asked. His shoulders hunched a bit and his eyes lacked any spark that used to complement the abundance of energy of his youth. His blonde beard was neat and cropped square and his head was shaved, exposing the flat top of his skull that pronounced the angular shape of his head.

"No. He's still very weak. Today he drank a little bit of water, but nothing else," reported Rakash.

"I'm so sorry that we've accelerated his end by removing him from the village," Nayan expressed the remorse of the entire team.

"Don't be. What happens is my responsibility. He trusted me," Rakash said with an even tone, aware that he had taken advantage of his teacher's love for him.

Nayan picked up a shovel that hung from a peg and started to remove the feces by pushing it out in the rain. The loud screech of metal on cement woke Otan up. He opened a lazy eye.

"Hi, Otan. Sorry for the noise," Nayan said, but continued on with the chore.

He finished quickly, then he grabbed a hose off the ground and turned on the faucet of the pipe coming out of the wall.

Rakash moved aside and let his friend finish cleaning. "Any updates from Prakit?" asked the villager.

Lately, Rakash was spending more time by himself than with the team that was only reviewing old data from which, they thought they could extract additional information. "No. I've heard some whispering that if they don't come up with concrete evidence on the technology in three or four months, Martinez might dismantle the team," Nayan explained.

"What about Otan and I?"

"You should talk to Hando directly. I have no other details. But we can't go back to Laeta. I assume you feel the same. I'd rather stay here or head east. I've always wished to see that part of the world." Nayan dropped the hose back on the floor, dried his hands on his pants by wiping them several times, and then he grabbed a stool and sat beside Rakash, looking at Otan. "How much longer does he have?" he asked, pointing at the elephant.

"Depends on his desire to live. He's a strong one, but being away from the herd could bring down even a tenacious spirit like his. I hope he will still be around to witness our achievements with the *state of bliss*. I still have faith that *One Who Created All* understands our cause." Rakash knew how much Nayan admired his unwavering belief.

"Have you had any more strange dreams lately?" Nayan changed the subject.

Rakash turned his gaze to the downpour outside, not ready to reply. He had the urge to go out and let himself be washed and purged of all the destructive thoughts and patterns that had changed him since he first arrived in Laeta. There was a palpable layer of dirt covering both his physical and ethereal bodies, keeping him dull and incapable of any subtle channeling.

"Yes, almost every other day. The same *Orange Soul*, no older than four, tormenting me about my past mistakes."

"Did you remember if you met him in a previous life? How are you connected?" Nayan asked.

"I still can't recall even a single instance when we interacted. I demanded an explanation, but he disregarded it. He's persistent in inflicting constant anguish in me. It's been two years since I first saw him. He has a very troubling message for me: I am the evil that through unreliable behaviour and stubbornness is ready to throw off the balance that *One Who*

Created All maintains between these two worlds, yours and ours. It's his duty, assigned to him by the *Supreme Being*, to reincarnate as a savior charged with abundant positivisms and love to counterbalance the effects of my mistakes. It's insane! Have I really done so much damage?" Rakash hoped to hear his friend's objective point of view. He just didn't know what to think of himself anymore.

Nayan kneeled down beside Otan and patted the area of faded marks that signified the number of children he had taught and the castes they belonged to. "I won't judge your actions. You were an innocent child when you arrived in Laeta. You know how protective master was of you. The *less contact with outsiders, the better,* he always said, instinctively knowing how they could transform you. This new *Orange Soul's* view on what you've done is a perspective that I just can't put myself into. He has a much deeper understanding of the implications that take place in the village and in the world that the *Trees of Life* are guardians of." Nayan paused for a moment before continuing, "You always mentioned proudly how *One Who Created All* forged the jungle as a perfect environment for living beings, a symbiosis that also needs protection from unexpected events. Maybe involuntarily, through your exposure to us, you triggered a crisis that requires a rebalance within the village and the castes. But there is no way to confirm if the *Orange Soul* is already born or if he will be born in the near future."

"I've tried to block him from entering my private space, but he's made of a pervasive energy that infiltrates and finds me no matter where I hide," Rakash confessed. "I'm going back to the lab," he said. He stood up and left the garage without looking at Otan. He knew that Nayan would comfort the elephant a bit longer.

* * *

FROM THE PORCH OF HIS HUT, Danish watched Bagham who gently grabbed Herven by the waist and put him on his large neck for a ride around the village. The *Orange Soul's* precarious balance forced the elephant to keep his trunk curled backwards, so Herven could hold onto it. The two of them had a harmonious connection and the entire community felt a powerful wave of positive vibration since the special soul's arrival.

The *Commoner* envied them. His relationship with Taber proved a bit colder than expected, even if he knew that no other teacher could match Otan's love for him. Four sunrises ago, Herven celebrated his third cycle in this incarnation and officially announced that he was a fully aware *Soul* now. It was the moment Danish was waiting for. He only had to remind Taber of the promise she had made for his own artistic disclosure to become a joyous milestone validated by Herven.

The latest three cycles had passed for him almost uneventfully. Alanda perished while she was still carrying for the *Orange Soul* and Baqar followed her shortly after, giving himself the opportunity to finalize the artwork he was creating under the *Commoner*'s guidance. Danish didn't stop from conceiving his own proof of worthiness as an *Artist*. Hidden behind the tall grass on the shady side of the garden, he kept the prolific effervescence going, using any spare moment to further his goal of being declared an *Artist*. There should be no excuse from either the community or Herven to refrain from bestowing on him such an honour. A daring thought protruded from his mind.

'*Why do I need Taber to make the request on my behalf? Who could explain it better than myself?*' He smiled, enchanted by the possibility. Bagham and Herven had already circled the east side of the village and now they were approaching the *Commoners*' huts, the boy laughing at thoughts sent by his teacher.

Danish jumped in the middle of the path, waiting for them. He put his palms together and bowed when the elephant stopped in front of him.

"Bagham, my dear friend, with your permission I would like to address Herven," the *Commoner* said out loud.

He was following the instructions given by Altan to all the children on how to convey messages to an *Orange Soul* younger than four cycles who might not be fully aware of his purpose on this astral level yet. And even if Herven was awakened, Danish decided to comply.

The elephant confirmed with a soft thought, still letting Herven hold onto his trunk.

"Right after your birth," Danish began, "I shared with Taber a unique experience I had: fragments from my previous life in which I was an *Artist*. It is my belief that this recollection happened because of your influence on all of us."

"What is your request?" Herven asked mentally, cutting the *Commoner* short. His laughter had vanished, his orange eyes gauging at Danish's mind. He let go off the trunk, straightened his back, and tightened his legs around the elephant's neck.

"I've created intricate pieces of art to prove what I just said. Recognize me as an *Artist* in front of everyone. Let my name be mentioned under the *Artist* caste," Danish pleaded. He scratched the skin of his forehead under a sudden pressure he felt on his head. Children from various castes that were passing to and from their chores, interrupted their walk, hoping to hear words of ancient wisdom that could help them on the spiritual path.

"And why is recording your name under the *Artist* caste so important? Is it more important than staying on the path you're already on?" Herven asked loudly this time, his voice sounded unnaturally grave, coming from a young boy. Too fixated on what the *Orange Soul* had to say, Danish didn't notice the gathering that had formed around them. It was his chance to convince an elevated soul of his own worthiness.

"You heard how Baqar, your caretaker and also an exhausted *Artis*t, recognized the creativity that eluded him all these cycles. He transitioned pleased that he wouldn't be forgotten. In my case I had dreams that intimated that a change might happen to me. It was not a coincidence that it materialized around the time of your arrival," the *Commoner* replied, his voice bringing out as much passion as he could muster.

Taber arrived silently on the path from behind Danish. She nodded her head at Bagham and waited for the conversation to continue.

"Is this what happened to Baqar?" Herven asked in a tone that somehow indicated that he already knew the answer.

"What do you mean? This is what he told all of us. Isn't it!" Danish said, looking over to his right where he noticed the brothers and sisters that could have confirmed his words. They acknowledged by nodding their heads. "See!" the *Commoner* said triumphantly.

"But this is not the truth," Herven thundered and the orange triangles on his cheeks sparkled violently. "It was you who put that idea into his mind and corrupted the last bit of decency of his elderly life. His soul is even heavier now. As is yours."

Danish wanted to deny it, but Herven stormed over his words.

"Tell them how Nagoti disappeared! Tell them! Tell them!" the *Orange Soul* drilled the command aloud into Danish.

"I don't know," the boy yelled, moving his head frantically in a desperate attempt to protect the intimate thoughts about his deceiving actions.

Everyone was staring at him, waiting for answers. The depth he had buried his guilt was not safe anymore. Spikes of pain overtook his mind, lessening the little control he had left on mental barriers raised with painful effort.

"Tell them! Tell them!"

He couldn't remove the echoing of Herven's demand that was vibrating into his whole body.

The entire community gathered around them, the elephants sitting in the background like pillars of silence. Only Taber moved one step forward when she heard Nagoti's name called by the *Orange Soul.*

"You betrayed your family and *One Who Created All* who gave you another chance to reach the *state of bliss.* This community is tainted by your impure thoughts. Humbleness and love are lost on you," Herven continued to chastise Danish, who shrank under an invisible pressure.

Taber issued a short trumpet. She wanted to know about Nagoti.

"He tamed her mental scream and pushed her down in the latrine while still alive," Herven thundered, quieting everyone. "*One Who Created All* is saddened by the blasphemy that took place in this sanctuary established by *Him.*"

The horrible truth was out in the open now. What looked like a child moments ago had turned into a leader that was determined to restore a broken balance between the community and the *Supreme Being.*

Taber took another step forward, the children parting in front of her.

Her ears and head held up aggressively gave her a larger appearance. Danish didn't turn around, but could sense her dangerous presence. An energy wave sent by Herven signaled her to stand down.

"We'll recover Nagoti and give her a proper burial," the *Orange Soul* said, being in full control of the crowd.

Altan, one of the last elephants to join the gathering, was also waiting for the verdict on the *Commoner*. "What should we do with Danish?"

As *One Who Created All*'s messenger, everyone had to rely on Herven's command.

"He will be released to the jungle for justice to take place. His physical body won't have the honour of a burial in the holy ground by the *Trees*, and his soul, torn apart by heavy sins, will wander in the astral, neglected by *One Who Created All*." Then, looking at Taber, he added, "This is how we punish our own kind, and you know it. Danish is an anomaly to our way of being, but he is not the only one. Rakash and Otan are alive among the humans."

A general muttering started, all the children were puzzled. The elephants moved their heads furiously as imminent danger was upon them. They exchanged frantic thoughts, inquiring of Herven for more details.

"Rakash was taken away from us, and, living without our moral guidance, he slowly forgot what's important. His intentions were good, but his mental strength, even with help from the *Supreme Being*, couldn't overcome the ignorance of the humans that may look like us, but have no belief. Otan, blinded by his love for Rakash, followed him. They both foolishly think that they can induce the *state of bliss* to non-believers. Our records are correct and there is nothing we can do to help those still attached to anything else but *One Who Created All*."

There was no reaction to the *Orange Soul*'s disclosure; they sensed that he was not done talking. For a moment, Danish's sins were less important than the whereabouts of the other two loved members of their community.

"No amount of effort will bring Rakash and Otan back to us. They are lost forever. But maybe, with *One Who Created All's* blessing, their souls will return to the astral plane to cleanse themselves," Herven continued.

The circle of children and elephants formed around Danish and the pair of Bagham and Herven was tight, as if attempting to keep secret what was just shared. Danish's behaviour and Rakash's involuntary betrayal stained their way of living by the simple principles of *One Who Created All.*

"Are you in communication with them?" Altan asked.

Herven knew that no matter the wrongs of the community members, they would still be loved and prayed for. So the lead bull's question revealed concern for their wellbeing.

"I was allowed to contact Rakash while in the astral plane, preparing for my incarnation. Our *Spiritual Father* sensed a strong build-up of negativity, and with the release of more knowledge about us, we were more at risk to have the humans come our way in greater numbers and with wicked intentions. Rakash never had the chance to understand the purpose assigned to him," Herven explained out loud.

Then, he gently pushed his knees into Bagham's neck, giving him the signal to move forward and force Danish out of the human enclosure.

"Open the gates," Herven shouted. "From now on, the *Commoner* known as Danish is banished from the village. His soul will wander in this world until his misgivings are forgiven by *One Who Created All.*"

No one challenged his decision except Danish.

"Please, don't send me away. I'll repent!" he blurted out, and fell on his knees in front of Bagham. Panic overtook him completely. His face was livid and his eyes wide open, looking around frantically for help from his brothers and sisters. There was no sympathy he could cling to, no warmth that could have encouraged him to deepen his plea. The jungle, even during the day, could be a dangerous place without the protection of the elephants.

"Help him up," Herven ordered.

Immediately, Janka and Nakori, two *Commoner* boys, that, like Danish, had Taber as their teacher, stepped forward and grabbed his arms, lifting him off the ground.

Danish didn't resist and let himself be led towards the gates. Everyone followed. He finally had to accept that *One Who Created All* had ceased *His* support and there was no more hiding of his ill behaviour, justified by an obsession that took him over and destroyed a fair chance to reach the *state of bliss.*

They let go of him just outside the surrounding walls. The gates closed. He looked at the path ahead and felt that the jungle had halted its tumultuous rhythm at his approach as additional punishment for his betrayal. For the first time in this life, the emptiness inside emboldened him to move forward to whatever was left for him to achieve.

Leaving the jungle behind crossed his mind for a moment, and an even deeper love for Otan than before, raised consciously in his being. The teacher he always yearned for was still alive in a bizarre world that the villagers knew nothing about, only in ancient warnings, in a generic language that would maintain a justified fear.

He looked back one more time at the high bamboo walls that had contained his entire existence; a small universe whose physical dimensions would always be the same. Only his internal universe could expand indefinitely when in synch with *One Who Created All.* The realization that finding Otan could ease his pain and swell his spiritual development brought a certain clarity to his thoughts. It was a path known only to those who left the community, never to return. He decided to become one of them, hoping that continued prayer to the *Supreme Being* would secure him safe passage to wherever Otan and Rakash were.

The boy took off his shirt, tied the sleeves into a knot, making an improvised basket for the two papayas and a bunch of bananas he picked off the ground. The jungle's edge drew near and the spring in his steps grew stronger, pushing him forward almost involuntarily. He tried to drive out of his mind any alarming thoughts sneaking on him and nibbling at his meager confidence.

He maintained the tempo even if the sun was scorching his exposed skin. In the distance, he saw low hills that could offer refuge from the heat until dusk would arrive. He kept walking while biting into a juicy papaya. Suddenly, the stillness surrounding him propagated a low toned scratching. Something was brushing against the hard, dried ground with a fast cadence. He turned around. In an instant, he understood the retribution *One Who Created All* had chosen for him.

There was no escape. Still standing, he had the time to mutter one more feverish prayer of forgiveness to his Spiritual Father before two of the four dapanees running towards him plunged their claws into his thin body. Redemption escaped Danish in this lifetime.

* * *

THE ENTIRE RESEARCH TEAM GATHERED inside the garage where Otan seemed to draw his last breath. Not even the improvement of the weather could bring any strength to his shrunken body which became skin and bones in a matter of two weeks. Sometimes, he would open his eyes halfway to check if he was by himself, then go back into a deep lethargy induced by overall weakness. An assuaged agony made his frame its permanent home.

He hadn't taken in any water for the last several sunrises as there was no more vigor in his trunk. Maybe he could bear the physical pain if Rakash had shown him the unconditional love required for a perfect teacher–pupil link. But the boy distanced himself the moment Otan's refusal to share the jungle location of the priceless seeds became firm. Otan still couldn't fathom the radical change that had taken place within Rakash, and no matter how many times he asked the boy what caused it, he only received an unintelligible moaning.

Back in the village, the elephant had intuitively sensed the importance of being part of the herd. Only his departure that disconnected him from the common consciousness proved how significantly healthy the feeling of belonging was. He couldn't integrate into an environment in which the only familiar point of reference, Rakash, was off balance and way beyond his help. Otan had no more expectations from this existence, just the vague disappointment of leaving behind a group of *Commoners* with unfinished training, that other teachers had to take care of.

One Who Created All might look down on him with pity at a second wasted chance to reveal Rakash's purpose as an *Orange Soul.* Otan somehow thought that he could continue the teachings from where he had left them, not anticipating the rift drawn in Rakash's behaviour. Even though the boy was taken abruptly away from him, the *Supreme Being*, using *His* unlimited wisdom, aligned the vibratory energies for the teacher to meet his pupil again, in a world run by principles that totally contradicted those of the village. Otan had no strength left in him to question once more if *He* had known from the beginning about his failure to ignite Rakash's hidden potential. It was pointless anyway, now that he felt his soul barely hanging on to his battered body.

There was nothing Otan could do for Rakash and himself. The boy would soon be alone after he drew his last breath.

Otan felt hands touching his dry skin and someone covering him with a blanket. The hay underneath him became thinner and thinner, and no one bothered to move him around to clean the smelly spot. He forced his eyelids up again, hoping to see Rakash caress him one more time, before the final goodbye, but the boy was on the other side of the garage, keeping his distance and talking to Nayan.

Images of happy moments in the village aroused his mind, giving him the chance to get mentally ready for his soul's ascension. Instead, he was drawn in steep ecstasy in a last attempt to redeem himself. A quaint fragrance engulfed him, inserting a wave of energy in his wasted muscles, and a refulgent vision displayed in his inner mind a message that he had to deliver before transitioning.

One Who Created All still wanted Otan to be part of *His* universal plan in one more attempt to block the expansion of this world's wickedness into the pristine patches where humans and nature understood the ample benefits of a behaviour based on love, compassion and humbleness.

This newfound vitality allowed the elephant to raise his head and produce a low toned trumpet that took everyone by surprise. Otan had enough strength to initiate a thought decoded not only by Rakash, but by the entire team, as reassurance that his closing statement in this life, issued through him by *One Who Created All*, would be inferred by many and implemented as *Divine* law.

Then, his head fell back with a thud and he was gone.

Rakash stepped closer to his teacher, probing for any sign of brain activity. There was none. Suddenly, it hit him that the message he just received was the last Otan would ever deliver. Tears still evaded him, subjugated by the pain caused by his conduct towards the elephant.

Breaking Otan away from the collective consciousness of the herd and killing him slowly had, in the end, brought no visible benefit to Rakash's spiritual path. He clenched his fists in desperation while each team member approached and patted him on the back consolingly.

"Otan touched my mind with his last thought. I know how we can generalize the *state of bliss,"* Nayan said, bewildered.

"I received the same message," confirmed Merlaya, who was not sure initially if the powerful energy that tickled her brain was indeed real or just an impression. Naranta and Prakit added that they had also *mentally heard* a similar directive.

Rakash looked at them sternly. He was supposed to be the chosen one that would deliver the holy instructions. Otan purposely deprived him of such an honour, belittling the years of his sustained effort in reaching the *state of bliss.* Suddenly, the previously affectionate glance at the elephant's lifeless body, was swept away by an utterly cold look. His sunken eyes peered at everyone's blithe attitude, not sure if he should scream his delusion of what the revelation should have been or scamper to his room and gather his composure.

"When can you have the device ready for shipment to all locations?" Rakash asked coldly, in a last attempt to reclaim ownership of the initiative.

The clarity of the message left no room for misinterpretation: they were told to create a mesh of copper and silver wiring from which two sensors would be attached to the base of the skull. The properties of the materials combined with their brain waves and the body's electromagnetism would generate a magnetic field which *One Who Created All* would be able to attune to and enhance *His* transcendental power through.

But the *Supreme Being* required a critical mass of people wanting to experience the *state of bliss.* They were supposed to hold in their mind feelings of love and compassion to overcome and disintegrate the heavy burden of their accumulated sins. The *Omnipresent Father* very well knew the motivation behind most of these humans' desire to try to reach such an elevated state, but nevertheless, *His* concern seeing them roam aimlessly through their lives forced *Him* to apply the universal love that the jungle community was so appreciative of.

In a flash of a single moment, Rakash, somehow awakened by Otan's message, understood that *One Who Created All* would allow everyone to repent. *He* would etch in their mind's eye the infinite possibilities existing behind the veil of illusion that they thought real and worthy.

"We need at least several months of hard work," said Prakit. "There is not enough raw material in Korobat and the only other source is in the east. Hando will have to reach out to the White Tiger. He might also want to negotiate new contracts with all these parties. It will take time."

"I'll talk to Martinez immediately to provide as much silver and copper as possible. Everyone should wear a device. Everyone!" Rakash stated forcibly.

The team gathered around him, forgetting too easily of Otan's passing.

"Why the urgency? Why everyone?" Nayan inquired, not sure if he missed any of the message's essence.

The villager's lips quivered involuntarily before he replied. "It's what the *Supreme Being* dispatched to me at a subtle level. You've all deciphered the physical interpretation about the device, but the finer details were meant only for me."

He had to be back in control; this was a necessary lie to maintain his status within the group. A spark of hope tingled his mind, exposing an unexpected leverage that could bring everyone closer to the *state of bliss.*

"Will *He* be involved in the demonstration?" Merlaya asked.

"Our *Spiritual Father* would not miss an opportunity of such grandiose importance. I think *He* holds everyone in the utmost regard by showing *His* support in this almost insurmountable task of enlightenment. Even if people and travelers to Korobat might consider it a joke, let's provide them with the mesh and the instructions. They'll be changed after this experience," said Rakash. He wasn't sure of *One Who Created All's* intention, but, faithfully, he delivered the faint signal that his mind decoded promptly as a *Divine* request that all humans had to follow. '*Is my subconscious giving me this message or is it really my Creator?*' For once, he doubted himself.

"What should we do with Otan's body?" Naranta asked.

The villager had noticed that even if she was listening to their conversation, the woman's gaze hadn't left the pile of skin and bones, of what was once a mighty beast that dominated the jungle. It was possible that she felt more attracted to his former glory than the other team members.

"I'll ask Tonio to bury him behind the hills across from the highway. Let his body return to the ground that gives life to all of us," Rakash answered, and, after a short pause, he added unconvincingly, "He will be missed."

Rakash had nothing else to say about a symbol of wisdom, knowledge, and paternal care that didn't have the chance to significantly mark his existence as an *Orange Soul.* Gone were the days of freely roaming through the jungle connecting with the other forms of life birthed by *One Who Created All.* Gone also was the deep feeling of being an integral part of that universal organism moved by the will and energy of the *Spiritual Father.*

The individualism characterizing his new family clung to him stubbornly, staining his once innocent thoughts, pouring sludge over the sophistication of what little he was able to remember as an *Orange Soul.* The negative influence of humans pulled down his recently opened vibrational channels, and not even Otan could balance the overpowering darkness.

Tasting the *state of bliss* was finally within reach! He would have to use his energy and power of persuasion to keep everyone in motion, Rakash considered. The group dispersed and only Rakash stayed behind. He knelt by the lifeless body and, in a slow motion, his fingers touched the faded orange triangle on Otan's hip, the sign that had identified him, and of which, the elephant was so proud. But that sign had no meaning anymore, just a patch of cold, wrinkled skin with no more identity. Tears evaded the boy once again. He patted the large ear, slowly moving his hand over the forehead, then along the soft trunk.

"*One Who Created All* will understand my decision," he thought, "and help me take my rightful place in the astral plane." That justification blocked any other effusion of empathy. He stood up and left the garage to find Hando.

* * *

HANDO RECEIVED THE NEWS about Otan's passing and the unexpected message from *One Who Created All* with mixed feelings. The town's duties, numerous and complex, prohibited him from making any significant strides in cleaning his mental clutter that would positively tune his mind with that of Otan's. No real closeness had developed between the two of them; nevertheless, the leader felt sad that the only elephant they ever came in contact with had perished. He expected that an event of such magnitude would impact Rakash's mood, making him unreachable for several weeks. Otan was not any ordinary elephant but his teacher that gave up everything to pursue a rare soul lost among strangers.

The words offered as consolation were shrugged off by the boy, leaving Hando with no other option but to get down to business, asking for as many details as possible on the decrypted message.

After confirmation from the team that an unlimited supply of silver and copper was all they needed to mass-produce the device, the leader drafted a plan to keep his mind focused and visualize all the self-imposed dates for accomplishing them. He not only had to find the raw material, but also coordinate with the leaders of cities spread along the west-east coast highway about how the devices would be distributed and used on the day indicated by the *Supreme Being* when the *state of bliss* could be achieved.

He couldn't trust anyone to sell the benefits of a concept that not even Korobat had believed in until a few years ago. Therefore, long trips ensued, punctuated for the most part by half-day long meetings with local officials. Funds were required for aggressive marketing campaigns to convince people to sign up and make a deposit in anticipation of the big day. Hando loosened the contractual terms as incentive to get officials on board, and even topped it up with additional free devices if the entire adult population enlisted.

In Laeta, when meeting the council, he had to tread carefully. He asked to see Rakash to bring him the good news personally, but "the boy is not feeling well at this time" Kanar explained and Hando didn't persist his inquiries, allowing Kanar to keep up the pretext of the villager's imaginary presence in Laeta. He offered the president some made-up details about how *One Who Created All* probed the mind of one of the more advanced team members, whispering to him the information they were looking for.

"So having Rakash in Korobat is not necessary anymore. The *Supreme Being* is helping out on that particular day. We have to be ready, that's all."

Documents were signed, hands shook, forced smiles exchanged, appearances kept.

Wherever he went, Hando had to describe the overall experience as a shattering event for anyone's life, a mental orgasm, more potent than any sexual flirt one had ever had. The hype was real.

Hando was now back in Korobat, looking at the assembly line in one of Banaar's buildings. His face, reflected in the window separating the offices from the main production floor, had a newly grown beard. The sagging below his eyes was more pronounced from the string of sleepless nights working on adjusting the strategy with each separate council. The curly hair left down on his shoulders was whiter and receded more above his forehead.

"We've been working three shifts for the last four months. Laeta was supplied first and also three-quarters of the east. As you instructed, the White Tiger took care of the delivery so there were no incidents. Every single municipality signed on delivery," Banaar provided the update. His moustache was dyed a strong brown to contrast with his green eyes.

When Hando had a final design for the device in hand, the assessment of the technical team was that one of Huitan's older facilities that produced parts for water treatment plants, could be refurbished quickly for the less complex manufacturing process of the mesh.

"When do you expect to have all of them finished?" Martinez asked. "There are only two weeks left before the deadline and we need a buffer for delivery."

"No more than three to four days. We kept optimizing the process and now we can crank them out much faster," Huidan said proudly. He didn't get any ownership percentage of the licensing agreement, which was in the city's possession, but the profit that would slowly come back to him from the huge volume, would be more than enough to allow a permanent retirement in Laeta and enjoy a wicked life that could be customized to his needs. "You look frail," Banaar noticed loudly, looking at Hando.

The leader barely smiled. He couldn't deny the fact that the erratic schedule had thinned his frame to the point where his clothes were just hanging on him, like he was wearing items from an older brother that were several sizes too big.

"I'm too worried about what's going to happen next. We've delivered on the device, but is *One Who Created All* going to show up? Such an entity is beyond any doubt, and while I believe in *His* enduring existence, there are still rebel thoughts nagging at me. I can't wait for it to be over. Our reputation would shoot up and revenue secured for at least twenty years, so we can keep improving the technology without anymore outside help."

"You've done a great job," Banaar said. "I've read the print today and everyone, far and wide, will drop everything on that particular day. Schools, shops, and businesses will be closed. Life as we know it will cease until we either experience the *state of bliss* or receive meaningful advice to move forward. Either way I'll be pleased. I don't have high expectations, so even if my brain gets a good shake generating some interesting ideas, I'd be satisfied," the businessman explained his point of view, then moved away from the window and sat behind his desk.

"Anything less than the *state of bliss* won't do it for me," Martinez replied. "I've put too much effort into it," he trailed off, staring at the workers' organized activities, then, a moment later, said: "Please send me daily updates on the production numbers and the delivery. Between now and then I have to supervise the outdoor locations for those who don't want to be by themselves. We'll use all the parks and public markets. The council and the team have decided to use the space outside the lab. Are you going to join us?"

"Count me in."

* * *

"WHY WERE YOU SENT BACK? Do you remember now?"

Bagham and Herven were facing each other in the open space in front of the *Trees*. The boy didn't want to leave the village that day, instead he suggested a new place for their daily talk. He still felt attracted to the portal like a baby to the mother who had given birth to him, and their closeness conferred a certain internal peace, much needed after the tough decision he had to make on Danish. '*A brother who was a brother no more*,' he thought, half listening to Bagham's question.

After the bamboo gates closed behind the outcast, Herven instructed the *Commoners* to retrieve what was left of Nagoti's body, and told Nukua to erase any mention of Danish's name from the historical records. '*From now on, no newborn will carry this name*,' the *Orange Soul* announced, the skin on his narrow forehead furled, his eyes still squinting furiously.

He sensed many questions on everyone's lips about Rakash and Otan, but he was not ready to share with them more disturbing announcements until he had his *Father*'s blessing. "There is a build-up of negativity in the world that *One Who Created All* sensed and, somehow, my role is to balance it," Herven replied. "Revealing Danish's twisted plan was only the first step. I'm here to continually guide the pristine consciousness of all the other children after our *Spiritual Father* cleanses this world in *His* own way."

"What do you mean?" asked Bagham, intrigued, and flapped his ears anxiously to hear the answer.

Herven didn't reply right away. His mind was prodding the infinite ethereal space for a sign from *One Who Created All*. '*Repentance for the world at large is near*,' his *Spiritual Father* told the boy two sunrises ago, and now, he yearned for more of the wisdom that would unveil the faith of those Rakash and Otan mingled with. "No trick can escape the omnipresent *Being*. No fake love or desire for spiritual enrichment may pass *His* filter, and those who try will be disappointed." The boy paused, and looked up at the spotless sky, searching for confirmation that *He* was listening, then continued. "Confused by his new life in a strange place, Rakash thought that his purpose was to spread the word about us, *One Who Created All* and the *state of bliss*. A good intention but wasted on those humans. There is no depth in their understanding of such a concept, just a quick way of pleasuring themselves. Our *Father* won't allow that."

"What will happen to them?" the elephant pushed the question.

"Everyone's soul will be lifted into a lower astral level and kept there until they realize that they are spiritual beings caught in a material form. That realization will shake them and reignite long forgotten beliefs. It's not the gratification they expected to have over and over again as a potential replacement for their scintillating pleasures. But this action will ease the pressure mounted by the negative vibrations of the decadence they are drowning in."

Herven pushed his head backwards to look at the magnificently coloured *Trees*. The blue and purple patches on the bark were larger, a sign that, as soon as they released the newborns, the portals started to slowly gather energy required for the lengthy process of giving birth again in the years to come, a cycle which they had followed for millennia. Leaves had fallen, dotting the ground, and Herven, with a delicate gesture, picked up one of each colour and looked at them intently, as if he were trying to read his *Father*'s future plans.

"Are we going to meet Otan and Rakash again?"

Still looking at the precious items he was holding, the boy replied, "I don't know. My *Orange Soul* brother has to wait many cycles before he will be allowed to return even as a *Commoner. One Who Created All* won't share with me *His* decision. But our lives will continue to unfold undisturbed as *He* is always watching over us."

* * *

WHEN CONVEYING THE MESSAGE ABOUT the *state of bliss, One Who Created All* didn't specify any particular timing. The unanimous decision was for the gathering to start early in the morning, allowing the latecomers to settle in and put their mesh on before the first prayer of the day. A detailed schedule of activities was delivered to each city council ahead of time for mass distribution. With Rakash's help, the difference between an affirmation and a prayer was explained, and why they were important in the preparatory process of welcoming *One Who Created All* into their lives.

Hando was well aware that most of the concepts didn't make any sense to those asked to participate; nevertheless, he hoped that everyone would go along for once and follow the guidance of the person designated to lead the procession from the stage.

Only city employees gathered in front of the city hall, about one hundred of them, covering the street and the cobbled sidewalk. Each of them brought a folding chair, forming ad-hoc rows for a show created for by invisible actor. On the adjacent streets, people were hurrying to the places they selected to be for this event.

As the main voice of the Supreme Being, Rakash was chosen to deliver the prayer and announce through his fine-tuned channel with his *Spiritual Father*, that these lost children were ready to repent.

Martinez was standing in the first row, hands crossed over his chest, assessing the participation. He smiled, pleased with the size of the crowd. The light of the early sun played on the wires of the meshes, creating countless twinkles. An eerie silence blanketed the city, telling him that he should give the signal. He raised a small trumpet to his mouth and blew into it, his cheeks reddening quickly from the effort. Then, he sat down beside his wife, the Clapel family and the entire research team.

It was Rakash's turn now. He would have to pray to *One Who Created All* before asking the crowd to repeat an affirmation after him. The boy put his palms together and pressed them on his heart. Everyone followed suit.

"Our *Spiritual Father*, on this majestic day that *You* choose to cleanse our battered souls and flawed minds, we open to *You* unconditionally, offering *You* these physical shells that mean nothing to us without being touched by *Your* love."

He stopped for a moment to clear his voice, then continued.

"We desire a taste of the nectar of knowledge encased in the depth of our consciousness that can only be unlocked by our fervent prayer and unconditional faith. As *Your* spiritual children, we have that right. Please listen to us!"

Hando kept his eyes closed, taking in the vibration that the words produced.

"We are love, we are love, we are love ..."

One hundred voices reverberated by the building's glass façade, joined the tens of thousands across the city, lifting to *One Who Created All* a request whose potency couldn't be denied.

An invisible signal changed the affirmation.

"Unconditional love, unconditional faith, unconditional love, unconditional faith ..."

The roar grew louder and louder. Infused by an energy they had never experienced before, they repeated the words with ecstatic zeal. The rhythm unveiled the hidden meaning behind the script, opening at the same time, their hearts and energy channels, normally concealed from non-believers. The tempo of the chanting increased again, and Hando couldn't feel his body anymore, but it didn't matter.

His forehead opened into an explosion of rainbow colour, so intense that he involuntarily squinted his eyes. It seemed as if a dark window broke into thousands of pieces, letting in a wave of pure light that instantaneously healed any physical pain and dissolved worries and stubborn thoughts, determined to keep his mind at ease.

His perception of weightlessness inserted itself subtly into his consciousness and for a moment, he hesitated to open his eyes to confirm the sensation of flying. He finally did. A lighter and semi-transparent version of himself left behind his physical body. His panic was cut short by a warm voice telling him to relax. Looking around, Martinez spotted his wife below him, almost ready to detach herself too, and Clapel, Rakash, and Nayan a little bit higher than him.

Every soul was going up to join the birds for a magical flight above the city. Then, he looked down. There was no fear of heights. He calmly observed all the bodies, including his, immobile and leaning back in their seats, like they were waiting for a command on what to do next. Several young children that pulled off their meshes before the Supreme Being's intervention were tugging at their frozen parents. They quickly gave up and started playing together, enjoying the freedom.

It dawned on him that Laeta and all the other cities in the East living the hype of the *state of bliss* experience were going through the same purification process as Korobat. *One Who Create All*, in one gargantuan swipe, was purging one of *His* worlds of souls, tricked into the ephemeral and trivial trap of the human existence, by lifting them up for *His* judgment.

In the distance, he could see many souls ascending. It occurred to him that *One Who Created All* was a spirit of *His* word. He chuckled silently at the joke that he couldn't share with anyone else and let himself be pulled upwards to his newfound *Spiritual Father*. It never crossed his mind that this would be a one-way trip.

– THE END –

Thank you for reading my book. If it challenged you in any way or opened new creative channels within your consciousness, please take a moment to leave me a review either on my web site (www.claudiumurgan.com), at goodreads.com or at your favourite retailer.

Thanks!
Claudiu Murgan

Friend me on Facebook: facebook.com/cmurgan